CIGAREETS an

By C

Volume five of t HREADS'

Also in this series.

THREADS. Volume one.
YES,SERGEANT VICTOR. Volume Two.
THE OTHER 'ARF. Volume Three.
CARELESS TALK. Volume Four.

Polladras publishers
Trew, Breage
Helston. Cornwall.
England. TR13 9QN
writerconnieteal@mail.com

Published 2016

A catalogue record of this book is available from the British Library.

ISBN 978-0-9562599-6-7

Printed and bound by Berforts Ltd.

Cover by Knight Design. www.knightdesign.co.uk

CHAPTER ONE

Early June 1953

"Yer don't have to stand up every time they play the anthem Mam, they can't see us." Rosie turned to Celia and smiled, each time the familiar strains of 'God Save our Gracious Queen' filled the small living room with that urgent sense of occasion, Audrey Potts had at once got to her feet to proclaim her loyalty.

"It's only proper, the poor lass buried her grandma but two months ago, and her father God rest his soul, not long afore that, now she's got to put up wi' all this bowin' an' scrapin' an' oathin' an' vowin' afore she's been wed five minutes," said Audrey with genuine feeling.

"She was married over five years ago Mam." Rosie sighed, in that instant recognising how much could happen through such a space of time, to any family.

Audrey sat down with a purposeful 'huff' that seemed to imply her unquestionable authority on the subject of marriage.

"Five years is nothin', not time enough to wear out the bed sheets, by ten years you've turned 'em sides to middle an' by twenty you're polishin' the brass wi' 'em."

Celia had a mental image of a bespectacled Queen, seated at the royal sewing machine, extending the life of her bed sheets by cutting them in half and stitching the sides to the middle! It had been a strange morning, in fact Celia had mixed feelings from the start, she had barely touched the television set since it was delivered. William had explained the simplicity of it, just turn the knob on to play and off to shut down, pull out the aerial at the back of the set if it thunders and the plug from the socket at bedtime, no more complicated than the wireless. Despite his casually delivered assurances Celia's nervousness persisted, when she'd dropped a cup from the new tea service and confessed over a dustpan of fragments he'd spoken to her so harshly that she'd walked round Wollaton with a bewildered Tilly until after dark. Aware of how much he must have paid for the television and riddled from dread of something going wrong with the thing, Celia dusted it daily as though she had charge of the crown jewels no less, praying that such homage might save her from yet another damning prosecution. It was only the company of her closest friend, Rosie Spooner, which enabled her confidence to 'turn on' the coronation ceremony. She wished Annie had been able to come too but Charles was being particularly difficult, resentful of Annie's time spent helping both Hilda, and Myra Wainwright, any opportunity to grasp some pleasure for herself he stamped upon and his brooding moodiness, if defied, lingered about their house like a mould, a menacing presence, which might do its harm as and when it pleased. In fact when Annie had coughed her way through last February, Celia felt her father in law's threatening menace infected the air at No.1 Winchester Street with little chance of anyone finding resistance to its strain.

"Can I have another biscuit please Aunty Celia?" Young Beryl's eyes had scarcely left the television screen so absorbed was she, not only in the actual ceremony but in the wonder of this piece of furniture at the corner of Celia's living room from which magic appeared. Beryl could see the real Queen and it was all happening now, this very moment as she watched. Although her mam had said that the Queen couldn't see them Beryl wasn't entirely convinced as aunty Celia had put new covers on her cushions and the biscuits were in a very fancy dish, which she'd not seen before. Determined to prove it one way or another she took two paces forward and touched the screen with her finger.

"Don't you put your sticky fingers on there our Beryl," said Audrey sharply, "you could be electrocuted."

"I wanted to see if she'd look at me, why can't she see us if we can see her?"

"I'm confused too Beryl," said Celia, "I don't really understand how it works, William tried to explain, it's to do with transmitters, whatever they are, anyway have another custard cream."

"Do yer think Emily might have a chance to see the coronation? It does seem a pity for her to be in London where it's all goin' on and not be able to watch," said Rosie.

"She did say that they'd probably have the day off from studies, but London will be thronged with people so I don't know if she'll even catch a glimpse. It's the gold carriage she particularly wants to see, 'what a spectacle that gold carriage must be Mam' she said. Celia's thoughts drifted to the Batemans next door. She had asked if they would like to come round to watch the ceremony on television. Dear Arthur Bateman had struggled with deteriorating sight for several years, now sadly he was virtually blind and Doris, with a sentiment that Celia found touching, had declared that they would stay at home and listen together, to the wireless, then she would be no more 'coronated' than Arthur.

As this morning progressed, along with Audrey's fervent display of loyalty to the crown, Celia began to wish that she had simply joined the Batemans as they calmly listened to events and reached this stage of the proceedings possibly less awed but mercifully less coronated!

"William didn't want to watch then?" Said Rosie, inwardly relieved this was the case. She never felt comfortable when he was present and rightly or wrongly, she believed he disapproved of Celia's friendship with her. But she and Tommy were Mathew's Godparents. Rosie clung to that heartening fact, it entitled her. William Eddowes might be considered a successful businessman with connections but fine leather shoes didn't always take a man along the ways of righteousness and William's association with Dick Woolascroft had ever failed to impress Tommy. One evening he'd sat reading the Evening Post, an article regarding the new housing at Bramcote, he'd spoken his thoughts out loud when he'd said, ' I hope Will knows what he's doing, there's something unsettling about Woolascroft, I observed him at his father's funeral, deep, his mind finds places deep and murky, Will needs to stay in the shallows'.

"William's gone to Derby," said Celia, "there's a derelict warehouse that he's decided to look at, more than likely it has most value in the site rather than the building itself." She sighed but her long breath was immediately overwhelmed by a fanfare of trumpets.

"That crown looks heavy on her head," observed a thoughtful Beryl.

Audrey was on her feet in a trice. "You show respect our Beryl, it's her Majesty's head."

Rosie couldn't resist. "Her Majesty was a poor lass ten minutes ago Mam." She winked at Celia, reached for a biscuit from the fancy dish and before taking a bite whispered. "For Queen and country, God bless her cotton socks."

"Amen," whispered back Celia, "Amen to that."

William sat back in the seat of the car, took the silver cigarette case from the inside pocket of his jacket and allowed his eyes to focus on the engraved initials, W.C.E. He smiled, a smug sound of self satisfaction followed his fingers as they removed a long sleek Player's Navy Cut, 'the better kind'. Reg Yeats was long gone, a shame, how gratifying it would have been to parade his success, William Eddowes' upward advance, past the withering vision of factory manager Reg Yeats. William tapped the end of his cigarette precisely over the letter C. It was his habit, his ritual, always exactly over the C., for Charles. "Take note dad, take note." He'd persuaded himself that so often did he repeat these words, somehow his dad heard them and felt pain. Not an actual bleed but a smarting of the skin where chafed Charles' regret. His father had amounted to nothing, a miserable, retired shopkeeper who had once imagined that an amount of money could compensate for a lie. Whenever William lit a cigarette he first scorned the past, then relished the satisfaction of the present. He wound down the window, looked across the small yard at the crumbling warehouse, sent a whirl of smoke into the air and was about to drive off when a sudden clatter caused him to swivel round in the seat and look behind. A cat, presumably scavenging in a bin must have tipped it in the process, now the creature scarpered and the battered bin rolled from side to side, agitated. William's own thoughts had swung this way, then that, and as yet found no firm place. One way drew him towards bigger and better, an enticement. While the other way cautioned him to steer his own course, albeit narrower.

'Chew on it for a bit Eddowes, if you come to the conclusion that it's too big to swallow, then spit it out'.

It was like throwing down a gauntlet to William, but that had been Woolascroft's ploy, William was no fool, he'd recognised the craft in Dick's approach. But the words had lodged in his head, should he or shouldn't he? How many such chances would likely come William's way? At turned fifty surely the answer to that question must be few.

When Fred Woolascroft died last year he'd left the business to his three sons. Dick's brothers had served in the war and thankfully survived, though Frank had been injured. Their mother was well provided for in the family house, the worry of the business, not surprisingly, Fred had chosen to spare her. Dick Woolascroft had placed a generous shot of whisky in front of William, one day in his works' office and said.

'The other two want out Eddowes,' he'd given a scornful laugh before adding 'they've never shared the old man's vision in the same way that I have.

We've already done business William, you and me, nothing earth shattering but I reckon it turned out beneficial all round'.

William had pressed him on the subject of finance, buying out two third shares must require a significant investment.

Dick had revealed the readiness of one other to stake an interest. Gordon Cheetham, Robert Cheetham's eldest son, and the possibility of his approaching Patricia Bradshaw, she was after all his aunt through her marriage to uncle Anthony and furthermore, since selling out to the coal board, she was awash with funds. Better for her to grow her wealth within the family business than to be at the mercy of the banks.

William drew on the last of his cigarette, opened the car door and dropped the butt to the ground. The bin at last having ceased its unrest lay on the old concrete yard, motionless. He slammed the door shut, turned the key and with a brief glance one way, then the other, drove off.

Annie's pace hastened, since Billy had given in to Susie's pleas and moved in with her, Joe and the girls, whenever Annie needed to walk by No.24 her feet propelled her along the pavement and past the window as though trying to outrun a torment that determined itself to pursue, then it would catch up again as she drew level with the old workshop gates, her breathing tight, her chest sore. Edna's death, almost six years ago, had created an emptiness in Annie, deep inside her was a void through which memory could neither pass, nor find its way round, unable to advance, memory returned again and again, each time as potent as before.

Billy had smiled for his girls with a courage, which Annie saw as selfless devotion to his daughters, those most precious gifts granted him by his Edna. But grief, the intense and relentless pain of it, Billy had shared with Annie behind the kindness of closed curtains, crying into her open heart 'til she needed to call on every last ounce of strength to bear its weight. After losing

Daniel, then years later John, Annie had clung to that unspoken understanding between Edna, Billy and herself, it held her fast, it enabled her breath and the will to live for her other children. Billy had so needed to cling, to hold on to life, somehow, someway. When he'd finally agreed to give up No.24 Annie had wept from relief. Yet that small house, so much a part of her own past, challenged her senses still, and walking along the other side of the street did nothing to lessen the heartache.

The birth of Myra's baby at May of '46, following all the dismay of Edna's operation and her severely impaired speech had been cruel through its anxiety. Undetected at the time of Myra's accident, the pelvic bones had been distorted, creating the most alarming and extended period of labour. Finally delivered by forceps the infant had been without breath, the skill of the nurses and doctors had achieved to make the tiny lungs pump but the possibility of some brain damage had to be spoken of. Now at seven years of age, Michael Wainwright was a happy, lovable child possessed of all the usual mischief, though with a slight deafness which may or may not be due to his difficult birth.

However, given that Myra almost died she and Jack had been told by the doctors that she should not risk another pregnancy. Eighteen months ago, through a labour that stretched every nerve to breaking point, Myra had given birth to a baby girl, Louise, with no need of forceps and breathing normally, but Myra had been left weakened and without her mam there to give strength, as mams do, the young woman had sunk into a deep depression.

Billy had been stoic but the absence of one arm limited what he was able physically to do for a baby. Jack needed to work so his mam Gertie and Annie, between them, with additional help from Myra's sisters, gently and patiently coaxed her along to recovery, constantly aware of the strain disturbed nights and everyday tasks placed on Myra's damaged leg. Jack somehow found his way through the minefield of nervous tension, the tears and tantrums, and emerged sorely bruised but constant and dependable. Now back to her old self, Myra could find happiness in the days and much joy in her children but Annie continued to help whenever she could, if only some ironing, the dusting or a bit of baking. Myra was always grateful but while Annie didn't voice it, she nevertheless did what she did, as much for Edna as for Myra.

"Hello Mrs.Eddowes, good day for the celebrations."

Annie smiled and agreed. Mrs.Sealey was a pleasant woman, inclined to look on the bright side, though Annie suspected that not everything was sweetness and light at No.19. Fred Sealey had a temper, it could flare up in an instant, neighbours couldn't fail to overhear his sudden outbursts but the enduring Lizzie, his wife of many years would loyally explain, ' 'tis his old war wound plays him up, give it ten minutes an' he'll be whistlin' like a Billy blackbird'. As a result, whenever Fred Sealey's raised voice was heard, folk would await the whistle, sounding the all clear and every blackbird frequenting the backyards of Winchester Street was a 'Billy'. For Annie the significance ran deep, Billy Dodds' nature had ever been uplifting, he'd whistled his way through years of struggle, what name other than Billy could anyone give to that cheerful little bird, which perched on the highest bough of the tree or chimney top, sending his notes of encouragement over those curiously distracted creatures scuttling about below. Billy Dodds whistled still for his daughters and grandchildren, yet suffered the pain of a wound inflicted by a fate that decided to take from him his own dear Edna, a wound that could never fully heal.

Charles had taken himself to The Standard, he would be occupied for the next couple of hours so Annie made her way to the bus stop, she could at least spend a little time with Celia. William's latest acquisition, the television set, was for Annie an incidental, lavish ceremonies and pageantry, while irresistible to some, failed to claim her enthusiasm to the same degree. In fact she felt sympathy, a measure of regret for the young Queen Elizabeth, destined to be constantly scrutinised and answerable to duty. Just how much normality could her future allow, Annie secretly hoped the palace garden might be blessed with a Billy blackbird, casting his notes of encouragement over those abiding there.

The bus held the usual mix of passengers, some engaged in animated conversation about the coronation, others preferring to sit quietly, doubtless making the most of an interlude in their busy day. As the bus approached the roundabout, which had they taken the left exit, would have led them past Bobbers Mill, Annie's thoughts turned to Freddy. Nothing remained of his dreams, all his plans for the farm. Instead rows of housing either side of the railway line, even half a dozen shops. Freddy had been 'an unfortunate casualty of circumstance', that was how the council described his situation. He and Annie recognised it as something else, he'd not been a casualty but a victim, and not of circumstance but of scheme and intent. She missed Freddy. Since a desperate Anthony Hemsley, driven into a corner by Charles, had voiced those revelations with such painful consequences, William persisted in keeping Charles and herself at a distance prescribed by his judgement. Hardly ever did he refer to her as mam, or mother, rather he avoided calling her by any title. More and more she felt devalued and his unkind attitude towards his dad troubled her constantly. As for George, unlike Freddy, he truly was a casualty of circumstance yet William's sympathy was slight to say the least.

For a little while Annie had dared to hope that an easy friendship, reinstated from childhood, might have blossomed between George and Liza Ollerton. Perhaps it would have, but after Edna died, poor Liza grieved so for her mam, the misery engulfed her, she near drowned in it. Losing Harry to the war had already turned her from a happy young woman to a withdrawn widow. Finding themselves in one another's company when George called at No.24 to see Billy and Edna, as he frequently did, they appeared relaxed, comfortable. George had driven Liza to the countryside a few times where they'd walked and talked. But despite all efforts, Edna's health had declined, in the later stages, quite rapidly, she'd died at home, in her bedroom at No.24 and Liza couldn't bear to remain there. She'd returned to Halam, to the farm where the daily tasks were demanding of her physically and mentally, that tried and tested salvation, work, no time to slack, no opportunity to dwell on misery, just hard work. George had said nothing but Annie recognised his disappointment, his loneliness.

Samuel had met a lovely young woman, they were spending time together at weekends, dating, if not quite courting. Four years ago George had bought a house off Weston Boulevard, No.8 Pelham Crescent, Margaret Coupland was a daughter of the family next door. The situation served to advance George's loneliness and although he hid it well, Annie was aware and it saddened her.

"Next stop Wollaton Park."

The conductor called out, standing with his finger poised over the bell. Annie clutched her bag and made her way along the aisle, thanked him as was her custom and watched from the platform the passing scene become more defined as the bus slowed down.

"Mam, thank goodness you've managed to come, you've missed most of the ceremony but you have arrived at just the right time for a bite to eat."

Celia stood at once, genuinely delighted to see her mother in law and to know that Annie had managed to escape, if only for an hour.

"I let myself in at the back door, I caught the 52 so it dropped me almost right outside. Hello Rosie, Audrey," she cast a warm smile about the room.

Beryl deemed herself to be the best informed, having watched intently the coronation and so launched into a detailed description for Annie's benefit.

"They behead her with the crown an' gave her an orb, I didn't know they were called orbs, aunty Kathleen gave me one Christmas afore last but mine's got a snowstorm inside it. The Duke, he's her husband an'all, gave her a kiss in front of all them people, even the Archbishop wer' watchin', she couldn't kiss him back though 'cause he wer' kneelin' down on the floor an' if she'd tried the crown might have slipped of her head an' she daren't risk that happenin' 'cause it's an heirloom, donkeys years old, like grandma's fancy sugar shaker, I'm gettin' that when she dies, aren't I Grandma?"

Annie felt obliged to turn to Audrey at this point, who now appeared to be nodding off. Rosie had gone with Celia to the kitchen. Beryl's chatter continued regardless and by the time they returned with a tray, Annie's head was spinning with a version of events, which Mr.Dimbleby would likely have felt aggrieved to have missed, so entirely removed must they surely be from the gracious, yet less profound ceremonial witnessed by himself in the splendour of Westminster Abbey.

"For goodness sake Mam, what must 'her Majesty' think asleep on duty, you've missed three anthems, it'll be the tower for you." Rosie prodded Audrey's shoulder and chuckled.

Somewhat affronted poor Audrey endeavoured to redeem herself by displaying the wisdom of age.

"I'm sure you should turn that thing off now Celia, it'll be gettin' too hot, I've heard that anythin' electric can catch fire when it's on long enough to overheat."

"Thank you Audrey," said Celia, "it's kind of you to make me aware."

If truth be told Celia was only too delighted to find some quietness, there was only so much trumpeting and horn blowing an ordinary mortal could stand in the confines of a small living room.

They had eaten the sandwiches and Celia was about to suggest she put the kettle on for some tea, when the sound of a door closing noisily, then heavy footsteps, alerted them to William's arrival. Within seconds he put his head around the living room door.

"Ah, a gathering," he said.

The atmosphere within the room was immediately tense. Rosie got to her feet.

"We were just off William, weren't we Mam, say thank you to Mr.Eddowes Beryl, for letting us watch his television."

The previously talkative Beryl now whispered nervously. "Thank you."

"Oh dear, please ladies, don't let me disturb the coven."

William crossed the room to the armchair and sat down. Celia gave him a stern look but accompanied an anxious Rosie, Audrey and Beryl to the front door.

Annie wanted to correct him, to admonish him for his rudeness, instead she enquired after his health and ventured to ask if all was going well with his acquisition of a plot of land at Stapleford, she only knew about it through Celia but felt obliged to speak and it seemed a reasonably benign subject over which to converse, given that family matters were best avoided when in his company. The mere mention brought down the wrath of the almighty on any unfortunate individual showing lack of tact. This was how Samuel described his uncle's unceasing bitterness, William in this instance being the 'all mighty' referred to.

He stared at Annie, his expression vague, for several seconds he was silent.

Here was his mother, the only one he had ever really known sitting not three feet from him, there was no one else present but his mam, Annie, unselfish, dependable, the most sensible of people who in the past had advised him and never been wrong. Why couldn't he bring himself to ask, should he or shouldn't he buy into Woolascrofts? She would know, of all people mam would know. He unfastened his jacket, leaned back in the chair, turning his gaze to the television set.

He couldn't help himself, that arrogance possessed his tongue.

"There's nothing you need to concern yourself with. What do you think of the television set then, not many of those in Winchester Street I imagine?" His words lodged in his throat momentarily, causing him actual pain. 'If it's too big to swallow then spit it out Eddowes'. Damn Woolascroft, what could a man do but take up the gauntlet.

"Take care of yourself William," said Annie. She left him to his devices. Winchester Street may not claim to hold a single television, but everyone abiding there had their very own Billy blackbird.

CHAPTER TWO

Late June

"How's your David gettin' on? Bert reckons it's the best thing for any lad, a spell of army discipline, nothin' like a bit o' barrack room livin' to free 'em from their mams' apron strings 'e says. 'E's a good one to talk mind you, first time I went to their house to meet his mam I could scarce believe it. Three lads and not one of 'em under six foot an' built to stand the weather, but she only had to snap her fingers an' they'd come to heel. Then I met his father, 'tis no wonder they did as their mam said, yer wouldn't have crossed him. Chainmakers, that's where 'e worked, had muscles up his arms like ships rope an' shoulders wide as sideboard. Bert told me 'e only walloped him once wi' a slipper but not 'til next mornin' did 'e feel pain, 'e wer' numb 'til then. I think I'll have it cut a bit shorter this time, so it'll last longer. It's our Jimmy's 21st next month, we're all goin' to Butlins for four days. I've told his mam we'll put some money towards his motorbike, I can't bear the damn things but now he's got that job at Ruddington he does need one, he's gettin' a Raleigh, Bert reckons they're the best, how he knows so much is a mystery to me, Bert's never progressed beyond pedal power. I went out wi' a lad once, full of it 'e wer', afraid o' nowt, ended up in Australia, did alright for hisself, his sister lives in Arnold, I bump into her sometimes at the market."

Hilda lifted Mrs.Whale's head from the wash basin and wrapped her hair in a towel, it seemed to be the nature of hairdressing, that flow of chatter, as though positioning the head back, with nothing to distract the eyes beyond the plain ceiling above, released a store of information, which prior to had been stuck in a queue behind more immediate observations.

"David writes and his letters suggest he's adjusting. It's early days after all, he only left five weeks ago tomorrow so he's sure to be finding things unfamiliar but his dad had a good chat with him before he went, he's always listened to Jack. Besides, once he makes friends, some mates as men prefer to call them, he'll be fine. I was surprised he was called up so early, his 17th birthday was last February, still, like he said, 'better this way Mam, gets it over with, then I can get on with life'. He's doing mechanics, Jack says the army might further his knowledge, all the services introduce practical skills, it isn't all square bashing. I thought it a strange coincidence that Gregory Tozer got called up at the same time, they've always known each other so at least something's familiar, they're both at Aldershot.

A little bit shorter then Mrs.Whale, and a medium strength perm, must have you lookin' smart for your grandson's 21st."

Hilda cast a glance at Janet, the two exchanged amused smiles. It had worked out well. Sixteen when her grandma died, shy and withdrawn at the best of times because of her hair lip, Janet Yeats needed something to build up her confidence. It was Hilda's mam, Annie, who suggested the young woman might be ideal as a trainee. Now competent and showing a real flare for the job, Janet was an asset to the business, working alongside Hilda and most days, Sheila Croft. Today was Sheila's day off, a character the very opposite of Janet, the salon would doubtless ring with enlightening accounts of her activities when she came back to work tomorrow.

Looking back over the past eight years Hilda acknowledged the strain her plans had placed on the family, yes, she had some regrets but they'd got through and now the days progressed happily enough with Jack at the mine still, having survived the changes brought about by nationalisation of the coal industry. In fact Hilda believed the Coal Board had unknowingly helped her persuade Jack that the time was right, three years ago, for them to buy a house of their own. In '47, when miners had been advised of the changes, a sense of liberation spread through their ranks, they were no longer the servants of wealthy, insensitive, driven individuals who made their own rules but employees of the government, with a recognised rate of pay throughout the coalfields, fairness at last. Suddenly there was a belief in better things, an end to war, the beginning of recovery, a wage packet that had not first been squeezed through the wringer of mastery 'til it slid into a man's pocket as thin as his hope and as flat as his dreams. To some extent the men's buoyant mood was due to rose tinted spectacles, a psychological issue, arriving with each envelope confirming their new status.

'If we don't do it now Jack then we never will'.

That had been Hilda's not unreasonable logic and Jack, acknowledging her patience over the years of their dwelling on Forest Road and her achievements at the salon felt he could not deny her. It was true, they were living in changing times, there were fresh opportunities within the sight of ordinary men. Jack like the rest, welcomed nationalisation but ever cautious, as his experiences so far had taught him to be, he chose not to adopt those rose tinted spectacles, preferring to stick with his old, plain lenses that enabled him a defined reality, no subtle blurring about the edges, no softening of the light but clarity, a man might foresee an obstacle if his vision remained unclouded.

The house on Bliss Street had three bedrooms and a bathroom, with a small garden at the back and an area of paving at the front, requiring little to be done beyond a lick of paint here and there. Hilda had been charmed by the name of the road and on moving in Rosemary had written a letter to aunty Francis at Bonthorpe, just so she could declare her new address as 27, Bliss Street.

To the other extreme her brother David had been ragged mercilessly by Corporal Battersby at Aldershot who'd learned that Private Haynes lived at 'Bliss Street' no less. There existed little in the way of bliss round about Battersby, though David's youthful optimism had managed to instil in him the belief that their constantly tormented Corporal would surely find relief from whatever ailed him one day before their duty ended, a soft spot, everyone had a soft spot.

Hilda had confidently cut and shaped Mrs.Whale's hair in readiness for the perm. It had become almost automated, the sequence so regularly followed. Placing the waterproof cape around Mrs.Whale's neck she poured some solution into a bowl, selected the right size of curler and with a small sponge, carefully coated each lock of hair before wrapping it with the thin paper strip, then rolling it like a fat, obnoxious smelling cigarette around the curler and clipping it tightly in place. It transformed the appearance of the tolerant individual undergoing the treatment to such a degree, Hilda often thought that folk looking in through the window might hurry past completely put off and resolutely curl-less. It had proved the opposite, confident in their mind that such unattractiveness was temporary, 'the perm' had become increasingly popular.

Mrs.Whale was blessed with a thick head of hair, unlike Celia, whose scalp was visible unless her hair was styled and pinned in a particular way. As she said, her mother, Gwendolyn, had always been troubled by woefully thin hair, even resorting to a false hair piece at a comparatively young age. It was unfair and undeserving but Hilda's sympathy was slight. William had received all of John's money, William and Celia, Hilda knew that Celia took no part in pursuing it, only William could be so avaricious, yet it rankled and whenever Celia sat in the salon, in her way being loyal to her sister in law, a resentment found its way into Hilda's thoughts and Celia's thinning hair seemed an appropriate consolation for Hilda's own sense of injustice. Jack had dismayed of her attitude, 'let it go Hilda, for goodness sake, you did very well, Mrs.Wright was more than generous, William will never be satisfied and that's his misfortune, because it means he'll never be happy'. Hilda knew Jack's words were true, but even more disturbing was her unspoken regret, that John had not come home from the war instead of William, and this induced guilt within her to wrestle with that foolish consolation, every time the innocently unaware Celia sat down in a chair at the salon, smiled at every one and said, 'just as you always do will be perfect'.

"I noticed the Queen's hair wer' a bit shorter than she usually wears it, I saw coronation on neighbours television, the Morrisons, he's an accountant, I polish her silverware for her, she's allergic to the cleaning stuff, only once a month it's not hard an' it pays paper bill. Anyroad I thought the Queen's hair suited her a bit shorter, happen it wer' to make the crown sit better on her head. We shall be havin' our meals wi' a lot of other folk when we're at Butlins, they feed yer in one big dinin' hall so I want to look respectable, if yer can make me hair look like the Queen's, that'd be nice. Jimmy's mam goes to the other place, up Sherwood, it's not for me to say owt but I know Lizzie Symonds goes there an' her kids are forever bein' sent home from school wi' nits an' yer can't be sure they wash the towels regular can yer?"

At last Hilda completed her task, encased Mrs.Whale's rolled up hair in a plastic cap and looked at the clock, for the next twenty minutes, with any luck, dear Mrs.Whale might give her tongue a rest.

"Have a read of the Woman's Weekly," said Hilda, taking it from the magazine rack and putting it in Mrs.Whale's hand, "it's this week's, I think there are one or two nice recipes in there."

Meanwhile Janet was putting the finishing touches to her customer's shampoo and set. Could any two people be more different, Mrs.Reeves was deaf and dumb and made herself understood mostly by simple sign language though she did attempt some speech, which Janet sometimes was able to understand. Hilda felt it was likely that Edna's severely impaired speech enabled Janet the ability to recognise certain sounds and their meaning. The young woman herself had never been without a slight lisp due to her hair lip. She had spent as much time as she could with her grandma through those two tragic years, witnessing Edna's frustration. One day it had all become too much, Edna had taken a pencil and paper and written, 'Who'd have thought that having a bit of tongue cut off could turn you into a dribbling dummy'.

Apparently Billy had found the piece of paper and continued the sentence with words of his own. 'Who has put up with being married to a one armed, short sighted, deaf old bloke with not much in the way of brains, for years'? Then he'd added a kiss for every one of the years he and Edna had been together, they numbered forty one.

"Any chance of a cup 'o tea? I'll read out your horoscopes if yer tell me your star sign." Mrs.Whale's tongue could remain still no longer, "it says I'm goin' to find me true niche in life, Mars is aligned wi' Neptune creatin' powerful influences in me astral orbit. I must follow where me confidence leads, both at work and in relationships, accept compliments as they'll be sincere and meaningful." She laughed, then sighed, but read on. "Time to shake off self doubt, the path ahead is paved wi' opportunity, but beware a wolf in sheep's clothin' an' that one raised pavin' that could trip you up. Listen to those celestial voices murmuring in your head, good things are just around the corner, waitin' especially for you. Oh aye, I know what's waitin' for me, a pile of ironin' an' I shall tell doctor when I see him that it's not bloody Tinnitus, its celestial voices. I'll have two sugars in mine Hilda love, but not too much milk."

It was a curiosity that folk referred to Dick Woolascroft as his father's son when in appearance any similarity was difficult to spot, the notion vaguely occupied William's thoughts as he walked away from the works' office across the yard, past piles of building materials and general evidence of the trade. A miserable looking dog sat on its haunches by a stack of drainage pipes, observing William's progress, while the sound of timber being sawn inside a Nissan hut by an individual intent on singing his way through the task, sent the lyrics of a popular song out across the yard with a cheerfulness that eased William's niggling anxiety.

"Cigareets an' Whisky an' wild wild women, they drive yer crazy they drive you insane."

The dog barked a token gesture of its authority then on seeing William leave though the gates, sank to its belly as if it too was soothed by the light hearted rendition drifting from the open door of the Nissan hut.

Woolascroft was sharp, there could be no denying that, the prefabricated estates that had sprung up like mushrooms after the war had been the builders' bread and butter, now bolstered by the assurance of such schemes, underwritten by the government and virtually risk free, the likes of Woolascroft sought to speculate a little in pursuit of a more lucrative plan.

For every score of working class mortals there was a rising number of middle class, for these property was more than a home, it was investment, they were prepared to pay for the right house in the right place and one or two refinements, whilst not adding too much to the cost of the build, nevertheless enhanced considerably to that sense of attainment, which in turn was typically calculated into the price. Bread and butter had found some jam and Dick Woolascroft liked to spread it thick.

William had put his signature to a legal and binding stake in the business, 20% of all things Woolascroft. Neilson and Bradbury was the firm instructed, the relish with which they supped a little cream from the top of the glass had been evident around the smiling mouth of Anthony Neilson as he shook their hands. Entering the fray along with William was Gordon Cheetham, he too had staked 20%. Dick had firmly held on to command with the majority stake. When William had enquired as to whether or not Patricia Bradshaw had chosen to invest, Dick's response had been simply, 'We are without female influence Eddowes' and he'd laughed but William had sensed a note of resentment in those few words and it had served to undermine in an irritating way, the confidence of which he'd persuaded himself over the course of the past month or so.

The episode of confusion following both the death of her father and husband, in the event appeared to have strengthened Mrs.Bradshaw's character, surprisingly over the years since she had successfully dealt with affairs of the pit and managed to redeem herself in the eyes of most folk who had hitherto considered her to be Basil Stanford's replacement, personally coached in the ways of extortion. She was no fool and while he'd never openly admit it, William would have welcomed her involvement and her reasoned approach. Aunt Patricia would surely be entitled to some measure of authority over her nephew as despite differences in the past, Cynthia Woolascroft and her younger sister in law seemed to have overcome any division, Dick was now obliged to acknowledge 'family' whether it served his purpose, or not, at least publicly.

The 'Business', as a result of the new order, now had access to a number of sites for possible development. William owned land at Strelley, Clifton and was currently at the final stage of securing the deed to an old warehouse at Derby. Gordon Cheetham had shrewdly got his hands on the parcel of spent colliery land at Colver. That had galled William, his approach, twice, of Caroline Tozer and her sister Julia had got him nowhere, to be thwarted by none other than his own wife's cousin added insult to injury. It was ironic therefore that indirectly, he now had an opportunity to make money from the torment, which Colver had become. 'Swings and roundabouts', an expression he'd heard used many times at Lodge meetings.

Driving away from the yard he glanced at his watch, 12-30, he'd call at Moreleigh, Diane would likely be at home, life offered some simple interludes, rent and repast. The first time he'd felt guilty but it harmed no one. Celia wouldn't suspect, she was far too distracted by women's trivia, letters to Emily and Mathew, shopping with Rosie Spooner, matronly concern for the Batemans. Provided he fulfilled his role in the household, attending the table for meals, placing housekeeping money under the mantel clock each week and warming the bed at regular intervals all would be well. Diane Roper understood him and every once in a while when the absence of her husband left her lonely, they satisfied each other.

William's foot applied a little more pressure to the accelerator pedal. Wasn't it a trait of men? It had been so for his errant grandfather, and the way of Anthony Hemsley. William used events of the past to mitigate deeds of the present, he so easily dispensed with conscience. Without any real intention he broke into song.

"Cigareets an' whisky an' wild, wild women, they drive yer crazy they drive you insane," and the irony yet escaped him.

Celia hurriedly hung her jacket on the hall stand, there was post on the mat and one envelope caught her eye as being a likely letter from Mathew. Her heart had sank one day last September when he'd come home from work with news that clearly excited him but rendered Celia bereft. Management wanted him to take up a position at the Dublin plant, it was the factory at Hanover Quay that produced Sturmey-Archer hubs and Raleigh was turning its attention to more lightweight sports models in order to continue growth in the export market. Mathew had shown a great deal of interest in the development of speed transmission and Stewart Hyde, who had taken over from Percy Pollard soon after the end of the war, had recognised Mathew's eagerness and deemed it beneficial to the Nottingham operation that Eddowes spend some time in Dublin on their production line. The bicycle must compete with the fast growing popularity of the automobile, likeable young Eddowes was a suitable candidate for the role of co-ordinator, taking to Ireland the goodwill of the English concern and in due course bringing back vital insight regarding Irish working practices. The largest export market by far was America, the modern lightweight bicycles crossed the Atlantic in a joint endeavour, a success story.

Many a shamrock was to be found in the States, that symbol of Irish pride, Mathew Eddowes represented the future, a better way, whichever side of the Irish Sea a man stood.

Celia carried the post to the kitchen, sat at the table and opened the precious envelope with fingers so impatient, 'more haste less speed' seemed like an adage most apt as the seal proved reluctant to yield. It was dated June 21st.

Dear Mam and Dad,

Thanks for your letter, I was pleased to learn that Emily managed to see the gold coach. For obvious reasons I haven't spoken of the coronation to the men here, it is impossible not to be aware of the tension that exists in some areas, though at work it seems to be absent. In a strange sort of way I do believe that a bicycle is unifying, the more we concentrate on improving design the more it appears to engage with everyone's sense of advancement. Liam Boland, one of the men I work with, until recently could talk of nothing but emigrating, industry here has been slow since the war, the economy almost stagnant and even I have noticed how much more some goods cost in Dublin compared to home. The factory is running pretty much at capacity however and a small pay rise has definitely lifted sprits, although I rather suspect Liam's mind to some degree has been influenced by his meeting Rochella, a very pretty young woman originally from Cork who works at a shoe shop in town. Apparently he tried on six different pairs the first Saturday afternoon, left without buying any, then went back the following Saturday to try on the first pair again, just so's he could look at her. When he reached home and took them from the box he discovered she'd given him two left feet. It seems she'd done it quite intentionally, knowing it would bring him back to the shop, a mutual attraction.

When he related these events to the rest of us at break time one of the older men, Jonjo, told us how he'd been smitten with two sisters, both having desirable qualities, his description would suggest of the physical kind! Apparently he proposed to the younger one whom he considered slightly ahead in the rankings but she refused him, so he immediately asked the other and she accepted. My first thought was, 'how shallow'. Then he went on to say that just days before the wedding she changed her mind. Well the frock was bought and paid for and the younger sister was almost of the same dimensions with a squeeze here and there, so she reversed her original decision and with a short delay to satisfy the Priest they were duly wed. I considered the arrangement too flexible to be worthy yet they've been married twenty five years next month and they're going to spend a long weekend at Wexford where his wife might choose a cut glass vase to mark the occasion. The crystal produced at Wexford has the reputation of being superior in every way.

I have a week's holiday due the early part of August so I shall be home with all news then and many photographs. The camera I bought from Mr.Fitzgerald's shop has travelled with me on my jaunts most Sundays. I have had to discipline myself not to take anymore pictures of Grottos, they are curiously beguiling but I'm sure the Virgin Mary must tire of constantly being a spectacle, all ladies need peace sometimes and her face seems to shrink from the camera with endearing shyness, so I have directed my lens toward other less sensitive features of this fascinating place. I write a short 'travelogue' on the reverse of each snap so I can take you on a guided tour as it were. It will be good to spend some time with Emily, I'm assuming she will be home for the summer break. We both now reside in Capital cities yet I imagine them to be quit diverse, it will be interesting to exchange knowledge of our surroundings. Tell grandma I came upon a lovely little dwelling with the charming name of 'Annie's Hearth', I think that grandma would enjoy Ireland, it's not afraid to let folk glimpse its soul. Here the people wear their culture and heritage at all times, woven into the fabric of their everyday work clothes and familiar, like kin. Back home we tend to keep such things in the press, on a hanger with the

Sunday best and bring them out only on special occasions. I have always felt the most comfortable when in work clothes, their fit is easy and they present less fear of mark or stain. Perhaps it is something so simple, which creates the differences, we need only to change the weave in our everyday.

Take care, much love to everyone,

Mathew xx

Celia smiled down at the notepaper, her son's nature traced through the words as though he'd actually spoken them. The letters that arrived from both Emily and Mathew encouraged her more than they could ever guess. William could be difficult if things were not going his way, he'd not been successful in his bid for land at Stapleford, it led to days of sullen grumpiness and when, two years ago, he'd learned that Robert Cheetham's son had secured the parcel of land at Colver his mood had been as barbed as a thorn bush and persisted for weeks.

Celia slid the letter back inside the envelope and propped it against the sugar pot. If William came home for some dinner he would perhaps be heartened at the prospect of having his children back for a while.

Emily had settled well to her studies at St.Mary's, teacher training had been considered vital after the war and Emily's results at school were commendable, her first love was music but she also excelled at English literature and pursued the subject of history with a passion. She had always made friends easily and though London must have seemed daunting at first, now she wrote confidently about its landmarks and citizens without any hint of regret. When she'd left to take up her place last September and Mathew had departed for Ireland last October, the overwhelming sense of emptiness had been as much as poor Celia could bear but both her children had able minds and strong convictions. The pictures of devastating destruction caused by the blitz on the Capital, which Emily had seen in publications at the library, determined her to achieve academically and play a part in the process of rebuilding a wounded society. It was her firm belief that education was liberating, it freed the mind by dispelling misguided opinions and replacing them with sound logic and hard fact. If the war had proved anything to Emily Eddowes then it was surely that ignorance in high places was the real threat. What travelled down the gun barrel was first released in a room occupied by the so called, 'brains behind' and the apostrophe between the n and s, which she had written into her essay, had not been an error of punctuation.

The sound of footsteps approaching the back door caused Celia to look at the clock, just after half past two. He may have eaten, William would sometimes arrive at around this hour and declare he'd stopped for fish and chips.

His eyes fell at once on the envelope. "It's stuffy in here Celia, leave the door open for some air." He observed the Irish stamp.

"Mathew is coming home for a week, early in august." Celia's expression revealed her delight.

"How busy you will be then my dear, so much preparation, I must endeavour to keep from underfoot."

His tone held sarcasm but Celia ignored it and simply asked if she should get him something to eat. He stared at her for several seconds.

"You begin to look like your mother. I felt peckish so I stopped for something earlier but I could drink a cup of tea." He took off his jacket and sat down taking the letter from where it rested by the sugar pot.

"Your shirt is fastened on the wrong button?" Said Celia with a degree of curiosity.

"Well I don't imagine Woolascroft noticed, too busy in his counting house. So Mathew is coming home for a week, Emily will be here too surely. Then we shall all go off somewhere, a family day out, whilst we have the opportunity. Leicester, how about Leicester? You could choose a new summer frock at Lewis's, I dare say Emily and Mathew could find something they'd like to wear, young folk always can. We could have a nice meal at the café."

William had mastered the art of subtle diversion. Celia beamed.

"Oh yes, that would be perfect." She set about making tea, while the kettle boiled she cut a slice from a ginger cake and carried it to the table. "Arthur Bateman is growing mushrooms in the old Anderson Shelter, they like the dark, Arthur refers to it as his dark room. He can't see yet he wants to do something useful. His grandson built some staging for the shelter and managed to obtain some mushroom spore from the nursery at Chilwell. You should call round and offer Arthur encouragement, I know he'd appreciate it and you'll feel less guilty when Doris gives us some results of his labour, as I'm sure she will."

William paused in his reading and looked at Celia with an amused expression.

"In the dark, at times my dear I think many folk are in the dark but if it produces mushrooms then what a bonus. I shall visit Arthur as soon as I've drunk the tea and finished reading Mathew's letter."

Women's trivia now apparently extended to the growing of mushrooms. With one hand he reached for the cake and took a bite, assured of his unquestioned place as head of household. He felt pleased with the day's events, especially the satisfaction of finally seeing Colver yield to William Eddowes' designs. It was such a pity that he couldn't make the devious Basil witness it.

Celia placed a cup of tea by the plate of cake, he offered up a smile that was no less of a mockery than Stanford's own. She hummed happily in blissful ignorance, her children would soon be with her once more, if only for a short time, that was more than enough satisfaction for Celia.

CHAPTER THREE

"Won't you have another piece of shortbread Annie?" Florence chuckled, "I'm not very adventurous in the kitchen, do you know, I've been making that same recipe for years, it's from the Be-Ro book, not during the war of course, how we did adapt our culinary skills, the old saying rings true, 'necessity is the mother of invention'. More than anything else it was that dreadful fish we were all encouraged to eat, 'Snoek', even its name suggests something to assault the stomach, surely it must be the most unpalatable source of protein. In any circumstance where there was nothing available for consumption other than Snoek I do believe I could countenance cannibalism, just imagine the fun one could derive from making up a list of the first to go in the pot."

Now Annie chuckled.

"Very well, I shall take just one more small piece of shortbread, given your present mood I wouldn't want to offend.

Talking of fish, Billy took Michael fishing for the first time last Saturday, Jack went too, it's difficult for Billy, Victor used to be his other arm. Those two were never happier than when sitting quietly by the Trent. I don't think catching a fish was the object of their expeditions, it was simply one another's company, shared along with a bag of toffees. Edna would pretend to be vexed and say, 'those silly beggars have gone off wi' arf me bread an' arf their brains'," Annie let out a deep sigh.

Florence reached over to pat her friend's hand.

"Who do you think Mrs.Dodds might have put in her pot first? I did so enjoy talking with her on the odd occasion that we met, mostly at the shop. She had a wonderful way with words, she called a spade, a spade but always with a little additional description that made her every account much more interesting than the usual exchange of conversation."

Annie's face broke to a smile.

"I miss her a great deal, but sense that she still knows the nature of our days and if Edna had any control of the situation then she would have arranged for a fish to take young Michael's bait just so she could see the broad grin spread across Billy's face.

Her list for the pot would be made up of all those pompous, blustering figures from officialdom who so irritated her, but when the time to render them to a stew actually arrived she would have given them a very large piece of her mind and required them to swallow it whole before sending them away suitably chastened. Then she would have poached her Snoek in the pot and sent a string of curses up in the air with the steam."

The sound of the front door and Patricia's voice calling out. "You'll never guess who I've been chatting with Mother." Prompted Annie to stand up.

"I should be going Florence, Patricia will want to spend time with you now."

Within seconds Patricia appeared, she crossed the room with an air of almost excited delight.

"Hello Annie, don't go just yet, I'm sure you'll be interested too. I know Mr.Smithfield has long been a friend of your family and I'm sure you'll remember Rex."

Annie sat down again, it was curious that the mention of his name made her nervous, she saw him seldom, since leaving the shop no reason presented itself. Yet if when in town, she happened to bump into him the memory of Edna's revelation, even though she had told herself it was embellished by Edna's own wishful thinking, nevertheless caused her to tremble a little and to consciously hide her awkwardness beneath a very correct cordiality, he must surely puzzle over her manner yet she could do nothing to alter it. At her age how utterly foolish and unnecessary but the nervousness persisted, along with a genuine regard for that kindly man, a concern for his well being, which never lessened.

"Is there enough for another if I squeeze the pot?" Asked Patricia casting her eyes over the table, "I'll fetch a cup and saucer."

She hurried to the kitchen leaving Annie and Florence feeling confused, after all this time could it really be Rex Madden to whom Patricia referred and if so, what was the connection to Andrew Smithfield? Florence slid her fingers inside the tea cosy.

"It's still quite hot," she said, looking at Annie with a bewildered expression. "It must be all of twenty years since Rex left."

Patricia returned, poured herself some tea and sat down beside them.

"He was walking across Slab Square towards me, I think we both hesitated, just for a second or two, after so long I suppose a doubt is understandable. His face is older, yet familiar, after all grey hair and a few wrinkles can't change the features. He spoke first. 'It is Mrs.Bradshaw isn't it?' Apparently over the years he and Mr.Smithfield have corresponded, not frequently but an exchange of general news, along with a card at Christmas or Easter. Rex is staying with him at Brassington while he looks for somewhere to live. He asked after you Mother, he was aware that father had died, I imagine through Mr.Smithfield's letters. He seemed really pleased when I told him you were well. I think we should invite him for tea one day, he is undeniably a part of our past and so much has happened since he left, such change. I'm sure I used to be less than hospitable to poor Rex."

Patricia paused, took another sip from her cup and drew her teeth over her lower lip quite harshly, as though needing to feel the discomfort of a rebuke.

Annie got to her feet. "I really must go now. I do of course remember Mr.Madden very well, it was after his wife sadly passed away and he left Mr.Stanford's employ that William became........," Annie's slight hesitation before saying, "your father's driver Patricia," caused Florence to utter.

"Stanford's man." She smiled, "but he returned to Mr.Smithfield's employ when Basil died. Now Rex is back and staying with Mr.Smithfield, how we are all connected by events, which thread through the past so significantly and yet quite random. I shall see you to the door Annie."

The two women stood by the open back door, Annie's favoured place of arrival and departure.

"Take care my dear and regards to Charles. I wonder if William and Rex will recognise each other, it's a while since either of them was so 'owned', I can't think of a more appropriate word Annie, Basil owned us all."

Annie kissed Florence's cheek and swallowing hard walked away. Basil Stanford owned many more than dear Florence could know, even now, all these years after his death he ordered Charles' troubled mind and drove William's relentless ambition, pulling Celia into the cruel mix that Basil's devious ways had created, just as Annie herself, day on day lived within its turmoil.

Rex gently moved the globe with his forefinger, tracing his passage across its surface. Andrew briefly turned his head to observe, then returned his attention to pouring a tot of whisky.

"The world appears much less alarming displayed that way doesn't it Rex? Yet I would listen to the wireless, to the reports of Allied advance and just as you are doing now, I would follow their progress with my finger, barely moving it more often than not but ever with them in thought. Names of towns, rivers, bridges, unknown to me before the war, all then became familiar, I'd imagine the faces of frightened people, in my head I knew them, that globe was more than graphic, it was alive."

Andrew crossed the room and passed a glass to Rex. “A great deal has changed since you left but I imagine England to be much less complex than South Africa. I would read your letters as keenly between the lines as along them. Man and his insistence on ‘colour coding’. Value, denomination, according to a given shade. We employ it in so many areas of life, money, politics, rank, even stamps. At the factory we were obliged to pay considerably more for the vibrant coloured dyes and when did we ever see such brightness in the slums, ‘richly’ coloured garments sat about the shoulders of the wealthy while the dull, muted shades allowed the poor to blend with their background, unseen, easily passed by. Colour coded, perhaps applied in South Africa it is more obvious but the system to some degree is employed throughout the world.” Andrew spun the globe rapidly until the individual colours on its surface became blurred, one shade, without definition.

Rex took a sip from his glass. “I saw Patricia Bradshaw in town, she seemed different to the way I remembered, quite pleasant, I didn’t know whether I should speak or not when I saw her approaching, but after a few seconds hesitation, which I believe we both displayed, I found myself saying, ‘it is Mrs.Bradshaw isn’t it’? She came across as quite naturally surprised but genuinely pleased to see me.

Her father could have found his utopia in South Africa. Following the war changes came but none that would have impeded Stanford’s progress, rather he would have fed off the back of them, gorged himself. The political melting pot has grown hotter and hotter ‘til the heat from it sucks up the air and saps the ability to think rationally, and still the contents refuse to dissolve to a smooth blend. While I worked my mind was occupied, I concentrated solely on getting through the days without complication. I worked hard and honestly.

You see Andrew, I had always felt denied my natural affiliation to the black faced men at the pit when bearing the title of Stanford’s man. In South Africa I was amid a throng of black faces and that suited me, I was myself, I was no one's 'man', I was Rex Madden." He smiled, "I had escaped that coding system Andrew and it felt good. I didn't know what to expect on reaching the Transvaal, nor did I appreciate how significant was Witwatersrand, gold, vast deposits of gold. It was easy finding work, you have to remember that Claude Stanford took me from the coalface to drive him when Doris was so ill, but I worked underground, in the thick of it, at Colver and Birchdale, I went to South Africa a miner. Wherever in the world might be found a deep hole in the ground, it will have little to distinguish it from another, blackness, stifling heat, nauseating smells, dangers, universally the same. Before the war labour was less divided, after all, down in the bowels of the earth all faces are grubbied and dark. People don't realise how much poverty existed in the white population over there, they sought work and the mines provided it."

Rex took another sip from his glass, leaned back in the chair, as if gathering his thoughts. Andrew remained quiet, Rex's account was gentle, though not of a gentle place, it fell upon his ears with no urgency and Andrew wished it to continue. So many hours he had spent alone since selling the factory, to have company and to be told, in such a fashion, the story of his friend's travels was a rare pleasure.

Rex spoke again.

"After the war that change was swift and harsh, apartheid, just a single word, but how loaded with effect. I was about to step aside, make room for a younger man in the workplace. I'd served my time, done my duty as I saw it. I left for Johannesburg, in my naive way thinking I could now enjoy retirement, be Rex Madden with time to spend in sunlight, honestly earned and deserved.

The young black men were roused, emotion drives with more force than a whip, their passion raged, through the streets and tracks, devouring any obstacle, aflame, all consuming. The more I learned and witnessed the more I could understand why, I could relate to these young men. All those years I was under Basil's thumb and how he pressured, you know the truth of it, if I'd defied him the consequences would have killed Doris, but the men, they believed I chose to be Basil's lackey, that I was apart from them by choice! I existed in no man's land, Rex Madden could be a man nowhere, oppressed by Stanford and segregated, forced to be apart from the men I used to work with, demeaned, and there was nothing I could do to change things. Liberty, I can understand sheer desperation when a man's liberty is denied him through oppression. In Johannesburg that damned colour code tracked me down, I'd escaped it, down a deep, miserable hole in the ground I'd escaped it, but in Johannesburg, in sunlight, I'd become, 'a white man'.

I thought of home, of England, I didn't want to die out there like dad and it was too far away from Doris and John, Basil was gone." Rex smiled, he chuckled as a thought amused him. "Just before Patricia Bradshaw turned to walk away she said, 'mother would love to see you again Rex, you must come for tea, one day soon'. Now I know that I have truly arrived Andrew, it has taken only seventy years but Rex Madden has arrived."

"Perhaps for that family the changes have been particularly severe," said Andrew. "Anthony Bradshaw was killed in Italy, her father was gone then her husband, she became ill, a deep depression, she was hospitalised, I can't imagine it possible to bring about quickly a recovery from such illness, she remained there for some time. You will remember the youngest daughter, Caroline, who married Edmund Tozer, two sons, he too was killed, air force, shot down."

Rex let out a long breath, his eyes held concern but willed Andrew to continue.

"The middle daughter returned from Italy, I understand she'd worked there for years, that she'd met and married an Italian long before the outbreak of war. Through the conflict she'd been interned, her husband too is dead. I wrote to you of Basil's death, I felt you should be aware of that, but the rest," Andrew paused and sighed, "the rest seemed personal to Florence Stanford and her daughters, I couldn't write of it, too much tragedy had been broadcast one way or another.

The animosity spawned by Basil couldn't continue to thrive under these changed conditions, for the most part I think the four widows have been granted peace. I've had little cause to be in the company of any one of them except for Mrs.Stanford. She came to see me, seeking advice, I believe Patricia inherited the greater part of her father's estate, her sisters were to have a parcel of land at Colver. Florence asked if I would let her know when I considered it a good time to sell that land, it obviously had the potential of development status. Of course when the collieries were nationalised, Mrs.Bradshaw was obliged to sell Birchdale to the Coal Board, such a transaction would have made her a very wealthy woman. But you are right Rex, she does appear to have shed her father's influence and the result is quite startling. Although I don't believe her deeds are common knowledge she has sponsored two scholarships at Clarendon College and created a bursary at the university, I only know of this through an acquaintance who is one of the governors. I felt sure they would carry the name of Basil Stanford, to perpetuate his memory, but no, they are without title.

I imagine she will have invested wisely, there are a number of men with reliable knowledge of local business, even valuable information regarding companies from further afield, some acting officially, others on the fringe but with connections. The chamber of commerce is rather like that globe," Andrew's gaze travelled to the informative item of furniture that had enlightened him so many times. "Spin it just a little and more than likely the information you seek will be found."

Rex rubbed his palms down over his thighs and sighed.

"I do hope the invitation to take tea was merely a vague pleasantry, soon to be forgotten, what could I possibly say to them, a family reduced to four widows?"

Andrew was slightly amused. "I can't help thinking Rex that their quandary might be greater than your own. A widower, a travelled man at that, respectable and not entirely a stranger, in their midst."

"Good God I shan't go."

Andrew spun the globe roguishly. "Another tot of whisky is called for surely. Henry Wicks would use the expression, 'without fear or favour', it enabled him strength of purpose. We shall drink to that Rex and raise our glasses to his memory."

Francis read through what she'd written, she sent a letter to Annie as often as she could, keeping her abreast of events at the farm. This month had been a spell of feverish activity, saving hay and lifting the first of the potatoes, not to mention lime washing the dairy between calving and overseeing the arrival of two litters of piglets. How she had managed to progress the sewing of the bridesmaids' dresses amazed even Francis herself, without the help of Ivy and Molly the pretty rose pink taffeta would likely be reposing still on the sitting room table.

The date of the wedding had been fixed, September 26th at the parish church at Skendleby, where Faith was christened. When the young couple had got engaged last year Freddy had declared it to be more than he could have hoped for. Richard Gillpin was a herdsman at a neighbouring farm, that way of life familiar to Freddy was equally so for his future son in law, hard, honest labour, an industry answerable to nature before the influences imposed by mankind, decent at the core and his elder daughter Faith would thrive within its goodness.

Leaving Bobbers Mill all those years ago, despite the heartache at the time, had proved a blessing, events had somehow found a sensible order, slotted into place as though following a plan, yet none such had been devised. The family had made a good life, only one regret thread its way through the past, for Freddy particularly, letters could do little to compensate for the distance in time and miles he had lived away from his mam. The war had galvanized everyone's spirits, defeating the enemy, defending all that was dear had taken charge over every single day and night. Losing John had inflicted a pain that stabbed the heart and crushed the mind, time healed to a degree but grief could suddenly erupt from the most innocent, everyday moments, a ray of bright sunshine, the call of a newborn calf, the first head of apple blossom. One day Freddy had wept over a pail of milk, with a pain deep inside him so sharp he sank to his knees on the dairy floor, it came from nowhere, like a sudden gust of wind that could cause the rooks to take flight. His mam was seventy two years old, how much greater must the pain be for Annie, and Freddy saw too little of her, they all did, Francis, the girls, months went by so quickly and all the time Annie grew older. Whatever might prevail Charles' mood the marriage of Faith to Richard Gillpin would surely bring occasion for happiness and with no shop to worry about anymore there was no reason why Freddy's mam and dad couldn't stay for a while. Nottingham could manage without them, William could manage without them, his brother took too much for granted.

Francis could understand her husband's feelings, while he held no jealousy over circumstances surrounding Davina's legacy, the situation as described by Hilda had sickened him. Always his mam suffered through William's selfishness and his dad seemed never to oppose it. Some nights Francis would be aware of his wakefulness and knowing how hard Freddy worked every day, concern for him kept her from sleep too. But now they must look forward to the wedding and she embraced the hope of better things. William and Celia would surely attend, it was the first truly happy event for the family since the war ended, George would come with Samuel, Hilda and Jack with Rosemary, perhaps David if he was granted leave. Mrs.Gillpin, Richard's mother, maintained that happiness was infectious, Francis prayed William and Freddy would succumb to its spread and display every symptom for the sake of all, but especially Faith. The forthcoming wedding delivered not only a measure of comfort over the ideal union between her daughter and a wholly dependable young man, but a degree of anxiety for those taut emotions that kept Freddy from sleep, should they snap under the pressure of William's presence. If there was any way of excluding him then Francis would clutch at it but Celia wasn't deserving of such upset.

With a hefty sigh Francis folded the letter and slid it into the envelope, she would walk to the post box before bringing in the cows for milking. When the girls were infants she would take them along the lanes around Skendleby, often calling on Ivy, the two women had grown close, in recent weeks spending every spare hour together, sewing. The bridesmaids' dresses were now complete, one for Grace and a smaller version for Pauline, Ivy's young granddaughter.

Harold and Elizabeth had waited until the end of hostilities before trying for another child with the result that Frank Boucher was ten years older than his sister Pauline. He'd not grown to share Harold's liking for farm work. Ivy had recognised quite early on, the boys' preference for more sociable activity, once school work was done he'd be hitching a lift to the coast making himself useful at the hotel or cafés in return for a few bob. Now he was employed officially by Mr.Holloway of the sea front hotel at Ingoldmells and lived in during the main summer months, kitchen portering and washing up, or 'pearl diving' as Frank chose to call it. Francis suspected it was unlikely to be permanent, national service aside, she sensed he was a young man who wanted to spread his wings. His dad worked still at Huttoft where he and Elizabeth had occupied a worker's cottage since they were married. The business there had grown considerably, the war had demanded so much of all farms but the Shipmans had seized the opportunity to expand in recent years and were now not only a significant milk producer but one of the largest growers in Lincolnshire. Faith worked in the office at Huttoft which she described as being 'busier than Skeggy's funfair on a bank holiday'. Grace had found work at the local bakery, the early mornings seemed never to faze her and Freddy's delight on learning that any bread too stale to sell she could take home for the pigs had sent him whistling about the farmyard in anticipation. Francis had one day heard him telling a sow, overdue to give birth, that the 'very' crusty bloomer loaf she was determined to consume, through the sheer effort of defeating its resistance to her jaws, should set things in motion. Within four hours she had produced a healthy litter of eighteen piglets. Freddy rewarded her efforts next day with two thoroughly dried iced buns and one virtually indestructible Eccles cake over which she'd shown no discernment.

Both girls continued to help about the farm as much as they could, the female farm worker was now a common sight as many had stayed on after the war ended, but Freddy had encouraged their daughters to gather some experience outside of family affairs, believing it broadened their knowledge and allowed them a choice, something denied to so many women in the past.

Ivy and Reggie worried over Molly, since losing Walter she'd become almost reclusive outside of her work, cleaning at the vicarage and the school. Reggie had hoped a spark might ignite through friendship with Jimmy Payne but as yet Molly chose to spend her free time sewing or knitting, in fact she had almost commandeered the task of embroidering the necklines on the bridesmaids' dresses, sitting for hours with fine needle and silk.

Reggie had reluctantly stepped back from his work with stained glass, arthritis in his hands had now so distorted his fingers they could no longer achieve the precision, the perfect accuracy, which every stage of development a masterpiece in glass demanded.

Many years ago he had taken on an apprentice, providing the young man with lodgings at home with Ivy and himself at Skendleby. When Jimmy's call up papers had come, the likeable addition to both business and household had shaken Reggie's hand and said, 'get this damn war out of the way Reg and then

I'll be back to make a window that big an' bright folk in Berlin will have to shield their eyes from its magnificence'.

Jimmy had survived the war, Walter had not, Molly had returned to the family home, dwelling under the same roof as Jimmy, his affection for her, a patient, caring fondness had encouraged Ivy and Reggie to hope, but Molly existed in a world of her own and her smile, when cast at Jimmy seemed to hold no more actual meaning than did her pleasant attention to the cat.

Next week the women were to begin making Faith's gown. Ivy had sighed long when she'd told Francis of her concern, surely stitching a wedding dress would be a painful process for Molly. Francis had to agree that very likely it would be so, but life went on, time healed and she was convinced that Jimmy recognised Molly's scars, looked beyond them and patiently awaited her recovery. The wedding would not be an easy occasion for Molly but she was cared for constantly and no one, including Faith, would allow her to feel lonely in the midst of that day's happiness, Molly was loved, perhaps more than she realised.

Ivy would recall the despair she suffered all those years ago, the first war that had robbed her of her Frank, her desolation. Then she had met Reggie and somehow found happiness again. Ivy willed a similar salvation to find Molly, Francis could understand yet ever felt afraid to give Ivy false hope. While cities were being rebuilt lives lay waste still, their restoring outside the reach of urgent plans and designs.

Francis reached the post box only to find a notice attached, it read, 'blue tits nesting inside, please use box at post office'. Even the birds were displaced. She put the letter back inside her pocket, it would have to await mailing until tomorrow.

CHAPTER FOUR

Early August.

"It's a picture of the palace Grandma, I thought Wollaton Hall was grand until I stood in front of Buckingham Palace, it seems to go on for ever, rows and rows of windows, there must be a window cleaner who's only place of work is the palace, by the time he'd shone the glass in the last one, the first would need doing again."

Emily had brought back from London a small gift for each of the family, it was difficult to know what to give her grandma, Annie's taste was ever simple so a linen tea towel, a souvenir of the Capital, Emily had considered that at least useful.

Charles sat at his claimed spot, to one side of the hearth, drawing on a Park Drive cigarette, the packet was close by, on the table in front of the wireless set. His appearance Emily found curiously different to the last time she'd seen him, he'd taken to using Brylcreem, rather too liberally and his hair, though very grey but as thick as ever, sat atop his head like it had been poured from a jug. He no longer bothered to attach a collar to his shirt or to fasten the buttons at the cuffs.

"This is for you Grandad." Emily handed him a wooden matchbox holder with the royal standard printed onto the front. "Around the time of the coronation so many shops were selling mementoes, I thought it would look good on the mantelpiece."

"You don't need to be spending your money on me." That was to be the extent of his gratitude, while Annie hugged Emily and declared her delight at receiving such a lovely present.

"If you two are going to chatter then do it outside, I want to listen to the play." Charles leant over to turn on the switch of the wireless, dropping ash from his cigarette as he did so, he brushed it from the table with his hand, sending it to the rug beneath.

Annie cast a reassuring smile at Emily. "Come along, I promised Nora I would pop in, she would be so pleased to see you, I try to call each week, I knew she would be lonely when Ted Furniss left. Mitchell Street is due for demolition, it survived the bombing but subsidence is causing the problems, cracks have appeared in all the houses, too severe to be ignored. I believe the landlords have been sent condemned notices and the tenants will all be offered places elsewhere, mostly the prefabs at Bilborough, Nora will find it strange, not knowing her neighbours, unless she's fortunate enough to occupy one close to familiar faces. She could have moved in with Gertie and Jean but after all these years I think she's too set in her ways, 'we'd end up squabblin' Annie love', dear Nora, she's probably right."

Charles turned up the volume on the wireless and muttered something under his breath. Emily thread her arm through Annie's and steered her to the door, outside the sun shone, it beckoned and both women sought its cheerfulness.

"I overheard dad speaking on the telephone, he mentioned Mitchell Street," said Emily. "Mam told me he's gone into business with Dick Woolascroft. Mathew doesn't have much regard for the man, I suppose he's overheard the men at Raleigh expressing their opinions, it's the way of men, they talk about such things, hold court and pass judgement when most of it is tittle tattle and hearsay. I'm quite sure that we women are far more ordered and sensible, we get accused of gossiping but it's the men who sit in dark corners of the pubs weaving yarns. Mrs.Lander my landlady in London, reckons anybody listening in to conversation at the Pig an' Whistle would think they were at a wet nurses' convention, 'men spout a titful o' wind Emily love', she said it over a mixing bowl of bread dough and gave it a firm slap of the hand before covering it with a cloth and putting it to rise. Mathew went to see Mr.Smithfield yesterday, they talked about Ireland, I do believe Mathew is quite taken with the place and the people. Mr.Smithfield lived there years ago didn't he? I can't imagine any conversation with him being remotely like a titful o' wind." Emily chuckled.

"If we hurry we can catch the bus." Annie's mind needed to skip past the virtues of Andrew Smithfield, 'a good man going to waste', how frequently Edna's words echoed in Annie's head, Charles could unknowingly make them all the more compelling through his perpetual moodiness, yet she dismissed them with haste and bore her reality as she'd ever been taught to do, 'remember what you are my girl'. We could call at the salon, just for a few minutes to see your aunty Hilda before going to Nora's. Rosemary is making herself useful, brushing up the hair trimmings and making tea for the clients, school holidays have been problematic in the past but Rosemary is now old enough to perform simple tasks and she seems to enjoy it."

Annie had been amused, when following the first visit to the salon of Patricia Bradshaw, to have a trim and perm, Hilda had elevated her customers and even the down to earth Mrs.Whale had become clientele! Annie was so reminded of Mabel Rashleigh when meeting Mrs.Whale at the salon, those wonderful accounts in 3D, vivid, lively and thoroughly enlightening. Annie could never have considered Mabel a client, she brought to the shop so much more than she carried away. Annie was pleased that the Co~op didn't inherit the resourceful Mrs.Rashleigh the memory was Annie's and she valued it.

Sherwood Road displayed the usual mix of people, a queue outside the butchers suggested a special offer of some sort. Cheetham would knock threepence off mince or sausages, often on a Thursday when housekeeping could be getting low in the purse, only the astute would note how much fuller was the basin kept for dripping after cooking a Thursday 'offer'. Folk spread

Cheetham's shrewdness on their bread and while it could be deemed no more than good business, Annie always resisted joining the queue, out of loyalty to Freddy more than anything else.

Mathew had hurried to Winchester Street on his first day home, eager to tell his grandma all about Ireland. The look of relief on his face when he learned his grandad was out hardly surprised Annie, Charles' manner made it hard for anyone coming to the house, even the man who came to empty the gas meter appeared nervous until his task was done and he could escape. When the new vicar paid a visit explaining his wish to meet as many folk as he could within his parish, Charles had remained mute throughout. As Annie stood with the puzzled man, by the back door, he'd placed his hand on her arm and recognising her embarrassment said, 'an excellent start my dear, at one house I was none too politely asked to remove myself, silence I can work on'. But Charles denied himself the pleasure of his grandchildren's company and unlike the vicar, they hadn't the confidence to attempt to convert him.

Mathew's description of Southern Ireland Annie found fascinating, his work, the people, his surroundings and the countryside, all tumbled from his lips in his desire to tell her as much as he could in what time he had. Though another subject obviously occupied his mind, out of the blue he cast the question. 'Do you think dad was wise to throw his hand in with Woolascroft Grandma'?

Annie measured her response carefully, Mathew's thoughts shouldn't be troubled as her own had been when Celia told her what William had done, neither did she want him to become cynical. She ventured to reply, 'Fred Woolascroft, Dick's father had the ability to manipulate circumstances, it would be logical to suppose that Dick learned from his father. If your dad had asked for advice I would have tried to persuade him that a cautious approach might serve him best but he seems confident in his judgments and certainly not afraid to be harsh where he feels entitled. We must hope all will be well'.

Cheetham, Woolascroft, Birkett, those names challenged Annie's mind still. Most folk knew Dick Woolascroft as a womaniser, it didn't necessarily make him a poor business associate but there could be no integrity written into any contract in his name, and to whatever William had put his signature Annie could feel only fearful.

The bus was comfortably full, Emily bid her grandma to sit on the inside by the window so if more passengers got on then it would be easier for Emily to give her seat to someone older but at the next stop more alighted than boarded so she remained in place, intent on feeling down the back of the seat.

"What are you doing," asked Annie.

The young woman grinned. "We always do this in London, you'd be surprised how many small coins can be found, they must slip out of men's trouser pockets, usually halfpennies and sixpences, though I did find two Irish shillings once. I wasn't sure what to do with them so I kept them to give to Mathew. There are a lot of Irish labourers in London and I believe some seek out the 'Sally Army' when they first arrive but I imagine most would be from Northern Ireland. I've heard it said that whenever there's an incident at the border you can sense the tension amongst the Irish community in London. 'If they all had emerald green faces we'd be surprised at their number', I overheard that comment one day at the newsagents, oil on troubled water doesn't seem to be the first policy folk think of. You would hope that by now everyone had more than their fill of strife yet it erupts sometimes over the most incredible things. Mr. and Mrs.Lander have an ongoing dispute every year at this time apparently, she looks forward to seeing the first daisies spring up in the lawn but he can't abide them and rushes out to mow them off. It can become quite heated and what they fail to grasp is while they sulk and brood that cussed little flower comes up again in the exact same spot, they fight but the daisy always wins. What hope can there be for peace on earth if folk even argue over a daisy?" Emily let out a long sigh.

Just then the bus came to a halt, traffic in front and behind but none moving. For several minutes they remained stationary, then the driver lowered his window and could be heard speaking to someone while the conductor hovered behind the cab, looking agitated.

"It's a copper summat's up," observed a man at the front.

Eventually the driver turned in his seat and slid back the small glass screen, his frustration travelled down the aisle of the bus, past his colleague and a rough looking youth who'd tucked himself away behind the conductor at the mention of a copper.

"The No.39 has broken down a quarter of a mile ahead of us, we've to wait here for another policeman to direct traffic then they'll let us through, a few at a time, while they hold back the oncomin'. Anybody as can't wait for that best get off an' walk. Yer can blame City Transport, arf the fleet are due for scrapyard, this bugger's not much better, I've told 'em, anywhere uphill an' you'd think I wer' pedallin' the ruddy thing, a set o' plugs is likely all it needs but it'd be quicker for the missus to knit 'em than to tell the pen pushers at depot."

He sat back in his seat and promptly lit a cigarette. With the exception of one or two of the older men eager to start a debate on local authority spending, the rest deemed it sensible to continue their journey on shanks's pony. Noting the driver's apparent disregard for the 'no smoking on lower deck' notice, one old chap took out his pipe and baccy.

"Can't yer bloody read?" Said the tetchy conductor, before hurrying back to the stairwell where Emily and Annie were about to get off.

"Mind the step missus, would yer believe it, I was due to knock off at arf past." For whatever reason he chose to voice his frustration to Annie. "It's me lad's last day, he's off to do his National Service in the mornin', Lofty swapped shifts wi' me so's I could finish early. His mam'll give me what for, she's made a cake an' her brother Courtney, the lad's uncle's comin' round. He's one o' the top brass at Welfare office, the best china'll be out this afternoon you mark my words. I told her, it'll be the last bit o' nicety the boy sees for two years, there'll not be much fancy china nor sugar lumps where he's goin', an' I still reckon a couple o' pints an' a sing song at The Salutation 'ould be a better send off, but what do I know, I only issue bus tickets, it's not down to me who gets a share o' the loaves an' fishes, Courtney almighty Craddock decides that."

"Perhaps the traffic policeman will be quick," said Emily, trying her best to rescue Annie, "my cousin is at Aldershot, David, David Haynes, tell your son to look out for him."

It seemed to soften the conductors demeanour, he sighed.

"Two years is a bloody long time to march on one piece o' Madeira cake. Me brother copped it in '44, not enough left of him to send home, never even had the cake, poor sod." He sniffed. "David Haynes yer say, my lad's called Phillip, Phillip John Watkins, he wer' eighteen last May, you tell yours an'all, Nottingham lads together eh."

Annie smiled. "I promise we will."

"I can't sit with me back to the engine, it makes me feel ill, are yer goin' far? I get off at Long Eaton, me sister has just had an operation," the talkative woman leaned closer to Liza and whispered, "piles, nasty," she immediately cast her gaze at the other occupant of the compartment, presumably to reassure herself that he showed no sign of having overheard, then launched into a blow by blow account of the trouble she was having with her neighbour, or more specifically, the neighbour's cat and its persistent scrabbling and fouling in the middle of her godetias. "I chuck it back over the fence an' I'm not the only one as complains. Bill Symons on t'other side lost half his seed bed to the damn thing. He's got hisself a catapult now, reckons a few stings from that'll make it think twice. I've told our Rene I can only stay a week an' I don't suppose there'll be a single flower left by the time I get home, but I swear I'll shovel it all up, they can have the lot back, I can't help the fact that their patch is concreted over, they did that the'selves, so the lads could have somewhere off the street to park their motorbikes. The daft cat'd likely do its business there if they'd left a bit o' soil in a corner. You should have heard him, language well! Our street's always been respectable, Mr.Nugent at No.12 takes Scouts an' Lilly Maitland on the corner writes poetry. As if a shovel a cat's mess could hurt a motorbike but my godetias look like they've been struck by lightnin'."

Liza nodded and 'uhmed' at what she hoped might be the right moments but the woman's voice droned on and on, dulling the senses like an anaesthetic.

At the farm they had reached a brief period of respite before the long days of harvest, hay was saved and stored for winter but the wheat crop not yet ready so the opportunity to spend a few days with family Liza must seize now. Susie's house was full with their dad being there and the girls at home still, Annie and Alec were redecorating their living room so it was with Myra and Jack that Liza was to stay. She looked forward to seeing the children, her visits were infrequent and they grew so quickly. It was a welcome change to feel feminine, the work at the farm left her no less grubby and smelly at the end of the day than the men. Today she'd actually put on a pair of stockings, the string of beads that Annie Eddowes had sent her last Christmas and a dab of Yardley's perfume behind each ear. Every once in a while she received a letter from George Boucher, simple lines of family news, of events in Nottingham, nothing romantic but a continuation of the friendship they had known from childhood, yet she'd found herself reading his words over and over. It was true, time did heal. After losing Harry and then her mam she'd wanted to hide away, turn her back, offering even the faintest smile was more than Liza could stand to do, Halam had provided sanctuary while demanding all of her effort. But of late the wider world again engaged her thoughts, she wanted to be a part of it, Liza needed to love, and be loved.

"Next stop Burton Joyce."

The ticket inspector walked the corridor, calling out for the benefit of passengers either intent on their reading matter or nodding off. The man seated opposite looked at his watch, then gathered his jacket and holdall from the rack above before making his way to a door, he smiled at Liza, a sympathetic smile, as though acknowledging the constant assault on her ears, then he addressed the woman, politely and pleasantly.

"Pepper, they say that a liberal dressing of pepper deters cats from scrabbling." Without waiting for a response he was gone through the sliding door and out of sight.

The train pulled in at the station where a group of youths appeared to be about to board. In high spirits their laughter and chatter amused Liza, how carefree were the young. Their activity aroused the curiosity of the guard and he could be heard asking them where they were going. One of the youths replied.

"We're off to the fisticuffs in Nottingham, boxin', bantam weight fight." He punched the air enthusiastically, right fist, left fist and danced from side to side.

The guard laughed. "More like sparrow weight you are lad."

The man from Liza's compartment hurried along the platform, past the youths, towards a young woman, they embraced, it was a simple display of happiness, quite every day, nothing at all unusual about it in the eyes of most folk but for Liza it was a reminder of how long it had been since Harry's arms had held her, warm, safe and satisfied.

The noisy young boxing enthusiasts were finally on board, the guard blew his whistle and the train gathered pace.

"Shouldn't be long now," said the woman, "I'm glad them lads have sat somewhere else, their antics 'ould likely make me fidgety an' I'm tryin' not to move 'cause I could do wi' spendin' a penny, I'll have wait till I get to Rene's, yer never know what yer might pick up from the lavatory seat of a train, them

Americans used the railway an' I've heard they had fleas, not to mention that 'gonawotsit' business foreign folk get down below," she cast a disconcerting look into Liza's lap, "my Fred, God rest his soul, reckoned them G.I.'s couldn't keep it in their trousers."

Liza sighed, "I think it would probably be wise to take your chances rather than develop cystitis." She was about to add that the war had surely been over long enough for the train to once more be free of foreign bodies, infectious or otherwise, when conversation was halted by the sudden appearance at the sliding door of a youth.

"Sidney don't feel very well, can yer come an' look at him Missus?"

Liza was only too happy to get to her feet and follow him, relieved to have an excuse to vacate her seat, she could hardly have been so rude as to leave the woman and sit elsewhere but the incessant chatter grew tiresome. She reached for her small case, clutched her handbag and bid her travelling companion, "Goodbye, I don't suppose I shall be back, I best stay with the boy until we reach Nottingham, I hope your sister recovers well."

The youth led the way to a compartment a few yards along in third class, where one lad sat with his head forward over an upturned cloth cap, which he held between his shaking hands.

"He feels sick Missus, he wer' alright until a few minutes ago, then his lips turned grey an' he come over right peculiar."

Liza sat down beside him, he murmured feebly, beads of sweat began to escape from his 'pudding basin' haircut, trickling down the side of his neck and into the funnel created by his open shirt.

"Do you have a stomach ache?"

He shook his head.

"Have you eaten anything unusual?"

Before the lad had chance to reply one of his mates asked. "What do yer call unusual Missus?"

Liza thought carefully about how best to explain. "Some folk if they eat a little differently can become unwell, an allergic reaction perhaps to a certain thing. I have a friend at work who can't eat mushrooms without being very poorly and I know someone else who's allergic to duck eggs, although they can eat a hen's egg."

The youth poked poor Sidney's shoulder, "What did your mam give yer for dinner Sid? You heard her, if it wer' a duck's egg then that's why yer need to puke." Then he turned to Liza, "There's no mushrooms about yet Missus, if there was we'd pick 'em."

Sidney at that moment retched violently, the cap caught most of it but some was propelled onto the boot of the other lad.

"Ugh shit, we'll be outside in the corridor Missus."

The hasty exodus left just Liza and the unfortunate boy.

"You've been on a train before haven't you Sidney?"

Liza recalled the talkative woman's remark of earlier in the afternoon, when she declared that sitting with her back to the engine would make her ill.

He uttered a miserable, "No," then within seconds retched again.

"We're almost there now," said Liza, reaching into her handbag for a hanky, "the train is slowing down, you'll be alright, let me wipe your mouth."

When he raised his face Liza felt nothing but compassion for Sidney's plight, he looked truly dreadful. Thankfully someone had left a newspaper on the luggage rack, Liza took it down and spread it on the floor, lifting the cap and its contents from Sidney's trembling fingers she wrapped it in the paper, the spatters on the floor she could do nothing about. At last the train stopped. The voice of one of his mates called in through the door.

"We'll wait on the platform."

Liza deemed it sensible to let the other folk get off first, to ease the boy's embarrassment.

“You’ll soon feel better, the fresh air and a walk on solid ground will do the trick, you’ll see.”

Liza encouraged him along, aware that they both smelled of sick, so much for feeling feminine she thought.

The group of youths stood leaning against the waiting room wall, they made an amusing spectacle, there was something endearing about these young males, still reliant on their mams yet determined to put on that big front for the casual observer.

Liza led Sidney towards them, a voice alongside her made enquiry.

“Is everything alright, I couldn’t help but notice your somewhat unsteady progress.”

Liza smiled at the kindly looking man who’d taken the trouble to ask.

“Travel sickness I rather think. Sidney’s first train journey, he and his friends are going to watch the boxing, I don’t suppose they knew what to do when he became so poorly so one of them fetched me from another compartment.”

“So you’re not his mother but a good Samaritan. Well fate is kind, I might be able to help, presumably the lad has a return journey to make later.”

Sidney groaned at the notion and the man chuckled.

“Let’s go over to that bench, I have something in my case.”

He flipped the catches on a small suitcase and lifted the lid. It appeared to contain various items of medication, briefly passing his fingers across their surface he homed in on a packet, plucking it from among the rest almost triumphantly.

“How do you feel now son?” He asked.

With a sniff and a long breath Sidney answered. “Alright, I feel okay now, whatever it was has passed, it weren’t a duck egg Mister, nor a mushroom, I had bread an’ cheese for me dinner.”

Liza thought she should explain, the man's expression showed his puzzlement. By now the other youths had gathered around, far too curious to miss a sight of what this man carried in his case.

"I'm a sales rep. for the Boots Drug Company. I'm lucky I don't suffer with travel sickness, couldn't do my job if I did, I seem to be forever on a train. These tablets are to stop someone like you Sidney from feeling sick on a journey. When do you have to catch the train home?"

One of the others answered. "Eight o'clock, we'll be skinned if we miss it."

"Well then Sidney, take two of these tablets at half past seven and when you get home tell your mother, you'll grow out of it, at least, most folk do."

"Ta Mister, an' you an'all Missus."

Liza and the man watched the youths, now animated, eager for the boxing. He laughed and held out his hand.

"Steve Roper's the name."

"Liza Ollerton, it was very kind of you." The two shook hands.

"Best be on my way or the wife'll skin me, goodbye Liza."

What an eventful time it had been since leaving Halam. Just then a welcome, familiar voice called her name. It was Jack Wainwright, waving and beaming all over his face.

"Am I late, town's busy, folk leaving work but we'll soon be home an' Myra'll have the kettle on."

He took her case, she smelled odd, a bit sickly, he put it down to the farmyard. Must be something to do with her work.

As they made their way from the platform to the street Liza related the afternoon's events from 'gonawotsit of the nether regions to travel sickness and vomit.

"Bloody hell," said Jack, "poor little sod, what a way to lose your cap."

Celia admired the two piece outfit that lay on the bed, a pretty shade of blush pink, dress and jacket. The hat wasn't quite what she'd wanted but it would do well enough. If they'd set off for Leicester in the morning and made a day of it, as was the original plan, then perhaps there would have been time to look in another shop but William had gone out after breakfast and not come back until almost midday. The promised meal at the cafe in Lewis's had been abandoned for sandwiches to eat on the way. His mood was tetchy, and determined that nothing should mar Mathew's all too brief time back home, Celia had bitten her tongue and donned her 'happy hat' for her children's sake.

It seemed the golden opportunity to buy outfits for the forthcoming wedding at Skendleby. Emily planned to attend but for Mathew it would prove difficult to travel again from Dublin, so he'd taken great pains to find what he believed might be a wedding present to please both bride and groom, which he would send with the others on the day. After much searching and pondering Mathew finally found an item to satisfy him, not in Lewis's department store but in an antique shop, down a side street.

A landscape in watercolour, stooks of corn in a meadow, the hedgerow bearing those signs of fading summer, a stand of elm trees against a sky of early evening light. A simple frame made from oak, the medulla rays patterning its surface providing all the decoration needed. The elderly proprietor had seemed almost reluctant to take it down from the wall of the shop. 'You have fine taste young man', he'd said as he wrapped it most carefully in thick brown paper and tied it around with string. 'For a wedding present you say? Then may it grace a new home for many years to come'.

Emily, quite early on in the afternoon, had spotted a dress in the ladies wear department of Lewis's, which fitted her perfectly, even William had let out a gasp of surprise as she'd emerged from the cubicle wearing the figure hugging creation in blue. Perhaps it was the sudden realisation that his daughter was no longer a girl but an attractive young woman, for a moment he allowed fatherly pride to spread across his face in a wide grin. He'd opened his wallet to pay for both Celia's two piece and Emily's dress, also a simple summery hat, the only one Celia could find that wasn't too expensive, given that seldom did she wear a hat other than on such occasions. As the start to their 'so called' day out had been a little tense, she had been relieved by his apparent mellowing and any slight she herself had felt, soon melted away through observing the happiness on the faces of both their children. In fact while Emily distracted her dad for five minutes, Celia bought a particularly smart tie for William, he had a fine suit already and a number of perfectly good shirts, but the tie she felt compelled to get for him to wear at the wedding, he looked handsome when all 'done up' as Rosie would say. She'd left him downstairs dozing in his armchair, the young ones had gone into town, to the pictures, meeting up with Samuel Boucher and Christopher Spooner.

Celia lifted her new outfit from the bed and hung it in the wardrobe, while her hair might be woefully thin and the odd line be advancing across her forehead she nevertheless maintained a trim figure, even without a girdle, she knew some women her age who displayed a much larger outline, those childbearing hips and a bosom surrendering to gravity.

Just then the front doorbell rang, no one was expected, Celia hurried downstairs, if it was Rosie William would be none too pleased at being disturbed.

"Is he in?" I had a quick look round the bar at The Standard, seemed only sensible, old habits an' all that. We fellas tend to pick 'em up from our fathers, like you women learn at mothers knee, been the same since time immemorial."

Dick Woolascroft was the last person Celia expected to find at the front door and rightly or wrongly she could raise no genuine welcome, but politeness prompted her to respond with.

"Yes, William is here, we had a family day out, Leicester, we drove to Leicester, Mathew and Emily are both home at the moment you see. Come through he's in the living room."

William looked surprised, inwardly he felt perplexed. Dick Woolascroft necessitated a man to be prepared for any conversation with him, mentally in particular, having succumbed to weariness and nodded off for a while, William was caught off guard. Assuming it wasn't merely a spur of the moment social call in passing through Wollaton, unlike many men folk, they weren't inclined to share any commonplace activity such as fishing, pigeons, sport or that male place of escape, the allotment, whatever brought Woolascroft to the door must be business related. The look William passed to Celia spoke as loudly as words, obviously her presence wasn't wanted, she left them to their designs, remembering William's sarcasm the day of the coronation when he'd put his head round the door and discovered Rosie, Beryl, Audrey and Annie to be present, 'don't let me disturb the coven ladies'. This must surely be the male equivalent, a meeting of two sorcerers about to covertly cast their ingredients into the bubbling cauldron, to stir until thoroughly combined and then await evidence of potency.

Closing the door behind her she felt the need of a brew, the harmless, everyday kind.

"Can I pour you a drink?" William now stood by a small side table on which he kept a bottle of Scotch.

"Aye, why not Eddowes, you've drunk more than one o' mine in the past." Woolascroft showed amusement and his manner unsettled William all the more. Unfastening his jacket Dick sat down and scanned the room with his eyes, it was a strange thought to suddenly come into a man's mind but William imagined that if Dick had been playing that silly childhood game of glimpsing briefly a number of objects and remembering, he would be able to name everything contained within the living room, even down to a bobbin of cotton which Celia had been using to mend Emily's blouse.

"So you've got the wonder of British Broadcasting then," he said, "we bought one for mother but I don't think it's been on long enough to move the needle on the meter, prefers a book." He took the glass from William's hand. "I won't piss about Eddowes, it's better I talk to you here, ears can flap at the office." He took a drink, put his head back as if savouring the satisfaction, then took another before settling himself in the chair, the tumbler and remaining whisky he held casually on his thigh. "Mitchell Street, two landlords, each owning the houses on either side respectively. The whole lot's coming down soon, I reckon they'll be glad to take whatever they can get. I'm only interested in Charlie Holbrook's side, the odd numbers, now he's an odd number if ever there was one. The old man had a run in with him once, years ago, somethin' an' nothin' as they say. Anyroad, he won't know that you an' me are associated. If I approach him he'll dig his heels in just to be bloody minded but you, I reckon if it wer' you danglin' the carrot it'd disappear down his neck an' be out as wind at t'other end afore the ink wer' dry on the paper. My money Eddowes, not the firms, you'd be broker so to speak."

William forced his mind to concentrate for a moment, what was Dick's reason for wanting Mitchell Street. Back filling and underpinning were costly procedures, the housing there was very old, built at a time when foundations were not always as substantial as should have been, not surprising therefore that mining had tested its endurance. The area wasn't especially attractive either, a view of the gasometer few would consider desirable, if they were to build more select properties for the better off, then Mitchell Street could offer little enticement.

"Why Woolascroft? There's method in your madness, has to be, even you wouldn't sink money into a scheme simply to settle an old score of your father's." William was curious, perhaps more intrigued than suspicious. "As development land it comes with big problems, too many to recoup the additional building cost through a return on average type construction and not lending itself to a superior plan, wrong area."

"You let me worry about such things, as I said, my money so no skin off your nose, I'll make it worth your while of course, I don't expect you to act as my mouthpiece for nothin'. By the time Holbrook realises that you an' me are associated, the deal'll be done, signed an' sealed, sweet as a nut." Dick downed in one gulp the last of his whisky. "Best be off, mustn't keep your good lady wife from her own living room. Keep it under your hat Eddowes."

He got to his feet and crossed the room to put the tumbler back on the table, William sensed the subject was now closed.

"I'll show you out, Celia's probably upstairs, today she chose an outfit for our niece's wedding, you know how the ladies like to dress up on these occasions, it'll have been tried on, put on a hanger with a lavender bag and covered about the shoulders with tissue paper by now. How is your wife? Her illness she bears with great dignity I understand."

Dick made no reply until reaching the front door. "Yes, dignity is a virtue Olive has much of, enough for both of us I dare say." For a second he appeared pensive, his brow furrowed, then striding over the threshold he cast back a surprising remark. "I left dignity somewhere at the curb side, many years ago, never bothered looking for it, too late now."

William watched him walk out of sight. Hard man to fathom, Dick Woolascroft left too many gaps for another to have any hope of reading him.

"What does he want?" Celia stood behind William her expression demanded an answer.

Obliged to offer her something William said simply. "A carrot, a mouthpiece, kindly fate and dignity."

All thoroughly stirred together over low heat until brewed to perfection, thought Celia, but she didn't voice her thoughts, instead she said.

"It's Mathew's last day tomorrow, make the most of it William, we can't know how long it will be before we see him again. Already a sinking feeling had begun to test her emotions, she could understand so well how much Annie missed Freddy but she would wave Mathew goodbye wearing her 'happy hat', while the cream straw bonnet with blush pink ribbon could sit on the top shelf of the wardrobe to await the wedding.

"It's been good having Mathew back for a while, just as you'd expect, he came into the factory to see everybody, his week off naturally included a chat with Stewart Hyde, he's a bright lad and sees life through very different eyes to William. I know Celia misses him, I can understand that, I'd feel gutted if Samuel were sent to the Dublin factory."

Liza saw the real dread on George's face when he spoke the words.

"Is that likely to happen?"

"No, I've no reason to suppose that it will, and it's wrong of me to feel that way, I can't expect him to be with me all his life, he's twenty one, all young men must spread their wings. He's very fond of Margaret from next door, she's a lovely lass, mam's a good judge of character and she says the girl is 'copper'." George chuckled, "Apparently that was one of Mabel Rashleigh's expressions, for someone with ability. Good old Mabel, she lives on."

Liza was quiet for a moment. "Jack and Myra are hoping to buy a place of their own, she was awarded compensation after the accident, I'm sure our mam would have told yours, they shared everything, the good and the bad, I wish I knew where to find such a friendship, they don't grow on trees do they? Anyway, over the years Jack and Myra have put away what they could, only small amounts but added to the original sum the interest has accumulated and they've enough for a three bedroom bungalow, no stairs, to make it easier for Myra, well thinking about it, for Jack too, it's so easy to forget that he has a false leg. They won't want to move far away from family, it'll be Sherwood I imagine, certainly within a sensible distance of Susie because of dad."

"You're happy at Halam still Liza, no thoughts of coming back?"

"Until recently I don't believe I gave the slightest consideration to happiness, much of the farm work is routine, almost automated, a constant process repeated over and over, day after day, emotion doesn't really feature in the way of things, even losing a calf becomes accepted as an integral part of that process. Lately I've found myself wanting to feel...." Liza searched for the right words, "To feel something at least, it's not natural to neither laugh nor cry. After mam I was cried right out, drained of every drop of emotion, it's not normal,"

Her voice tremored as heartstrings, for so long unmoved, now tugged from deep within. George understood only too well the desolation of loss, he gently wiped an emerging tear from her eye and speaking softly said.

"Come home Liza, if for no one else, then for your dad. I call to see him most weeks, he looks old and tired, he'd never tell you how much he misses you, he's the most selfless man. Perhaps it's disloyal of me to think such things but the difference is stark, if Charles Eddowes, my stepfather, had just a grain of Billy's kindness how much more bearable would be my mam's life."

Liza rubbed a hanky across her face, she was about to say something when the sound of the back door being opened and, "Only me", declared Samuel back from the pictures, he came into the living room whistling happily. "Hello Liza, it's good to see you and to know that my old dad had company after all, we tried to persuade him to come with us, Norman Wisdom film, 'Trouble in Store', we laughed 'til we cried, me Mathew, Emily and Christopher Spooner, but he wouldn't, see if you can coax him out of his shell, grandma and I have both tried but stubborn isn't the word for it," he laughed and crossed the room to plant a kiss on Liza's cheek.

"You can see what I have to put up with," said George, pretending to clip Samuel's ear, "he's bigger than me now, thinks he can tell me what to do."

Liza recognised the deep bond between them and before a foolish tear could again erupt to embarrass her, she got to her feet.

"I should be making tracks, Myra and Jack will be waiting to lock up and get to bed, Louise is wakeful some nights, her back teeth I think."

"I shall take you in the van," said George, at the same time looking directly at Samuel, as though seeking permission, he was rewarded with a roguish wink, why then did he feel so nervous, it was Liza, they'd known one another all their lives. Holding her jacket for her to slip her arms into the sleeves he was aware that his hands were shaking. Through all his time as a soldier strength had stayed with him, yet here, now, he felt vulnerable, less worldly than his own son. George picked up the van keys from the shelf, smiled at Liza as confidently as he could and led her to the back door calling back to Samuel, "Won't be long," while inwardly struggling under the hampering weight of his age hardened shell.

"The time has gone too quickly Dad," said Mathew, "it's a shame I can't get back for Faith's wedding but all being well I should be back for a few days at Christmas. Grandma really enjoyed looking at the photos I'd taken, I wish I could manage to get her over there, what has she ever seen beyond the roofs and chimney stacks of Nottingham. She so readily opens her mind to other places and peoples that she's only ever read about in books. Grandad has worn a path between Winchester Street and The Standard, there's no harm in a man taking a drink, I can enjoy a pint myself, but it's as if he's blinkered to everything around him. I sat with him yesterday as grandma made the tea, I could have been invisible, staring into the empty hearth, what goes on in his mind, whatever it is lies far away from grandma, no wonder she spends time with aunty Hilda and Myra Wainwright, couldn't you take him along sometimes, when you're driving about the place, raise his interest, he's not that old. Take Arthur Bateman, poor chap can't see but he still shows an interest in life, does something with his days."

William's fingers clenched the steering wheel tighter. "Your grandad wouldn't take kindly to being told what to do, by me or anyone else, if he chooses to sit in his chair staring into the empty grate, or tuck himself into a corner of The Standard then it's up to him. Whether he condescends to speak or determines the silence is his entitlement, if he's worn a path to the pub then at least he trod it of his own volition, no one drove him there with a stick. Your grandma would likely be skivvying for Jack Haynes and Hilda even if dad were Mr.Cordiality himself, and she was always going to watch over Myra after Edna died, wild horses couldn't keep her away. She's never been able to resist 'a cause', every lame an' lazy scrounger this side of Derby used that shop on Gregory Street, they all knew she was a soft touch, it's little wonder the damn place barely gave them a living let alone a comfortable old age."

Mathew had no wish to part company with his dad amid unpleasantness so he chose to ignore William's unkind remarks and quickly changed the subject.

Mr.Smithfield's mother came from Tipperary, he's familiar with much of Ireland. 'You should visit Connemara Mathew, a man can stand on ground at Connemara and recognise his own insignificance', that's what he said, I think I understand what he means but I shall go there one day and discover for myself.

Rex Madden is staying with Andrew, although I believe he's intending to rent a house on Denman Street from Mrs.Stanford. He asked after you, they both did."

"What time is your train?" William snapped the question and honked the car horn at traffic.

"No panic Dad, It's not 'til ten past seven." Before Mathew could speak further William issued a caution.

"Smithfield might know his way around Ireland and wax lyrical about the place but he didn't stay did he, couldn't get out fast enough once his face didn't fit, you keep away from the border and never mind his poetic nonsense, watch your back, keep your head down."

Mathew felt amused by his dad's concerns. "You know me Dad, I never look for trouble, besides the factory is miles away from the border. Dublin is alive with music, men go out in the evening for 'the craic', it's like our light hearted banter but uniquely Irish. I shall ring to let mam know that I've arrived, she'll fret 'til then but Emily being home will help."

William pulled up by the curb. "I'll say cheerio here Son, no point in my parking the car and coming on to the platform." He glanced at his watch. "Its 7o/clock so you best make your way, the Liverpool train is sure to be busy on a Monday morning."

Mathew leaned over and took his case from the back seat, opening the car door he turned to William, held out his hand and said, "Mind how you go Dad, even this city has borders."

William gripped Mathew's hand so firmly that for an instant it actually pained. Within seconds the car was lost in traffic, Mathew gathered his case from the pavement, hurried through the concourse and into the station, he needed to cross the bridge to the other side of the tracks.

A good number of people were waiting, mostly men. There was a woman holding a small child by reins and the hand of another a little older, with no luggage apparent Mathew presumed they were travelling a short distance only. Two young women stood together, their animated chatter and bursts of laughter suggested a conversation about their past weekend's activities! How draughty are railway platforms, thought Mathew, though the air was warm and summer sunlight dappled the ground beneath the canopy. The familiar pigeons were this morning joined in their search for morsels by a dishevelled rook, his was the first triumph and he flew off with an apple core in his beak, which when discarded had missed the waste bin and lain unnoticed by the less beady eyed birds that paraded their colourful plumage amongst the feet of those regular travellers inured to their presence.

The train came into view, the mother at once stepped back, keeping her children a safe distance from the edge of the platform, while almost all the others moved forward, trying to identify the carriage markings as the train passed by before coming to a halt. With a minute of patient good manners whilst folk alighted and their place of boarding was matched to the price of their fare, the waiting number got aboard. Mathew found a quiet compartment in second class, almost immediately he was joined by another man, his appearance and case suggested a sales rep of some sort. They sat opposite each other.

"How do, nice morning isn't it? Not too crowded yet, that will change when we stop at Crewe," he smiled pleasantly.

"I'm on my way to Ireland," said Mathew, "Dublin, I catch the ferry this evening."

"Ah, off for the craic as they say," he chuckled.

"Work, I work at the Raleigh factory, been home with the family for a break." Mathew unfastened his jacket and settled back in his seat.

"I get about a lot but never the emerald isle, Boots Drug Company, that's me, it's Liverpool for the next three days, to see what I can shift there. I wouldn't mind a chance to kiss the Blarney Stone, a chap needs the gift o' the gab if he's to get anywhere in this line o' work."

He unfolded his newspaper and began to read, an easy quietness rendered the compartment surprisingly comfortable, until the next stop anyway they would be untroubled by others, Mathew's travelling companion presented no challenge to his peace but neither could know how miserably they were connected through 'rent and repast'.

CHAPTER FIVE

September

As was his practice, Tommy stood quietly while the vicar spoke his final words over the coffin, with one hand he'd gently rubbed a palmful of soil until it was as fine as breadcrumbs, now unobserved he let it fall into the small bowl. Over the years Tommy had watched this same scene more times than he could remember, only the faces changed but almost without exception, it was the sound of that first scattering of earth when it fell onto the coffin, which visibly challenged those closest to the deceased. There was little he could do to ease their pain but to render the soil so fine as to fall in virtual silence from the hand to the lid of the coffin, a simple act of compassion through years of privileged understanding.

Now Tommy held out the bowl to Dick Woolascroft, in turn family members sent a small measure of earth into the grave before moving away. Tears had been evident on the faces of some of the women, Patricia Bradshaw lingered, dry eyed but for a few moments appearing oblivious to others, Tommy thought he saw her lips move, as though she mouthed words without sound. William Eddowes stood to the rear of the assembly, acknowledging Tommy with a brief nod of the head. Present were all those individuals so familiar to Tommy when the deceased in his care had been, in life, part of that 'removed' section of society, one of those 'other folk' less compromised by the common touch.

It was a curious fact, sombre black attire, considered only fitting at a funeral, whilst cladding everyone likewise in respectful livery, failed to disguise any individual attending, not to mourn but to witness, one such was Valerie Oates.

Joyce had begun to suspect that Edgar was not Elizabeth's father when Valerie had seized her position as wages clerk at Woolascroft's with such assuredness. Dick's reputation went before him, he'd likely sired a number of such innocents, blamelessly ignorant of their actual kin. Only in Tommy had Joyce confided. Edgar and Elizabeth Perry were father and daughter in every true sense, but it was the irony and Tommy understood his sister's need to voice her thoughts. All those years ago Joyce had ejected Dick from that miserable room on Peverell Street, determining herself to be better, to rise above all that he represented, now it was entirely possible that the little girl whom Joyce adored and so readily helped Edgar raise, the same little girl who called her grandma, was a child of Dick Woolascroft. It mattered not an iota, whatever blood travelled through Elizabeth's veins, flowing with it was deepest love and that indisputably pure, unfaltering Perry.

Tommy now observed the look on Valerie's face, standing as she was to one side, apart from the rest, dressed in black but present not to mourn but to witness.

Cynthia Woolascroft had died in her sleep, when Dick had come to Handley's it was to Joe that he spoke. Composed and showing no distress he'd issued the family's instructions, the funeral arrangements were to be much the same as for his father but no need for the most expensive handles, and a lighter wood could be used. When Joe had sought to confirm that Mrs.Woolascroft was to be buried with her husband Dick's reply had been typical of his mentality. 'Good old ma, came out top in the end'.

Finally the last of the mourners left the scene, Tommy spoke to the sexton, instructing him to place the wreaths and flowers carefully over the mound, arranging them so as to make the attached cards easily visible, one caught Tommy's eye, tied to a bunch of white spray carnations it read simply, 'from Olive'. It wasn't the undertaker's place to question yet when Tommy cast a last glance at Cynthia Woolascroft's resting place he sensed many past troubles lay buried there, while above ground, for such a family, more would surely come.

"Aye up, looks like they've sent 'er on 'er way, must be time for the eats an' drinks now then." Bob Budgeon looked across the road to the cemetery gates where a shiny black limousine was about to emerge. "Wonder who's place they're goin' to, likely be Dick's, arf the bloody 'andshake brigade'll be there. I've heard it said that the nobs, whenever they 'ave a do, only put on the table what's bite sized, them funny little canapé things an' sandwiches no bigger than postage stamps. Me mam 'as a theory on it, she reckons it's so nobody drops crumbs on the carpet, if it goes right in wi'out 'avin' to bite yer get no mess, they wouldn't let the dog lick 'em up like ordinary folk do would they?"

Charlie had paused in his work, the process of burning off old paint with a blow lamp and to carry on scraping seemed too lacking in respect, even though the funeral was over, not to mention the unfortunate smell that accompanied the task, no one would want that to assail their noses as they walked away. The two men were working on the upstairs windows, Charlie stripping the old paint and Bob following on with the sandpaper.

Almost four years ago, while sitting in the cab of the bin wagon bemoaning the monotony of his existence over a Spam sandwich, Charlie had proclaimed himself, 'sick to death of other folk's muck, paintin' an' decoratin' Bob that's the way forward'.

It had been the sight of his dad's ladders, laying redundant in the back yard that first put the notion in Charlie's head. He'd already borrowed them to do up the house he and Maureen had moved into when they got wed and what she said was true, he was good at painting. It was only common sense after all, get the preparation right, use good materials, make a proper job of it and charge a fair rate. Bob had needed little persuasion on the subject, at the time he'd been desperate to woo the shapely Barbara Baines, an usherette at the Odeon, any chance of appearing a half decent catch Bob had grasped with both hands.

'Your poor old man's knees givin' out wer' a stroke o' good luck', was how Bob put it the day he raised a ladder to begin their first commission, yet he'd been unable to walk past the dustbin at the side of the house without putting the lid straight. 'Idle buggers on this round Charlie', he'd said, 'first gust o' wind an' that'd be arfway down Monsall Street'.

As it happened the fickle Barbara glimpsed richer pastures when she'd gone on a works outing to Mablethorpe. Eight months later she'd struggled up the Registry office steps in a subtle beige maternity frock to become Mrs.Rowbotham. The philosophical Bob had shrugged his shoulders and remarked 'that she weren't all that to look at in daylight anyroad', then moved his attentions to Glynis Hopwood who worked at the fish and chip shop.

'There's only so many tubs of ice cream a bloke can stomach Charlie but them parcels o' fish an' chips, by the time you've got outside the shop the smell, that vinegary drippin', a mouth waterin' 2/9d worth is through the newspaper an' up your nostrils like nothin' else an' that Glynis wraps 'em up like she wer' wrappin' a baby, 'tis a joy to behold'.

So far, so good, Bob's appreciation seemed to charm the friendly Glynis and apart from putting on a couple of pounds weight, Bob whistled his way happily through the days with little to dampen his spirits.

Maureen had blessed Charlie with a daughter, now almost three years old the child was the apple of his eye. Jack and Myra Wainwright were Shirley's Godparents, Charlie had so proudly said to his best mate. 'I know now what I wer' put on this earth for Jack'.

Perhaps that was it, the reason Charlie halted his work and watched the funeral car drive away, why his gaze travelled up and down the rows of gravestones, spread out across his line of vision from where he was perched, high up on the ladder.

Maureen and Shirley were his world, he couldn't imagine life without them. Deep love created a reverence, compassion for those bereaved of it, while Charlie felt slight regard for Dick Woolascroft it was impossible to ignore the heartache which must surely overcome those grieving the loss of a mother.

Bob however, obviously considered that more than enough time had been spent on 'respect' and now began to rub, somewhat haphazardly, the sandpaper over the window frame with one eye still on the opposite side of the road.

"That's William Eddowes, him an' Gordon Cheetham, gettin' in that car, yer can tell their sort a mile off. Do yer remember that freezin' cold mornin' when we found Patricia Bradshaw, arf dead an' arf daft in Driscoll Street, she wouldn't 'ave give us time o' day if she 'adn't been doolally. I reckon their family must still 'ave nightmares over that, she's Woolascroft's aunty yer know, ridin' in a bin wagon wi' the likes o' you an' me, one o' theirs travellin' the streets wi' the city's rubbish!" Bob looked at his watch. "Dinner time Charlie, mam's packed us some o' them nice canapés, so's we don't drop crumbs on van floor."

"You're a sarcastic sod Budgeon," said Charlie, "besides, I remember we both got a letter o' thanks from Mrs.Stanford."

Bob was already at the bottom of his ladder. " Aye, an' for a bloke who's forever claimin' to 'ave nous it sounds like you still believe in bloody fairies."

"What's he up to Eddowes? That smug grin of his, even today, burying his own mother it was on his face before he left the cemetery, something up his sleeve but when we shall get to hear about it is another matter."

Gordon Cheetham chuntered his concerns as William drove along. Not wishing to become engaged in conversation regarding Dick's affairs, Mitchell Street was not yet conveyed, William asked.

"Where do you want me to drop you off, back home or in town?"

"It's a fine house, Fred had a lot done to it over the years, I've heard me dad say that the hallway is oak panelled and he had some kind of heating system installed years ago, when most folk were considered affluent if they had more than one hearth, even if they only lit second one at Christmas. Dad would call there from time to time, both being in business I suppose they shared interests. Wonder what will happen to the place now, put up for sale and the proceeds divided I suppose, should fetch a fair sum," Gordon chuckled, "likely the thought of that was what spread Dick's grin."

William felt uncomfortable. At the graveside his thoughts had been with John, memories from childhood had returned, vivid, blotting out sound, just a hazy awareness of the vicar's final prayers. He'd found again the present just as his gaze fell upon Tommy Spooner, then the moment was sharp and clear, he'd nodded briefly, Tommy was so much a part of William's past yet something inside him allowed no more than that brief nod of the head. He'd actually felt remorse. Now Gordon's remark galled and that chuckle assaulted William's conscience. Cheetham was a hypocrite, he'd donned his father's mantle and paraded it with no less smugness than Dick Woolascroft yet here he was making scornful asides.

"I'll drop you home then," said William.

"I've heard on the grapevine that Patricia Bradshaw's put money into Courtaulds. Her sister in law was no fool, some say that Cynthia was the brains behind Fred but her problem was persuading him to listen to her. My missus leaves all that alone, provided the housekeeping allows her a few little luxuries she's happy. What about cousin Celia, is she the quiet spectator type or does she like a turn with the bat?"

Gordon seemed unable to still his tongue, William chose to ignore the question, considering it churlish. Sensing William's irritation, although not entirely understanding the reason for it, Gordon at last declared his intent.

"Well you must do what you like Eddowes but I'm not missing out on a 'light luncheon' at Dick's place, a man can learn a surprising amount when folk gather together without their armour, the women especially let slip a few tit bits after one or two glasses of sherry."

William inwardly cursed his own weakness, he'd planned to deposit Gordon and simply go home but now the thought of being absent from the proceedings at Dick's place and possibly being less informed than Gordon as a result, changed his previously accepting mind.

"Courtaulds you say, that's interesting, perhaps we too should consider putting a number of eggs in another basket."

William slowed down the car as they approached traffic lights, a woman walking along the pavement beside them looked briefly their way, Diane, it was Diane Roper. The light turned to red as if prompting a flush of embarrassment to redden William's cheeks also. Cheetham didn't notice, he was intent on lighting his cigarette, he sent a puff of smoke through the open window.

"Can I light one for you Eddowes?" He asked before putting the cigarette back in his mouth.

"No thanks." William in that instant regained all the confidence the last hour had sapped away. Cheetham had taken the cigarette from a packet of Park Drive, while in William's own pocket lay his engraved silver cigarette case containing 'the better kind'. "There was little chance to speak with the family at the cemetery, I would like to give my condolences to them, not least to the Bradshaw's side, to her brothers, decent folk I understand, well thought of in Hull, from where Dick's mother came, but I shan't stay long, they'll need their peace and quiet, the day will already have been long for them."

Gordon muttered some vague agreement as he brushed ash from his trousers, sent there by the sudden movement of the car as the light went to green.

Diane had walked out of sight and that eased William's awkwardness but the presence of Gordon Cheetham, sitting beside him stirred his emotions, guilt and regret vied with self satisfaction and William's perceived justification for his behaviour. Why in God's name did Celia have to be Cheetham's cousin? There had been a time when the fact impressed a young, ambitious William Eddowes, but that was long ago, pre Stanford and pre war, two elements of William's life, which achieved to diminish the relevance of anything that went before.

"I'm goin' out for a bit, the place reeks of mothballs and scent, they all come out from the woodwork on days like this, have a good nose around, shake your hand before they go an' leave nowt behind but what travelled from the cemetery on their shoes."

Dick took down his jacket from the hallstand, briefly glanced in the mirror and was out through the door before Olive could enquire after his likely time of return.

From a level of such noisy chatter as to grate on her ears, Olive Woolascroft now found herself in total quietude. Dick was at least correct in his description of the smells, camphor didn't mix well with the fragrances of Yardley and now an unfamiliar, unpleasant air lingered about the house even though the last, overly gracious guest left more than an hour ago.

Mrs.Plowman had helped Olive to clear away the dishes and unbeknown to Dick, gratefully accepted her invitation to take home the sandwiches and odds and ends of cake, left over from the luncheon, the hard working woman had four children, and a husband at the pit.

'There's no fillin' 'em Mrs.Woolascroft, our Ronnie must have hollow legs an' his sisters aren't far behind in appetite neither, I'm in an' out o' the Co-op like a fart in a colander'.

Dorothy Plowman came in twice a week to do some cleaning, Olive's health was not good, her illness could be fickle, sometimes presenting little discomfort, at others causing considerable pain and a need to be close by the bathroom. It was debilitating and not a condition to be spoken of easily with the result that Olive seldom ventured further than the town, to the shops or the library, home was the least challenging place to be and she had grown used to her own society. Dorothy Plowman however was a welcome injection of 'life', she brought normality to the house, honest, uncontrived conversation, an ordinary woman with an ordinary family, no axe to grind and Olive enjoyed her company, Dorothy's informative commentary on Plowman life was nothing short of medicinal, especially on days when Olive felt unwell.

In the early months of their marriage Dick had been as Olive imagined any new husband might be, pleasantly attentive, expecting satisfaction when his mood desired it but generous enough with peace once his need was met. In the second year she had miscarried and for whatever reason, had not conceived again.

Then doctors had diagnosed her worsening health as being the result of Crohn's disease. Dick didn't cope well with illness, she wasn't infectious, nor could he catch it through touch but more and more he would spend time away from the house and physical contact became no more than the slightest meeting of fingers when passing the cruet or sugar pot. Gossip had come down through the years and was now as much a part of their marriage as the familiar furniture and ornamentation that bore witness to its indifference. They didn't row or challenge one another, he'd not once raised his hand in temper or denied her money but as Dick aged he'd become a mystery to Olive, just what went on inside his head she could no longer fathom and what might be the nature of his business affairs caused her to feel anxious.

Olive's mother in law had confided in her years ago, probably because she'd considered Olive to be the only person able to understand.

Fred Woolascroft had feathered his own nest lavishly and Cynthia had come to realise that not all the feathers had been naturally shed, he'd shamelessly plucked bare the unsuspecting. Dick had many of his father's ways, though when it came to women they differed, Dick's philandering vexed his father, Fred changed the principles of business to suit himself and saw no wrong in it, yet a moral standard he applied to dealing with women. At times Cynthia had actually felt it was because Fred considered the female to be trivial, too insignificant a subject on which to waste time and effort. Fred judged women to be irrelevant to business, they had their place, he regarded his wife as 'keeper' of their home, he respected her role as that and remained faithful.

Cynthia however resented Fred's attitude, she was able minded, competent and determined not to be ground down, yet Dick, her own son, achieved to do that very thing, he wore her away and observing Olive's diminishing existence, she'd chosen her daughter in law as a sympathetic listener, through frustration and the need to vent it. Cynthia could be no more than a 'silent' partner where the business was concerned, yet she should be entitled, her own father had been more than generous at the time of their marriage and that money Fred had ploughed straight away into his building firm, young as it then was and little known. Lionel Bradshaw had instructed all his children, daughter as well as sons, in the ways of the world and instilled in them the merit of honest gain. In her own right she had acquired property, only to let it go in order to save Dick from himself, his loose lifestyle had cost her dear. Circumstances had led Cynthia and Olive to a genuine friendship, when alone they'd felt their lives eroding, in one another's company some resistance to Dick's chafing briefly held firm. Now Olive had only the reassurance of Dorothy Plowman's chatter, those obvious stares and whispered exchanges Olive experienced on the streets she must bear alone.

Someone was knocking at the back door, Olive sighed, she was halfway through a book that Cynthia had given her, relieved to have thanked the last of their company for attending and having smiled a kindly goodbye, the thought of sitting quietly with her Monica Dickens held much appeal.

"Buy some lucky lace dearie and I'll read your palm, lucky lace and ribbons."

The gypsy woman stood at the threshold holding a basket. Each year they came and foolish superstition, as Olive deemed it to be, prevented her from saying 'no thank you, not today'. Always the tracing of her palm with a finger too keen to grasp money predicted a journey.

'You will go on a long journey and meet a dark stranger, a man whose name will begin with W or E'.

Why should this day produce anything other, yet Olive held out her hand, palm side up, inwardly challenging this gypsy woman to tell her something different.

The gypsy put down her basket and as she bent down Olive noticed the silk square she wore over her hair was fraying, loose red strands mingled with black waves at her shoulder. She stood, took Olive's fingers with one hand while with the index finger of the other she slowly traced each line on the surface of Olive's palm. Momentarily she stopped, looked at Olive then lowered her eyes and followed the line around the base of the thumb. It was done so delicately and with not the slightest haste, unlike those past performances, which left Olive feeling annoyed at her own lack of will, 'not today thank you', was the sensible response delivered by most other folk. Now the woman spoke.

"No children," she looked directly at Olive as if for confirmation, Olive nodded her head. "You will always have enough money but never a fortune, troubles, many troubles, illness," she stooped to pick up her basket, "you will live long, your palm reveals that you will live to a good age." Only then did she release her grip of Olive's fingers. She held out the basket. "Lucky lace, three shillings a yard."

"I'll fetch my purse." Olive hesitated, normally she would latch the door until she returned but what could this gypsy woman do, run off with a saucepan, or the kettle, grab the soap powder from the shelf, steal a potato from the rack and even if she did, what of it. Leaving the door ajar she went to the living room where she kept her purse in a drawer. Three shillings, fingering the coins she hurried back, the woman smiled and held up a length of cream coloured lace, pretty. Olive dropped the three shillings into the gypsy's hand and took the lace, the 'lucky lace'. No journey, no dark stranger, today Olive considered it a fair exchange. She glanced at the hall clock, almost a quarter to four, settling herself in the easy chair by the living room window she picked up her book. A long life of troubles with little else, it summed up Olive's past as well as her future, and the title of the book seemed to apply quite accurately to the role of a Woolascroft wife, '*My turn to make the tea'*.

Cynthia was gone, Olive would miss her. The obnoxious mix of camphor and perfume had at last faded, swallowed up by the fabric of the house, confined in the folds of the curtains, inert unless disturbed. Until the next episode of pain and discomfort from her illness Olive would shut out the world and its vagaries, turning to chapter ten of her Monica Dickens' autobiography she began to read of another's life, she couldn't help wondering if Monica too had a drawer in her bedroom holding numerous lengths of 'lucky lace'.

Dick stood at the corner, for a few minutes he let his eyes follow the row of houses, by Christmas they would be razed to the ground. Years of quiet observation, all the comings and goings, the domestic upheavals, misery and joy, success and failure, life and death, events that coloured the passage of time until even the exteriors of these modest abodes could no longer deny the evidence. Past life seemed to have somehow permeated the brickwork and now they wore such a wearied expression it felt almost a kindness to relieve them, to finally grant them peace.

The deal with Holbrook was close to completion and Dick had designs on the future of Mitchell Street, the odd side at least. He lit a cigarette and allowed himself to wonder if Margaret Holbrook had given birth to a boy or a girl, whichever, he or she must be all of twenty two by now. Charlie had gone to Fred with a clarion ready to sound, he'd drag Dick's name through the mud and all of Woolascrofts with it unless Fred stumped up. She was old enough, and willing, if it had been down to Dick then Charlie would have left empty handed to do his worst. Yes, Dick had found trouble at the curb side one night, but he wasn't the only one, neither would he be the last, that one fall from grace and the black mark was never to be erased. Charlie Holbrook considered him to be the devil incarnate yet Dick had actually liked Margaret, looking back, he might even have married her had Charlie not damned him, damned them both. Fred paid for Holbrook's silence, though not before their verbal exchange had reached a volume so heightened by dislike and resentment that the air turned blue.

Dick had suffered a tongue lashing from his father that cut deep, the episode created coolness between them that prevailed for several months. 'You're a disgrace, in God's name do you have to serve every bitch on heat'? Words which rang in Dick's head for a long time. Yet it was always Dick whom Fred favoured over his other two sons when it came to business, in that area of life they shared a like mindedness and Fred had recognised the need to 'bring Dick in', for the future of Woolascroft's.

Charlie Holbrook was now an old man, a widower and as for Margaret, well she'd disappeared from the scene soon after Fred had paid up, Dick had heard it rumoured that she was in Ireland with relatives of her mother, but folk made up what they didn't know, the Irish connection could be nothing more than a nosy postman's speculation over a picture postcard he'd delivered from the emerald isle or a tea towel hanging on Mrs.Holbrook's clothes line bearing the words, 'a gift from Ireland'. It was the way of folk, tittle tattle, a picture drawn from imagination and coloured in with what few crayons the old candle box offered up, that was the nature of things.

Halfway along the street two boys were kicking a ball about, while a young girl sat on a tricycle sucking half an orange, soon their view of life would be changed, a scene less gnarled by age, at Bilborough or Bramcote most likely.

Dick began to walk a little further along until he drew level with the small girl on the opposite pavement, he smiled, she briefly lifted the orange from her mouth and cast a smile back to him, across the cobbles, now Dick chuckled, the juice had coated her mouth and chin in bright yellow stain while the bodice of her frock declared its stickiness through a yellowy wet patch, she appeared wholly content, the innocence of babes.

Dick made his way slowly past the numbered front doors, what was here to inspire anyone, the place needed a face lift, deserved to be part of post war regeneration. Heat from the last of his cigarette nipped at his fingers, he sent it to the ground and trod on it before kicking it into the gutter. A sudden thud as the ball struck a window of a house on the other side caused Dick to look across, in an instant the front door opened and a pinafore clad woman appeared waving a carpet beater, "I'll put this across your backsides if yer don't buzz off to play somewhere else."

Dick grinned, amused by the notion that soon it would be a much heftier ball striking the glass and with much greater effect, construction took time, demolition was quick. As he walked another yard or two something caught his eye, etched into the brick and weathered by time but surprisingly obvious still, a smiley face. Dick looked closer at the image, two round eyes, a neat nose and a deeply curving mouth, a happy face. What poor optimist scratched this years ago? Dick spoke the question to himself with a trace of derision yet he made note of the number, 69, a dreamer had once lived at 69 Mitchell Street, probably before the gasometer cast its shadow.

Now the ball came Dick's way, rolling by his feet and bouncing off the front doorstep. "My pass," he called to the eager lads, standing hopefully in the middle of the cobbles, socks about their ankles, knees scuffed, boot laces swinging loose but growing shorter with each determined kick of the precious ball. Dick dribbled it around the lamppost then for a second pretended to aim it at the woman's door, he kicked it hard into the entry.

Relieved cries of, "Nice one mister," and thumbs up before the lads ran to retrieve it suggested that for a moment they thought he might confiscate the ball out of sympathy for the harassed woman.

The girl had pedalled her way along the street to the storm drain and was now intent on pushing the soggy half orange through the grille, her blonde curls only just managing to hold fast the pink ribbon bow, lovingly tied by her busy mam no doubt.

Margaret must have had one or the other, boy or girl, Dick's son or daughter. She was old enough and willing. Dick let out a long sigh, but regret served no purpose, Charlie Holbrook was a nobody, he'd amounted to nothing more than a row of cracked, crumbling houses and Dick would relish the day they all came tumbling down.

He looked again at the smiley face and traced it with his finger, speaking as though it could hear.

"Wonder what became of you, dreamer at number 69, don't you worry, Dick's goin' to shake things up round here, Woolascroft style."

Annie felt amused by Florence's need of her company, Rex Madden would surely recognise the sincerity behind her visit, Florence wished only to establish that he was happy with the accommodation and settled at Denman Street, it was after all a very different place of abode to the one in which he'd been living since his return. Andrew Smithfield was the most unassuming of men and no doubt lived modestly within that large house at Brassington but there the space and outlook were a far cry from the small rooms and cobbled surroundings afforded Rex by the house on Denman Street. Dear Florence, ever correct, considered it inappropriate to call alone on him and so Annie now accompanied her as they made their way.

"You must be looking forward to the wedding Annie," said Florence, "are you all travelling separately?"

"William and Celia will be coming back to Nottingham afterwards so they are to travel independently, Jack and Hilda, with Rosemary are giving a lift to Mr.and Mrs.Ripley, Francis's dad can't drive at present, he has the curious condition of dropped eyelids. Charles and I are going with George and Samuel, we couldn't very well cover the distance in the van but one of George's colleagues at Raleigh is lending him his car. Emily is travelling up by train the day before, Freddy will meet her at the station, it's a shame that neither Mathew nor David can attend but Faith understands. It will be good to see Ivy, Reggie and the family, reading between the lines of Ivy's letters I don't think Reggie is well, he's been a very hard working man and though they say hard work hurts nobody it does take its toll. Freddy would like Charles and me to stay for a few days, as it is we are all, bar William and Celia, spending Saturday night there. It will be a squeeze but Jack, Hilda and the youngsters are sleeping at Ivy's in Skendleby while the Ripley's and ourselves will be at Bonthorpe. Charles won't commit to more than one night and I think that Freddy will find it hard to persuade his dad to stay longer, at least we shall have some time to look around the farm, George and Samuel must be at work on Monday but Freddy would put us on a train later in the week if Charles relented," Annie sighed, "you wouldn't think Winchester Street would lure him back with such urgency would you?"

Florence sensed Annie's disappointment so chose to lighten the conversation with an enquiry that always cheered her friend.

"Talking of farms how are your relatives at Ruddington, whenever you speak of them I at once imagine an idyll, a place of perfect peace," she chuckled, "isn't it strange, a farmer must, in every sense be a 'man', such physically demanding work made even more so by the contrariness of weather, and constant, Christmas, Easter, every day of the year without respite, yet I picture them in serenity. I don't believe Basil ever did an honest day's work in his entire life but how he laboured the demands of his 'man's world' and gullible folk thought it must be true, to use one of my mother's expressions, 'it is all cock-eyed', mother comes to mind a lot lately, because of making ready the house for Rex I suppose."

"Little changes at Ruddington," said Annie, "Seth seemingly sows content along with his crops and Doris takes from the harvest what she needs for the family, pickling and preserving, baking and boiling so that each of them receives their share of that contentment everyday of the year. Many would say their way of life is too basic and outmoded but the evidence contradicts that, they display complete happiness and I don't believe the word envy could be found in the dictionary that sits on the bookshelf behind Seth's armchair."

"The green eyed monster," said Florence with a hefty sigh. "Mother had a cat for years, tabby with green eyes, I never liked it, you couldn't stroke it, not if you valued your skin, it would scratch with a vengeance every time anyone made the mistake of trying. I was convinced the creature existed as a reincarnation and I used to imagine who it might have been in a previous life. I came to the conclusion that uncle Greville was the most likely. As a child I was terrified by him, I don't think he cared much for children. He kept his fingernails far too long for a man and he wore a monocle, which made his eye look enormous, a big green eye, the lens somehow reflected the shade of aunt Evie's curtains, he always sat opposite the window and the curtains were the colour of Izal, that green disinfectant folk put down the lavatory when it first came out, pine, we all relieved ourselves while imbued with the essence of pine forest. Mother should have called the cat Izal instead of Tibbs, it never seemed like a Tibbs but Izal would have made it sound suitably Prussian, scratchy and irritable. Uncle Greville died in his fifties, a strangulated hernia mother said."

Florence chattered on, it was easy listening and Annie walked alongside with a mind comparatively free of those concerns, which often occupied her thoughts as she went about the daily tasks at home. But Florence was quite right, she looked forward to the wedding with a degree of excitement, the nature of it, all family together warmed her like a comfort from the past before they grew up and the wider world imposed its influence. Charles gave no hint one way or another of his feelings, his suit she'd had dry cleaned and he'd been to the barber but enthusiasm seemed absent, dear Billy had shown more. Annie had fought back tears when he'd handed her a parcel and said 'somethin' for the young couple from me an' Edna'.

Denman Street had a pleasant air about it, so far spared any threat from subsidence perhaps the residents expressed an unspoken gratitude through their simple pride, pretty curtains, fresh paint, scrubbed doorsteps and letterboxes bearing evidence of regular polishing with Brasso, even a hanging basket by the door of one house, its blooms stubbornly defying autumn. A Jack Russell sat on the windowledge looking through the glass at the two women, quite motionless, like one of those china dogs that along with its twin, looked down from the mantelpiece of so many homes, the would be heirlooms of future generations.

"This is it," said Florence, "oh dear there's a car parked outside, he must have company, we needn't stay long."

Annie suspected the car might belong to Andrew Smithfield. Florence's knock at the door was soon answered.

"Come in Mrs Stanford," said a surprised Rex, and Mrs.Eddowes surely, that kindly face from all those years ago when I collected the groceries."

At that moment Annie felt awkward, it must puzzle Rex, the fact that he was required to collect from the shop the items of Florence's order and now the two women stood together at his threshold, apparently friends, but times change, situations become altered by circumstance, Rex himself must have found a great change to his life. Winnie Bacon's profound observation came to Annie's mind, 'every day the same, never two days alike'. Rex led them to the small sitting room, as they entered Andrew Smithfield got to his feet, it had been some time since Annie last saw him, his smile and manner were warm and polite as ever but he'd aged noticeably.

"I think we are all acquainted," said Rex, "please do sit down, I shall make us some tea."

"Oh no, really you mustn't trouble yourself, I have come merely to ask if you are comfortable Rex, and do stop calling me Mrs.Stanford, Florence please. Annie kindly keeps me company when she can, we have been busy in recent weeks shopping for the wedding at Skendleby, her granddaughter Faith is to be married there next Saturday." Florence declared the news with a flourish of delight, it quite touched Annie, Florence was sincere in everything she said and did.

Rex chuckled, "Very well. I shall call you Florence and to answer your question, yes, I am very comfortable thank you, but you surely have time for a cup of tea, Andrew is the best of company, he will be host until I return with the tray."

Annie could detect a glimpse of amusement in the look that Rex cast at Andrew, perhaps like herself he imagined a suitability between their mutual friends, it was as well they were unsuspecting, Florence would likely turn into a recluse and Andrew would be unwelcoming of such interference. His pleasure was genuine however when he said.

"Freddy's daughter, the wedding is of Freddy's eldest daughter? You must extend my best wishes Annie."

"Yes, Faith is to marry Richard Gillpin, a local farmer's son, at Skendleby parish church where she was christened."

Andrew's memory returned in that instant to the evening he'd sat in the car, outside the church at Skendleby waiting for Charles, when Freddy had offered his hand and spread relief over Andrew like a baptism of forgiveness.

"I enjoyed very much the company of young Mathew recently as I'm sure you will know, as well as our conversation about Ireland, happily I learned news of your family Annie, first hand news is really the only kind worth heeding, I've come to realise over the years that the more news is passed about the more it loses credibility so I try to dismiss the travelled versions, how is William?"

Andrew had heard numerous 'travelled' versions of William Eddowes' affairs, Dick Woolascroft attracted the scrutiny of older men both in business and out, their inquiries usually furnished them with a dangerous mix of truth and speculation, Andrew steered clear, if at all possible, of their eager revelations.

"William is in good health, Celia copes with his comings and goings, just as with Charles and me I think she has resigned herself to not knowing what he's up to, perhaps it's for the best, he doesn't encourage involvement of the family, we are spared, William takes it all upon his own shoulders.

Unfortunately Mathew isn't able to attend his cousin's wedding, but Emily is travelling up from London for the weekend. Freddy is the opposite of William, we see him infrequently yet we learn of the farm and all its events, from the everyday routines to the unexpected, just as if we lived next door. I shall give him your best wishes of course and I know they will genuinely please him. Freddy is an open book and I fully expect to find him looking a little worn, whereas William allows us not a peep between the covers, no one must thumb the pages of William's book, brothers yet chalk and cheese."

Andrew was about to respond when the door opened wide and Rex reappeared.

"There we are, didn't take long did it? Now do you ladies take milk and sugar?" Rex carried the tray to the table.

Florence was stirred by a memory and smiled. "Mother used to forbid me sugar, she had curious notions and expressed them with unusual turn of phrase. 'It's all very well being sweet but too much sugar and you'll be sucked away', that's what she'd say, sucked away. Today I shall take two sugars Rex, after all I am still here."

He poured her tea, inwardly feeling glad that Basil failed to reduce this woman through his overbearing ways.

Andrew caught Annie's eye, she could read his thoughts, Florence and Rex had both survived Stanford, he could know nothing of the misery that man had inflicted on her own family. "I don't take sugar thank you Rex, just a little milk."

Conversation was relaxed and a half hour passed pleasantly, anxious not to overstay her welcome however Florence declared they really must be going.

"Then surely I can give you both a lift," Andrew got to his feet, put his cup and saucer on the tray, then to Rex said, "I'll see you on Friday, about ten o'clock," as if feeling obliged to enlighten the ladies as to why, "we're putting on walking boots and stretching our legs in Derbyshire, before we become too feeble of age." He laughed but Annie sensed there lay some truth behind his words. "Yes, I shall give you both a lift home, I have nothing else to do so it will grant more purpose to my day."

Goodbyes said Andrew stood by the car holding open the passenger door. Even if her attention had not been diverted Annie would have encouraged Florence into the front seat but a woman had just stepped out from a house opposite, it was Lillian Sulley, Annie had not seen or heard word of her for a long time but it definitely was Lillian.

"Please Andrew, would you mind waiting for just a couple of minutes, I must speak with the young woman across the street, she used to be a neighbour of Edna." Annie looked at Florence.

"My dear you run along before she walks away, neither of us is in any haste." Andrew nodded agreement and Annie hurried across to Lillian.

"Perhaps I should have attended the funeral this morning," Andrew spoke softly, almost as though he were thinking aloud, "I went to her husband's, it was only at odd times, council meetings mainly that I found myself in the company of Fred Woolascroft, amongst others of course. It becomes expected of those who move in similar circles, a formal attendance. That was my difficulty, I felt no similarity to Fred Woolascroft whatsoever and during the service I shrank from my own hypocrisy. I'm sorry, I know that Cynthia Woolascroft was your elder daughter's sister in law but I really didn't have any association."

Florence sighed, "I did ask Patricia if she would like me to go with her, obviously I knew Cynthia but the occasions on which we met I could count on one hand, I was relieved when Patricia said no. I didn't attend Fred's funeral either, a strange man in some ways. Dick is at the helm of Woolascroft's now I understand. He approached Patricia you know, with a view to her investing in the family firm, thankfully she declined."

Annie reappeared, hastily climbing into the back seat. "What a coincidence, Lillian has lived here since she married, I remember Edna telling me that Lillian had met a man from one of the road gangs, her first husband died when their daughter Norma was very young, now she too is married and living at Long Eaton. I am glad to have seen Lillian again, or Mrs.Arthur Dunstan, as she now is, she's so deserving of some happiness, goodness knows she found little enough of it all those years ago."

Annie related this account as if both Florence and Andrew were familiar with Lillian. It was Andrew who ventured to ask if the woman was any relation of Jack Sulley.

"Yes, so you remember him?" Said Annie.

"I remember only that he was Mrs.Bacon's grandson, the night of the chimney fire, when Edna sent me to Mrs.Sulley's, a young woman was there, Lillian."

Annie imagined he remembered much more of Jack but it was his way, not to perpetuate the bad. He started the car and drove off.

"I shall drop you first Florence then on the way to Winchester Street, to take Annie home, I can stop to buy an Evening Post, it should be in by then. I confess it's not so much for the news content but for the crossword, that and the one in the Sunday Telegraph keep my brain cells alive and if there's a clue to which I can't get the answer, then I torment Rex with it."

It took a bare ten minutes to reach Castle Road, Andrew helped Florence from the car and walked her to the door, Annie looked on, they could be taken for a couple so alike they were in manner and nature. Edna's disapproval rang like an alarm bell in Annie's head, 'he's loved you for years'. Now Annie clung to her place in the back seat of the car, it was but another fifteen minutes or so to Winchester Street even allowing for a stop at the newsagents, it would be foolish to join him in the front, yet she felt unkind. As they again made their way Andrew was tempted to ask if it was true, that William had thrown his hand in with Dick Woolascroft. Despite William's apparent unwillingness to speak with family of his affairs he would likely have confided in Annie, she of all people would offer reasoned guidance, but something he couldn't define prevented him and instead he enquired after Edna's family, word of Billy and the girls. Annie was able to impart a piece of news which truly delighted her.

"Liza is coming back, she will see the harvest through at Halam but then she is coming home, to stay with her eldest sister and family until she finds a place of her own, and work, Liza needs to work of course. She writes not infrequently to George, they have remained friends since childhood."

Andrew recognised the pleasure in her voice. He pulled up just short of the corner, as was her way, Annie opened the car door and was outside on her feet before he had the chance to be attentive.

"Thank you Andrew, I won't forget to give Freddy your good wishes. If you have time one day I know Billy would appreciate your calling at Susie's, for just a few minutes of conversation, apart from his family, and George and myself he sees hardly anyone, since losing Edna he goes out seldom, I worry for him." She spoke through the open window of the car, here Mrs.Charles Eddowes sought no escorting to her door.

"My regards to Charles," he said, "I shall visit Billy tomorrow, I have such memories of Edna it will be a privilege."

Annie watched as the car turned the corner, raising her hand to wave.

Andrew held tight the steering wheel, gripping it as firmly as he gripped the past, 'you won't give me away will you Edna?' Dear loyal Edna Dodds, larger than life, and keeping of his secret. Andrew drove home to Brassington, an Evening Post his only companion on the seat beside him. Good luck to George and Liza, it did happen for some, just not for Andrew Smithfield.

A silly song came into his head, a popular nonsense folk sang without thinking. *"Cigareets an' whisky an' wild, wild women, they drive yer crazy they drive you insane."* He sang to himself as he drove along, though Andrew did think, and the words taunted him, *"they drive yer crazy they drive you insane."* He was an old man and it was nonsense, nothing but nonsense, yet it still tightened his chest to the point of pain.

September 26th Skendleby

For the last few minutes of the service Annie's eyes had been fixed on a butterfly that had settled on William's shoulder, wings outstretched it had remained quite still, only when the young newlyweds emerged from signing the register and the congregation stood did it take flight and even then Annie's gaze was drawn to it as the delicately beautiful creature rose high above the gathering, circling briefly before seeking the sunlight at the opened door where it lingered, hovering over the heads of the exiting procession. Elegant, airborne, free of earthbound hindrances, not ever growing old and losing lustre, short lived in sight of man but enduring in memory.

All the years that had passed, the family's now aging features, grey tiredness disguised only by their colourful apparel, so stark was the contrast. Enid had been like a butterfly, too delicately beautiful to suffer the ravages of age yet far too curious to be absent from events on earth to which she had rightful invitation. Where else would Enid position herself, but at the shoulder of her first born son?

"What a lovely service Mrs.Eddowes, doesn't she make the perfect bride, like her mam before her? Oh dear, here I go again." Mrs Ripley dabbed tears and sniffed up any that might be pending. "Her dad managed to see most of it, his eyelids only dropped twice, we've tried holding them up with Elastoplast but his eyebrows get stuck in it, his left one was plucked almost bare and he didn't want to come looking peculiar so we stopped doing that last month. Like I told him, you often see folk in church with their eyes shut, nobody thinks anything of that but a man with plucked eyebrows, now that would look strange and we didn't want to embarrass Faith."

"I think they want the family to gather for photographs," said Annie.

Charles hastily made his way past those intent on dawdling and had disappeared beyond the open door at the first opportunity. He and William had barely exchanged words, in fairness they'd not had much chance, Celia and

William had gone straight to the church, while George and Jack had driven first to Bonthorpe, Freddy had greeted them with a smile so broad that his cheeks swelled to proportions worthy of nothing less than a kiss to equal them, Annie had felt the warmth of his pride and happiness. If Enid had slipped inside the church today and briefly occupied William's shoulder then perhaps it was as it should be, there she would feel in place. Yet Annie doubted William had been aware, seldom did he notice subtleties.

The photographer's voice sounded above the hum of chatter.

"Move up closer, parents of the bride and groom, grandparents too."

Mrs.Ripley steered her husband into position, the unfortunate man was to be immortalised in print with his eyes closed. Mrs.Gillpin beamed out from under the most fetching hat, while Francis, by now showing in her face the evidence of her 5am start, smiled her love over the group. Annie stood beside Charles feeling awkward as she ever did when faced with a camera.

"Squeeze up a bit more, that's right, now say cheese." All duly delivered the magic word designed to ensure a lasting memory of the happy day. Several more photographs followed, Charles obliged just once more with a helping of cheese considerably reduced then retreated to a spot from where he could observe but be free of any requirement to converse. Annie followed him, aware that what came so naturally to others poor Charles struggled with.

"All this fussing about gives me a headache, why must he take so many photographs, he's a professional, I bet he's costing a packet so every shot should be perfect without the need of spare."

"You'll feel better when you've had something to eat and drink," said Annie, "breakfast was a long time ago." Here he was in the company of family yet he couldn't hide his nervousness. "This is Faith's day, you are her granddad, it is our role to make it special, for her, no one else has command of it, William can be but a quiet bystander, he's come simply to wish the young couple well. Play your part Charles, you are entitled to smile, even to laugh."

He made no reply, on the opposite side of the pathway William stood with Celia and Emily, the two women animated and involved, while he used a cigarette, sending smoke into the air about him, in his attempt at excusing himself from dutiful pleasantry.

There was a moment of excited anticipation when Faith turned around so's not to face the gathering and threw her posy of flowers over her shoulder. Molly could do no other than catch it so close to her did it descend. For a moment there was a hush, but she laughed and handed the posy to Pauline. Francis and Ivy exchanged smiles of relief, Faith had surely identified her chosen recipient and the spot at which she stood, Molly could suspect no other but she'd laughed, Molly had caught the posy and laughed.

The reception was to be at the Beach view Hotel, Skegness, though it was a fact that only from the east facing windows at one end of the building could any guest glimpse the sea. It was however a popular venue for such occasions, affordable and with a reputation for good food. Annie had wondered if when the day came William might decide to overnight in a room there but the conversation she'd had with Celia just last Thursday didn't suggest any real likelihood. He'd been very preoccupied of late, Celia was satisfied that his health presented no problem to him and so assumed his quietness was due to whatever business he and Dick Woolascroft were currently engaged in.

"Come on the cars are leaving now." Freddy walked over to where Annie and Charles stood. "You are to ride with the bridesmaids and Francis's mam and dad, the rest will follow but everyone has a seat in a vehicle of some sort." He chuckled and lowered his voice to say, "But no tractors Mam, I thought of parking one outside the church gate, just to see William's reaction. Bought a tractor the other week Dad, the old one is beginning to wheeze on damp days, this one isn't new, second hand, but she's a good 'en. I'll show you tomorrow, you ought to drive her across the barn field Dad, there's no better feeling than sitting up on the seat of the tractor, looking over the hedges." Annie willed Charles to show some interest.

"You should put your brother on it, he's always looking into the distance, spots things a mile off. Put him on the seat of a tractor here and he'd likely see a plot of development land to take his fancy in the Netherlands, can't imagine a bit of water like the North Sea getting in his way." Charles laid his hand on Freddy's shoulder, sighed and walked away.

"What's William up to now Mam?" Charles' response had troubled Freddy, even Annie had been surprised by it, seldom did Charles speak of William's activities.

"Not now Freddy, come along, look, Francis is beckoning to us and everyone must be getting hungry."

Freddy took her arm. "Do you remember getting the chickens Mam? They'd be cockling away out the back at Hood Street, those lovely eggs every day. How soon Will lost interest in them, too simple for William Eddowes, too ordinary. I reckon our family holds no more attraction for him than did those hens, but he ate the eggs." He smiled and Annie understood, William would take but show little regard for the giver.

The young waiter, obliged to remain cordially silent, held the tray of sherry glasses before the guests, maintaining his very correct demeanour but unable to contain a roguish wink when Frank Boucher paused beside him and under his breath said.

"I'll wait for a beer."

The two knew one another from school and had begun to work at more or less the same time, Frank at Ingoldmells and Derek at Skegness. Neither intended the hotel trade to be their future but it was local, paid a wage and granted them a spell of thinking time while National Service loomed ever closer. It felt strange to Frank, he would normally be one of the unseen, besieged kitchen staff on such occasions, but today the ongoing procession of dirty pots and pans, the intermittent mopping of a potentially lethal floor and the less than courteous instruction broadcast by a harassed chef were borne by some other poor mortal low down the pecking order. Frank's chest rose to match his feeling of some status and he sought aunty Molly, a familiar female on whom to practice his previously unaired charm.

Annie quickly cast her eyes about the dining area, hoping William was not placed too close to Hilda and Jack. She had resisted actually asking Francis to keep them a reasonable distance apart when arranging the seating, it seemed unfair to mention friction when the planning at Bonthorpe was entirely happy. Her discreet glance at the tables delivered relief, the name cards revealed, George to be seated alongside William, then Samuel, Emily, Rosemary, Hilda and Jack. Annie had noticed the best man, Richard's brother Colin, looking at Emily, it wasn't surprising, she was pretty and her personality couldn't fail to engage the interest of any young man, especially in this situation where folk tried to look their best and naturally pursue conversation.

At last everyone was seated at the table and welcome bowls of soup were quick to arrive. Charles took a spoonful as though it would deliver a vital antidote to the threat of some dreadful affliction. Mrs.Ripley sat at his other side, upset over a spot she'd made on the tablecloth and achieving to make it worse by dabbing at it with her serviette. Francis could see her distress.

"It's alright Mother, no one will worry about it."

She was more concerned that her father's eyelids might drop before the spoon reached his mouth and quickly tucked the serviette into his collar ahead of his next attempt. Freddy sat by Faith, mentally going over his speech as he spooned the vegetable soup, and briefly wondering if a calf, due at any time, might decide to enter the world before he got back to the farm, with any luck Clover would chew the cud until then.

Only the sound of knives and forks touching plates could be heard throughout the main course, except for the moment dear Ivy, unable to bear the thought of waste, asked Frank if he'd like her Yorkshire pudding as she wanted to save room for dessert, the latter taking everyone to the point of satisfaction, in fact Pauline had declared herself 'fit to burst' having happily finished the last two or three spoons of trifle to ease her grandma's predicament.

Now quietness fell upon the scene as tradition required both fathers to speak in turn, before the best man. The waiters had ensured that each guest had a glass topped up in readiness for the toast and Freddy got to his feet, cleared his throat, for a second looked down at Francis and began.

"Firstly I'd like to thank you all for coming, especially as most had to travel a distance. Not nearly often enough do we all get together and the irony today is what unites us at this place, the marriage of Faith to Richard, the day she will leave home to live with her husband, in their own home. I shall miss her. I remember the day she was born as clearly as if it were yesterday. A farmer witnesses a lot of births and we're not the unfeeling, thick skinned men some folk imagine us to be, it comes naturally to him, a soothing palm over the cow's rump, a sincere, 'how do little 'en', when the first piglet leads the others into daylight. But when his own baby enters the world, now that's something entirely different. Nothing welds a man's strength to his determination like the first sight of his child, in that instant he takes a silent vow, to nurture, protect, to be the best dad while ever he draws breath. Just a couple of hours ago I gave Faith away, it's what a father must do, it's how a family grows." He paused and looked towards Grace. "There'll come a second time and it'll be no easier then. Although they say it's better to give than to receive I reckon young Richard is on the receiving end of a pretty good deal. Not only is his bride beautiful, intelligent and hard working but she comes with the Eddowes' stamp of quality that guarantees she'll increase in value with age, like her mother." Francis blushed and smacked Freddy's sleeve, smiling he continued. "We joke, make fun, but occasions like these are all about family. Soon after Francis and I came to live at Skendleby an older man of the village came up to me and with no preamble said, 'Which family are you?' Later, when I thought about it, I realised he'd probably lived there all his life and considered himself familiar with everyone, so seeing me drove him to ask the question. His approach was so direct that he surprised me and I must have taken several seconds to answer. I've recalled his words many times over the years. 'Good God boy', he said, 'if it takes you that long to remember who you come from, how are you ever going to know where you're going'. So I would ask you all to stand and raise your glasses in a toast."

The sound of chairs rubbing the parquet floor hid from anyone's hearing a mumbled remark made by William. Freddy held out his glass and beamed at his daughter.

"Faith and Richard, may they always remember who they come from and know only happiness wherever they go."

Speaking in unison, everyone made the toast. William swallowed a mouthful of port and ungraciously looked at his watch. George saw and was thankful that no one else appeared to have noticed. Mr.Gillpin was obviously a man of few words and simply chose to share an anecdote taken from the Readers Digest. It was Colin Gillpin, who in typical best man tradition caused just the right amount of embarrassment to the groom and dared to inject a measure of comedy into the orderly proceedings, which made all present, both old and young alike, laugh with abandon. He began.

"Round these parts you'll find a good many farms and men to work them, it's always been thus. Kids grow up knowing the way of farming before their ABC and times tables. Now some years back the schoolmaster had in his class of boys one lad who struggled with his sums. So one day he took young Bobby aside and tried out his idea, a different method, to help the lad grasp arithmetic. You see the schoolmaster thought that if he incorporated a farming element into the sums it might naturally reach young Bobby's logic. 'Think carefully before you answer lad', he said, 'and pretend you are at home on the farm instead of in school'. 'Yes Sir', said Bobby. 'Now if your father decided to divide one pig sty and fetched wood and nails to build a wall down through the middle of it, what would he get?' Thinking carefully before speaking, as he had been told to do, Bobby said, 'Two sties Sir, he'd get two'. 'Well done lad, well done. Now if your mother went to the chicken coop and picked up ten eggs in her basket, then carried them to her kitchen and subtracted two so she could bake a cake, what would she get?' Bobby thought for a few seconds, 'Eight Sir, she'd get eight'. 'Well done lad, well done. Now if your father put his bull in the shed with a young heifer so they could multiply and produce a calf, what would he get'?

Bobby knew this one, without hesitation a confident Bobby said, 'Shit Sir, he'd get shit everywhere'.

When the laughter finally died down Colin continued. "Our Richard has never had any bother with his sums, in fact over these past months he's divided his time between work and play very successfully and he can do his takeaways, he managed to subtract a wardrobe and dressing table from the spare bedroom with no difficulty whatsoever." The amused gathering chuckled at the fun. "So at multiplication I reckon our Richard'll be a natural, but perhaps Faith better put a few dust sheets around just in case!"

Even Charles could not resist the humour, Mrs.Gillpin shook her head in pretence of dismay over her son's less that sophisticated wit while the two brothers embraced with all the warmth of genuinely close kin.

The hour by now almost 7o/clock folk had begun to leave, William had been chafing at the bit since the last greetings card had been read out. Not surprisingly Celia was enjoying the company, especially Emily, someone would drive Emily to the station to catch her train in the morning. William had retreated to the lavatory, the general good humour that surrounded him finally proved more than he could bear, enough was enough and William had long passed that point of sufficiency, a quiet cigarette in the mens was his immediate need before driving away from it all. For a minute or two he'd savoured the satisfaction of his own society, it was Freddy who then appeared.

"Wondered where you'd got to Will, the day's far spent and it's the first chance that I've had to ask how things are with you? We do try to keep abreast of city news, the wireless can be informative but you'd be surprised how often, in the middle of a report something occurs on the farm, sheep over a fence or a call from a neighbour needing an extra pair of hands. Besides, you know me, more interested in crop rotation and milk yield than expansion of the suburbs. Good to see Emily looking well and sounding so happy, mam tells me in her letters that Mathew has really taken to Dublin, perhaps the words of the song are true, *'Dublin's fair city where the girls are so pretty'*, goodness knows he's bound to look at his age." Freddy chuckled.

William stood at the wash basin, stubbing out his cigarette in the bowl, he turned on the tap and ran water 'til the butt disappeared. Not turning his gaze from the drain he spoke.

"Family, all about family is it Freddy, I wonder what went through dad's mind, you must have taken great satisfaction from your little aside, 'remember who you come from'. Does it still gall, do you weave resentment through those thoughts of crop rotation, do you grieve for all the cows you could have bought when you measure that milk yield. He gave the money to me, yes dad favoured me, it wasn't my doing, when it comes to family ours couldn't claim title to the word, we're a farce, the whole bloody lot of us, the difference in you and me is you pretend, I call it like it is, a bloody farce."

Freddy pulled at William's shoulder until he faced him.

"I meant no slight against dad, he knows that but your mind is twisted Will, you got John's money, it's never occupied my thinking, more it was a relief. Do you honestly believe I could use John's death to further my life, I weep for him still, a penny of John's money would have drowned me. But mam, our mam, the one who reared us, sat by our beds when we ailed, met us at school gates in all weathers, put wisdom in our empty heads so we knew right from wrong, fed us, and never asked for a thing. She gave life to John he was truly hers, her flesh, her blood Will. You take, you always take. Mam and dad live out their days in that miserable house on the corner of Winchester Street but you don't even see it. You're so busy thrusting William Eddowes into every lucrative scheme, every money making deal, no one stands in your way do they Will, especially not family, how conveniently you scorn family. Well you're wrong, long after bricks and mortar crumble, after you and me have departed this earth and turned to dust there'll be a generation of this family surviving and they'll know who they come from. The higher you climb Will the further it is to fall, remember that. She's never said a word but I can guess that mam has caught you more than once in the past, saved your bones, yet you'd deny her what was John's to give, we owe mam, but you only take, come the day of reckoning Will you'll struggle to reconcile the balance sheet."

The door opened.

"Here you are, they're looking for you William, Faith and Richard are leaving to get changed into their going away clothes, they want to say goodbye."

George sensed an atmosphere but Freddy's expression cautioned him to say nothing. The happiness of earlier had been washed away down the drain with William's cigarette end, Freddy forced a smile.

"Coming George, we were just coming."

An uneasy silence possessed William, Freddy's words had stung and now goodbyes held much attraction, it was time to leave.

Freddy had spoken only the truth, William drove a man to harsh words, the sooner he was on his way back to Nottingham the better, yet their exchange tormented Freddy, it was hard to feel close to such a brother, flesh and blood, family, who you come from. Freddy would be glad to reach the sanctuary of his cow shed and the simplicity of Clover, right now he needed to rub his palm over her rump, he wanted to sit on the seat of his tractor and look over the hedges. Bloody hell, Freddy Eddowes was weary.

CHAPTER SIX

Late November.

Jack scanned the room, if Woolascroft was present it would likely go beyond their means.

Myra's compensation money following the accident they'd determined themselves not to touch but instead add to the amount, a little whenever they could, in the hope that eventually it would enable them to consider a place of their own, rather than renting. Jack had sought guidance of their bank manager, he could show a good regular wage and the fact that he and Myra had managed to save the all vital nest egg achieved to convince Alec Drummond of their reliability. The name too had helped, Wainright, 'are you a relation of Henry Wainright by any chance?' Drummond asked the question with only a slight stammer in his voice, during the five years Henry had worked as teller under Alec Drummond's management, the two men, apart in age by several years, nevertheless struck up a friendship and when Henry left the bank in Nottingham to take up a more senior position at a branch of Barclay's in Leicester it had been through Alec's recommendation and goodwill. Henry had become engaged to Judith Shaw, they'd married and two children had come along in quick succession, Henry was deserving of promotion and the higher wage that came with it, a position at Leicester offered an excellent opportunity for the young family. Despite Henry's initial reservations, his work at the bank had suited him. Now living happily at Leicester but regularly visiting his mam and aunty Jean things couldn't have worked out better.

Discovering that Jack was Henry's older brother Mr.Drummond had felt no qualm in agreeing the terms of a relatively small mortgage, should it become necessary.

A guide price of £1,250 had been placed on the property being sold at today's auction, it was likely to be a low estimate but the bungalow did need redecorating and some structural problems with a chimney were obvious because of damp in the front bedroom.

Myra tugged at Jack's sleeve.

"William is over there, in the corner, standing alongside a man with a big moustache."

Jack had looked that way no more than a minute ago, now William Eddowes took up position there, at least Woolascroft hadn't made an appearance.

The low drone of men's voices petered out as James Cochran mounted the stand at the front, a curious individual in the eyes of some, it was his sombre, expressionless authority over auction house proceedings that had earned him the title, 'Jolly Jim'. Jack however was disinclined to make judgement of the man, a colleague at Bonham's had been a prisoner of the Japanese, while his hands mastered the job with co-ordinated dexterity it was as though his mind could not embrace the simple demands of a smile, of extended conversation, the slightest requirement of mirth. The end of shift saw him disappear to some distant place of sanctuary where time might find a remedy for what ailed him. James Cochran had also been a prisoner of the Japanese and no doubt it had been the death of his father last March that thrust the gavel into James' hand before the time was right.

He cleared his throat and even the most unobservant couldn't fail to notice his long intake of breath.

"Usual terms apply, 15% deposit today, the balance payable at completion, deposit non refundable. The property is freehold, acting solicitors being Chaucer, Caffin and Holt, there is a reserve in place. I am obliged to make clear the existence of a local authority dictate which applies to the entire of Thorpe Road and neighbouring Treadwell Drive, banning the keeping of all domestic poultry, excluding pigeons. However imposed upon the latter is a restraint of number, all relevant details must be obtained from the public health department of the council prior to any such pursuit. Are there any questions?"

"Who the bloody hell is Dick Tate?"

A ripple of laughter spread across the gathering, the expressionless Cochran responded with.

"I shall start the bidding at twelve hundred and fifty pounds sterling."

Silence prevailed.

"Alright then, eleven hundred and fifty pounds."

"Twelve hundred," a voice from the back of the room caused every head to swivel.

"Twelve fifty," the man with the large moustache entered a bid.

"Thirteen hundred," another showed his hand. It continued rising, more or less at fifty pounds a bid, the activity regularly punctuated by someone's deep seated cough, until the be-whiskered gent alongside William called out, "Fourteen hundred and seventy five."

A tense moment brought a hush to the room, James Cochran spoke. "I repeat, a deposit of 15% is non returnable, am I to conclude?"

Jack had waited until the very last second as he judged it to be.

"Fifteen hundred."

Myra could barely contain her excitement as she watched that large moustache shake from side to side.

"I am selling then, going once, going twice," Cochran brought the gavel down hard on the wooden stand with an emphatic, "Sold."

Jack turned to Myra with a big grin on his face. "We've done it now love, just don't crave too many pigeons." He laughed and planted a kiss on her cheek. "We need to do the necessary business with Mr.Cochran, I don't suppose he has the faintest idea who we are. Rank, number, religious denomination, service record."

Myra in her innocence looked puzzled. "Why does he need to know all that?"

"Only kiddin'," said Jack, "but he does need two hundred and twenty five pounds and to shake hands with Mr. and Mrs.Wainwright."

Jack felt undeniably proud leading his wife forward as everyone else made their way to the door.

"I was watching William," said Myra, "he didn't make a single bid, but I think the man alongside him thought it was to be his. Then you produced the surprise, I thought I'd explode until Mr.Cochran called out 'Sold'. No. 14 Thorpe Road, our bungalow Jack, our very own. Do you think William didn't bid because he saw us there? I know we see each other seldom these days but I've always felt somehow related to him, although I'm not of course, you must be a sort of relative, Mrs.Eddowes' husband who died was your uncle wasn't he? Anyway, Annie couldn't be more of an aunty to our family if she tried, deep down I bet William is a big softy, he just likes folk to think he's a stern businessman."

Jack listened to Myra's words and welcomed them, it was good that she believed in the loyalty of friendship, yet Jack couldn't share her conviction, William had left swiftly without even a wave of his hand.

James Cochran led them to a small office at the rear of the building, he made no attempt at conversation and Jack respected his need of quietness, what it was necessary to say would doubtless be said, but as it was for Jack's workmate at Bonham's, memories alone could create too much disturbance for idle chatter to find an airing.

Meanwhile, outside on the pavement William stood lighting a cigarette, he'd no real intent of buying the property on Thorpe Road, it was just a passing interest, useful to know who was in the market place as it were. Men harboured mistrust of the banks and since the Wall Street crash stocks and shares had become no more than a game of chance to many, like aiming a gun at a pop up duck in the fairground, a few got lucky while most walked away with pockets much less occupied. Bricks and mortar were favourable to under the mattress.

'So Jack Wainwright took it, there's a turn up for the books, wouldn't have thought he had the means, probably played the wounded soldier card, even bank managers might be swayed by that.' William muttered his thoughts as he walked to where he'd left his car, hastening his pace, it was 'parky', Celia had been sniffing and sneezing for days, the cigarette began to sting his throat. 'Damn, a bloody cold.' He had considered calling at Moreleigh, Steve Roper was in Manchester but perhaps he'd drop by at Woolascroft's instead, the thick skinned Dick would be impervious to common ailments. Next week was to begin the demolition of Mitchell Street. William puzzled still over why Dick had been so intent on buying the place off Holbrook, a colourless individual William considered the man to be. Something connected Woolascroft and Holbrook, it was a source of intrigue and William hoped to discover the origin, inside information could prove a useful tool, Stanford had taught him that. As William turned the key in the lock of the car door a sudden violent sneeze erupted without warning, it sprayed the car window with droplets of spittle and for an instant William saw Basil Stanford's face staring back at him. A shiver propelled him into the driver's seat, turning the ignition William drove off, cursing.

"I could scarce believe it, they walked in with big grins and Myra was like a child on Christmas Eve. Jack was quite clearly delighted, a bungalow will be so much easier for them, it has three bedrooms and an area of garden, even a small bathroom. I haven't mentioned anything yet but I think I could afford the rent so if their landlord is agreeable I'll take over the tenancy. I'd like to have dad stay sometimes, it would give Susie a break and I think he'd welcome the chance to do that, I know it bothers him, he believes he makes extra work for her, the only problem will be persuading Susie to let him out of her sight." Liza chuckled and squeezed George's arm.

Since leaving Halam Liza had been living with her elder sister Annie and brother in law Alec Yeats, she was not in the least bit unhappy there but she couldn't presume to remain at their home indefinitely. Last Thursday on her afternoon off she'd looked after little Louise and met Michael from school while their mam and dad attended the auction. It had occurred to Liza then how convenient it would be if when Myra and Jack moved into their new place she might be able to rent the house on Northolt Road. Liza had secured a position at Burton's in the ladies fashion department, she'd declared that transforming herself from farmhand to potential shop assistant had challenged her far more than the actual interview. Her fingers had required intense and valiant efforts with a manicure set and almost hourly application of lanolised hand cream, while her hair was virtually in need of house training, so wild had it become through being abandoned to nature with no measure of redemption beyond a simple shampoo. At Burton's looking healthy and wholesome was possibly considered less of an asset than appearing cultured and precise, indeed one of the pre-requisites, as serenely demonstrated by Mrs.Warneck, the department manageress, was a spine like a poker with a neck extended like a goose. 'Chest out, bum in', a sort of motto to be instilled at the outset, rather like the words of wisdom that occupied the classroom chalk board in bold capital letters at the start of each new term.

George was happy for Liza, time had healed, listening to her cheerful chatter and laughter filled him with genuine relief. Again they were spending time together, some evenings and at the weekends. This Sunday afternoon George had asked Liza to come with him to Mitchell Street, tomorrow that place which had been such a big part of his early life would succumb to the bulldozers, before it was gone forever George wanted to stand in front of the smiley face in the brickwork, etched there all those years ago by his dad. He needed to trace it with his finger, honour the sincerity of its cheerful message to the world. He was far too young when his dad was killed to have any recollection, he had a sepia photograph, an image of the young Harold Boucher, which George treasured, yet it was that smiley face by the front door of No.69 Mitchell Street that held a place in his heart like no other.

They turned the corner, although a distant sound of traffic denied the silence Mitchell Street was unearthly still. The council had removed the street lamps, which used to stand like stern sentinels, all brass fittings had been taken from front doors, the letterboxes, latches, knockers, now gone, only the deeper colouring from once fresh paint or oil remained to bear witness to their previous existence. Windows had grown in dimension through the absence of curtains and nets, while the starkly bare interiors seemed to shrink from George's gaze as he peered inside, as if they were ashamed of their demeaned status, their failure to resist rape, all had been stripped of anything salvageable, flagstones, lead from grates, oak mantels, nothing but walls remained and those showed their utter despair in faded wallpaper and flaking plaster, the window ledges on the inside displayed sad collections of dead flies and daddy longlegs, resting on one, a spider, as yet defying the odds, moving between the debris with almost respectful, dignified attendance on their passing from this life. George felt such sadness, grief, it was painful, a lump came to his throat as they neared No.69. Liza thread her arm through his but didn't speak. There it was in the brickwork by the door, George reached out to touch it, to feel that lost age and all it represented. Now he could do nothing to prevent a tear rolling down his cheek and if anyone had asked what caused him to weep he could not have answered in any way that made sense. A weight of emotion bore down on him, so much had happened, but here, at this spot, his real dad ever smiled back at George, throughout the heartache of losing Alice, the ugly war that destroyed so many lives including his dear brother John, the furore released upon the family by Anthony Hemsley, the realisation of his mam's uncomplaining weariness, abiding still at No.69 had been his dad's comforting, smiley face and tomorrow it would be lost forever.

"Will you marry me Liza?"

The words passed from his lips before he could stop them.

"Yes, George I will." Mitchell Street was granted one last memory.

"Your mam, my dad, they're never really far away Liza, come along, time to go."

George put his arm around her as they made their way back to the corner, the bulldozers could do their job, Harold Boucher had left Mitchell Street, he walked along side them, every step.

The sound of traffic became less distant, a car passed them, slowly, Dick Woolascroft glanced at them from inside but George and Liza took scant notice.

'A last nostalgic look at beloved dreariness before progress transforms the place', thought Dick of the departing couple, though Dick himself had felt a pressing need to see the smiley face at No.69, his smiley face as he now deemed it to be, ere the advance, before the march of Woolascroft's trod it asunder. Whilst Dick would never admit to such it was a lonely march with more than a few regrets in its name.

He sensed the onset of a sneeze but could barely stifle it in time, his head reeled from the force. 'Eddowes and his bloody germs'. Dick sniffed up his annoyance, William Eddowes managed to get up his nose at the best of times, that ideal family, father, mother, a son and daughter, normality, things as they should be.

He pulled up at the curb and for two or three minutes simply sat quietly, his mind now strangely calmed, his thoughts inert, a dreamer at No.69.

18th December.

Myra chuckled at the sight of Louise busily packing her dolly's clothes into the shoe box, understandably part of the last few items to be gathered up. Today the family was to vacate the house on Northolt Road and move into their bungalow, to be installed before Christmas made the whole activity even more exciting.

Jack's best friend, Charlie Jones, had insisted on helping, it would require several runs in Charlie's van along with the trailer, which on work days he towed behind filled with paints, thinners, brushes and ladders, the equipment necessary for him and Bob Budgeon to pursue their trade. Today it had arrived empty and brushed clean for the purpose of transporting 'Jack and Myra's worldly goods' as Charlie chose to describe the undertaking.

Raising the money to secure the Deed had taken virtually all that Jack and Myra had, and that along with a small mortgage, so removals posed a problem of cost, until one day Jack had unwittingly spoken his thoughts in the company of his old mate Charlie.

'No problem Jack, piece o' piss, you, me an' Budgeon'll have the lot shifted afore the streets are aired'.

That had been his verdict and no amount of argument from Jack could change it, case closed, Charlie's word was final.

Myra glanced at the clock, which sat on the floor ready to be put inside a bag at the very last, the men would be back soon to load all that remained, apart from the furniture in the house when they took up the tenancy. Over the years the simple house had been kind to them, in its quiet way supporting them through the trauma surrounding first the alarming circumstances of Michael's birth and the difficult months of Myra's nervous depression following the birth of Louise. As a home it had gently absorbed the unrelenting tears shed for Myra's mam Edna, catching at sunlight and shedding the warmth over those grieving within until that hurt from loss was soothed by the all knowing constant No.19 had become.

Yet since Miss Pennifold died even Jack had felt the need of change, one morning while standing at the back door, looking out across the yard before leaving for work, he'd sighed and said.

'It's a tired view Myra, too weary to smile back at me anymore'.

Louise was up at the window, she could see the van approaching, her feet danced up and down on the big cardboard box in which Myra had packed all the bed linen and towels. The men would want a cup of tea before setting off on the last run, Myra was to follow on with Louise, by bus, 'I'm not having you sitting among all the stuff with your leg, if you knock it an ulcer could develop, that's what the doctor told us'. Jack was firm on the subject, besides it was the last thing Myra wanted, with so much to do at the bungalow she couldn't risk being laid up.

Annie Eddowes had insisted she meet Michael from school and along with the makings of a meal for them all, take him to Thorpe Road. Dear Annie had been stoic, helping Myra to empty drawers and cupboards, methodically packing and labelling boxes, entertaining Louise while Myra removed pictures from the walls, protecting the glass with thick brown paper, goodness knows how many cakes and buns Annie had arrived with. Myra regularly asked after Charles and was ever assured of his good health, thankfully his humour wasn't questioned and so Annie had no need to dilute the truth, Myra was Edna's daughter and possessed the same intuitive wisdom.

The kettle was on the gas, a quick cuppa to 'wet the whistle' then, when the last of the bags and boxes were loaded the key could be turned in the lock one final time for the Wainwrights, no doubt they would be replaced with little delay, Myra sincerely hoped that whoever followed might know the kindness of the house as they had.

Charlie and Bob now squatted on the floor with their tea. Wearing their decorator's white bib and brace overalls, which sported every imaginable shade of gloss and emulsion, they made for a colourful sight, Bob especially with his mop of ginger hair reminded Myra of a clown at the circus.

"The new place needs paintin' Jack," said Charlie, "outside an' in, wi' winter weather on us the woodwork is vulnerable, inside don't matter but outside, too much wet an' the window frames'll likely turn to rot. A couple o' fine dry days to rub down, undercoat an' gloss, that's all we need, Bob an' me'd soon tick that off. I know money's tight at the minute so the bill can wait, we'll think of it as an investment, a bit put away until we need it for summat in particular, like Budgeon's weddin'."

Bob grinned, still dating his young lady from the chip shop he regularly declared to Charlie.

'While ever the door opens Jones wi'out havin' to ring the bell there's no point in disturbin' the peace'.

Charlie admired Jack and while Bob said little, he too felt regard for a man who's every other step was taken on an artificial leg. 'You'd never know', was how he'd heard folk describe those men fitted with a leg like Jack's, but the men themselves knew, they bore the aches and pains, yet never spoke of them, an entirely different 'never'.

Jack got up from the old chair, one of those pieces of furniture that had been in the house when they first moved in, along with a small side table, two dining chairs, a very unstable dresser, which Jack had strengthened with some urgency and a single bed in the smaller of the two bedrooms. At least these items they had no need to manhandle out to the street. Jack's mind had inevitably travelled back to their first night as man and wife at No.19 Northolt Road. They had eaten supper at the side table, happily cuddled up in the single bed and in all honesty lacked nothing that mattered. He glanced at the clock.

“Come on lads, me mam’ll be on the doorstep gettin’ tetchier by the minute if we don’t get a move on,”

Gertie had insisted Jack take the measurements of each window in the bungalow at the earliest opportunity, so’s she could begin stitching curtains.

‘You can’t be without curtains in a bungalow, folk’ll be gawpin’ at you in the bed’, had been her genuine concern. Gertie had been quite definite when she’d told Myra that by midday the last pair would be completed and she would be at Thorpe Road to hang them up.

Charlie chuckled. “Quite right is your mam Jack ‘tis only decent. I remember me dad comin’ in from work one day shakin’ his head in disbelief, ‘now I’ve seen the lot’, he said. He told us how he was cleanin’ the windows of a house on The Ropewalk, one o’ them mansion houses, three stories high an’ a basement. Well he got the extending ladder up to one o’ the top bedroom windows, climbed up there wi’ his shammy an’ a bucket o’ water, drop o’ vinegar in it to cut through the bird mess, me dad reckoned that if man’s waste wer’ proportionate to that o’ the pigeon this city alone by the end of a week’d be sittin’ on top of a mound the size o’ Ben Nevis, anyroad he got up to the bedroom window and couldn’t believe his eyes, there wer’ a man an’ a woman in there havin’ a bit of ‘how’s your father’! Now riggin’ himself up wi’ the extending ladder, ‘cause you have to remember the bottom of it wer’ at basement level, wasn’t easy an’ it wer’ the afternoon he allus did that house, last Thursday afternoon of every month, so he thought sod it an’ carried on, an’ so did they. When dad had finished and put all his stuff back on his cart he knocked on the door, ‘cause he needed his money. After a couple o’ minutes the door opened an’ there she stood, bold as brass, in one o’ them silky housecoat affairs, now their sort hate partin’ wi’ money an’ she had the cheek to say ‘you missed a bit’, so me dad said, ‘I don’t think so missus, unless it wer’ at the start ‘cause I saw the finale an’ heard the encore’!”

Myra thought she should at least pretend to be embarrassed but she couldn't hide her amusement, while Jack pulled at Charlie's bib and brace.

"Yer daft beggar."

"It's true," said Charlie, every word of it, that's posh folk for yer, they think the likes of us don't do same, that it's too good for the workin' classes."

He picked up a box and began to sing, Bob and Jack looked at each other, grinned and did likewise, Northolt Road bid farewell to the Wainwright family amid cheerfulness, the melodious tones of Charlie Jones rendering '*God Rest Ye Merry Gentlemen*' travelled its length and breadth.

With Louise clutching her doll Myra scanned the room, whispered under her breath, 'come with us Mam', picked up her bag and locked the door.

"Your fingers are cold," she took the doll from Louise's hand and put it in the bag, cupped the little hands together and breathed warmth into them, "lets hurry up, it's only a week to Santa coming and we've to get the house ready."

The child beamed her delight while Myra felt pained at the memory of Edna warming her hands as a child, just as she had done with Louise a moment ago. Again Myra whispered as they walked to the bus stop, her leg aching, 'come with us Mam, be sure and come'.

Dick somewhat subconsciously observed Olive as she gathered up the breakfast dishes and carried them to the scullery, why did she never ask about the business, not ever display interest in the sale of his mother's house, could a wife really be so indifferent to her husband's affairs as to genuinely seek no knowledge of them. She returned to the table and picked up the butter dish, Dick found himself revealing what was to be the nature of his morning.

"I've an appointment with the solicitor, half past nine, Bradbury has been engaged in securing compensation from the Coal Board, for housing on

Mitchell Street, and he'll probably have some idea of when we're likely to exchange contracts on mother's house."

Olive looked surprised, he never spoke to her of the business, even when she'd sensed that not all was well. She put down the butter dish and lowered herself to a chair. Dick continued.

"Once the sale is complete Bradbury can finalise probate and divide the Estate. Mother was fond of you, she specified that you receive three hundred pounds. Of course you will be sent notification, a letter as to the fact, the law doesn't rely on word of mouth."

Dick smiled half heartedly, perhaps his revelation might incite a response.

Olive's finger traced the pattern on the tablecloth, she was pensive, then she raised her face to look directly at him and spoke.

"I don't imagine you ever realised how frustrated mother became, your father denied her a voice, she was a bright woman, she felt entitled to be heard. Over time, as we are seemingly disregarded when it comes to matters of importance, we cease to make any attempt at involvement, rather we watch from a distance, say nothing and learn from man's mistakes. Much of a woman's wider knowledge is gained in this way, we consign our discoveries to wisdom while men hastily shed their errors, disown them, as though a kindly lift of air will carry them out of sight."

He prickled, mistakenly believing Olive referred to his time spent outside of business, Dick was well aware of what folk thought of him, his 'reputation'. While most folk felt a need to live up to such, Dick had cynically felt obliged to live down to his, continue to sport the colour in which folk had so generously painted him. Yet not since his marriage to Olive had he actually slept with another woman, he'd flirted with more than a few, bought them drinks, even the odd present or two, it was his pathetic need to impress, to cock a snook at those sanctimonious, goody-goodies who pointed a finger when in truth they knew nothing. Intimate moments between man and wife had, rightly or wrongly, been dominated by Olive's illness, the nature of it brought fragility to her, partly actual and on Dick's part, perceived. He had tried to overcome, to silence the gremlins in his head but every time their tormenting voices sapped his intent, until eventually he banished them, allowing them no quarter. Spirit, of the bottled kind served the purpose, it dampened ardour but at cost to the pocket. More than once his mother had raised her voice to shout the cutting words, 'what in Heaven's name do you do with your money'?

How could he have answered her with the truth, how could he have shrieked back at her, 'I drink to stop myself wanting Mother, to keep it limp'.

His father's words, the memory of them caused him anguish still. 'Do you have to serve every bitch on heat'?

Dick had only ever wanted to be like his dad, to be successful, strong in business, ruthless even, if that was what it took.

"So dear wife, what do you consider to be your entitlement, beyond a meagre three hundred? He snapped harshly.

Olive sought no argument.

"Unlike your mother I brought nothing to the business when we married, I know that your grandfather, Lionel Bradshaw, was generous at the time of Cynthia's wedding, his generosity enabled Fred's developing business some stability, that is why your mother felt entitled. But I do have intelligence, I've not ever considered 'my' entitlement or even if I had such, but where you go, what you do and why, I have spent days and nights considering those things, can you really wonder at my surprise when just now you told me of your appointment with Mr.Bradbury, as though it was your habit to keep me informed."

Dick now calmed a little.

"I went to the bank for some money when I bought a row of houses on Mitchell Street, I had funds but not sufficient, it's only a small loan. I used the

Deed of this house as collateral, until mother's Estate is paid out and I knew that wouldn't take too long, it won't happen this side of Christmas but we should exchange contracts in the New Year. I wanted to keep the Mitchell Street deal separate from the firm, my purchase, with my money, my profit. Compensation from the Coal Board will make it a good deal, if the collieries were still in private hands, chasing some, any recompense from Stanford and his ilk would see a man in his grave without satisfaction. It's different now, the government can't afford to portray themselves as the proverbial stone, they need to allow the sight of a little blood now and then, evidence of humanity within the corridors of power, besides it's become a legal requirement."

Dick stopped short of declaring Charlie Holbrook old and out of touch. Just as he'd predicted, when Eddowes had made approach the old bugger had been only to keen to be rid of his condemned houses. But Holbrook was Dick's 'thorn in the side', he had nothing to do with Eddowes and Cheetham, buying the houses on Mitchell Street in the firm's name would have diluted the cloying smugness Dick granted himself.

Olive got to her feet.

"You don't see enough of your brothers, I thought we might ask all the family round for supper on Christmas Day, I could order some nice things from Burton's, I think mother would have approved, family was important to her."

"But today is Monday," said Dick, "isn't it a bit late for that, Thursday is Christmas Eve surely?"

Olive walked towards the scullery, butter dish in hand, casting back her remark as if randomly.

"It's never too late, so they say."

"Let me have that bag Grandma, I feel lost with nothing to carry."

Home from Aldershot on a fortnight's leave David had met his grandma in town, accompanied her to the Co-op and now insisted on seeing her safely back to Winchester Street, Annie could only hope that Charles might for once welcome him, how he managed with such ease to disregard his only daughter's family was a mystery to Annie. Jack Haynes was a good man, solid, dependable and over the years had given Charles no cause for resentment. Charles' own son William on the other hand, had for so long created problems, ill feeling and upset. Charles attitude towards Jack was irrational and not surprisingly Hilda was remote from her dad, yet still Charles uttered no condemnation of William, while harbouring that senseless animosity for Jack.

David took the shopping bag from Annie's hand.

"Your fingers are cold Grandma, why didn't you put on some gloves?"

Without giving her chance to reply he continued speaking, his voice and manner so much more matured than before he went away, confident, grown up.

"I've come to the conclusion that it's the first, the umpteenth and the last army regulation, every man, throughout his waking hours, must bear weight. We carry endless buckets of water, back packs fit for mules, lengths of timber, each other and guns, we transport them bodily from A to B then back from B to A, time without number. In fact everything is repeated over and over, the army adopts the same method employed by young mothers with their babies, I've observed it often on the bus, in the park, in the home, they all do it. 'Say, da da, da da, da da', until the infant finally comes up with the desired result but has no idea why he or she is making the sound. Repetition, drilling it in, running with a heavy weight from A to B then B to A and at the end wondering, for what? Discipline, endurance, teamwork, all good enough words, all relevant, yet I'm sure I'd have felt a much greater sense of accomplishment if I'd actually produced something or served a real purpose. At least we're not carrying these groceries to Winchester Street only to turn around and carry them straight back to the Co-op."

Annie laughed. "I take it you're not too enamoured with army life then David?"

"It's not for me but Gregory Tozer has an aptitude for it and no mistake. When he salutes, his hand is that sharp it's a miracle he doesn't slice the top off his head and by the time he's finished polishing his boots Trinity House could use their shine to direct shipping safely round the Eddistone Rock. He marches up and down the parade ground like a bantam cock, Battersby looks at him like a cat watching a canary, though sometimes I think Gregory's not trying to satisfy our corporal or even sergeant Walker but doing his very best to honour his dad, I know it's not the RAF but I could understand why he might feel that way."

Annie had bumped into Caroline Tozer at the Post Office when mailing a parcel to Skendleby, 'They're both coming home for Christmas Annie and we're all spending the day at Patricia's'. She'd spoken the words with excitement, her sons with her again and Annie understood, her own spirits had been lifted, her heart warmed by the news George had whispered in her ear, but she had kept her promise and mentioned to no one that he and Liza intended marrying in the spring.

'We're not in the first flush of youth Mam, neither are we without past loss so it will be a quiet wedding, at the Registry Office'.

Annie could appreciate their need of quietness, it was a part of their need for each other, they understood one another's thoughts, memories, little anxieties, they shared them. Annie's relief was immense, it warmed her from within and the bleak, midwinter weather, this year would not find her bones.

"I'm glad you're doing your national service with Gregory," said Annie, "time will pass quickly and you'll be back to pursue your ambitions before you know it. Perhaps next year might be more instructive in a practical sense, I remember someone telling me that their son had learned how to do welding."

"Now that I would enjoy," said an encouraged David, "but I think Gregory's mam might find that he wants to become a regular. His dad was a professional man wasn't he? You never know Gregory might turn out to be officer material, his brother Jonathon was always going to be something beyond the ordinary, I'm not surprised that he's studying medicine. Some folk are destined for the professions and others, like me and dad naturally lean towards industry of some kind, that's how the world works, co-ordinated effort, white collar, blue collar and in many cases collarless but all a necessary part of the whole."

Annie relished David's company, his philosophies, his young, cheerful enthusiasm, Mathew too would be home for Christmas and Emily, bright young minds, they were the future and Annie loved them dearly.

David put the bag down on the scullery table, looked nervously at his grandma and for a moment hesitated, the smell of tobacco confirmed Charles' presence, if he was man enough to be a soldier then the grumpy nature of his grandad shouldn't alarm him.

"Hello Grandad, how are you?"

For several seconds until David stood immediately in front of him Charles seemed confused. Over the years his grandad had been an intimidating character, while not ever knowing the background to the obvious tension existing between his mam, dad and grandad, David nevertheless avoided trouble and seldom called at Winchester Street. Today he felt able to withstand whatever might be his reception, for his grandma's sake.

"It's me, David, surely seven months of army life hasn't changed me beyond recognition Grandad?"

"Oh it's you, I've cataracts on my eyes, they're going to do whatever it is next month, in General Hospital, old age lad."

Annie was concerned over how much Charles' eyesight had deteriorated since Faith's wedding and now the daylight hours were so short, he seemed to have abandoned all efforts at reading The Evening Post under electric light. Until now she hadn't realised he relied on the familiarity of a voice to identify company, David through most of his growing up years had barely seen his grandad and today, with no hint of youth left in his voice it was hardly surprising Charles had squinted through a haze of cataracts, his clue to identity being the word 'grandad'.

When the official looking brown envelope appeared on the doormat and Annie had handed it to him she at once recognised his anxiety, when the content revealed he must bring with him to the hospital, slippers, dressing gown, pyjamas and a wash bag his face drained of colour. 'It's a well practiced procedure Charles, you'll be kept in for no more than two or three days and your sight will be so much improved'. She had done her best to reassure him, in all his life so far he'd not been hospitalised, the prospect actually frightened him she could tell.

Of late he'd spent his days either in his chair by the foot of the stairs or in bed, like some recluse. At least the wireless offered him the pleasure of listening to a play, even the news provided a distraction, a fact Annie had taken pains to point out when his mood confined him to his bedroom. His response was always the same.

'I'm not doing any harm to anybody while I'm up here'.

William's attitude, his distance preyed on Charles' mind. Annie wanted to correct William, to speak sternly, pour shame on his selfishness. But it was knowing Celia would suffer as a result, that Celia would bear the brunt of William's ill temper that prevented her doing so. Annie was familiar with the kind of existence a wife had to endure when her husband needed someone on whom to shed his frustrations, not physical blows, they were too noticeable, too damning, but an assault on the nerves, cruelly dealt for days, weeks at a time. Celia missed her mother, dear Gwendolyn had passed away still in her world of make believe. After the funeral service Celia had turned to Annie and said, 'how confused St. Peter must have been when mother arrived at the gates, another Queen Victoria', then burst into tears.

William had his own way in everything and while it troubled Annie constantly she'd resisted speaking out, she was forced to weigh one emotion against the other, Charles' depressed spirit or Celia's hope of happiness, she could not sentence her daughter in law to the kind of life so familiar to herself, and so Charles' dilemma proved the lighter and William proceeded unchecked.

"We've a fortnight's leave," said David, "two weeks of respite away from corporal Battersby, the best Christmas present any of our platoon could have. You were in the army during the Great War weren't you Grandad?"

Charles visibly tensed.

"Nothing great about it lad, but yes, I was in the army and even after all these years I can remember the corporal at training camp. Sugden, corporal Sugden, hard as nails. He had a stare that could send your chin whiskers into retreat, he'd fix his eyes and you'd feel them boring into your head, but then he'd open his mouth and verbal abuse would bring pain, pain to your ears, like cannon fire. It was one of the first things he said to us, 'you're in the British Army now and I've got to turn you all into soldiers of the King'. That was the difference between him and us, we were in the army but the army was in him, a man possessed. Happen your man Battersby is possessed an'all. It took no more than a few weeks to make soldiers of us, there wasn't much time back then."

Charles threw what remained of his cigarette into the fire and fell silent. Annie cast a smile at David, while their conversation could hardly be described as uplifting, it did take place, if only Charles could have brought himself to ask, 'how's your mam'?

For the small mercy that it was Annie felt thankful. Corporal Sugden would never know what a significant role he had played in this day's advance.

CHAPTER SEVEN

Annie had just finished buffering a shine to the toasting fork when a knock came to the front door, she looked at her hands despairingly, black as the grate, quickly putting the lid back on the polish she went through to the front room, the knock came again, using her pinafore as a glove she turned the door catch.

"I hope I'm not disturbing you Annie. Having heard that Charles was in hospital and finding myself close by I felt compelled to ask after his health."

Andrew Smithfield was the last person Annie expected to see, the moment reminded her of the day, many years ago, when he'd called in the midst of her packing up at Hood Street, her hands grubby from the activity. Here she was again, fingers like those of a chimney sweep and bearing the obnoxious smell of metal polish.

"Not at all, please, come in, you must excuse my disarray, it's a job well overdue, my aunt Bella used to say that brassware, when shining was proof of an industrious housewife but when woefully tarnished, evidence of apathy. Edna had her own thoughts on the subject, she so disliked the task. She would rub the rag vigorously over her three brass monkeys, hear no evil, see no evil, speak no evil, then laugh and say 'so you can mind your tongue Edna Dodds or you'll be turned into a brass monkey for some industrious housewife to cover you in Brasso and rub you all over with a pair of old knickers', I think of her every day."

Annie let out a long sigh, told Andrew to sit down and hurried to the scullery to scour her hands. Returning to the living room she sat down by the table, smiled and said.

"Billy does enjoy your visits, I know he was a little anxious at first, Billy has never walked amongst gentry and considers himself lacking in education, I'm quite sure you never think of yourself as 'different', I can't find quite the right way to put it, but you know what I mean."

Before Annie could utter another word Andrew burst into laughter.

"I would rather spend an entire day in Billy's company than five minutes biting my tongue or stifling yawns when amongst the so called upper class. Gentry I am not, nor have I ever been. Through no wish of my own I have been obliged to tolerate their company but confess to inwardly seeking means of escape. Billy Dodds is a man with whom I can sit and be completely at ease, I haven't known that pleasure since losing my friend Henry Wicks. Rex Madden is fascinating to listen to, his travels and experiences, I do enjoy our walks and conversations but Billy has a wonderful simplicity about him, which I warm to so much, and of course the memories I have of Edna soothe me like a Psalm, a source of unfailing wisdom to keep me ever on the right path 'surely goodness and Edna shall follow me all the days of my life'! He chuckled.

"Charles has been struggling with cataracts," said Annie, "his stay in hospital was planned, there was no emergency and I fully expect him to be discharged tomorrow. George will drive me there and bring him home, unless when I visit this evening I am told otherwise."

"If it means George must take time off from his work then please let me drive you tomorrow, there is nothing at all pressing on my time."

"You are very kind Andrew and I am grateful, but Charles will expect one of the boys to do it. William is so busy these days we hardly ever see him so George explained to his manager at the factory and they understood, besides it will likely take no more than an hour."

An urgent rapping came at the back door.

"Mrs.Eddowes, are you there Mrs.Eddowes?" The door was thrust open before Annie could reach it.

"Whatever is the matter Mrs.Sealey?" Annie was alarmed by the woman's obvious panic.

"Fred's been in a fight, I can't stop his nose from bleedin', anybody'd think I'd stuck a pig in our scullery, I can't manage him on me own will you come?"

Annie cast a worried look at Andrew, speaking softly she said, "I shall have to go I'm sorry."

"We shall both come with you my dear," Andrew got to his feet, "I might be of help Mrs.Sealey in calming your husband." He felt sorry for the harassed woman.

"Oh dear God no, he wouldn't touch Mrs.Eddowes, I know he wouldn't but he'll likely use his fists if I come back with a man an'all, bless you for offerin' but he's a lot younger than you, one fight's enough, he's had a drink I reckon, or several, I just need to stem the bleedin', he'll go quiet then, he allus does."

Annie pulled on her coat, Andrew refused to be swayed and hurried with the two women along the street, cold air nipped at their cheeks and challenged their breathing.

Fred Sealey sat slumped forward, a pool of blood at his feet, vomit too covered the flagstones, the sight and smell brought instant nausea to the onlooker and Annie swallowed hard as she held out her arm to deter Andrew from crossing the room.

"Give me a minute, it will be alright." Moving forward she spoke softly to the pathetic figure of Fred. "It's Annie Eddowes Mr.Sealey, you've had a nasty nose bleed, they happen sometimes, I had a series of them some years back, let me see if it's stopped now." She ventured to touch the side of his face.

"It never bloody stops," he raised his head and in that instant saw Andrew standing there. "I don't need a doctor," he glared at his wife, "yer daft cow, get rid of him, get the hell gone man, I don't need owt from you."

His head fell forward and if Annie had not been there to steady him he would have toppled from the chair into the mire at his feet.

Andrew rushed over, putting Fred to lean back, the man had now sunk into a state of semi consciousness, a drink induced stupor.

"Do you have old newspaper Mrs.Sealey, a bucket of water, some rags? Boil a kettle Annie, find a face cloth and towel if you will, Mr.Sealey's resistance is passed, perhaps I can restore him to some degree then I think it best to leave him be, I doubt enough remains within on which he could choke." He didn't voice it aloud but to himself he added, 'other than his shame'.

Despite the women's protests Andrew cleaned the floor and washed Fred's face and hands. "I'll take off your husband's jacket Mrs.Sealey." He smiled to reassure the poor woman. "I'm afraid my knowledge of how best to redeem cloth is likely to be much less than your own, you ladies have expertise in such things, then perhaps you can find a blanket to cover him until he wakes." Lizzie Sealey's eyes showed her anxiety. "He'll sleep for some time, alcohol I do believe does as much to weary the onlooker as it does the drinker, you should take the opportunity to sit down quietly Mrs.Sealey, I'm sure that when your husband stirs his mood will be subdued."

Annie helped Andrew to free Fred's arms of his jacket, it took her mind back to the night Edwin Garbett brought May Watkinson to the house, his patience and kindness.

Peace came to the Sealey household at last, Annie and Andrew were about to leave when Lizzie said.

"It wer' a blessed good fortune he thought you wer' the doctor, Fred would never strike a medical man, them army doctors saved him from bleedin' to death, that's why I panicked, all that blood, I thought he'd die on me."

Annie then realised that in all the confusion she'd not introduced Andrew.

"I'm sorry, I should have said, this is Mr.Smithfield, an old friend of the family. Charles is in hospital having cataracts removed, he should be home again tomorrow, Andrew called to ask after him."

"Oh dear, whatever must you think of us? I come to fetch Mrs.Eddowes 'cause I knew she wouldn't say owt," Lizzie's eyes made an appeal of Andrew to be equally discreet. "Folk round her tittle tattle an' it's not his fault, 'tis his war wound plays him up, when he comes to he'll be whistlin' like a Billy blackbird."

"I'm glad I could help Mrs.Sealey, and have no fear the incident has already gone from my mind." Andrew felt pity for the woman, he'd vowed years ago never to let drink be his master, he wasn't like his father, he'd led a good life, at times unbearably lonely, but decent. That was to be his consolation prize, he'd go to his grave in all things respectable, but a runner up.

They walked back to the corner sensing that behind the nets they were being observed, it seemed to impose a silence, neither wanting to betray Lizzie's trust they sought the privacy of No.1.

"I'm sorry you had to be involved in such an awful mess, I truly am." Annie felt awkward, such goings on must be far removed from Andrew Smithfield's experiences.

He sighed. "Do you imagine me to be so feeble, so delicate Annie, to be somehow apart from the problems of other people, cloistered in that big house, serenely untroubled and unaware. Are you sure I can't drive you to the hospital tomorrow?"

"Thank you, but George has already cleared it with his boss at Raleigh. I shall of course tell Charles that you called especially to enquire after his health."

He sensed that Annie wished to return to the brasses, which sat across the newspaper covered table awaiting a good housewife's industry.

“I shall leave you to your task, and we must observe the ways of Edna’s brass monkeys, hear no evil, see no evil, speak no evil, for Mrs.Sealey’s sake.”

Annie led him to the front door. “They say it is unlucky to leave by any other door than the one through which you entered.”

He laughed. “Then I shall claim my good luck.” He leaned forward and kissed her cheek, promptly walking away to his car.

‘You can grant me that one kiss Edna Dodds, for surely it shall last me all the days of my life’. He was in no doubt that Edna was watching, Billy had convinced him of that.

He drove off leaving the residents of Winchester Street to await the welcome whistling of their own Billy, especially Lizzie Sealey.

“Brrrrr.... it’s bloody freezing up here.”

Diane Roper shivered as she pulled on her skirt, fumbling with the buttons in her haste.

“Well what do you suppose the fireplace is for?”

William reached for his jacket, his immediate need being a cigarette.

Diane prickled. “And how do you suppose I would explain to Steve the reason for my lighting a fire in the bedroom during the day, he should be home by half past five, even if it died down and went out I couldn’t disguise the smell of fire, he works for Boot’s remember, not down the pit, we have to buy our coal, not like your sister and brother in law, what with his pay, the proceeds of fancy hairdos and free coal, they must wonder what to do with their money.”

Her words grated on William’s tolerance the thought of Jack Haynes’ successful charge over Birchdale caused his hackles to rise.

“You can’t be that badly off for goodness sake, other women go out to work you know, you’re a kept woman Diane, no clocking on and clocking off for you.”

He waved his cigarette at her like a cautioning finger of authority.

"Bastard." She snapped her retort and glowered at him.

"What's the matter? If I thought a sack of coal would remedy your malaise then I would fetch one and tip it in the bunker myself, but you're a woman, and women talk in riddles so at least throw me a clue." He lit his cigarette. "Do you want one?"

"No, not now, stand up, I need to straighten the covers before my 'malaise' renders me incapable."

She virtually thrust him from the edge of the bed, pulling at the eiderdown and pummelling the pillows as if avenging some terrible offence against her, at which they played a significant part.

"We're moving, oh don't worry, he'll give you good notice. It was his big surprise, a New Year present, I don't know whether to be delighted or dismayed." By now she had crossed to the window and stared into the street. "Grey, miserable grey fog, what's the climate like in New Zealand, providing it's never cold grey fog, I suppose I should be thankful?" she turned to look at William, his expression revealed his bewilderment. "They've offered him promotion, he's good at his job, they're expanding the retail business in New Zealand, more responsibility with more pay. Apparently he is the ideal candidate for the post. Unbeknown to me he's been arranging our emigration, our new life! Just so long as the powers that be agree I am a decent, upstanding individual, worthy of entry, then I shall be automatically included in the firm's guarantee and travel to New Zealand with the necessary endorsement." Her eyes widened. "Unless you can't bear to see me go?"

"Surely it's what you want, more money, better prospects, and whilst I'm no expert on the subject I'd venture to say, no miserable grey fog. You can't really expect me to plead with you to stay, we both knew our arrangement would eventually cease, I'm surprised he didn't quit this place a while ago, new houses are being built all round the city, affordable, good investments, but if he had any inkling of this move being a possibility it would explain why. I could have raised the rent you know, for six years it has remained unaltered, we've exchanged favours you and I Diane, you were always aware that I had a wife and family, it's too late to protest your innocence now."

"Then go home to them, sign the 'oh so glorious' rent book, in receipt of services rendered over and above your dues as landlord and sod off. Steve will call round, give you good notice of his intention to leave, he'll shake your hand I shouldn't wonder. I'm sure you'll have no difficulty letting the house again despite all those wonderful opportunities for investment, but when you issue a new rent book don't neglect to state the favour clause, it could lead to regrettable confusion otherwise."

Diane's sarcasm, for a moment reached William's conscience and he felt a pang of guilt, but it passed from his mind as quickly as the thought of Colver entered it. Development of the site was to begin in March, Moreleigh had served as a stepping stone to that end, a small but significant part of William Eddowes' plan, whereas Diane Roper had ever been an incidental, requiring no appearance on the balance sheet.

Outside on the road he pondered his misconception, he'd believed Diane had understood, no strings or expectations, simply a mature approach to those oft times irritating 'ties that bind'. Women, how they wallowed in sentimental slush, they read so much fiction in time they came to believe it. New Zealand, land of opportunity, how much of that is fiction thought William.

His convenient logic managed to put together a good case for his defence and by the time he reached his car William Eddowes had been cleared of all charges and drove away a free man.

Celia was chopping vegetables, sniffling up the wateriness of onion induced tears. The wireless played quietly, she looked over at the clock.

"The news will come on at two, there's been trouble at the border again, a place called Crossmaglen."

William sighed impatiently, "Mathew is nowhere near the border, you fret too much, to hear you talk anybody would think that Mathew was obliged to walk around Dublin with the union flag and a portrait of the Queen stamped across his forehead. He's only there until October or thereabouts, a couple of years Hyde said, the lad's happy enough, you make it your day's objective to worry about Emily or Mathew depending on world events, troubles in Ireland or incidents in London, let them breathe their own air for gracious sakes." He went into the living room where Celia could hear him muttering to himself. "Do you know where my reading glasses are?" His patience when looking for something was almost none existent.

"They're where you left them, on the shelf in the bathroom. Your dad will be out of hospital by now, you didn't visit him in the General so the least you can do is go to see him at home, one day it will be too late and you'll regret it William."

Celia the tipped the vegetables into the pan with the meat, put the lid on and went through to the living room to listen to the news, William was ferreting around in his bureau.

"Why must you be forever tidying up, I can never find anything?"

"I'm listening to the wireless, trying to anyway, I've not been in your bureau, I never touch what's in there, that way I can't be blamed if you lose something."

William was tetchy, he crossed the room and switched off the wireless.

"Just in case you might be interested, the Ropers are emigrating and will be giving up the tenancy on Moreleigh, I'm looking for the agreement they signed when they first went in."

Celia turned the wireless on again. "I'll look in just a minute, it can't be that urgent, they're not emigrating tomorrow are they?"

"And Mathew is nowhere near the bloody border." William shouted the words purposefully to deny her any chance of hearing the news report.

A hissing, spitting noise erupted in the kitchen where the pan of stew was now boiling over. Celia ran to the stove, turned off the gas, grabbed her coat from behind the door and left. Tearful and aware that she had with her not as much as the bus fare to Caroline's she wandered up and down, numbed, aimless too miserable to even take note of which road she walked along.

Someone was tapping at a window, a muffled voice called out. Turning her head towards the sound she saw George, he was beckoning, within seconds the front door opened.

"Come in Celia."

His cheerful expression achieved to deepen further her own misery. George was sufficiently intuitive to recognise that she was upset and when she drew closer he could see that she had been crying.

"I would have gone back into work but Mr.Hyde said I may as well take the afternoon, he's good that way. One of the men has a wife who suffers with her nerves, sometimes a neighbour calls the factory, Wilf goes home for a couple of hours, sorts things out as best he can but Stewart doesn't dock his pay and Wilf makes up his hours somehow, I shall do the same. Mam and I collected dad at half past one, he seems okay, I sat with him for a bit and brought in the coal and sticks for mam, she looked tired, although a letter from Bonthorpe had cheered her. All's well at the farm, the geese proved profitable, most of them were taken by the hotels as part of their Christmas menu, so no doubt come spring Freddy will have a pen full of goslings. Dad will need to sit quietly for a day or two, lately that's all he seems to do anyway. Samuel goes round to give him a game of cards, as often as he can, but I don't think he feels confident enough to introduce Margaret to the table, mam would love that but you know what dad can be like. I try to put it down to his age, advancing years but if I'm honest then I have to accept that he's always been like it." George looked directly at Celia. "William is his father's son isn't he?" She nodded and endeavoured to raise a smile. "You sit quietly for a minute while I put the kettle on."

Whatever caused Celia to shed tears was almost certainly down to William's moodiness, if she wished to talk about it then George would lend a sympathetic ear but he'd always steered clear of actually asking. It wasn't the first time he'd seen Celia looking miserable, she said little, her loyalty and reluctance to burden others was touching yet George would have preferred her to shed at least some of the troubles weighing heavily about her shoulders.

"I shall go to Winchester Street over the weekend," said Celia, "I have told William he should visit his dad, he's not really that busy, I wonder some days where he spends his time, engaged in his man's world I suppose. That was one of Basil Stanford's favourite expressions, 'a man's world', as though we women trod a totally separate and inferior earth, suited to those lesser mortals born female."

Celia sat at the kitchen table watching George move about as he made the tea, his entire demeanour so different to William, his tread lighter, his manner always mild, even his voice ever pleasant through its softness. George carried a tray to the table.

"Have a bourbon, in the past I've sat here alone and been thankful for the comfort of a bourbon cream, I think it must be due to army biscuits and rationing, content so frugal that it wasn't so much a comfort eating them as a relief when finally they got swallowed! Now able to enjoy the luxury of a sweet chocolaty bourbon they can be a substitute for company, a pleasure to linger over." He gave Celia an intriguing sort of smile. "You can be mother while I tell you a secret."

His teasing lifted her from the doldrums and she poured the tea, took a biscuit and awaited his confidence.

"Mam knows but no one else, don't say anything, we decided to keep it to ourselves for a few weeks yet. I've asked Liza to marry me and she's said yes."

"I'm so glad George and Annie must be thrilled, I won't breathe a word, I promise." Celia's hand trembled as she picked up her cup.

"Liza shall call to see you on her afternoon off next Thursday, now you are holder of the confidence she can talk about the wedding, she misses Edna, we all miss Edna," George chuckled, "it's strange isn't it, how someone who never held office, not once trod the corridors of power but dwelt on an ordinary back street, ever counting the pennies and utilising the old, could have such a lasting effect on all she met," he let out a long sigh. "I was only just turned a year old when my real dad died so I have no recall, but God only knows how I would cope if I lost mam."

Celia squeezed his hand and picked up a second bourbon.

"I shall take another helping of comfort if you will too." She dipped it in his tea, he laughed, took a biscuit and dipped it in her's. In a strange way, the simple act of sharing tea and biscuit met the need to share a trouble. Celia said nothing to George of William's selfishness, to speak of it would spoil their peace. Perfect peace, a rarity in Celia's world, her ordained place.

"Come on, hurry please, where is the ambulance? Moira felt frantic, desperate to hear the sound of its bell. She tried again to get some response. "Charlie, it's me, Moira from next door."

Charlie Holbrook's eyes gave not even a flicker at her harassed attempts to make him speak, yet he breathed, the slight rise and fall of his chest Moira willed to continue, she watched so intently every stitch of his ribbed jumper became animated in her mind, alive, Charlie was alive. She had only gone round to see if he needed anything from the shop and found him in his chair with a fixed expression on his face, a look of alarm set in the moment like a wax work. His hands were cold, the fire had lowered in the grate. It had been at least a quarter of an hour since she telephoned for an ambulance. At last the sound of it approaching.

"You'll be alright Charlie, help's here now." She hurried to the front door, disturbing the cat that had been curled up on the sideboard, when the door opened it sped through missing the legs of the ambulance man by no more than a whisker.

"Mrs.Holbrook is it?"

"No, no I'm the neighbour, Mrs.Holbrook died years ago. I found him when I called for his shopping list, it's not that he wasn't able, I just thought it a neighbourly thing to do, I was going to the Co-op anyway. In here, he's alive, I know he's breathing but he hasn't uttered a single word nor moved a muscle, not as much as a blink."

"Hello Mr.Holbrook, I'm Reg." He took Charlie's hand as if to shake it when in fact he was trying to gauge the measure of response. By now his colleague had entered the room, anticipating the need he brought forward a wheelchair.

"A bleed I reckon Bill, we need to move him." Reg turned to Moira. "What about family, will you be able to tell them that we've taken him to City Hospital?"

"It's complicated," said Moira, "I don't really know much except that he has a daughter in Ireland, not close, as family I mean, I presume there was some sort of upset, years back. Since his wife died I've tried to keep an eye on him, a man on his own and not young, well you must know what that can be like in your job. These last few weeks he's let himself go a bit, I don't think he's been eating properly."

"Call the hospital in a couple of hours Missus, I'll tell them you're the contact until we trace family, what's your name?"

"Lacey, Moira, and my husband's Bob, he works at Handley's for Tommy Spooner."

Reg leaned forward and spoke reassuringly to Charlie. "Alright Cap', we'll soon have you sorted, you leave it to Bill an' me."

Moira was physically shaking, she pushed the front door closed and for a moment felt like the only remaining soul on the face of the earth. The cushion where Charlie had sat was wet with urine, it made the room feel all the more desolate somehow, she picked it up by one corner and deposited it in the coal shed. She carried a plate and cup to the scullery, sighing at the sight of an old basin on the floor by the sink, the cat's feeding bowl. The fire was almost out but she pushed in the damper and put the guard in front.

Poor Charlie, she couldn't help wondering if he'd ever return, her own mother had died from a stroke. Would his daughter come? Folk had a way of manifesting, of miraculously forgetting grievances when there was no longer need of involvement.

Moira took the key from inside the door and leaving, locked it behind her. Several women had gathered on the street, curious more than concerned Moira judged them to be. She waved but disappeared inside her own home without enlightening them. Whatever was in the cupboard would have to suffice, to be pursued to the shop by a bevy of nosy parkers held no appeal.

"So what will you do now that you're a woman of means?"

Olive slid the money order back into the envelope, she couldn't embrace the satisfaction that came so readily to Dick.

"First and foremost, I will remember your mother, then when I'm ready I shall deposit it at the Post Office, in their savings account."

Dick looked surprised.

"What's wrong with the banks, why put it in the Post Office?"

Olive picked up his breakfast plate and stacked it with her own.

"There's nothing wrong with the banks but for me the Post Office is convenient, there I can buy stamps and stationery, plus it's effectively guaranteed by the Government, 'National Savings'. I've not before had an account of my own, whilst you are confident in all matters of finance, I think as a beginner I prefer the Treasury to be my bank manager."

"Well at least you can go shopping, all women love to shop, it's their equivalent to sport, I've seen them in Griffins when there's a sale on and any referee who valued his life would run a mile, competitive is too mild a word."

Olive got to her feet.

"Then I best stay at home, such a passionate pursuit would find me gasping and a long way behind at the final whistle." She picked up the dishes. "What will you do with your money, unlike we women who can think of nothing better than shopping, men seem to choose from a whole range of activities? Have you paid off the loan and redeemed the Deed, that might be sensible as a first transaction?"

If his attempts at discovering his wife's intentions were to lead to an inquiry after his own then he'd pursue it no further. A sudden need to check the time and to declare himself late enabled his release. Olive listened to the sound of the front door, actually laughed out loud at his predictable response and hummed happily as she washed up. Cynthia would have approved, a Woolascroft woman at last finding her voice.

Dick drove to the yard, his need for haste was not entirely untrue, and while it was quiet he wanted to go over, one more time his outline plan for Mitchell Street before approaching the Council.

The site would require considerable work at foundation level, costly in both materials and labour, not to mention time, his father had often remarked when pricing a job that 'time is money', in the trade it certainly was.

Dick's plan would do away with the old fashioned entry between every two houses, the gardens would be no more than small courtyard areas with enough space for a few flower pots, a dustbin and a clothes line, outdoor area would be sacrificed to create more actual living space within. A ground floor flat and one above, effectively putting three houses where once stood four but thereby creating six dwellings in the process, each one having their own access. Multiplied the length of Mitchell Street it coincided with the local authority's desire for more inner city housing. It was a package Dick needed to sell them, less became more, more tenancies, more rents.

He unlocked the yard gates, Sid Bayliss would be first in. He'd worked for the firm ever since he left school. For years foreman of the workshop Sid could take a length of timber and turn it into more or less anything the architects designed. The dearth of wood during the war and the proliferation of prefabricated housing since its end had put Sid's skills to one side, of necessity he'd adapted to the changes but Dick now needed Sid's craft for those select builds, which enabled the all crucial 'honey pot', that source of sweetener into which Fred had dipped when officialdom's palate required tempting.

Plans for Colver had been approved, the firm had bought the site from Gordon Cheetham on paper, the cost having been factored into the overall build, with Cheetham to receive his 'bulldog's share' at the point of sale. Estate type housing but privately owned, aimed at middle class buyers. The men were currently working at various locations, small stuff in the main, Mitchell Street, if Dick could convince the powers that be at council would secure a good deal, the site was his to sell while the contract to build would be 'Woolascroft's'. Modern local authority accommodation, the cost of the site again factored into the overall build, thus taking immediate pressure off the council's coffer but in return a guarantee of contract regardless of other tenders, and of course that bulldog's share for Dick at completion.

Not having to put up money for Colver at the outset granted the firm a healthier cash flow, Peter was ever robbed to pay Paul and vice versa, it could be no different where matters of the council were concerned, that shuffling of funds to best advantage.

Dick hung his coat over the hook and switched on the electric fire. The office seemed always to hold within its walls some residue of his dad's authority, not yet trustful of Dick's management his spirit lingered.

A rattle outside confirmed Sid's arrival, at least that was Dick's presumption, but the office door opened and William Eddowes entered.

"I saw your car so I knew you were here already, I'm on my way to Derby, got a bit of business to finalise. Last night in the pub I overheard something I imagine might interest you Dick. Apparently Holbrook was taken to hospital last Friday, a neighbour called for the ambulance, don't know what of but he died Sunday night."

William scrutinised Dick's face for a response, some clue to the intrigue surrounding Dick's connection to Holbrook, for there surely was one.

"Then the deal was done just in time Eddowes."

Dick spoke as casually as if he were commenting on the weather and proceeded to unlock the drawer of his desk. He looked up. "Derby yer say, not a bad place to sink a bit of money into Eddowes, good luck with it."

William sensed himself dismissed and sudden activity in the yard removed the possibility of a confidential exchange. He left, frustrated and none the wiser.

Dick leaned back in his chair. 'You can stop starin' at me from these walls dad, I'm puttin' it right, my way this time, your son's puttin' things right. He's gone, you're both gone, it's me sittin' here, my chair, my office'.

Dick spoke as if to ghosts, only he didn't believe in ghosts. He took the plan for Mitchell Street from the drawer and spread it over his desk. This he'd promised to the dreamer at Number 69, and a promise was a promise.

CHAPTER EIGHT

Dublin. Late January.

Callum came back to the table with a tray of drinks, he handed a glass to each in turn.

"Whiskey for Michael, a Murphy's for Liam, Guinness for Derry, pale ale for Mathew, a Miwadi for Jonjo, because of his problem an' a drop of the hard stuff for meself," then sat down opposite Liam. "Well lad, marriage is a soberin' experience, 'tis a fact that up to the event a man's fantasies are either brewed or distilled an' enter his head by way of his mouth. Now after the event fantasies join the realms of fairy stories, kiddies stuff so then he has dreams, an' they creep between the bed sheets on a Saturday night, but these dreams have a way of turnin' into sons an' daughters all needin' to be fed an' clothed, so after a while he has to swap his dreams for realities, nothin' sobers a man like realities." He laughed, "Silly buggers, we all do it. Raise your glasses, here's to Liam, dream for as long as yer can lad, for as long as yer can."

"To Liam." In unison they toasted their workmate Liam Boland, he'd announced his engagement to Rochella, his young lady from the shoe shop and revealed their intention to marry in the spring.

"Busy in here tonight," said Derry, "usually a crowd like this would descend upon Hoolahan's when there's music but there's no band."

The air was thick with tobacco smoke and the barmaid was besieged.

"How many hands do you think I've got Douglas Dooley, not as many as you that's for sure, the likes o' you can hold a glass wi' one hand, a fag wi' the other an' touch up every poor lass within a three yard radius all at the same time as pickin' your nose."

The harassed woman's voice rose above the clamour but made no impression on the impatient punters other than to respond with raucous laughter, though one called out encouragement. "Handcuff the bugger," it simply added to the frenzy.

Mathew's attention had been drawn to a group in the far corner, while the rest made merry half a dozen men appeared removed from the company. Callum noticed young Mathew's look of curiosity.

"Word of advice lad, we all know it, learned it long ago, you need to learn it as well. When yer see men huddled around a table, in a corner where the light's dim, when their eyes never turn right nor left, when their gaze is fixed on the centre of the table top as though at that very spot they expect to see the second comin', yer look away, do yer understand lad, yer look away an' stay away?"

Mathew nodded. "Yes, I understand Callum." He swallowed down the last of his drink. "It's my round what are you all having?"

He felt obliged to move conversation swiftly along as Callum's remark had brought a sudden, sombre mood to the others, now pouring down their throats thc last drop of liquid from their glasses like the good cowboys in the film, just before the fight breaks out.

Mathew repeated their requests to be sure he'd got it right, adding a Miwadi for himself. "I'll keep Jonjo company," he said. While not voicing it Mathew considered the implications of Callum's advice to be far more sobering than holy matrimony.

"So have yer changed your mind about emigratin' Liam?" Asked Michael.

Liam grinned. "Now at my age, the world is me oyster don't they say? Rochella won't be fittin' folk out in shoes all her days, an' I might surprise even meself one day an' walk away from factory gates for the last time, but for now, work's constant, I've money in me pocket so I'll stay wi' the shamrock an' the little people."

Mathew returned with their drinks. "A man at the bar just asked me if I've seen Finnbar Galvin, I told him I don't know him so I couldn't rightly say."

Callum looked at his watch. "Best drink up lads or the women'll be sendin' out search parties, it's home to the realities." He pulled on his hat, stood up and made for the door, like the sheriff in the film, leading his posse.

Derry smiled. "The bugger's right, my missus'll be watchin' the clock, it's what they do, when everybody's in they can bolt the door an' thank the Virgin Mary for bringin' them safely back to the fold. I've watched Kath' time an' time again standin' in front o' the holy picture mouthin' somethin' an' crossin' her chest like a cat pawin' at a mouse. I stare at the picture meself sometimes, to see if her expression's changed, but it never has, she allus looks as if she's just had it for the first time."

"Bloody hell Derry," said Michael, chuckling roguishly as he followed on, Jonjo sniffed, nodded his head, as if in agreement and put a toffee in his mouth. Mathew didn't know whether to feel amused or mortified.

Once outside they went their separate ways and as Mathew walked to his lodgings he acknowledged passing folk with a cordial 'goodnight', his subconscious effort at redeeming a measure of sanctity, at the same time wondering if among them might be Finnbar Galvin.

Callum brushed his hand over Kathleen's hair, smooth as silk and the colour of barley, his eldest daughter was sewing the hem of a skirt, taking up the length so's to fit Maeve, her younger sister.

"Are you alright Dad?" She put down the needle and felt his fingers, they were so cold. "Why don't you keep them in your pockets?" She asked, knowing full well what his answer would be, so often in winter did he reply the same way.

"Because I need them to count me blessings with." They spoke the words together, it was Callum's fun and Kathleen always joined in. "Young 'ens are in bed I suppose," he said. There was a gap of six years between Kathleen and Maeve, then along came Eoin, a delightful little boy with a laugh that could transform glum to glee in an instant.

"Yes, we had the story of 'Struwwelpeter' tonight, Eoin's favourite. Maeve sang herself to sleep as usual, Seamus is on a night shift, he swapped with one of the others, they needed to be at a party of some sort, anniversary I think he said, and Connor," Kathleen sighed, "Connor is wherever Connor wants to be."

"Sit at the table Callum O'Shea, tell me if it's hot enough."

Callum's wife Margaret had emerged from the scullery with a plate of shepherd's pie. "I suppose you all wished the lad well at Hoolahan's, I saw Theresa Boland in town today, she seems pleased, a mother's always relieved when her son finds a good lass." She sighed and Callum knew his wife's anxious breath was spent on Connor. He put a forkful of potato into his mouth.

"Plenty hot enough Maggie, some take longer to settle than others, it's a big step," he looked up at her face, "you an' me stepped further than most but it was the right one, it's always been right."

He smiled fondly, it was true for the most part but of late Connor created worry, he was twenty three, impressionable, even in his early teens he'd challenged Callum's neutrality. These days he looked at his dad almost scornfully. Raleigh was a British company, headstrong Connor O'Shea gave slight consideration to the benefit in employment, he'd worked at Grapel's since leaving school, there they processed cattle feed and Connor deemed beef to be inherently Irish flesh and bone through and through, uncompromised, pure Irish muscle.

Callum sensed his wife was preoccupied by something but not choosing to speak of it suggested Kathleen's presence might be the likely inhibitor. He knew Maggie inside and out, her mannerism tonight told him she carried a concern, she would open up when the time was right, he could wait. Patience was a virtue often needed by parents and never more so than when willing their own infant son, Rowan to defy the odds. For almost a year they watched and waited, born severely handicapped, a belief in miracles enabled Callum and Maggie to patiently pray for his emergence from his chrysalis like body that seemed determined not to yield, not to allow Rowan life on earth. He died just three weeks before his first birthday. Sympathies had been genuine enough, it was their own knowledge, which intensified grief, a pain deep inside for their baby, the pain of loving, pain from fear. They were first cousins, Callum's mother was Margaret's aunt, their marriage had come about through compassion yet cruel fate took Rowan from them, that first big reality in Callum's life. It took a great deal of faith to try again, it was to be rewarded, four times over, granting Connor two healthy brothers and two bonny sisters, he had no need of knowing that what had threatened his siblings had caused no threat to him.

When Margaret's mother had asked her sister Agnes to take in her pregnant daughter it had been a big ask, especially given the reason. Becoming pregnant at the age of nineteen and out of wedlock was not what drove Margaret's father to such lengths, he would not contemplate any possibility of his daughter marrying the man responsible, he was older than Margaret by a good many years, of dubious character, and she was not of an age to defy her father.

While Charlie Holbrook in the beginning provided 'keep' for his daughter, a natural attraction that quickly developed between Callum and Margaret removed the need, a man provided for his wife, they'd married quietly when she was five and a half months on. Six weeks before the baby was due they moved from Cork to Dublin where no one knew them, it gave the young couple and the child a better chance.

Callum had heard stories, dreadful accounts of a vindictive authority over young women who'd made a mistake and fallen pregnant. He liked Margaret a lot, Callum had grown up with the violence, the troubles, he'd distanced himself, felt no urge for blood, a baby was an innocent beginning of life, he could love it, Callum could love and care for them both. He was of a Catholic family, at times as he'd grown up Callum had wondered why the church seemed ever to parade 'sin' before the congregation as though a genuine 'fear of God' might contain their souls between the pews, held there, confined in rows, liberated only during Mass, mortals obliged to return so's for a few moments they might be whole. Surely the childhood hymns they sang declared God's abiding love through the Holy Mother, the Eternal Father. If their marriage was sinful, if Margaret's mistake was a sin, then neither would be confessed, God would know, it didn't require a priest to tell him, and God would be the judge.

Kathleen put away her sewing. "I think I'll go up now Mam, shall I fill your hot water bottle too, you'll not sleep if your feet are cold?"

"Alright love, that'd be nice, we won't be far behind you, Connor has his key, I don't know what keeps him warm."

Margaret sat by the fire, Callum on the other side of the hearth. "I must darn those socks, I'd swear 'tis because you don't cut your toenails often enough, I'm forever doin' it Callum. I sit here week on week lookin' at your big toes pokin' through the ends of your socks 'til I'd recognise them anywhere. God forbid I should ever need to identify you but if I did I'd only need to see your big toes."

He laughed. "An' I'd only need to look into your eyes Maggie O'Shea."

"Get away with yer Callum, yer soft beggar." She grinned, it was their way, their pleasure, home and all it represented, probably more than most folk they valued home.

Kathleen stood between them clutching the hot water bottles. "Goodnight Mam." She leaned forward and kissed her mother's cheek. "Goodnight Dad." She lowered her head and positioned her face so's he could plant a kiss on her cheek. As a child the bedtime kiss had been the most important bit of the day, all was well, Kathleen would be safe from all dark dangers while her mam and dad kept watch. Now she'd reached the age of eighteen she felt strongly protective of her mam so the kiss was reversed but her dad she thought of still as the watch keeper while she slept, while they all slept and the feel of his kiss on her cheek each night was like a lock turning on her mind, barring all troubles from entering.

The sound of the bedroom door closing above them and alone as Margaret had needed them to be, she crossed the room and took an envelope from a drawer of the dresser.

"What is it Maggie?"

She passed the envelope to him saying simply, "Read it."

Just the feel of the paper was enough to confirm the content important, a water mark was apparent as the light from the fire illuminated the letter when Callum held it up to read, the official heading revealed the sender to be, 'Meakin and Kirk' solicitors, London Road, Nottingham. Callum was silent, his eyes following the words, his mind trying to absorb the information. It was signed, Julian Russe.

"Dear God Maggie, yer need to tell him, what else can we do. When you went to see your mother before she died, just three days you were away and we told them you were spending the time with their grandma in Cork because she'd been poorly. We can't keep lying to them, it's time Connor knew, he's no regard for me anyway an' shows little for you. I'm weak, I work for the British, that's how he sees it. Because I won't stir the quiet, join the huddles of militant minded agitators Connor considers me a source of shame. There'll never be a 'right' time to tell him Maggie but it has to be now, for his sake. It says in the letter that your father died on January 17th, it's the 29th now, he has to be buried Maggie, the house emptied of his personal possessions at least. You didn't attend your mother's funeral, I could understand that, it was only ten days before that you'd got home from seeing her, but whatever drove him to act in the way he did doesn't alter the fact that he was your father. The letter states that you're the sole beneficiary, he left all that he had to you, his daughter. I don't know, nor do I care about inheritance, be it a sum of money or his old watch chain but if ever there was a time to tell Connor that not a drop of Irish blood flows through his veins, then it's now. I see the way he's headin' Maggie, he's walkin', marchin' with the wrong sort an' if we don't do this, if we don't take away his 'cause', one night, God help us, the Gardee will stand at our door an' tell us that Connor O'Shea is locked up in a cell, an' I dare not think on what charge."

Margaret began to weep, her hands shook in her lap. "If we tell him he'll want to know who his real father is, after all this time it wouldn't be right."

"Maggie love, I've never asked about the man, I didn't need to know, not then, not now. I'm assuming' he's still alive but if you feel so strongly then tell the lad his real father's dead, the war, Connor wouldn't question that, he knows the war took men like a plague."

Margaret sniffled and dabbed her eyes. "And what if tellin' him only makes him hate the English more, have you thought of that?" I could write back to this Mr.Russe and request he make arrangements for father to be buried with mother at the cemetery, ask him to instruct an agent to auction the house and contents. There'd be more money than enough to pay their bills and the children needn't know of it."

Callum sighed. "Maggie yer can't expect a stranger to go into your father's house to sort out all the personal stuff, his clothes, photos, bits an' pieces like all homes acquire. I'd go with you, or Kathleen could go, she'd understand Maggie, either one of us could go with you, an' the other would look after the young 'ens for a few days." Margaret took the letter and put it back in the envelope, crossed the room to the dresser, tucked it underneath the tea towels in the drawer and was about to speak when the sound of the back door opening bound her tongue.

Connor came into the room, on observing their faces he said. "You two look like you've seen a ghost, perhaps you have. They were lookin' for Finnbar Galvin tonight, he went out this afternoon to get baccy an' didn't come home. His poor ol' missus raised the alarm. They found him literally stiff wi' cold, dead, oh don't be worried, not killed dead but died dead. On a bench he was, in the gardens, just sittin' there, his ankles crossed like a little leprechaun, an' some thievin' bastard had turned his pockets inside out." Connor rubbed his hands before the fire. "I took six frames tonight, had a break of sixty seven, the balls rolled into the pockets honey sweet. Sometimes they fall right for yer an' at others they'll stop short, just hoverin' on the edge, tormentin' little sods. Well I'm off to bed then."

Margaret stared into the hearth.

"Goodnight lad," said Callum, "six frames eh." He stood, looked at his wife with pained eyes before walking away to bolt the back door. Realities, there were too many realities, he couldn't remember one single thread of a fantasy, nor of a dream and tonight's reality hovered at the edge, tormenting him.

Julian Russe studied the letter carefully, as a lawyer it was important that he interpret correctly the content.

Mrs.O'Shea wished Mr.Russe to engage an undertaker, her father was to be buried at Witford Hill cemetery where her mother had been laid to rest eight years ago. It was also Mrs.O'Shea's wish that there be no notice of the funeral placed in any newspaper and there be no prior church service but simply a private interment. She alone would attend, thus requiring herself to know in advance the date and time as she would be travelling from Dublin. All other matters of her father's Estate she would discuss at an appointment convenient to Mr.Russe on either the day before the funeral or the day after. The letter was so cold he was glad to let it fall from his hand to the desk below.

Given the nature of things he considered Handley's to be the most suitable funeral director, Tommy Spooner was ever discreet, he sent souls on their way without questioning. Often it felt like a three act play, the embalmment, the sacrament and the testament, delivering a moral, a fable to those attending, and performed by undertaker, clergyman and lawyer, each familiar with their part but never truly knowing how their performance might be received.

Had it not been for the kindly neighbour, Moira Lacey, who had diligently searched through Charles Holbrook's papers in the hope of finding contact details, Margaret O'Shea would likely be unaware still of her father's death.

Russe was about to call his secretary but hesitated, the clock displayed the time at almost 10-30. He got to his feet, slipped the letter into his pocket and went through to reception.

"What time is my next appointment Ruth?"

She checked. "Nothing until 2o'clock."

"I have to go out but I won't be long, an hour at most."

On this occasion he would go himself to Handley's and convey Margaret O'Shea's wishes, unusual as they were a gentle Ruth might be tempted to puzzle over the irregularities and voice her bewilderment, albeit innocently, to others outside the office.

So often had Callum seen the head badges on the bicycles, they'd become irrelevant, Raleigh Bicycle Company, Nottingham, England.

Now Nottingham sought to overwhelm his family, despite his desperate attempts to maintain the calm, when they'd sat down with Connor, Seamus and Kathleen to explain events all of hell broke loose. Kathleen clung to Margaret and cried as if she believed the revelation might somehow take her mam away from her, while Seamus in his disbelief had stared at Connor as if searching his brother's features for proof, the physical evidence! But it was the reaction from Connor that near' brought the walls tumbling in on them, his shouting, hurling of abuse had woken Eoin and Maeve, both had appeared in the doorway, looking all the more innocent in their nightclothes, terrified and without understanding. Margaret's cries to God for help must surely have shook Heaven to the core and when Connor finally left through the back door, slamming it behind him, sending a blast of weather into the house to chill the soul, his mother had fallen to the floor in faint taking Kathleen with her.

Callum had sat up, waiting for the lad to come home, not until nearly 2am did the latch lift and Connor creep inside, not expecting to find anyone still downstairs he'd looked hard at Callum, pointed his finger accusingly and then with a voice lowered by fatigue said. 'I'm bastard English an' you're feeble Irish, we're a waste of the ground we stand on'. He'd sunk into the chair opposite Callum, brooding, silent.

Only the mention of money had turned Connor's mind from the destruction of family and peace to an advantageous outcome for Connor O'Shea, he was deserving of that, entitled, his was the injury, his must be the compensation. There would be an inheritance, house and capital. Callum had encouraged Connor's expectation, it offered a way forward, at twenty three he was an ideal age for spreading his wings, for taking off, finding a broader view and opportunities within it. The money, albeit his mother's in the first instance, she would give to him, enabling him to travel, see the world beyond the shores of Ireland, a solid independence on which to build a future. The economy of the country had stagnated but if a young man was fortunate enough to have the means he could then venture afield, use his head and succeed. Callum had tried to place himself in Connor's shoes, conviction, belief turned on its head, foundations undermined. He would be desperate to distance himself. Leave it all behind. But even if there were sufficient funds to support Connor in a bid to emigrate, so far away would leave his mother desolate, away from Ireland was one thing, the other side of the world, something else entirely.

Maggie was to catch the ferry tomorrow, she'd insisted on travelling alone to England, to Nottingham, the thought brought an ache to Callum's heart, his wife would step inside that empty house with only memories for company, and what would those memories be? She would stand at the cemetery as her father was buried, no other family member present, make her way to London Road, to Julian Russe, nervous, no steadying arm alongside.

It was dinner time, the men had knocked off for their break and the usual groups were sitting about the factory, flasks and sandwiches, along with observations on life, banter, always there was banter!

"You're from Nottingham aren't yer lad?" Callum directed the question at Mathew, "What's it like there?"

Before Mathew had chance to reply Michael piped up. "Why, are you thinkin' o' crossin' the water Callum, to dig them streets for gold, it's all been done before ol' son."

Callum put down his sandwich. "It's just that I've never made the connection 'til now, here we are puttin' together the bikes with the emblem on the shaft, 'Raleigh, Nottingham' and our friend Mathew actually comes from there, it's what yer call natural curiosity Michael, interest."

Mathew swallowed his mouthful of cheese an' pickle and chuckled. "It's not unlike Dublin except there's no waterfront, unless you count Trent side, the river Trent flows through, wide in places narrow at others. We've a castle built on the rock, caves run underneath, a university, a college of art, a grand library, theatre, picture houses, sport's grounds, all the usual places. When it comes to industry the biggest employers by a long way are the collieries, nationalised now of course. There's Player's tobacco, our own Raleigh, Vyella and Clydella, Nottingham lace, a few brides over here would have been married in our lace I shouldn't wonder. Briggs and Bonhams are the two main engineering concerns, and you must have heard the stories of Robin Hood."

"Aye, I've always thought that deep down the bloke wer' Irish. He wore green an' fought the King's men, robbed the rich buggers to feed them that had nothin', teamed up with a monk an' arf a dozen men who liked their ale an' met a woman on the side called Marion who he had his way with up an oak tree, sounds like pure Paddy to me."

"Yer daft sod Derry," said Michael, screwing up the greaseproof paper that had been wrapped around his sandwiches and throwing it at him.

"Well oak tree aside, they do say that all the pretty girls come from Nottingham, Marion was probably a stunner," said Mathew with a chuckle.

"Now I'd dispute that, yer can't beat a soft, Irish Colleen, melt a man's heart she will," said Liam.

Jonjo gave an almighty sniff then sank his teeth into a wedge of potato cake. They all looked at one another and grinned, thinking it was a great many years since Jonjo's heart last melted.

"What kind o' work does your father do lad?" Again Callum directed his question at Mathew.

He was thoughtful for a few seconds, mentally recalling his dad's past activities. "He's in property and construction, since the war anyway, before that he worked a short while for Mr.Stanford, a mine owner but for several years he was in the employ of Mr.Smithfield, a real decent chap, used to own a textile factory, weaving, but had machinists too, produced good stuff. Of course the shortage of cotton throughout the war years would have affected his business, he's retired now, must be in his mid seventies but such a nice man, no side to him at all. His mother was from Tipperary, he lived and worked over here for a number of years, with Merino wool. Dad is different, I love him dearly but he can be 'hard to fathom', perhaps it was the war that changed him but I don't remember him being so......" Mathew searched for a word, "moody I suppose you'd describe it, but harmless, he barks but never bites."

The bell signalling the end of break brought them all to their feet. Callum laid the flat of his hand in the middle of Mathew's back.

"You're alright Mathew lad, I wish our Connor could think like you."

His remark was accompanied by a heavy sigh, Mathew with perception beyond his years made no reply, was there anything more complicated than family, or more vital.

Margaret took the key from her bag, her father had insisted she keep one when she'd come to see her mother before she died. This house was where she'd lived and played as a child, she'd skip over the doorstep, eager, excited at the prospect of going into town with mam. They would stop to look in the toyshop window at the clockwork clown banging his cymbals and the farmyard set, Margaret's favourite animals had been the pigs, round bellied pink ones, spotty ones with their litters. The dolls with eyes that could blink and hair you could brush and tie up with ribbon. Sometimes mam would buy her a treat for 'being good', a salty tear found the corner of her mouth.

The door looked just as it had always looked except for the brass around the keyhole and letter box, her mother would polish them every week, even when the weather was icy she would don her coat over her pinafore and stand at the door with rag and polish until her nose turned blue. 'Fetch the milk in Margaret, don't drop it'. She could hear her mam saying it, yet here she was at that very same threshold and her fingers trembled too much to put the key into the tarnished keyhole. Something moved by her feet, a cat, it rubbed itself about her ankle and purred like an engine. Just that simple presence of another being, even a cat, was sufficient encouragement, Margaret turned the key and opened the door. The cat was inside first, plainly familiar with its surroundings, showing no hesitation, while Margaret stood still, a smell, not of damp or staleness but of demise, loss, of spent breath. The rag rug, it remained all these years on, the colours used to be vibrant, like a kaleidoscope, they would change depending at which end Margaret sat, and the tufts of cloth used to tickle her legs, especially her upper thighs where her skin was so soft. Now the colours were faded and blurred by the dirt of ages, the once cheerful tufts flattened by years of tread. The empty grate in the living room seemed to stare at her, open mouthed from surprise, 'where have you been all this time Margaret Holbrook'?

She rubbed her fingers over the worn fabric of the chair arm, her dad's hand had chaffed it almost bare, the antimacassar over the chair back held a shadowy stain where the grease from his hair had transferred to the linen, the lace trim at the bottom was coming unstitched and a length of cotton hung down woefully, calling her attention to its plight.

The cat had wandered along to the scullery and sat on a piece of old fraying carpet at the foot of the sink, washing its face and paws. Some kindly soul had rinsed up a few dishes and placed the dishcloth neatly over the edge of the drainer.

Julian Russe had spoken of Moira Lacey, the helpful neighbour, Margaret would thank her, make it right. She bent down to stroke the cat, it responded by looking up with eyes that had witnessed Charlie's loneliness, watched his ageing, Margaret had done neither yet she felt no rebuke from the animal, only gentleness.

Climbing the stairs to the bedrooms she found herself counting. As a little girl she would count each night when she went to bed, the treads of the stairs and call out 'nine' when she reached the top. Her bedroom looked out over the back yard and the small patch of grass, where her dad had put up a swing. Sometimes her mam would sit and swing to and fro, lifting her legs out straight, letting the fullness of her skirt brush the daisies. When Margaret was first in Cork, living with her aunt Agnes and the family she would often imagine her mother sitting on the swing back home, likely crying, just as Margaret herself did, night after night into her pillow.

Callum's kindliness, his understanding eventually dried her tears, Ireland was not familiar to her but a kiss was a kiss wherever she might be. It was hard to believe such a comfort found and soothed her mam, her dad was not a cruel man, not really, but if he ever kissed her mam then it was not done in Margaret's sight.

The bedroom was so cold, she shivered. A small piece of soap sat in a dish on the washstand, cracked along its length, dried out. The mirror above was pitted, losing reflection around the edges, damage advancing like a rash. The bed was still made up, almost as though the room had been expecting her, she touched the pillow, it felt clammy, black mould spots had begun to form on the wallpaper around the window as though confirming the mirror's affliction contagious, the curtains too had a feel of damp.

Someone was knocking at the door downstairs, she sighed and went to answer it.

“I saw you arrive, I don’t want to disturb you but I couldn’t not say hello, I’m Moira, from next door. I need to give you the key I’ve been using, I have tidied up a bit. When the hospital asked me to look for anything that revealed a family contact, I’m afraid I had to go through some of Charlie’s papers until I found something. It was his Will, it showed the name and address of his solicitor who then identified you.

Margaret felt awkward, she couldn’t sensibly offer Moira a cup of tea, not until she lit a fire at least.

“I’m grateful to you Moira, for all that you have done.”

“I know you have lots to do but before you make a start come round to mine, for some hot tea, I see you’ve met Minnie.” Moira looked at the cat, “I’ve wondered what you might do about Minnie, she’s a dear creature, I’ve been feeding her and I’d take her myself but my husband, Bob, is allergic to cats, they make his eyes water and itch and affect his breathing. He works for Tommy Spooner, the undertaker, if you need to find a home for her Bob reckons Tommy would probably have Minnie for his daughter Beryl, or for someone else in his family who’d like a cat, they’re a big family, the Spooners, between them I’m sure the problem would get solved.”

Margaret smiled, “Yes, that would be helpful, I can’t take her back with me all the way to Dublin, it’s Mr.Spooner who’s doing the funeral isn’t it? I’ll ask him afterwards. It is just a burial, there will be no church service.” Margaret saw the puzzled look on Moira’s face, “It’s complicated, and I wish I could explain but I really can’t. I know that you were very kind to my father and that it was you who found him and called the ambulance, Mr.Russe, the solicitor told me. If you’d like to be at the cemetery then perhaps we could go together.”

If truth be known, now faced with being the only one to watch the coffin lowered, other than the undertakers and the bearers, Margaret hoped that Moira might say yes.

“I would like to go tomorrow, Bob never says much about his work, understandably I suppose, so I don’t know at what time the burial is to be.”

“Ten, it’s at ten o’clock, I must sort through all dad’s personal things and empty the house of all but furniture, I don’t have to leave until Friday but I have an appointment with Mr.Russe on Thursday, you know how it is with the legal side of things.”

Moira found it difficult to judge this woman, in her mind to think of Margaret as a long lost relative seeking gain, she seemed gentle natured, timid almost and looked worn out, a woman wearied. No one escaped problems and Margaret Holbrook’s eyes showed strain, Moira put a hand on her arm.

“Come along, some tea first, something to warm us up and I’ve cooked some scraps for Minnie. She must wonder why everything’s changed, I think Charlie fed her bread and milk but she enjoys something meaty. I went to school with the butcher, I think he was sweet on me,” Moira laughed mischievously, “an old admirer can be useful, ‘no charge for the odds and ends Mrs.Lacey’ he says. If there’s another customer waiting then he says nothing but his wink must suggest a conspiracy of some sort to those who notice. I told Bob, now he’s a rogue if ever there was one, ‘have a bit of homemade cake in your bag love and hand it to him if anybody’s watchin’, that’ll set their tongues waggin’’, he’s no shame my Bob, you’ll see him at the cemetery, he’s sure to be one of the bearers.”

“I shall make it right, I must give you some money, tidying up, feeding the cat, searching for a name and address to contact, I’m in your debt.”

“Nonsense,” said Moira, “all my family have flown the nest, my time is my own, I enjoyed popping round to see Charlie and it’s been no hardship tending Minnie, besides, we wouldn’t be here chatting together now if I hadn’t got to know your dad. I’m genuinely pleased to meet you Margaret. All families have their troubles and complications, we can only do our best with whatever circumstances prevail.”

"Mrs.O'Shea is here Mr.Russe."

"Thank you Ruth ask her to come through." He had developed a mental image of Margaret O'Shea, from her letter, her voice on the phone and from the circumstances surrounding her father's, 'life and death', both held sadness, a lonely sadness. Russe expected to meet a stern, rigid woman, intent on the business of the Estate, it was not for him to scrutinise any client, regardless of irregularities, all things written in law passed across his desk to be dealt with dispassionately but even a lawyer was subject to 'opinion', albeit neither written nor spoken.

Margaret O'Shea now stood before him, slight of build, pale, hair greying prematurely, her expression revealing nervousness, not at all stern in fact her face held gentleness, a fading prettiness even, which when she smiled, momentarily recovered.

Russe shook her hand, it was a hand that had known hard work yet her grip was strong, despite her obvious anxiety. If a solicitor was asked to identify one thing which enabled him confidence in his undertaking it would be the firmness of a handshake.

"Please take a seat Mrs.O'Shea, I can imagine your tiredness, first having to travel from Ireland, the inevitable tasks that awaited you at your father's house and the rigours of yesterday so I shall not keep you long.

As you are the sole beneficiary I would anticipate getting Probate within a matter of weeks. It appears that your father had only one bank account, there is the house of course but unlike the situation, which arises when there are siblings, requiring a property to be sold and the proceeds divided, that does not apply here, I see no delay therefore."

Margaret hesitated before responding. "It will sound heartless to you I'm sure Mr.Russe but I do need to ask, what will be the likely sum of money, after all expenses are deducted of course?"

"I believe your father recently sold property on Mitchell Street, he instructed us to draw up his Will several years ago, however he didn't use this firm to act for him over the recent sale, whether he dealt with matters himself I'm not sure, he may have being trying to save costs as he saw it. I would have expected his account to show a greater balance. You see the properties had been condemned due to subsidence, therefore the value would have been in the site and in salvage, reclamation prior to demolition, a much lower figure of valuation. While subsidence creates huge problems, through more up to date building methods and a better knowledge of groundworks they can be overcome but at a cost. The sale achieved a minimal amount, but due to the owner would be compensation from the Coal Board which Mr.Holbrook should have claimed before selling. Any law firm acting for him would have pursued that on his behalf. As compensation was seldom agreed on when mines were in private ownership it is quite likely that your father was unaware and the solicitor acting for the buyer was under no obligation to inform the vendor.

I can more or less estimate the bill from Handley's and this firm's charges, I think it unlikely that your father had any outstanding debts but a notice in the Post, which I can place immediately should confirm that to be so. All things considered the bank account at Probate might stand in the region of seven thousand pounds."

Margaret turned from pale to ashen.

"Are you quite alright Mrs.O'Shea? Perhaps Ruth could make you some tea."

Russe was concerned at the draining of colour from Margaret, even her hands appeared lifeless, he felt the not unnatural urge to rub them feverishly with his own. She took a deep breath and clenched her fingers as though fighting a pain.

"Thank you but I'm alright, a family like ours doesn't often deal with money over and above the weekly costs, a little put by when we can, but thousands, never have we even thought in thousands.

Nearer the time perhaps you would recommend an agent, I've talked with my husband and we both agree that it might be prudent to keep the house rather than sell, rent it out. We'd like to help our eldest son, opportunities in Ireland are limited, prospects appear better elsewhere. Many young people are emigrating and that might be his choice but as a mother it would sadden me, so far away. Here in England industry is thriving, jobs are being created all the time. The money will enable us to help him financially but we have four other children, two boys and two girls, while ever we keep the house we hold future help for them also. Callum, my husband, believes bricks and mortar to be a safe investment. But could father's house become devalued as a result of subsidence do you suppose, advise me please Mr.Russe?"

"Whilst I can't guarantee it Mrs.O'Shea, I would venture to say 'no', I am not aware of any such problems in that area of the city, in fact this firm recently conveyed ownership of a property there at a very good sale price."

"Thank you, I go home tomorrow, I'm sure you will write when things are done." Margaret got to her feet.

"There will be one or two documents requiring your signature but I can mail them to you by recorded delivery and include the necessary return addressed envelopes, to which you must attach proof of registered post, to enable me due submission to the Probate office."

"By Easter, do you think it might be concluded by Easter?" Asked Margaret anxiously.

Why the significance of Easter he could not understand but he was able to answer her confidently. "Almost certainly Mrs.O'Shea, I would be surprised if it were otherwise."

The bus was busy, the breath from so many passengers caused the windows to run with condensation, the air outside being frosty. It was half past three and already the temperature was dropping fast.

Margaret's head was so full of thoughts each denied the next sufficient time to be properly considered. Connor was a troubled young man, his loyalties were now so muddled, his confusion manifested in outbursts of temper and spite. With money Margaret might persuade him to cross the water to England. It seemed the most unlikely place given Connor's political leanings, but surely that must change, he must accept the truth and live with it, a sum of money would ease the process, at least England would grant them the chance of seeing their son from time to time.

Connor had demanded to know who his real father was, just as Margaret had expected him to, thankfully her fib, the war's consequence, he appeared to accept but any day he could ask for a name. Dick Woolascroft was almost sure to be married, if in fact he was alive, over the years Margaret had made no enquiry about him, Callum and the children were her life, all else she'd left behind. Any contact now would be unfair, she'd never blamed Dick and she had no intention of causing trouble to his family now. The reason she'd specified there be no notice placed in the paper, of the funeral, and simply interment without a church service, had been to remove any possibility of Dick knowing she was in Nottingham, for all their sakes.

How kind Mr.Spooner had been, Minnie was to find her new home with his great niece Elizabeth. His daughter Beryl already had two rabbits to care for. He'd added the remark, 'she's not really my niece but sort of, and we love her lots', Margaret smiled to herself at the thought, the gentlest of undertakers and yet his words had suggested that even the Spooners, his large family, was not without complications, she felt strangely comforted.

Margaret wanted Connor to leave Dublin before the Easter marches, they incited men to violence, stirred emotions and brought about displays of resentment, one against another. This year Connor could feel only betrayal, he was too young, too intense to be rational. His grandad whom he'd not once met now would grant him a future, how sad that it came without affection, words on paper, formal, official, poor Connor, he was blameless too.

Yesterday when she'd stood in the back garden of her childhood home, watching a bonfire consume old papers, old worn clothes too ragged for even the Salvation Army, the many remnants of her mother and father's lives, Margaret had cried bitterly. Gone, all gone, but affection was gone long ago, her tears were for loss and loss of affection, not of life.

What was it Moira Lacey had said, 'all families have their troubles and complications, we can only do our best with whatever circumstances prevail'. At that moment the conductor's voice interrupted her thoughts.

"Next stop Aspley Lane."

Margaret fastened the top button on her coat and braced herself against the cold, in the morning she was to catch a train to Liverpool, to the ferry and to home, at least she was completely assured of Minnie's future, affection in abundance from young Elizabeth, a sort of niece whom Tommy Spooner loves a lot.

CHAPTER NINE

Early April.

"I don't think Samuel and Margaret will be far behind us, I hope that he doesn't feel that our getting married puts pressure on him to find a place of his own. George tells me off for imagining such nonsense and Samuel has always been welcoming but I can't help worrying."

Liza folded the last item in Celia's wash basket and added it to the pile already done, while Celia lifted a tray of currant buns from the oven and rushed to the table, the baking tray singeing her fingers through a small hole in the oven cloth.

"Ooh, just made it," she dumped it rather unceremoniously on a cork mat and sought urgent relief at the cold water tap. "I'm not surprised George tells you off Liza, I can't think of anyone less likely to be troubled at the prospect of his father's wedding. Samuel is delighted, the fonder he became of Margaret Coupland the more he was fretting about his dad. Put yourself in his shoes, Samuel loves the girl and must have known they would be married before too long, to think of his dad living alone would have put him in a dilemma but when you came back and things developed," Celia gave Liza an old fashioned look of mischief, "he was relieved to believe that his dad wouldn't be alone after all. So there you are Liza Ollerton, the fact is you've enabled a young couple to love and plan without feeling guilty at leaving George to a miserable solitary existence. Besides I happen to know that Samuel was approving of you from the start, he told his grandma and she told me." Celia chuckled. "Sometimes I think we are completely misguided in believing that it is we, the older generation, who steer a family through life, avoiding the bumps and potholes, the wrong turns and dead ends. Mathew's letters inspire me as well as comfort and Emily's long wordy descriptions of London are an education, I'd swear that since they went away my wisdom has increased, my two children keep me on track, without them I'd be lost."

"You do have William," said Liza, now carefully lifting the buns onto a cooling rack, "surely he's steady at the wheel, I've always thought of him as staid, not exciting but not reckless either."

Celia was grateful for the timely intervention, the saving grace of the front doorbell.

"I hope that's not another salesman, there have been two in the last week, one desperate to convince me that I couldn't properly sweep my carpets without the latest model of vacuum cleaner, he'd obviously been at some kind of training, 'Hoover beats as it sweeps as it cleans' madam!' The other offered me a feather duster entirely free if I purchased six tea towels."

Celia blew over the end of her finger where the start of a blister had begun to throb and went to the door with a huff of impatience.

"Mrs.Eddowes?" The man gave a pleasant smile but other than that Celia could see no evidence of a sales pitch, he carried nothing, not as much as a pamphlet. "Steve Roper's the name Mrs.Eddowes, I don't suppose your husband is at home this hour of the afternoon but I can just as easily explain the situation to you I'm sure."

Celia made the connection, Moreleigh, not until this moment had she met either Mr. or Mrs.Roper but remembering William's irritable announcement early in the year, of their intention to vacate the house and emigrate, she assumed the man had come to give notice.

"Please come in Mr.Roper, you're quite right, William's not here but I am aware of your plans it all sounds very exciting." Celia was in a quandary, if she led him to the living room then Liza would feel awkward but the kitchen seemed hardly the appropriate place in which to attend business. He solved the problem for her.

"That's a lovely smell of baking Mrs.Eddowes, Diane's not one for that sort of thing." His gaze bypassed the living room door and travelled with intent directly to the kitchen.

"Well if you don't mind sitting amidst a muddle of laundry then I shall put on the kettle and we'll all have tea and cake, my friend Liza is here."

"Oh I am sorry, I mustn't bother you when you've company."

By now they'd reached the kitchen anyway, Liza looked startled and Steve Roper's face showed surprise too.

"The train, that poor lad with travel sickness, it is the same lady isn't it?" He directed the question at Liza with a note of amusement.

"Yes, I remember you too, the kind man with a suitcase of remedies." Liza's expression was one of disbelief almost, three salesmen in just a few days yet he appeared to be without his trademark suitcase, she felt curious, though Celia was even more intrigued, how could Liza know Steve Roper, she'd obviously met him before today.

The next few minutes of conversation revealed all and Steve laughed heartily at the irony of him being in fact a sales rep.

"It's a small world isn't it?" Said Liza.

"Normally I would agree," said Steve, "but right now, just one month away from our leaving England for New Zealand, it feels very much bigger than it ever did before. Diane I'm sure is a little apprehensive but we don't have children and it is through my work that the opportunity has arisen, nothing ventured, nothing gained, England will be here still if it doesn't work out.

Now alone, Celia fingered the envelope, it contained official notice of the Ropers' final weeks at Morleigh and a month's rent. In addition a small sum of goodwill by way of gratitude for their untroubled years of tenancy. Celia felt thankful that it had been she who shook Steve Roper's hand today and not William. Pleasantry, a sense of friendship had been at the table with Liza, Steve and herself, the envelope and its contents merely a silent witness to their easy exchange. William would have torn the seal, scrutinized each and every word within and counted the notes at least twice in sight of the affable Steve Roper, then dismissed him for being no longer of use.

Thank God for the nearing of Easter, Mathew was coming home, just for the long weekend but bringing Celia a lodger, the son of a workmate at the factory, it was only a temporary arrangement, while the young man was taking a look at Nottingham, she hadn't asked the purpose of his visit, saving that enquiry for conversation when he arrived. Possibly three or four weeks, no more than that Mathew said. Emily would be back as well, for a few days, young company to steer Celia past the potholes and dead ends. Before granting consent to the accommodation of Connor O'Shea, William in typical fashion had established that the young man was expecting to pay for his keep. Celia couldn't help wishing that William too might explore, take a look at the world beyond Colver and Derby. New Zealand, it might as well be the moon!

She carried the envelope to the living room and placed it by the clock on the mantelpiece, where each week William put her housekeeping money. They had a joint bank account yet not once had Celia felt brave enough to withdraw a single penny, just as her fingers today had failed to open the envelope and look inside.

Annie waited patiently in the queue, the post office was busy, towards the front she could see Joyce Haynes next in turn after Olive Woolascroft. Annie's mind made a connection between the two women though nothing tangible bound them together, perhaps it was simply the name 'Woolascroft', it had a way of inveigling thoughts however hard one resisted, unwelcome, unsought yet so often present. Some days it seemed to vie with 'Stanford' for domination.

William had surprised both Annie and Charles by turning up late in the afternoon the previous day, seating himself in the chair opposite his dad and with no casual conversation beforehand asking, 'do you know anything about a Charlie Holbrook'? The name was vaguely familiar to Annie but she couldn't think why so said nothing. Charles had responded naturally enough by asking why William needed to know. 'Just something Woolascroft was interested in, that's all', had been William's veiled reply. With eyes now free of cataracts Charles had looked intently at William and said, 'can't help you with that one Son'. Later in the evening, after Annie had cleared away their tea dishes and settled herself with her knitting, Charles had abandoned his usual pre-bedtime silence to reveal knowledge of one Charlie Holbrook. 'I won't subscribe to William's 'Stanford type' schemes, that man knew too much and now William seeks to know too much, it's time he let other folk be'. Charles had spoken quietly when imparting to Annie his own knowledge.

'Holbrook had a daughter, she would have been in her late teens when she disappeared from the scene. You know what happens, anything remotely unusual and away go the gossips, tongues wagging ninety to the dozen. For a while it was the topic of conversation in the pub, young woman suddenly goes away, couldn't be anything else but a fall from grace, got herself pregnant. Folk shut their minds to all other possibilities don't they? As far as I'm aware the lass never came back. Dick Woolascroft's name was rumoured but if that man is responsible for all I've heard him blamed, then he must be beyond human, talk about giving a dog a bad name'.

Olive Woolascroft had completed her business at the counter and now made her way to the door. Annie had been surprised by Charles' unusual reluctance to further William's intrigue, she was quite convinced that in the past he would have been there, in the thick of that dangerous speculation, moving with the rest from one gossip to the next, perhaps not using it in the twisted way of some but nonetheless hungry for it. Anthony Hemsley's revelations had turned Charles away from such pursuits, more and more he clung to home, to privacy, not venturing out, not welcoming others in, while his seclusion troubled her at least he was becoming peaceable, she'd grown used to his moods, they occupied the house like a familiar creak of the stair, the rattle of the letterbox on a windy day. But Stanford and Woolascroft too seemed to take up residence at No1 Winchester Street, a product of the times, along with Huntley and Palmer, Brown and Polson, Cross and Blackwell, they looked down at Annie from the shelf, advertising their success, taunting her through association.

Joyce suddenly spotted Annie further back in the queue, she called out.

"I'll wait for you."

Annie mouthed a silent 'alright', and smiled to herself. Even after all these years aunt Bella's authority ordered her ways, to call out in a public place lacked all decorum. How silly it all was, Bella Pownall's life had decorum by the cartload, cold, lonely decorum and what difference did it make at the end? Yet here, almost forty eight years on, Annie stayed loyal to Bella's instruction.

Finally Annie reached the counter, quickly completed her purchase of stamps and envelopes and with her customary 'thank you' hurried outside to where Joyce stood talking to a pigeon.

"I allus say hello to it, knows my voice now, don't yer?" The bird was intent on a morsel of something lodged between two paving slabs but miraculously turned its head at just the moment Joyce spoke before returning its attention to the source of interest. "I reckon it's the same one as perches on the coal shed roof, it must follow me home. Now Elizabeth's got Minnie I'm surprised it hasn't cleared off, our house seems to attract strays."

Joyce was quiet for a few seconds, hesitant, Annie sensed the pause would lead to something more significant than the habits of a pigeon.

"Valerie's been callin' round, it started just before last Christmas. Edgar didn't seem surprised, I think they must have been seein' one another before then. First time I opened the door an' found her standin' there I didn't know what to do, it wer' only the odd evenin' at the beginnin', then more regular, now it's at the weekends an'all. I had to ask Edgar what had happened, why now after all this time. He told me neither o' them had expected it but when they'd bumped into each other in town, which I suppose they were bound to do sometimes, livin' in the same city for goodness sake, Valerie had asked about Elizabeth an' if she wer' with him she'd seem pleased to see her. I don't know whether to be worried, cross, afraid or forgivin' Annie. My William's washed his hands of it an' I can't bother Tommy, he's a family of his own to worry about. I see Edgar's smile when she comes, I can tell Elizabeth likes her. The lass wer' young an' Tom Oates was no sort o' father, they say everybody deserves a second chance, I got one didn't I?" Joyce looked at Annie with watery eyes.

"Valerie's older and wiser," said Annie, "I've heard nothing untoward spoken of her, she managed to lose herself in the crowd, like the rest of us, blending in as best she could. Edgar hasn't met anyone else, you've told me many times how devoted he is to Elizabeth. Valerie is her mother when all's said and done. I can't really advise you Joyce, it's you who observes them when they're together, you who recognises the child's feelings. For some folk happiness can be rare, simply living can challenge it, those everyday problems that beset a household, threaten contentment and whether rich or poor no one escapes them altogether. But if I were in your place I think I'd carry on as you've always done, Edgar thinks of you as his mam, Elizabeth loves her grandma and Valerie isn't going to change any of that. Quietly observe Joyce and if Edgar appears happy trust his judgement, a more level headed young man you'd search long and hard to find."

Joyce sighed. "That's true," then sniffed before saying. "She's allus very quiet, Dick Woolascroft's missus, I've seen her before at the post office, dignified I suppose you'd call it, she's smiled at me once or twice an' said good mornin'. Makes yer wonder what she ever saw in him."

That connection again, so Joyce made it too, nothing tangible yet how potent it could be.

"At this stage Ernie we haemorrhage money, machines like them earn Bill Whittle a fortune." Dick Woolascroft stood with the site foreman, Ernie Roddick, watching the bulldozers carve their way through the ground at Colver.

A heavy snowfall in February followed by a long period of rain in March had delayed the commencement of groundworks, that initial thrust into the sod, which stamped Woolascroft's intent on previously unfranked land. Not until Bill Whittle's men and machines had done their part could the build proper begin.

Mitchell Street's problems from subsidence had driven Dick to seek knowledge of Colver's workings. When he'd asked Gordon Cheetham if any plan or map of the spent coal seams had been included in the Deeds his careful check of all documents had resulted in his answer being no. The only person able to shed light on the subject was likely to be aunt Patricia, among her papers should be a record of the mine's operation, depths, levels, at which points of the compass. Dick had taken himself to Castle Road, armed with a bowl of blue hyacinths, while visiting a relative shouldn't really pose a problem, he nevertheless felt vulnerable, Patricia possessed a certain authority. Florence Stanford had opened the door, inviting him inside with no obvious surprise at finding him on the threshold. Patricia had been studying some papers but put them down immediately, greeting him with a pleasant smile. In the event he'd felt no actual need of a 'potted gesture' but presented the hyacinths with the appropriate generosity and pursued his mission. It had proved fruitless and two cups of tea and a slice of malt loaf later he was feeling frustrated, then Patricia made a suggestion. 'You should go to Birchdale, I shall telephone Jack Haynes and ask him to look out the old papers relating to operations at Colver, they will be there, records for both pits have been kept at Birchdale since Colver closed down. It would be wise to let Jack explain the plans to you, while a builder knows chapter and verse of his process above ground only a miner can fully understand what goes on below it'.

Thus Dick had found himself in the office at Birchdale studying old maps and charts of underground warrens, which in times past had led men to early graves. For the layman, unfamiliar with mining practices it was a shock to the senses, such deep shafts, and tunnels running for miles. Jack Haynes had lived and breathed pit life for years, even as a manager. 'I can't make a judgement if I don't see', was how he'd described to Dick the necessity of his 'going down'.

Dick had come away from Birchdale pondering the stark differences between Haynes and Eddowes, related through marriage only it was hard to imagine any common ground existing between them beyond the obligations of family. In fairness much the same could be said of Patricia Bradshaw and himself, though deep down he held an admiration for her that he shouldn't deny, a woman with a bright mind, he'd been unable to resist a quick glance at the papers she'd been studying that day at Castle Road, share statements, relating to Courtaulds, while his own wife Olive stayed with the safety of the post office.

Dick glanced at his watch, he had an appointment with the chief planning officer at 2 o'clock. Early afternoon meetings Dick favoured, viewing them as less prone to obstacles, if officialdom's stomach had been recently satisfied then it sat back, mellow and receptive. On the agenda this afternoon was Mitchell Street, he'd instructed the architect to draw in detail the finished design, interior and exterior, front and back. It had been costly and risky, few developers would approach the authority initially with more than an outline plan. But it was thinking of Jack Haynes fundamental policy that persuaded Dick to chance it, how could the planners who held court over his intentions make a judgement if they didn't see?

"Keep 'em at it Ernie," said Dick, "don't want Bill Whittle's gear on site an hour more than necessary, haemorrhaging we are an' Whittle'll bleed us dry if we let him."

Ernie muttered his accord with a more audible, "Right you are boss," added by way of insurance. Being a foreman brought responsibility, he was first in line for any criticism of performance, he was tasked to wave the stick, but it was a damn sight better than being a labourer, a man could soon learn yes sir, no sir, three bags full sir, if the benefit was his own.

Mathew's travelling companion proved to be a puzzling mixture of outspoken opinion and mysterious silence. On the ferry Connor displayed an almost reckless confidence, his chatter defending 'the cause', as though Mathew was the embodiment of British interference into Ireland's sacred Constitution. Yet on the train his conversation had gradually become subdued, tiredness Mathew supposed it to be until the restless tapping of his foot and the constant pick, pick of a thumbnail suggested nervousness, the closer to Nottingham the train chugged its way, the deeper became Connor's silence.

In five minutes they would reach the station, Mathew's dad was meeting them, perhaps not the mildest first encounter for Connor, it would likely be a quick handshake then a bustled deposit into the car boot of their baggage before an impatient drive through the city traffic, until finally nearing the warm, wholesome welcome, waiting in the arms of Mathew's mam, if anyone could ease Connor's nervousness it would be mam, as generous with her smile for the stranger as for family.

When Callum waved them off at the quay Mathew had sensed an anxiety, young man embarking on an adventure didn't feel quite right somehow, eyes often revealed more than the spoken word and the look father and son exchanged held pain. If Connor O'Shea was to accept Nottingham with all its challenges and differences then Mathew must show in his eyes confident delight and will his dad to do likewise, a bottle of Irish Whiskey snugly wrapped about with a Donegal Tweed hat should do the trick.

Emily wasn't due to arrive until Monday so Mathew's time with his sister would be very short, he must catch the early train on Tuesday. Travelling with Connor had been possible only because the manager at Hanover Quay had said, 'go on then lad, as a favour to Callum'. The factory was busy, American demand for the sports models kept production at capacity. When the time came for Mathew to leave Dublin and return to Nottingham he would have mixed feelings, there was great truth in the saying, 'there's no place like home', yet Ireland had a way of creeping softly beneath the skin, taking up a place not so obvious from the outside but there, staking its claim from within.

He'd not experienced any resentment, the men he worked alongside had not once struck the warning drum or waved the battle flag, they'd sung and danced pure Irish rhythms pulling him into their midst with hands of friendship, teaching him the words and steps so's he could live the moments as they did. Working hard, playing fair, being the best they could be.

"Need to collect ourselves now Connor, gather the bags and make our way along the corridor." Mathew got to his feet and reached up to the luggage rack. "Be careful with this one," he winked at Connor, "a drop o' the hard stuff for the old man." He handed him the bag. "I'll take you to The Standard tomorrow night, and buy you a pint of Wrenshaw's ale Connor O'Shea, you can sample a bit of English craic for a change, we'll go with my cousin Samuel, he's another Raleigh man."

Connor appeared less than enthusiastic but took the bag carefully from Mathew's hand saying only. "I bet your sister will be able to tell me a lot about London, now there's a place to think about."

"Give Nottingham a chance first Connor," said Mathew, "you've not yet seen the place it has a lot to offer."

"Aye, maybe it has." Connor sniffed dismissively, at that moment thinking of what it had already offered, money and opportunity courtesy of his late grandad and 'late' was a word most apt in the circumstances. "Sometimes Mathew a lot's still not enough, not when yer count the interest owed."

Mathew didn't understand Connor's remark and sensed he wasn't meant to, 'a puzzling mix' described accurately this young Irishman.

The train finally pulled in at the platform, opening the heavy door Mathew took in a breath of home, the familiar sights and sounds of Nottingham's Midland Station. It was Good Friday, that most holy day, the shrines and grottos in Ireland would be visited upon by the faithful.

"You're Catholic aren't you Connor?"

"That's what it says on me confirmation certificate an' me birth certificate says I'm Irish, they're just pieces o' paper when all's said an' done, Connor O'Shea is his own man." He looked intently at Mathew, then laughed. "Me dear old grandad left me some money yer see, thought the world of his eldest grandson so he did, wanted me to make somethin' o' meself. Now I can't let him down can I, I'm obliged to do him proud, be it here, there, or someplace else?" Connor looked about the platform at folk moving swiftly towards the exits. "Where's your dad?" he asked.

"Oh he'll be waiting outside, you've to pay to come on the platform, dad won't waste money on unnecessaries," now Mathew laughed, "don't tell him you've come into money or he'll try to sell you something or persuade you to invest in Woolascrofts. Now if it were me I'd give even London a chance before I'd do that."

“Why.” Asked an intrigued Connor.

But Mathew made no reply, if Connor O’Shea was able to be mysteriously evasive then so too could he be. Hurrying to the concourse he merely said.

“A pint in The Standard, you’ll learn more about this city by spending an hour in there than you would from reading a scholarly history book at the library, English craic Connor, English craic!”

Celia laid the table for breakfast, Emily wouldn’t arrive until tomorrow afternoon so her egg sat in a dish on the sideboard. William was sure to make some sarcastic remark but Celia was beyond taking notice and so she placed chocolate Easter eggs, brightly encased in gold foil, on Mathew and Connor’s plates, grown men who yesterday had gone to County Ground to watch the match and last night had taken themselves to the pub, for a quick one, as Mathew declared their intention to be though it was past eleven when they got back. William had been intent on going with them but Celia had persuaded him to let the young ones get to know one another first, Samuel was to meet them there, George had been of the same mind as Celia, Connor would likely feel happier in company of his own age until everything became more familiar. As a result William had gone into the living room and put on the gramophone a record that he’d recently bought, playing it over and over, knowing that Celia didn’t like it. She’d gone to bed with ‘*Cigareets an’ whisky an’ wild wild women’*, ringing in her ears, defying sleep and was wide awake still when the boys returned. For what felt like hours she’d lain wakeful, pondering Connor O’Shea, something about him troubled her, he was polite, mannerly, yet strangely distant. His Irish accent she found quite charming, it softened his speech as though his words had been anointed in some kind of soothing oil before escaping into air, yet his eyes seldom met her own, he must be feeling a little insecure, that was understandable at this early stage of his visit but at twenty three years it seemed unusual, a small child, in its mind would hide behind a diverted gaze but here was a man, in Nottingham to explore the possibility of work, to see new places, it made a great deal of sense, Mathew was thoroughly enjoying his time in Dublin, it was easy to imagine Connor doing the same in reverse. But Celia sensed there was more to it than that, it was a mother's intuition, Connor's mother was in Ireland, she would be feeling anxious so it was for Celia to be mother while he lived under her roof, just as Mathew's kindly landlady in Dublin applied herself to the role.

Celia was to meet Annie later, they were going to Chapel with Rosemary, the girl had a sweet voice and her grandma had encouraged her to sing in the Chapel choir. Hilda was often busy catching up on housework while the salon was closed so Annie would go with Rosemary most Sunday mornings, along with Mrs.Sealey who'd sit in the pew gripping her handbag as if life depended on it. Apparently she'd explained to Annie that any money in the house she put inside her bag and took it with her so Mr.Sealey couldn't use it for drink, like Annie Celia felt pity for the woman and kept all knowledge of the struggling Sealey household to herself and no other.

Celia couldn't manage to go every week, she tried to spend a little time with the Batemans and a Sunday offered the opportunity, even William in a curious sort of way accepted the Sabbath as belonging to a higher order. Sometimes she wondered if he was simply trying to curry favour with The Almighty, encouraging a degree of influence over William's part of a deal but then regretted such unworthy thoughts. This morning Celia needed the comforting strains of '*Christ the lord is risen today'*, to drive from her head the relentless intrusion of '*Cigareets an' whisky*'.

Movement above confirmed the boys were dressing, William was getting up too. Desperate to avoid anything that might make Connor uncomfortable she'd bought a box of coffee creams and put them by William's plate, they were a favourite of his, like the coffee gateaux that up until the war and rationing she'd bought at Burtons every October for his birthday tea.

By the time the kettle boiled and the porridge was ready they'd assembled at the table and found their treats. Mathew and Connor were pleased, Celia could tell. For the first time since arriving Connor spoke of his family.

"Eoin an' Maeve, the two young ens'll be findin' theirs, mam always buys them one each, in an egg cup, from Foleys sweet shop on Kiltey Street, like she did for us older ones. There's a whole line of egg cups on the top shelf o' the dresser, like a row o' Communion cups waitin' for Father O'Malley to come along with the raspberry vinegar. Thanks very much Mrs.Eddowes, it's been a while since I had an Easter egg."

William looked at his box of coffee creams. "I'm in lucks way, new hat, whiskey and now chocolates I best carry on as I am, must be doing something right."

Celia spooned the porridge into their dishes, ignoring William's remark. She asked what the boys planned to do this Easter Sunday.

"I thought we'd go to the Park Mam," said Mathew, "show Connor the police horses, such magnificent animals, it's not just the Irish who have good horses," he chuckled, "on a fine Sunday afternoon there's sure to be a few young ladies about too, I've told him that all the prettiest girls come from Nottingham. Samuel and Margaret will meet us there at half past two or thereabouts. This morning we'll catch a bus into city centre, have a quick look around there then go out to Brassington to see Mr.Smithfield. I wrote to tell him that I was bringing Connor over and he replied to say he'd be delighted to meet him. I know dad will show Connor around the development sites and take him to see the factories, give him every chance to see Nottingham's industries but I'm only here for one more day and I must call on grandma and grandad tomorrow, so I'll keep Connor company today then hand him over to Emily and dad thereafter."

Celia recognised William's peeved expression on hearing the boys were to spend time with Andrew Smithfield. It was a pathetic fact that his childish attitude required Celia to buy the peace with a box of coffee creams but from sheer weariness she ever rewarded his pique and chastised herself for being so feeble.

"You'll like my sister," said Mathew, "she has firm beliefs and if you ever fancy a good debate then seek out Emily. I've sparred with her many times and while I've come away thinking I'd held my ground, if I'm honest I don't believe I've even once scored points."

Connor was quiet, thoughtful, he walked alongside Mathew in silence, casting his gaze briefly over whatever Mathew drew his attention to. Poor Robin Hood was minus his arrow yet again. No matter how many times the local authority replaced the missing piece of statue, before long some vandal would prise if from the hero's hand and disappear with their trophy. Connor at last spoke, revealing the source of his pre-occupation.

"In the pub last night conversation seemed dominated by that name, Woolascroft, the one you mentioned on the train. He makes a few waves around these parts doesn't he? I couldn't help but overhear, men's voices grow louder with every sup, it's the same back home, except for those that scheme."

"Your dad warned me about them," said Mathew, "turn away and stay away is what Callum said. I don't think the scheming here goes on in pubs, it's pursued at more select gatherings, out of common man's sight and hearing. I can't really say much, dad invested in Woolascrofts, they're a big building firm, son runs it now since his father died, he's a similar age to dad, bit older maybe. Folk don't have a lot of regard for the man, perhaps it's a requirement of business, the ability to ignore sentimentality, to do whatever it takes, as they say. Dad might be moody but he's not ruthless, I couldn't understand why he chose to join forces with Dick Woolascroft, just to see a healthy return on his money I suppose and I dare say he'll do that alright, Woolascroft's seem to win all the council contracts, they must tender like the rest but being big and established I imagine they can afford to submit a lower figure. Like I said it's all done out of sight, the common man can only sup his pint, speculate and bemoan."

"Perhaps your dad will take me to one of their building sites, I wouldn't mind meetin' this Woolascroft fella, he'd likely look at me an' think, 'Irish navvy'. I'll be happy to debate with your sister but if I really wanted to pit me brains against another it would have to be him, there's a lot more to an Irishman than navvyin'."

Mathew now felt regret at having written to Andrew Smithfield and began to doubt that Connor would appreciate the wonderful Camellia house at Wollaton Park or be in awe of the magnificent police horses. His only hope must be the pretty young women and right now even that hope felt slender.

Mathew recalled Callum's words. 'I wish Connor could think like you'. Perhaps the bright lights of London would be a better option for Connor after all, according to Emily there were many Irish folk living and working in the Capital, anyway a month was long enough for him to spend at Mathew's home with his gentle mam, and be accompanying his dad on visits to the opportunist Dick Woolascroft. In that regard Connor should heed the advice of his own dad, 'stay away lad, stay well away'.

CHAPTER TEN

Early May.

Celia stared at the keys on the table, Mrs.Roper, just a few minutes ago, handed them to her with little more grace than a relay runner passing the baton. She wouldn't come in, 'he's waiting in the taxi, we catch a train at eleven, tell William he'll find the house clinically clean, no trace of the Ropers remaining, just as he likes it, clinical', she'd virtually thrust the keys at Celia then turned away with no goodbye and was through the gate and into the taxi before Celia could speak. As the vehicle drew away Celia could see Steve Roper waving, and he was smiling. His wife must have held the keys tightly in her hand from leaving Moreleigh to reaching Celia's front door, they were warm when Celia took them from her. Now she looked at them laying on the table with a fob bearing an image of the castle and puzzled over the woman's remarks.

She'd referred to her own husband somewhat coldly as merely 'he' while naming William. 'Just as he likes it, clinical'. Her expression had been sour, her words delivered so urgently and with such sharpness they might well have cut her tongue, the very opposite of Connor's soft, slow speech, which over the past three weeks, at times had drifted about the house on Spring's warmth. William had the habit of firing conversation as though always having a target in mind, so sure of his aim.

The more Celia puzzled over Mrs.Roper's manner the more troubled she became, it wasn't normal behaviour, Steve Roper had been in every way pleasant and courteous that day he'd sat with Liza and herself yet his wife had been most unpleasant.

William must know why, and when he came home Celia had every intention of asking.

He'd taken Connor with him to Colver yet again, William seemed obsessed with that place, they'd been there several times, surely little could change between such frequent visits. Celia had suggested that Connor might benefit from seeing Leicester, and Sheffield, at the latter the steel industry was thriving, partly due to the increased activity at the shipyards up north. Originally Connor's stay was to be a month, nothing had been said and Celia suspected it might be extended, she didn't mind, he was no bother, in some ways cooking for three was easier than for two, but there'd been no communication from his family and that felt odd. Emily had been bewildered by him, 'I can't dislike him, but neither can I really like him, he's a mystery beyond my solving'. While not voicing it to Emily, Celia was of a similar mind, she felt no dislike of Connor but neither did she feel any closer to him now than she did at his arrival, the mysterious Irishman.

She picked up the keys, put them in a drawer, took her jacket and bag from the hook and turned her back on housework, town, she would go to town, buy a wedding present for Liza and George. Next Saturday was to be the happy day, let in on the secret Celia had been tight lipped as promised, only ever speaking of it to Annie. Half past ten at the registry office, a delighted Samuel and now fiancé Margaret would be witnesses. The rest of the family would be told afterwards, along with Liza's family, though Billy was aware. Annie had explained to George that not to tell Billy would be unkind, he would happily keep their secret, but to deny him the chance to be with them in his heart as they became man and wife couldn't be right. In fact he already knew, just as George had confided in his mam, so too had Liza whispered in her dad's good ear, his response came from a source of abiding love, 'only one thing could have made your old dad happier an' that would have been you whisperin' first in your mam's ear an' then Edna whisperin' it into mine'.

Outside the sun shone, it lifted Celia's spirits and drove the episode with Mrs.Roper to the back of her mind. She would go first to Rosie Spooner's, if she wasn't too busy then perhaps Rosie would go into town too. It was impossible to feel downhearted when in Rosie's company, a household that was never tidy, evidence of 'family' everywhere, laundry at various stages of the process festooned the furniture, while the scullery table always bore the makings of a meal or the ingredients of a cake, often both. When Celia had called there last Saturday afternoon, two rabbits had been chasing one another around the living room to the delight of young Beryl, who made the perfect picture of contentment, sitting on the pouffé sucking a sherbet lollipop. 'I allus know when they've done their jobs behind the settee' said Rosie, 'I hear 'em clatter up the vacuum cleaner on a Monday mornin', they've dried up by then'! Happiness, Celia was envious, rabbit droppings and all.

"What do you think then Connor, is the building trade for you or not?" William stood by the driver's door speaking across the car roof to Connor, who looked back at the site, at the activity amid a maze of trenches, foundation work, which now turned Colver into a large scale development, the vital drainage system to take waste out and length after length of pipe to bring water in.

"Maybe, maybe not," said Connor, "it's a shame he's not here today, I've glimpsed him only once, the mighty Woolascroft, a man needs to know who he's doing business with."

William chuckled. "If you worked on the building site you'd be making business for him, not doing business with him, for me too as it goes and for Gordon Cheetham. Dick's the majority stakeholder but without our investment he'd have been in limbo. He had to buy out his two brothers you see, after Fred their father died. He's been tied up lately over plans for another development, with the best will in the world lad you'll not get much out of Dick. I come here to Colver to maintain a presence, not just to check on progress, which is what the foreman Roddick thinks, I see it in his eyes, 'here comes that pain in the arse, Eddowes'. I look to remind myself that I do business with Woolascroft and that makes me entitled, otherwise I could be no more than that man over there shovelling, ignorant of whatever goes on in Dick's head. He's bright, canny, my kind of bloke, but deep, so I don't turn my back for more than a few days at a time."

Connor's face broke into a smile. "Sounds like a man with a cause." He opened the car door and sat himself down in the passenger seat, William followed, the sun was directly in front of them, he pulled down the visor to shield his eyes from the glare before driving away. "Bright day today Mr.Eddowes," said Connor, "brightest day in a while."

Celia and Rosie walked to the bus stop, it had been a welcome interlude, no more than an hour but both had enjoyed a break from the chores.

"I'm a bit worried about me mam," said Rosie, "she's gettin' very forgetful. I made a boiled fruit cake an' took it to her last Sunday, I know I wer' there most o' the afternoon but when I got up to go she said, 'wait a minute Rosie, somebody give me a cake, I don't need it, take it home with yer for the kiddies, an' she give me back the cake I'd just brought for her. I don't know how she can imagine the boys as kiddies, Thomas an' Samuel are twenty five an' Christopher's nineteen. Thinkin' back I don't reckon she's been the full shillin' for a few years, me dad, God bless him, allus thought she wer' worse on a Thursday, she'd sometimes queue for ages at Cheetham's, for one of his specials, in his shop there's them bright strip lights an' dad genuinely believed it wer' too much electricity passin' over her brain. Tommy had a different theory, he reckoned it wer' Cheetham's prices, 'enough to addle anybody's wits' he'd say an' come to think of it yer never see a poor butcher do yer?"

Celia squeezed Rosie's arm.

“I think it’s simply old age Rosie, years of thinking, of puzzling about the family, what to do for the best, and when to do it, stretching the pennies when the purse is low.”

Celia clutched the large bag containing a pretty blue, satin edged, Witney blanket, which she’d bought at Jessops, sworn to secrecy she couldn’t tell Rosie it was a wedding present for George and Liza so she’d pretended it was for the home. It had cost a bit more than she’d anticipated, she’d not had cause to buy a double blanket in years. Now her purse was a lot slimmer but she would have to stretch its contents until housekeeping day, she couldn’t tell William of her purpose for the blanket anymore than she could Rosie, not until after the event and then she mustn’t let him suspect that she knew of the wedding before he did. Secrecy was difficult, though she could understand George’s need of it, everything about George was quiet and without fuss, Liza too had wanted to become Mrs.Boucher without the strain of having to beam at everyone while inside aching for her mam. Celia would let a few days pass then go with Annie to see the newlyweds, taking the blanket, from William and herself.

The time spent with Rosie, the pleasure of choosing a nice gift for Liza and George had restored strength to Celia, Mrs.Roper’s words had undermined her but she could not ignore them, she let out a long sigh. Now Rosie squeezed Celia’s arm, ever mindful of what a difficult character William could be.

“We’re a long way from goin’ doolally you an’ me, neither of us buys meat at Cheetham’s on a Thursday.” She began to laugh, it was infectious and Celia joined in, dear, unfailing Rosie.

“You can come in if you like,” said William, “I need to check the place, but they were good tenants, they’ll have left it as they found it.” William pulled up outside Moreleigh.

“When did they leave?” Asked Connor.

"I believe their journey commenced early this morning, taxi first then train, finally a flight to New Zealand, it would be easy to feel envious wouldn't it? I'm surprised such adventure doesn't tempt you Connor, if I were a younger man and Mrs.Eddowes were a braver woman then likely I'd venture further afield."

Connor said nothing, as a lodger he'd been made very welcome by Mrs.Eddowes.

William felt strangely nervous, the house was empty yet as he entered Diane's voice echoed in his memory, Connor followed him through the back door and from room to room.

"Nice house Mr.Eddowes, must yield a decent rent, the last lot didn't have kids then?"

"What makes you say that?" William was genuinely bewildered, Connor could have no knowledge of the Ropers.

"No odd little scribble here an' there with a wayward crayon or scuffs along the bottom o' the walls from bein' too eager with the broom when helpin' mam, no bare patches low down on the edge of the doors where them too short to reach the knobs wore away the paint with their fingers. Little 'ens leave traces yer can follow, tell where they've been, kids never cover their tracks, it's only grown-ups that do that, an' God knows they can be good at it."

"Children used to live here at one time," said William, "two boys, my nephews." The significance he'd not thought of until that moment. "It was Celia's brother and his family owned this house, his plane was shot down, Caroline, his widow, eventually moved into mother in law's house, it was bigger, more room for the boys, it seemed only sensible."

The many times he'd come to collect the rent, followed Diane up the stairs for his 'repast', as his conscience had ever described it in excuse, not once until this day had he thought of Edmund. Connor was right, this house had yielded well. It was to Moreleigh William had come to ask for the piano, to chase Colver, it was here, to this place that latterly he'd come to satisfy his ego, and all had been granted him, even Colver had finally come his way. He'd heard it said that everything must be paid for in the long run but so far he'd covered his tracks well. A strange observation by someone as young as Connor, a young man with an old head, a mysterious character, he intrigued William, so very different to Mathew, there was worldliness about him, better an ally than an adversary.

"When do new folk move in, can't imagine you'd want it empty for long, I'd take it myself if I had somebody to share it with? Kids that's what this house wants Mr.Eddowes, mam, dad an' kids. Long way to go, New Zealand, best o' luck to 'em, the Irish put a lot o' store in luck, the charms o' the little people, beaverin' away when you're not lookin', smoothin' your path with their dancin' feet, but the Irish flock to Mass, just in case."

They'd eaten and Celia had cleared away, hoping that Connor might take himself off to the pub for an hour, but this evening it was apparent, the quiz programme on the television along with his avid scrutiny of Exchange and Mart was sufficient to keep him happily occupied without leaving the comfort of the living room. Normally Celia would feel pleased by the fact that her young Irish lodger didn't follow that commonly pursued ritual, the manly hour with a pint or two. Mathew had never taken up the habit, once in a while, but not observing the ritual as so many did.

William sat reading the Evening Post, he'd not mentioned the Ropers and nor had Celia, she recognised the truth of the expression, 'conspicuous by their absence'. When the quiz finished it was Connor who brought up the subject of Moreleigh, quite innocently but in a way that did little to lessen Celia's unease.

"I was sorry to hear about your brother Mrs.Eddowes, I was only a lad when war broke out an' over there we felt removed from it. I can remember me dad an' some o' the men talkin' about it, like blokes do, chew the cud, an' I can recall mam cryin'. Me mam's not Irish yer see, she wer' born over here. It's a brave man who'll sit in a plane an' fight an airborne battle, his sons must be proud."

Celia felt quite touched, seldom a day went by that she didn't think of Edmund, William must have spoken of him to Connor, despite Celia often wondering if William ever gave her late brother even a passing thought.

"Thank you Connor, you must have been to the house." She looked at William, surely he must say something now.

He let the newspaper down onto his lap. "I thought I should check the place, I guessed Steve Roper would hand in the keys on their way to the station, the house is in good order as you'd expect of them."

"I wouldn't know what to expect having met Mr.Roper but briefly and his wife not at all, until this morning, it was Mrs.Roper brought the keys." Celia needed to see William's reaction at hearing that it had been her, the unpleasant one.

"Well just so long as one of them remembered, wouldn't want a set of keys to Moreleigh ending up in New Zealand." William laughed but he was uncomfortable she could tell.

"I don't know why Woolascroft doesn't get hold of some heavy plant, it wouldn't take long to pay for itself, second-hand would be alright, a machine is often better for bein' 'broken in' as it were. I reckon a man could do well sourcin' it from Ireland, there's not much buildin' work goin' on over there. Seems to me that round these parts houses are sproutin' up like weeds, the only thing multiplyin' back home are potholes in the roads, there's one on the road to Bray deep enough to drown sheep an' probably has by now," said Connor.

William leapt at the chance to steer the conversation away from the Ropers and when he went into discussion with Connor over the for and against of sinking capital into machinery, while Whittle met the need, albeit at a cost, Celia gave up and went upstairs for a bath.

"He's bright you know, cocky but he's a good head on his shoulders." William got into bed beside Celia, doing his best to talk his way over her very marked silence.

"Clinically clean, just as William likes it, those were her words, what did she mean?"

"The woman knew I'd expect the house to be clean, what do you suppose she meant." William took his book from the bedside cabinet.

"She referred to her husband as 'he', almost scornfully, yet you, for you she managed the courtesy of a name, not Mr.Eddowes but William if you please. How many rent collectors are so familiar with their tenants that they are referred to by their Christian names do you suppose?"

"For goodness sake, go to sleep if you can't talk sense." William barked the words angrily.

"Look at me, look me in the eye and tell me you did nothing improper with Steve Roper's wife, I'm not a fool William."

He threw his book onto the floor, turned off the bedside light and rolled onto his side facing the wall. Celia couldn't remain there, she couldn't bear it, creeping across the landing she sought the comfort of Emily's room, where she could let go the tears. For a while she'd suspected William was sometimes in the company of a woman before coming home, a lingering perfume about his clothes, his manner almost sheepish and the activity in their own bed she'd felt he dispensed, like a linctus to be swallowed quickly at given times, merely to soothe.

Whilst home at Easter Emily had tried to persuade her mam to visit her in London, at Whitsuntide, during the college break. 'You never go anywhere, never see a different scene, dad would be alright for a few days'. Weariness from thinking eventually took over and Celia slept.

It was just after six when a sound on the landing woke her, she lay still, listening, if it was Connor he would use the lavatory and go back to bed. But the stairs creaked as someone descended, it would be William, making his escape, disappearing to someplace where he might concoct a suitable story to impart later. It wasn't long before Celia recognised the sound of the back door being closed then the car starting up, empty headed and empty bellied, William was taking himself off, by the time he returned he would have remedied both, his head would be filled with imaginative explanations and his stomach with whatever he craved.

She tiptoed back into their bedroom to find her clothes and dress, hoping that truly remarkable, coma like sleep only granted the young, might have kept Connor in ignorance of the night's troubles. She'd thought a great deal about Emily and London, why she should worry goodness only knows but William had never so much as boiled an egg for himself so if she decided to go, if only for three or four days, he would have to go to Winchester Street for his tea. He should go there anyway regardless of any trip to London. He would almost certainly protest but even William cared about his stomach, going to Winchester Street each evening would provide him with a good meal and his mam and dad some long overdue company.

Yet what if Connor was still in Nottingham, the month was up on Friday and Whitsuntide was but three weeks away. As if reading her mind, at that moment he appeared in the doorway of the kitchen.

"Mornin' Mrs.Eddowes, goin' to be sunny again by the look o' things."

He pulled out a chair and sat at the table, his quietness and the fact that he made no enquiry after William told Celia that deep sleep had not spared Connor. She put two bowls of porridge on the table and sat beside him, not knowing what to say.

"It's time I wer' thinkin' about leavin' I reckon, can't be under your feet forever, I'll be off at the end o' the week, let you both get your peace back."

Celia sighed. "It's not you Connor, really it isn't, you don't have to go."

"Oh but it is Mrs.Eddowes, if you only knew just how much it is me. I need to go home anyway, sort out a few things. Whether the problem of Connor O'Shea will be solved in Ireland or England who can tell, but you've been very kind to me. It's a pity you an' me mother couldn't get to know one another, you remind me of her yer see, you're alike, both soft hearted. Life's never easy Mrs.Eddowes, perhaps it's not meant to be. If I come back to Nottingham an' likely I shall, although I'll be findin' a permanent place for meself to live I'd come to see you. I'd bring you a shamrock, for luck, to tuck under your pillow." He took her fingers and kissed the back of her hand, it was such a gentlemanly gesture it took Celia by surprise. "We're not all bloodthirsty renegades, between frustrations we can be as decent as you'd find anywhere, we all have mothers determined that we shall make good an' constantly prayin' for our souls.

I'll go to the station this mornin', get me ticket for Friday. Is there anythin' you need in town while I'm there?"

Celia smiled. "I have to go myself later but thank you Connor. I never for an instant thought of you as a renegade, Mathew wouldn't have brought to me anyone for whom he felt no regard." She chuckled. "In England we have highwaymen, there're usually well dressed and difficult to spot but they can be as fearsome as your renegades I'm sure."

"You're alright you are Mrs.Eddowes," said Connor, "I'm glad we had the chance to meet an' when I tell me mam about you she'll thank yer, if only in her prayers."

Celia felt emotional, she willed him to finish his porridge and not to notice. At last he carried his dishes to the sink and went upstairs. Celia recalled something Mathew wrote in one of his letters. 'Ireland's not afraid to let folk glimpse its soul'. For just a moment, a little of the young Irishman's mystery fell away and Celia caught a brief glimpse of Connor O'Shea's soul.

The closer to the bank Celia became the faster her heart pounded in her chest, but she was resolved, today she would withdraw money from their joint account. As she waited to approach the teller she felt everyone's eyes were upon her, 'William Eddowes' wife, foolish, naive woman', of course they were not, people were about their own business. It was her turn.

"I'd like to withdraw ten pounds from our joint account please, William Charles Eddowes and Celia May Eddowes."

The young woman behind the counter seemed a little concerned, Celia supposed her sudden appearance, requesting a withdrawal caused the teller to hesitate.

"The account was set up eight years ago, I was required to lodge with the bank a sample signature, which I did and although I've not before today made a withdrawal I wish to do so now." Celia smiled to reassure the teller, and to enable her own confidence.

"Of course Mrs.Eddowes, if you would fill in this slip and sign it where specified, I will need to check the signature against the one you lodged eight years ago."

"I understand, thank you." Celia now felt even more that all around her were observing the situation.

Within minutes the young woman returned, sat down, smiled her obvious relief and said. "How would you like it Mrs.Eddowes?"

Celia was bewildered. "Pardon me?" By now the nerve gremlin was taking a spoon and stirring Celia's stomach.

"In one pound notes or ten shilling notes, unless you prefer two fives."

“Oh I see,” said Celia, letting loose her suspended breath. “I would like five one pound notes and ten, ten shilling notes if that’s alright?”

The teller counted the money with incredible speed, handed the notes to Celia saying. “Thank you Mrs.Eddowes.” Then lowering her voice and leaning forward, whispered, “I get my hair done at your sister in law’s.”

Celia left the bank with a sense of liberation, in her purse she had ten pounds, to which she was entitled, now she could go to whichever shop she liked and buy whatever she wanted. Yet as she walked along the pavement she could think of nowhere else to go but to the war memorial, where she could read her brother’s name, feel him close by, not gone from her but there still, Edmund Tozer, simply speaking his name was a comfort.

The purse lay in her bag, the money meant nothing to Celia, but William must acknowledge his wife’s entitlement. In those past eight years she’d asked for nothing more than faithfulness, let her resolve today be a wakeup call, Celia Tozer had a mind and a will, she was not a fool.

CHAPTER ELEVEN

Late August.

"Are you comin' to the pictures with me tomorrow then Miss Pearl?" Connor took his wage packet from her fingers and winked.

"My name isn't Pearl as well you know, and why do you suppose I'd want to go out with you Connor O'Shea?"

"Because I'm askin' nicely and Connor thinks you're far more a Pearl than a Searle."

Beth could not maintain her stern look, he'd asked the same thing last Friday and the one before that, a smile crept across her mouth.

"If I say yes and go, will you leave me be and find someone else to torment?"

"No, me tormentin' belongs to you alone Beth Pearl, when I'm sittin' in that great, noisy brute of a machine with me arse shakin' an' me eardrums near burstin', I keep tellin' meself a yes from Miss Pearl an' me an' the earth shifter'll turn into a carriage an' horses to carry her to the Odeon to see a Jimmy Stewart film."

"What time does the film start, I'll meet you outside, just this once?"

Beth found it hard to resist the young Irishman, there was a charm about him, he was different, when he spoke his words were strung upon invisible thread so one rested gently against the next, adorning his smile. The first time he'd asked, the memory of her mam's caution, issued to the adolescent Beth along with mother nature's delivery of her first period, had enabled her a very precise 'no'. His second request had tempted her thoroughly instilled modesties to answer him with 'I'll think about it', but today his virtual plea, wrapped up as it was in persuasive Irish mischief Beth could not refuse.

"Need to be there by 7o/clock but I'll call for yer at home if yer like, 'tis the gentlemanly thing to do."

Connor beamed his delight as he thrust the wage packet into his pocket, Miss Pearl had agreed to go out with him, now Barry owed him ten shillings. 'Bet yer ten bob she'll say no, bolder than you have tried'. Well Barry could put his hand in his pocket now and stump up.

Beth laughed. "I'm not daft Connor O'Shea, if you discover where I live I'll not get rid of you an' me mam would turn you inside out 'til she was satisfied your intentions were honourable."

Connor paused at the office door and blew a kiss before walking away across the yard to the heavy gates. Bill Whittle ran an impressive set up, everything about it was outsized, the machines, the contracts, even Whittle himself. Connor had operated a mechanical shovel whilst working at Grapels, moving grain, ten minutes were all it took to prove himself capable at the controls of a Drott shovel.

'The job's yours lad providin' yer know how to turn up on time an' how to keep men in your sights, whether they be fore or aft of yer, only ever had one accident an' that wer' the fault o' the daft bugger that fell asleep in the sun sittin' back against the bloody roller'.

Bill Whittle's cautioned hiring had prompted Connor to approach the foreman with a question, anticipating the usual 'did it kill him', which all horrified newly employed asked after receiving the exact same chilling story from the big boss, the foreman, one grizzly looking Jed Unwin pre-empted Connor's enquiry with 'dead as a stone lad', breath mangled out of every orifice', but Connor had felt no curiosity over the wretched casualty, his question being merely 'fore an' aft, was Mr.Whittle in the navy then'? Unwin had looked Connor in the eye, his face no further away than a couple of inches from Connor's and said, 'Merchant Navy, tough as old boots, plaited rope out o' fellas bigger than you Paddy'. That had been six weeks ago and Connor had arrived on time for work every morning, kept his eyes peeled, his ears pinned back and now had some insight on Whittle's outsized concerns.

Nottingham suited Connor's purpose, for the time at least, he'd rented a small terraced house at the end of Denman Street, lodging was all very well but he'd stepped outside of family life, no sound of his younger sister and brother playing childhood games, no judging looks from Kathleen or probing questions from Seamus over where and why Connor followed the agitators, but most marked of all, the absence of his mother's face, that pleading look she would give him, which spoke louder than any words, 'leave trouble alone son, don't make me weep'. Then there was Callum, constant, dependable Callum, dad. If he must step away from all that then Connor O'Shea would have his own home and not make do with someone else's family. Almost immediately after moving in at Denman Street he sublet a bedroom and shared facilities to Barry Pointer, another of Whittle's men. The fish and chip shop met the need of three evenings each week but Connor was capable of making a decent meal, he'd observed his mother often enough and Barry was happy to pay for the privilege of being fed, as a consequence much of Connor's rent was covered through the arrangement and both men were content, though Barry had spotted an opportunity to claw back ten shillings by betting Connor he wouldn't achieve to persuade Beth Searle to go out with him, it felt like a safe wager, Miss Searle in the office was known for her standard refusal. It was a self satisfied Connor whom this Friday evening left Whittle's yard at work's end.

Emily spread the tablecloth and put out plates and butter knives, Charles watched quietly from his chair in the corner, his granddaughter was no longer a child, she had the figure of a woman, didn't schooling ever finish in this day and age?

"How much longer are you going to be studying, my mother was married at your age?"

Emily laughed. "It's different now Grandad, especially for women, we've stepped out of the shadows, we still marry and have babies but it's not our only function, do you know there are women in all the professions now and in London there's even a female undertaker." Emily put down the butter dish. "Just one more year then provided I pass my final exams I shall be qualified to teach." She cast a look of amusement at Annie, "Grandma would have made a good teacher."

"She was raised by one, even after all these years I can remember Miss Pownall's authority, she didn't much care for me, it was as well she didn't live to see me marry your grandma, perhaps if she'd lived longer she'd have expelled me from the classroom. I need to go to the privy before I have tea."

Emily was sorely tempted to say 'you should raise your arm and ask, please may I go to the lavatory Miss', but her grandad's sense of humour had abandoned him years ago, so instead she put the ginger cake and fruit loaf closest to his place at table and sighed as she saw him crossing the scullery to the back door without uttering a single word to her grandma, now pouring the boiling water into the teapot no more than a foot away from his shoulder as he passed by.

Perhaps it was an inevitable result of living together, eating, sleeping, growing old under the same roof until all sources of conversation were exhausted, years of routine, automation replacing the more natural order and with no challenge to its subtle advance. At home Emily had noticed a similar pattern developing between her mam and dad, at times she actually wished that one or the other would display an emotion of some kind, even if it were anger, periods of silence and a refined ability to ignore one another were worse than a full blown row, which according to those romantic stories in magazines enabled a marriage to find fresh momentum through an impassioned truce. More and more Emily began to think that such stories were nothing but witless nonsense, she would certainly be in no hurry herself to go down the path of matrimony, while surely it must work for some the evidence before Emily gave reason to question its vowed sanctity. Her grandad's words of a few minutes ago had added to her resolve, nineteen was far too young to be considering wedlock and babies, it might have been the way in her great grandma's time but not now.

With Charles seated at the table Annie poured tea.

"We were so long with hardly any sugar I don't think of putting it in tea now," said Emily, "I think it's more a childhood thing anyway. I don't have a sweet tooth these days but when I was little a bag of sweeties would disappear in no time. You always gave us Tom Thumb drops Grandma when we came to the shop, do you remember?"

Before Annie could answer Charles intervened. "You and all the kids in the neighbourhood, Lady Bountiful was your grandma and that made me Ikey Eddowes, I overheard a lad calling me that one day, ought to have clipped his ear but his father took up a daily paper and the Racing Times, plus two ounces of Golden Virginia every week, until he dropped dead beside the dog track."

Emily looked across the table at Annie but said nothing while Charles spread bramble jelly onto a slice of bread and butter. Annie frowned, he'd not ever told her that, 'Ikey Eddowes', the boy must have been Tommy Marsden, she recognised Charles' description of Mr.Marsden's weekly order, though more often than not it was Elsie Marsden who paid the paper bill, a waif like woman, timid, always in a rush.

"Samuel has asked me to go to with him and Margaret to the pictures tonight, a James Stewart and Grace Kelly picture called 'The Rear Window'. I said no at first, thinking I'd be playing gooseberry, but Samuel said, don't be so daft Em', I'll sit between the two of you with an arm around each."

She chuckled and bit into a slice of ginger cake.

"Your mam really enjoyed her time in London," said Annie, "she should go again next year before you finish at college."

Annie recalled the evenings spent with William while Celia was away, his unusual demeanour, not abrasive as so often he could be but subdued, especially at first. By the last night he he'd recovered much of his contrariness, whatever humbled his mood at the beginning William had overcome. Celia too had been sparing with words when asking Annie if she would make a main meal for William, 'four evenings, don't fuss over him, he'll always eat stew' was the extent of her concern. Annie worried about them, abiding day on day with William would test any average mortal who sought simply the comfort of a home. Celia was to the other extreme of William's selfishness, the typical homemaker and yet Annie had sensed an urgent need in her daughter in law to be apart from their home, to be apart from her husband, if only for those four days, and nights.

"Something's up, that's the second police car with its bells going," said Samuel.

There was a queue outside the Odeon, James Stewart always proved popular, Samuel smiled to himself as he thought of his great aunt Gertie's bewildering notion, 'he reminds me of my Henry', she'd say, just which feature of Henry Wainwright bore a resemblance to Jimmy Stewart only Henry's mother could know.

In the distance bells could still be heard but the people in the front continued to move along and Samuel's attention was diverted by Emily when she tugged on his jacket and said.

“Look, it’s Connor O’Shea and Beth Searle, I wonder if they’ve seen us.” Samuel caught a glimpse of them just as they were about to disappear inside.

“It hasn’t taken Connor long, good for him, we’ll try to catch them when the film ends, I don’t think they could have spotted us.”

Having paid for their seats, Samuel led Margaret and Emily up the stairs into the ever darkening interior of the Odeon. The usherette led them past the end of several rows before directing them with her torch along row eight. A low hum of voices as folk exchanged conversation ahead of the entertainment, and random giggles, mostly erupting in the back row added to the eager anticipation.

The first shaft of light travelled over the heads of the audience from the projectionist’s box and with the usual burst of life, the screen delivered those informative advertisements, ‘the must haves’ for a full and fruitful life. ‘Friday night is Amami night’, Tizer the appetizer, the Brylcreem shine’, and even the less inspiring but vital preparation in achieving a healthy glow, Enos fruit salts! The drone of voices now faded to be replaced by stirring music, all those needing to cough did so and at last the titles rolled.

It seemed hardly possible to have reached the interval already.

“Good film,” said Samuel, “for just a second when Jimmy Stewart lifted the binoculars to his face I could recognise the likeness to Henry Wainwright, he’s got four fingers and a thumb on each hand exactly the same, well would you credit it.”

Emily smacked his hand and laughing leaned across him to speak to Margaret. “You’ll have to house train my cousin, he’s incorrigible.”

“Ice cream or chocolate?” Asked Samuel as the usherette approached the end of their row. The unanimous verdict being ice cream, he squeezed past the other folk to secure three neopolitan wafers.

“Look, over there, buying something from the usherette, it’s Samuel Boucher, Annie Eddowes’ grandson, you stayed with his aunt and uncle when you first came to England didn’t you? My aunty Rosie told me, she and Celia are best friends, we must catch him before he leaves at the end, I expect he’s with his fiancé.”

“That’s Emily surely,” said Connor, catching a glimpse of her face as she turned to take her ice cream, “he’s with Emily and Margaret, I met her only the one time, lucky Samuel, sandwiched between the two of ‘em. I called to see Mrs.Eddowes last weekend but she was out with her daughter so I missed them both, not that Emily would be disappointed, I think Connor O’Shea is a far cry from the young men she’s surrounded by in London, not likely to pay the likes o’ me any regard.”

Beth felt disappointed, and dismayed at herself for being so foolish, it was quite clear that Connor carried a liking for Emily Eddowes, albeit not reciprocated. Presumably ‘Miss Pearl’ was merely a time filler until Connor clambered up into the cab of his machine on Monday morning. Yet through the second half of the film Beth was aware of his shoulder firmly pressed against her own and his knee, gently resting against her’s among the folds of her skirt, innocently, pleasantly and Beth couldn’t but warm to him. If only she could look like the beautiful Grace Kelly, but then, Connor didn’t look like the handsome James Stewart either, comparisons, always comparisons. She’d faulted Connor for judging one against another as he ever seemed to do, Whittles with Woolascrofts, Irish and English, even men against women, perhaps it was a natural trait of most people. His knee moved slightly against her own, small mercies, how often Beth heard her mam speak of those, ‘be thankful for small mercies’, Emily was, after all, five rows away.

“Let’s walk to the next stop,” said Connor, picture houses are always stuffy, a bit o’ fresh air will do us all good.”

They'd managed to meet before losing sight of each other in the muddled exodus of folk, bustling their way to bus stops. "How's your mother Emily, I called not long ago but you were out and your father was just about to go to Moreleigh, new tenants he said, a family with children?"

"Mother's alright thank you Connor, she's busy making jam with Mrs.Bateman next door, they've a glut of blackcurrants. Last week grandma and I went to cousin Seth's farm at Ruddington, to gather blackberries, we picked five pounds and there were still loads in the hedgerows."

The instant she finished speaking Emily despaired of herself, how could Connor possibly be interested in jam making, it was a silly thing to say.

"Just like me mother, by now there'll be a row of jars on the pantry shelf back in Dublin, all labelled up. I reckon it's a mother thing, the urge to be forever feedin' her babies, except mammy cuckoo an' she leaves it to somebody else, in human kind that's more of a father thing don't you think?" Connor's expression suggested he actually sought a reply. Samuel broke the awkward silence.

"I read somewhere that a cuckoo's egg is disproportionate to the size of the chick."

Beth chuckled. "Mam say's our Peter wer' no bigger than a sardine born but now he's the tallest and broadest of all Woolascroft's men, he can lift a hod of bricks like it was a slice of angel cake."

"I didn't know you had a brother workin' for Woolascroft," said Connor.

"There's a lot of things you don't know about me." Beth taunted him, threading her arm through his.

Margaret had been quiet since leaving the Odeon, content simply to listen whilst others chatted, Samuel wrapped his arm about her and kissed her cheek, it aroused a sense of fun in Connor, walking between Beth and Emily he put an arm around both.

“Tis the way we dance in Ireland, arms around each other, like the links of a chain, now you put your arms around my waist ladies, then we kick our heels and skip like them glorious little leprechauns who dance to the moon an’ the stars with every rhythm of their hearts. Come on Samuel, you join up with Emily, five links o’ the chain, we’ll show folk the Irish way o’ gettin’ to the bus stop, we’ll make the English pavements sing beneath our feet.”

His fun was infectious and they made quite a spectacle as they progressed along Parliament Street. But then a figure coming toward them in the fast fading light began to wave and call out, the street lamp revealed it to be Barry Pointer.

“Connor, Connor.” Breathless and agitated Barry stood before them, words trembling in his haste to deliver the news. “We can’t go home, there’s a gas leak in Denman Street, the police have evacuated everybody.”

“Slow down afore yer choke yerself on your own tongue, catch your breath Barry for gracious sake.”

Connor had heard the words ‘gas leak’, it wasn’t something he’d come across before and it sounded serious but Barry was gasping like he was about to expire.

“That explains all the police activity,” said Samuel. Where are they accommodating the residents of Denman Street, they must number a good many?”

“You can both come back with me,” said Beth, “mam won’t mind.”

Aware of Connor’s earlier place of lodgings with Emily’s mam she was determined to speak first, if it meant Barry Pointer must come along too then so be it but it was better than Connor going off with Emily.

“Most have been shepherded to Bentinck Road School,” said Barry, “I wer’ in the Standard when a bloke come in to tell everybody what wer’ happenin’ so I thought I best come and look for you Connor.”

Samuel was perceptive enough to recognise Beth's ploy and to sympathise with it but Connor and his mate needed to present themselves at the school, the police would have to account for everyone, no doubt they would knock on every door in Denman Street and if there was no answer they'd see fit to force entry.

"You're right Samuel," said Connor, his mind now racing ahead, "I'd rather know what they're doin' about the leak, I've got a few quid in a drawer back at the house an' two chump chops an' a knuckle in the meat safe."

"If there's an explosion tomorrow's tea will be the least of your worries," declared Emily, a little insensitively.

Beth appeared to have resigned herself as she waved at the fast disappearing figure of Connor who'd run off after Barry without so much as a peck on her cheek. Samuel felt obliged to rescue her spirits having been more or less responsible for dashing them.

"You'll see him on Monday Beth and he'll likely plan next Saturday evening then, I wouldn't be afraid to bet on it."

"I don't care if I do or don't," she said with a trace of pique.

"Come along this won't do, we must link up like a chain and dance like leprechauns, the Irish way, set our dull English pavements to sing beneath our feet." Emily's tone was sarcastic and even Margaret winced. Samuel sighed, Connor O'Shea seemed to have an unfortunate effect on the girls, Beth normally of habit indifferent to the advances of roguish Whittle's men, was quite obviously smitten, while Emily usually easy going and accepting of folk appeared strangely irritated by the Irishman. Margaret chose to stay quiet yet like himself, she would be feeling the tension both Emily and Beth had failed to hide. Samuel wished he'd suggested going to the Theatre Royal instead of the Odeon, that old faithful, 'The murder of Mariah Martin in the red barn', was being performed there, yet again.

"There aren't really such people as leprechauns are there?" Asked Beth. "I've seen that little man who lives at Sherwood, they say he's a dwarf, perhaps that's what the Irish call their dwarfs, so I suppose leprechauns are real then."

Samuel hastily trod on Emily's toe, to caution her, that was the only downside of a good education, it dismissed make believe, rather like growing up destroyed the magic of Santa Claus. It was dear Margaret who provided an unexpected diversion.

"Will you be my bridesmaid Emily when Samuel and I get married next Spring?"

Samuel's grin spread from ear to ear, he wanted to dance to the moon and stars with every rhythm of his heart.

"The leak has been located and the engineers are dealing with it, hopefully it won't take too long but make yourselves as comfortable as you can, there are plenty of chairs and of course lavatory facilities, it's a warm night but the elderly might still feel the need of a blanket, of which there is but a limited number, so will the younger ones please make sure they respect age and grant any mothers needing to feed their infants some privacy, thank you."

The constable looked about the assembly hall of Bentinck Road School, at the mixed gathering, all ages, some showing alarm, others trying to cat nap their way through the ordeal and a group of men setting up a game of poker. Only one elderly man caused Constable Elliot actual concern, he'd been very quiet throughout, his awkward, almost restricted movements suggested he was experiencing discomfort.

"Are you alright Sir, do you need a glass of water maybe?" The constable consulted his notebook, it was impossible to remember the identity of every individual so in such a situation as this he concentrated on the elderly and most vulnerable, jotting down references to aid his task, his entry for this resident being Rex Madden, navy blue pullover, seventies, looking poorly.

"Sharp pains in my chest Constable, don't often get indigestion."

Connor had been observing the scene, it reminded him of an incident at Grapels when Derry Doyle collapsed of a heart attack, and this was the pleasant old boy who almost every morning was standing in his open doorway with a mug of tea and would say good morning to him and Barry as they walked up the street to work.

"I reckon it's his heart officer, you need to call for the ambulance." Connor's confident assessment Constable Elliot seemed to be cogitating upon.

"Jeysus, hurry up officer, if it's his ticker there's no time to debate it."

"Is there no end to this night's troubles, I wer' supposed to be off duty, me an' the wife wer' goin' to watch our new television set, she bought a bottle of Babycham an' a Wrenshaw's bitter specially."

"For God's sake make haste man."

Elliot was about to protest such outright disrespect for an officer of the law, but Mr.Madden did look bad.

"Stay with him lad, while I use the phone, I'll talk to you later."

Connor sniffed his withering regard for what passed as a Gardee in England, back home they were the opposite, by the scruff first, innocence was secondary.

"You'll be okay old friend, me an' Barry'll see yer' right."

Rex breathed in short, fast gasps, he leaned closer to Connor. "Tell Mrs.Stanford I never blamed her," his words began to slur.

"What's he sayin'? Barry stood behind Connor shaking from dread.

Rex made the effort to speak again to Connor. "Tell her I never blamed her, nor Patricia." Briefly he raised his face, then slumped forward, Connor only just managed to catch him.

"Is he breathin', bloody hell Connor, I've never seen anybody die 'afore?" Barry stepped back as one of the women rushed forward, she spoke to the crumpled Rex.

"It's me Lillian, from across the street, can you hear me Rex?"

Connor gently set the old man back in the chair. "I think he's agonna, the poor ol' fella's breathed his last." Connor held his flattened hand to Rex's mouth, shaking his head he spoke softly, lowering his voice to little more than a whisper as he turned to Lillian. "Is your name Stanford by any chance Missus?"

CHAPTER TWELVE

Mid September.

"You will come back for some tea won't you, I don't imagine many others will, poor Rex, I do hope he wasn't unhappy in mother's house, it seems harsh doesn't it, so long away only to return to this place, which he surely must have always thought of as home and then......."

"Don't upset yourself my dear," said Andrew taking Florence by the arm to steady her. "Rex was wholly content, you made every effort to provide him with comfort, far more than he'd experienced in a very long time."

"You're kind to say so Andrew but Rex dwelt with you at Brassington for a little while, with the best will in the world Denman Street could never have matched that." Annie standing alongside them smiled, even Florence, who spent much of her time in that large house on Castle Road with Patricia, viewed Andrew Smithfield's surroundings as splendid, yet in conversation with him Annie had come to know that he continued his lonely existence there out of loyalty to his late aunt Alicia, when in fact he envied the simplicity, the sense of homeliness enjoyed by Rex at Denman Street. Annie also knew of Florence's own dilemma, with both Jonathon and Gregory absent Caroline made a lonely, worrying sight each time Florence called. Patricia had overcome a serious mental breakdown in the past and now appeared fully restored, but Florence had confided in Annie that one day she had discovered tranquilisers, on the carpet between the side of Patricia's bed and the bedside cabinet. It had come as a shock, until then Florence had believed Patricia's need of them to be long passed, perhaps they were old, unused and overlooked, the label confirmed them to be current, so dear Florence went from one daughter to the other, loyal and loving to both, writing regularly to Julia too, ageing herself through the effort and today shedding genuine tears for Rex, for whom Annie sensed Florence had felt grateful affection.

"We'll wait by the lych gate for Patricia and Caroline, they're speaking with Mr.Spooner," said Florence, "Julia would have liked to attend but to ask for time off, now at the commencement of term when of course the college has been closed for the summer holidays, she thought would be unfortunate but she's sent flowers. Teaching suits her I do believe, she lost her confidence after Luciano and she was convinced her application would be unsuccessful. Languages have always been her strong suit. Exeter is a long way from Nottingham, sometimes I think that was part of the attraction, a way of leaving the past behind. Ah, here they come." Florence patted Annie's arm. "We shall face the necessary sorting of Rex's things when we feel a little brighter, there's no hurry for that."

Annie was amused at the way Florence automatically included her in the task, which must indeed follow this day's events in due course.

"I have absolutely nothing more important to do than to help, Rex was a good friend, sad though the task will be I would consider it a privilege." Andrew spoke the words with intent and Annie couldn't help feeling relieved, she would gladly help Florence but going through Rex's belongings, inevitably papers, always there were documents, surely Andrew would be better suited to that while Florence and herself could deal with clothing and less important items.

"Are you ready to go now Mother?" Asked Patricia. "We best leave or someone might arrive at Castle Road ahead of us. Tommy Spooner will come for some tea, I told him that the bearers too are welcome, other than those few it looks as though the handful of Rex's neighbours have drifted away."

Annie had managed to say a brief hello to Lillian but funerals weren't really conducive to actual conversation, solemnity and awareness of loss prevailed such gatherings and despite Rex having no family to mourn him the acknowledgement of sadness had been evident today, perhaps because of Tommy's natural respect for those he laid to rest, regardless of their circumstances.

Andrew helped Florence into the front passenger seat of Patricia's car while Caroline and Annie got into the back.

"I shall follow on," he said, doing his best to assure them of company.

The women were quiet as the car carried them back to the house, they couldn't be aware of one another's thoughts but each supposed the other to be remembering Rex in their own particular way.

Annie couldn't drive from her mind the image of that tiny headstone beside the fresh earth of the grave. Rex had been buried above his wife Doris, their infant son alongside them, Annie's tears had fallen silently for John Madden and for her own Danny.

After several pensive minutes it was Caroline who first spoke. "Do you know yet when Mathew is coming home Annie, surely it will be soon?"

"Definitely by Christmas," said Annie, "I think Celia is counting the days."

"I begin to think Gregory is embracing army life, his letters give not the slightest hint of homesickness, perhaps I shouldn't look forward too confidently to having him back home for long," Caroline sighed. Annie recalled David's remarks but made no mention of them. "Jonathon has years more study ahead of him, the house feels so empty, I've thought of taking in a lodger, a young person, a student possibly. Jonathon has been obliged to take up lodgings, so too has Emily so wouldn't it be sensible for me to offer the same to someone else's son or daughter needing a place to live whilst studying?"

Annie felt so sorry for Florence who must be hurting inside, Caroline intended no distress of her mother and was simply thinking aloud for the most part. "I think it would be altogether sensible Caroline," said Annie, "providing you are able to cope with that and your job at the hospital, I can't imagine you wanting to give that up."

"Goodness me no, I need to work and the small additional income from a lodger would be useful I must admit, but it's the company more than anything, another person in the house, especially during winter months, I thought last winter would never end."

"I could ask them to put your details on the notice board at the university if you like," said Patricia, "in fact shouldn't we do the same Mother? With Julia settled in Exeter we do have plenty of room and a young face about the house couldn't be a bad thing."

Florence was surprised to say the least, not by Caroline's conversation, she'd wondered if money might become a problem for her youngest daughter. Colver had sold well but Caroline had immediately invested her half of the proceeds for the boys. 'It was never intended for me mother as we both well know but I shall take it for our sons'. Florence fought a tear at the memory. Caroline had her war widow's pension and the income from her hospital job but it was an old house, little maintenance had been done over the years, even when Jessie Tozer was alive the house seemed to display a weariness, but finances dictated how much nourishment could be granted bricks and mortar, Florence suspected Jessie quietly helped his children before the needs of the house, and Gwendolyn was in no fit state to even notice. Other than to sell her house on Denman Street Florence could see no way of helping Caroline, with dear Rex gone perhaps that's what she must do. But to hear Patricia speak of taking a lodger, Florence could not have foreseen that and yet it would be entirely sensible. Since the university had been established, year on year the number of students increased, this year's intake was the highest ever and all required accommodation. The more Florence thought about it the more agreeable she found the idea.

Patricia parked the car outside the house. "We'll anticipate one or two people back for tea besides Tommy Spooner and Andrew but afterwards, when they've left, we shall make plans, times are changing and we must adapt accordingly."

Florence was in full accord, Patricia had changed more than she could have believed possible, yet her wealthy, eldest daughter appeared not to recognise the actual necessity behind Caroline's plan to take in a lodger and Florence was fearful of enlightening her.

Annie was quiet but thoughtful, Andrew Smithfield had pulled up behind them, living as he did in a large house, empty of life but for himself since the Bevin boys left, perhaps he too would provide lodgings for young people, his housekeeper was a good woman, likely to welcome the chance of more hours. Some folk did say that the world belonged to the young, but for Danny Eddowes and John Madden, how fleeting had been their tenure.

"You seem better this evenin', at least you've eaten a half decent meal." Dick sat by the hearth idly watching Olive stretch a tapestry cloth over the wooden frame, trying to identify the design imprinted onto its surface. Cows, surely it was a scene of cows by a tree, a farmhouse in the background, rather different from her last accomplishment of roses in a bowl.

"Yes, it's eased, it usually does eventually," she said, "I saw Mrs.Eddowes today, William's mother, she mentioned a funeral, a Mr.Madden, apparently he worked for Basil Stanford a long time ago. I know she and Mrs.Stanford are good friends, they were all going to attend, Patricia and Caroline, Julia couldn't get leave from her work. Did you know this Mr.Madden?"

"Vaguely," said Dick, "he was Stanford's man, his driver really, I can't imagine the job title pleased him very much, it made him sound like a lowly manservant, in a way I suppose he was. Everyone referred to him as such, especially the miners, they were all Stanford's men but Madden was considered the old retainer, always at Stanford's beck and call. I don't know what became of him, he disappeared, but obviously he came back if it was his funeral here today, I presume the funeral was in Nottingham."

"Yes, at St.Andrew's, half past two." The cloth now secured Olive spread her skeins of woollen thread over the arm of the chair and took up her needle. "How is work progressing at Colver?"

Dick nodded as though affirming his response. "It's progressing well, we've seen the back of Whittle's services for the time, thank God. Buildin' is a curious process, first we excavate, diggin' down deep into the ground, then we build up, it occurred to me one day that if folk were able to see an entire build turned upside down they'd be amazed at just how much lies beneath." Dick sighed heavily. "Mitchell Street will take that to the extreme, underpinning and sheer volume of concrete alone. Where man determines himself to take the guts from the ground then at some point he's obliged to put back. It's not a money making project but a principle, Mitchell Street was without guts, I'm puttin' them back and it will make me or break me, only God knows which."

Olive looked puzzled, not before had Dick shown signs of being morally bound. "When will work begin at Mitchell Street, if you're having second thoughts can't you pull out?"

"Oh it won't start for a few months yet, there's the other side to take into account, that's owned by a chap in Derby, he'll be intent on securing compensation from the coal board before he sells. The council has approved our plans and accepted our tender, it won't be long before I receive official notification, then they'll pursue the purchase of his side."

"How can you be so sure, he may not sell, perhaps he'll instruct another firm to develop it, one from Derby?"

"I doubt that, you see the site itself isn't worth much due to the problem of subsidence. The council will offer him its value, no one else is likely to want it once he's creamed off the compensation, plus few people seeking to buy a house of their own would want to look across the street at council accommodation. Because our plans have been more or less rubber stamped the authority will be able to waive the requirement for tenders to build the other side, no one would expect a street to look odd no more than a woman would want a dress with two unmatching sides, or a man could consider shaving only one half of his chin. Mitchell Street must carry the same plan down both sides."

Olive put down her needle. "Didn't I hear you say that when you took out that loan against this house that you were to get compensation from the coal board?"

"Yes, Holbrook didn't claim it, possibly because he wasn't aware, though lookin' back his mind might already have been failin', he did die from a head bleed not all that long after."

"Is there any actual difference between a builder and an engineer?" Olive's expression suggested criticism. "It does sound very much to me like you're proficient at the latter."

"You don't understand," said Dick tetchily, "we employ a good many men, I do what I have to. Sometimes it's necessary to steer the council down the right path, they can't be expected to see what the developer sees, too many other matters come before them. Years ago my father recognised the potential of Bobbers Mill, to take development two ways, towards town one way, to meet the new boulevard the other. Anyone lookin' now would see the sense of it but at the time not everyone did."

"I wouldn't tell that to William Eddowes if I were you, it was his brother who farmed Bobbers Mill."

"Well then it's true to say that his brother was instrumental in furthering the progress of this great city."

Picking up her needle once again Olive thread a strand of green wool through the tapestry where the design portrayed grass.

"I can't believe he would see it that way, when your father set the council on that path, the large imposing figure it was, still is, at a spot not far along, would have met the smaller, milder brother of Mr.Eddowes trying to progress from another direction, do you suppose he eagerly leapt into the ditch to enable it unhindered advance or was he obliged to move out of the way or be trod asunder?"

"Well it doesn't matter now does it," snapped Dick, "because when you finish your tapestry we will have a bloody farmyard of our own, hangin' on the wall."

Late September.

Connor had put on his best clothes, from what he'd gleaned by means of casual enquiry, subtly injected into dinnertime chatter at work, Stanford was a significant name in the world of mining and Mrs.Stanford was obviously a lady of property as Rex Madden had rented from her the house on Denman Street. Connor had been discreet when seeking to discover where the good lady lived, the message that Rex had trusted Connor to deliver seemed to require discretion. Of course the fact that Mrs.Stanford was Rex's landlady satisfied Lillian's concern when Connor approached her, presuming that Rex had in some way been distressed over rent. While her late husband was reputed to have been a hard man, Florence Stanford was known for her kindly nature. Rex need not to have worried Lillian felt sure.

Castle Road was very different to Denman Street, each house stood apart from its neighbour, solid, elegant properties with front gardens protected by railings and shrubbery, pedestrian gates of ornate wrought iron and bold front doors, taller and wider than those of meek abodes where occupants had no importance to declare. He checked the directions on his piece of paper, eighth house along from the corner, there were houses like this in Dublin and walking past them made a man take his hands from his empty pockets and clutch at the railings in frustration, yes, he was free to walk the street, but he faced bars, he gazed at that other life through iron bars.

This must be it, Connor stepped back into the road taking a quick count of the houses he'd passed, this was the eighth one. Gazing up at the facade he thrust the scrap of paper into his pocket. "Jesus, Mary and Joseph, Mrs.Stanford has a grand place so she does." He spoke aloud and let out a breath of relief, it was a good thing he'd put on his tidy clothes sure enough. Looking respectable and feeling entitled, he was delivering a private message after all, Connor made his way to the front door and rang the bell, stretching his collar a little to enable a confident 'good afternoon'. His first press of the bell button brought no result, he tried again, after a few seconds the door opened to reveal and elderly lady. "Mrs.Stanford? I hope I'm at the right house."

"Yes, I'm Florence Stanford." She looked puzzled, Patricia had gone to have her hair done at Hilda Haynes' salon and Florence could think of no young man likely to be asking for herself on a Saturday afternoon.

Connor recognised the hesitation and at once spoke to dispel any anxiety. "I need to give you a message Ma'am, from Rex Madden, it's not your every day sort of message so I thought it only proper to let him be laid to rest and then deliver it personally."

"Oh, I see, well you best come in, please," said Florence holding the door open and stepping to one side.

"I should introduce meself first Ma'am, tis only right, me name's Connor O'Shea, I live on Denman Street."

"My goodness I know that name, you stayed with William and Celia didn't you, in the Spring, I remember my dear friend Annie telling me, Annie Eddowes, William's mother?"

“Aye that’s right Ma’am,” said Connor as he stepped inside the hallway, taking great pains over wiping his feet on the mat. “Tis a nice house Ma’am, a grand house.”

“I live here with my eldest daughter Patricia, the house belongs to Patricia, she’s not home at the moment, come through.” Florence led Connor to the drawing room, though these days she thought of it as the sitting room, the little used, tidy space, often at the front, like Annie’s at Winchester Street and her mother’s house on Denman Street, which folk ever referred to as their sitting room, as though it were kept for special occasions and important visitors. “Do sit down Mr.O’Shea.”

“That doesn’t sound right Ma’am, Connor’ll do, I reckon I need to earn a few stripes before I can claim to be Mister.”

Florence laughed. “And I have lost too many to warrant Ma’am, so as I know you a little through Annie shall we settle on friendship terms Connor. I must appear ancient, indeed old enough to be your grandmother but if you could bear to call me Florence I would like that. You knew Rex then? I was saddened by his death, it was no more than ten days before that I’d been to the house, to see him, he made no mention of feeling unwell nor did he show any sign of discomfort, it was so sudden.”

“The heart can sometimes just stop with little warnin’, I don’t reckon he’d been feelin’ poorly otherwise he’d have said what he needed to say before that night. We were gathered in the hall at Bentinck Road School, because o’ the gas leak, I couldn’t help noticin’ he wer’ in pain poor old chap. I went over to him an’ spoke, he was strugglin’ for breath an’ desperate to make me understand, an’ I did, caught every word.

‘Tell Mrs.Stanford that I never blamed her’, then he repeated it, ‘tell her I never blamed her, nor Patricia’.

They were his last words. I’ve waited ‘til now because it felt only proper. We walk up that street every mornin’, early on our way to work, Barry Pointer an' me, Rex'd be in his doorway with a mug o' tea, we'd exchange a courtesy like folk do but that's all, I didn't know him any more than that. It could have been any o' the others in the hall that night it just happened to be me he asked the favour of an' so I've tried to be respectful of his wishes, I hope I've done right."

Florence fought back tears, her hands trembled in her lap, smiling through her emotion she nodded her head.

"I'm glad it was you Connor, yet how puzzled you must be by such a message."

He found himself concerned for this elderly lady, she wasn't what he'd expected, not at all.

"Not for me to dwell on Ma...., Florence, I won't take up any more of your time." Connor was about to get to his feet.

"Please stay a little longer, Patricia will be back soon, she would want to meet you." Florence composed herself as best she could. "In the coming days I must brace myself for the task of sorting Rex's things, there's no close family that I'm aware of. Annie will help me, and another good friend, Andrew Smithfield has insisted he help too."

"I've met him," said Connor, "when I first come over from Ireland, to look at the place, with Mathew. He took me to meet Mr.Smithfield, because of the Irish connection, his mother was from Tipperary I believe an' for a number o' years he lived there, seemed like a real decent sort."

"Oh he is," said Florence, "unusually so in the realms of business and industry it's surely sad to say. He's retired now of course, textiles, a very well respected employer."

"I'm workin' at Whittle's, the boss, Bill Whittle, now he's big business, up there with Dick Woolascroft from what I can gather, both names crop up in pub talk more than any others."

Florence stood and crossed the room to the window. “Yes, it is Patricia, I thought I heard the car. Although she’s not so many years his senior Patricia is Dick’s aunt, she married Anthony Bradshaw, the much younger brother of Cynthia, Dick’s mother,” Florence sighed, “Anthony was killed in the war, that dreadful, mindless conflict made widows of all three of my daughters.”

Connor didn’t know what to say. The sound of the front door opening and footsteps in the hall took his gaze towards the drawing room door.

Florence called out. “In here Patricia.”

Her hair immaculate and just enough makeup to be tasteful Patricia cut a fine figure for her age. Connor was on his feet and extending his hand. Florence introduced him as though he were a guest of some note and he sensed her manner was sincere. Patricia took his hand and smiled.

“What a nice surprise, young company, our family is sadly lacking in young company Connor. Before I forget Mother, Hilda sends her best and I am to tell you that Rosemary is singing a solo at Chapel tomorrow.”

The following half hour or so was in every way pleasant, they drank tea, chatted easily and when Connor finally said “Goodbye” he walked away from the house scarcely able to believe he’d not dreamt it all. Connor O’Shea had actually taken tea with Dick Woolascroft’s aunty, rubbed shoulders with the great and good, though possibly the good had yet to be established.

God bless Rex Madden, may he dwell among the angels, Connor would go to mass and light a candle for him. Holy Mother Mary, today she was on Connor’s side. He made the sign of the cross over his chest, something he’d not done in many a month. I wonder what Emily Eddowes would say if she knew, he followed the thought with a sigh. Miss Pearl wasn’t so bad, he was taking her dancing tonight. A tune came into his head, which the men at work often whistled and sang. In lyrical Irish tones, as he walked along Connor serenaded the grandeur of Castle Road. *‘Cigareets an’ whisky an’ wild, wild women, they drive yer crazy they drive yer insane’*. Just at the very moment he reached the corner and was about to turn, curtains suddenly closed in a top window. He stood still, "Would yer believe that so, it winked at me, that big house winked at Connor." He blew a kiss and called out. "I won't forget yer, Connor'll be back," as though the elegant face of the corner house could see and hear him, still singing he turned the corner, and was on his way.

CHAPTER THIRTEEN

Late March 1955.

Valerie rubbed the tea towel over the last of the dishes. "You must give me the recipe for that pudding Joyce or they'll be lodging complaints. Mam never bothered much with afters, stewed apple sometimes or semolina, an' now me dads gone I don't think she'd make the effort for herself. Edgar says we'll make sure she's alright, have her round for something to eat at least once a week, you an' Mr.Haynes an'all."

Joyce reached for the towel to dry her hands. "You don't need to worry about us but it's hard for Peggy, she's on her own now."

Edgar had gone to the corner shop for a loaf, taking Elizabeth with him and William was working a late shift. Joyce had tried really hard not to show how much she missed Edgar and the child, the wedding had been two weeks ago and since then she'd feverishly spring cleaned the house from top to bottom with the sole intent of denying herself a minute to be miserable. 'We've not rushed into anything but we both know our minds and it's what we want, Elizabeth is happy and that's because she now has two homes, ours and grandma's'. When Edgar had spoken these words to Joyce and explained that he and Valerie had agreed to be married at the registry office, quietly, William and herself to be witnesses, Joyce had felt mixed emotions, a dread of emptiness and a measure of relief also. For weeks she'd been expecting it and living day on day with the uncertainty of when, wore away at her nerves. With Valerie spending more and more time at the house the two women had developed a friendship, which Joyce wouldn't have believed possible to happen given Valerie's unfortunate past failings. Edgar had secured the tenancy of a pleasant little house not far away. The night before the wedding he'd sat Joyce down, held her hand and asked her to please be happy for him, for Elizabeth too, 'you're my mother Joyce, I'm your son, circumstances of birth didn't make it so but no one will ever say other than that to me'. Joyce knew beyond all doubt that Edgar meant every word and she couldn't have loved a son anymore than she loved Edgar. Elizabeth was a delight, a joyful bonus and albeit surprising, Valerie had added to that blessing of family.

This evening they had come for their tea, all part of Edgar's determined plan to make everything gradual, no immediate upsetting change but a gentle easing into different routines, 'can't do without your cooking 'til Valerie's picked up a few tips', tonight was the third time they'd come for a meal since the wedding and Joyce was perceptive enough to realise it had little to do with Valerie's culinary skills.

"You could have brought Peggy with you," said Joyce, "I bumped into her the other day, outside the post office, she was sending a parcel to one of your brothers."

Valerie chuckled. "A pullover for our Frank's birthday, mam's been knittin' it for weeks, she saw the pattern in a magazine, it was a fancy fair isle at the front, plain at the back, I think if that had been fair isle an'all she'd have chucked it on fire back, she said it wer' double Dutch. Then Mrs.Eddowes came to her aid, she's a wonderful needlewoman, it was Lizzie Sealey told mam to take her knittin' to Annie Eddowes an' to sit with her til' she'd done a few inches. Mam went home thankful that her Fair Isle pattern wasn't as complicated as Mr.Eddowes. 'He's a rum 'en', for mam to say that given what me dad wer' like, God only knows what poor Annie Eddowes has to put up with."

Just then the back door opened and Edgar's voice called out. "Guess who we've come across on our travels?"

"Hello Aunty Joyce." Beth was first to step inside, leading Elizabeth by the hand followed by Connor and Edgar.

"Hello Valerie, and congratulations, we were going to call on you in the next few days but Edgar insisted we say hello now, we shall still come to your new place one day soon, at Easter I expect."

Joyce could tell that Beth was feeling awkward, even after all the years that had passed since Elizabeth was born, still insensitive folk passed unsettling remarks, never specific and always behind the family's back, the secret nature of the wedding too did little to counter the gossip.

Joyce had met Connor for the first time at Christmas and Beth had called round several times since, with Connor. He'd seemed comfortable and easy to talk to, Elizabeth liked him and children were a good barometer of character so Joyce was happy for Beth. Elizabeth skipped across the floor to Minnie, curled up on the armchair, planting a big kiss on the cat's head.

"Just look at those two," said Edgar, "Minnie's no fool, she's got the best of both worlds, because we're living only two streets away she spends time at both places, an' I reckon she gets fed at both places an'all."

"Well we eat at grandmas and at Milton Street," observed Elizabeth, "Minnie's only copying us."

Joyce laughed, the cat did appear at some point every day and always got a titbit, but they all did, Edgar would pop in either early on his way to work, in which case Joyce would slip a slice of cake into his dinner bag, or he'd call later, on his way home to Valerie and Elizabeth, then it would be a couple of oranges or a bit of chocolate. William would pretend to despair of it but deep down he missed them too. Unbeknown to Elizabeth, 'grandad' was doing up a bicycle, working out in the shed whenever he could.

"Sit down Connor," said Joyce, "you know by now that nobody stands on ceremony in this house."

Valerie busied herself putting the kettle on while Joyce stacked away the dishes and Beth gave in to Elizabeth's pleas to plait her hair, "Like Barbara Waters', just to see what I look like."

The two men, finding they were for the time superfluous, made themselves comfortable and embarked on a typical male conversation.

"How's work progressing at Mitchell Street then Connor?" Asked Edgar, "I overheard somebody sayin' that Woolascroft was bringin' in enough cement an' aggregate to construct a pyramid, they reckon that it's not to be council housin' at all, that notion was wishful thinkin', what they're buildin' is a mausoleum for Dick an' his progeny, except he doesn't have any, not official anyroad."

Edgar's voice lowered as he spoke the last few words, Connor didn't appear to notice but Joyce did and despite Edgar's hushed remark she heard, and automatically glanced at Valerie, who showed not the slightest sign of embarrassment or emotion. Perhaps his words had been just too faint for her to hear over the rattling of the cups and saucers.

Knowing one way or the other would make no difference now, yet like all unsolved mysteries, underlying was a need to find an answer, to solve the mystery once and for all.

Connor laughed. "A pyramid eh! Now that could challenge the gasometer in sheer size an' novelty but I reckon if Woolascroft set about buildin' himself a mausoleum he'd choose some place different to Mitchell Street. Though havin' said, he's there every day an' nothin' gets past him, but it's true what they say about the mighty volume of underpinnin' he's puttin' down, think what you will about the man, he's set on a good build, no one in a hundred years from now will be able to fault it. Perhaps he's not like his old man, I've heard one or two stories about his father that if true, should have had him in the confessional eight days a week."

"I don't believe he was a Catholic," observed Edgar.

"Well if he couldn't find absolution as he went along he'll likely still be sittin' in the Almighty's sin bin. Back in Ireland you've only to sneeze without puttin' your hand over your mouth an' you've to declare your mortal sin to the priest. I've never been able to understand it meself, the Irish were sinned against an' yet they're forever confessin'. Best o' luck to the likes o' Woolascrofts, that's what I say, father an' son."

"Tea up," said Valerie, "do you take sugar Connor?"

"No ta, sweet enough, isn't that right Miss Pearl?"

Beth blushed as she tied the bow around Elizabeth's plaited hair. "Well Minnie certainly thinks so, that cat has jumped onto your lap and purred her delight each time we've come."

Connor ran the palm of his hand along Minnie's back fondly. "Animals come free of complications, not like us humans, you've nothin' to confess have yer Minnie?"

"What do you make of that Connor O'Shea?" Said Valerie, as she climbed into bed beside Edgar, "I can tell Beth is smitten."

"He seems like a decent sort, works hard by all accounts, an' if Beth's mam is approvin' then he must be alright, she's Joyce's sister don't forget." Edgar chuckled at the thought. "Don't start readin' your book now, it's gettin' late."

Joyce looked at the clock and smiled, just after ten, not so very late. She turned to face him. He blew a wayward strand of hair from her brow and kissed her.

"I love you Valerie and I love our daughter, my Elizabeth, Mr. and Mrs. Edgar Perry an' their daughter Elizabeth, we're a family an' I thank my maker every day."

Valerie sensed there was a 'but' pending, sooner or later he was bound to ask, she was surprised he had not done so long ago.

"It changes nothin'," said Edgar, "you know what I mean. I was so naive back then, I actually believed it possible, that what I did in that telephone box with you could have made a baby. No one will ever prise Elizabeth from me,

I'd swing for any man that tried, but if I knew, if you told me then I could stop feeling so inadequate every time I heard his name spoken, he couldn't threaten my confidence anymore."

Valerie looked nervous, for a second she hesitated, then feeling for his hand under the covers she asked. "Every time who's name is mentioned?"

"Woolascroft, it was Dick wasn't it?" Edgar's expression seemed to declare the inevitability of it as he let out a long sigh.

All the years Joyce had wrestled with loyalties, at times wanting to shout a defence of Dick Woolascroft when the tittle tattle condemned him, yet if she had, loyalty for that someone who could not defend himself she would have betrayed, it defied all sense but war did that, it pilfered, it stole, it shamelessly took from good folk their precious things, war was a robber of the worst kind. Holding Edgar's hand tightly Valerie revealed the secret, an answer to the mystery.

"Elizabeth is nothing to do with Dick Woolascroft. I needed to work, to escape. Everyone knew I'd had a baby, how eager they are to put two an' two together, they don't stop to think, I don't believe they really care, Dick's reputation I suppose, and the fact that I got the job.

I thought if I dolled meself up he'd say yes when I asked for work, it would get me in through the door an' then I could prove meself capable, I wouldn't take any nonsense from him an' he'd find that out very quick. When I asked him if I could have the job of wages clerk he said 'no', without even considering it, such a definite no. I thought it must have been because of the baby, I was cheap, Valerie Oates had no shame. I wanted to cry but not in front of him so I walked away and had my hand on the door latch when he spoke again. 'You can give it a try, see how it goes'. Why he changed his mind I don't know. All the time I worked there not once did he behave in any way improper, perhaps he deemed me to be soiled goods. I did the work well an' he wer' always pleasant but I didn't see anything to justify what folk say about him."

Edgar felt bewildered, what he'd done that night in the phone box couldn't have made a current bun, let alone a baby, so who?

"You remember what me dad wer' like," said Valerie. "I grew up afraid of men, I imagined they could all be violent like him. One day I wer' in town when a young man asked me which bus to catch for Wollaton. It sounds silly an' I don't know why but I pretended that was where I wer' goin', Wollaton. We both got on the bus and he sat by me chattin', friendly, like we weren't strangers at all. He was American, one of the airmen based at Wollaton Park. He was nice, kind, I liked him, I suppose I must have thought American men to be different, never in a million years could he have been like me dad! We met again, twice, he was tender, I didn't understand tenderness, I couldn't reject it, tenderness was beautiful. The next day they were gone, the Americans, all gone, I think he was aware. They said the expected life of an airman was no more than weeks. I knew that what we did could make a baby, but it wouldn't, just that once it wouldn't. I can't regret it Edgar, nor can I judge him." Valerie's voice began to tremble. "He was probably killed soon after he left. I couldn't look after a baby, I was afraid of me dad's temper, for her an' for me an' if poor mam had tried to stand in his way he'd likely have killed her. The baby would be safe with you an' Joyce, I wanted her to be a Perry, not an Oates, me dad's reputation was worse than Dick's and I knew dad's wer' warranted."

Edgar gently wiped a tear from her cheek. "You've nothing and no one to fear now Valerie, not anymore."

He put out the bedside light, and all anxiety with it. He was alive, he had a wife and daughter. In that moment Edgar felt love, such deep unconditional love, it lay with them, wrapped them about in pure tenderness.

Emily flopped down onto the chair and kicked off her shoes, the shopping bags she'd abandoned at the foot of the stairs.

"Oh Mam, what a performance, a pin here, a tuck there, on, off, on again, turn about."

"In out, in out, an' shake it all about," Mathew overheard from where he sat in the kitchen, painstakingly gluing back together the pieces of a little bon bon dish that Celia had dropped on the bathroom floor, it's purpose of late being far removed from dainty confectionary but to hold the soap, a present years ago from her mother, Celia had been upset. 'I'll try to fix it as good as new', Mathew had declared in his bid to console her and true to his word his careful repair was the closest he could get to invisible mending. "If you will go doing the hokey kokey on an Easter Saturday it's sure to be hectic." He chuckled roguishly.

"It's alright for you men," said Emily, casting a look at her mam that revealed her frustration, "a clean shirt, a tie, a rub of polish over the shoes, the occasion suit from the wardrobe and Bob's your uncle, without leaving the house, you should try being a bridesmaid brother dear." Emily called out loudly so as Mathew couldn't fail to recognise her sense of injustice at the stark difference required in effort by women over that of men.

"That could appear a little avant-garde for the Couplands Emily," observed Celia, "perhaps acceptable in London but too shocking for the less sophisticated mortals of the Midlands!" A big grin spread across Celia's face, then realising what she'd actually said Emily burst into laughter.

Mrs.Coupland would understandably want her daughter's wedding to be special, it was but two weeks away, on the 23rd of April. Emily had been to the seamstress, Mrs.Dale, for a fitting of her bridesmaid's dress. Naturally slim and of average height it was to establish the need for any slight adjustments. Not possessed of the greatest patience, Emily had despaired at Mrs.Dale's endless fidgeting over a perfect fit. When at last that was done, shoes for the occasion had to be bought and adornment for her hair. Celia was amused at her daughter's dismissive attitude, feeling convinced that when the time came for her own wedding Emily would be completely caught up in the excitement of it all, just like Margaret.

The only unfortunate circumstance as Celia considered it was the date, College resumed the week before so Emily must travel to London only to return to Nottingham in time for the wedding on the 23rd, or miss five days of tuition, which in her final term she was loath to do. Already applying for teaching posts, subject to the results of her finals, Celia dared to hope that one of the schools in Nottingham might turn out to be Emily's immediate future. Harrow Road would be ideal and Emily had tentatively made approach of the headmaster with encouraging response. It wasn't possible to keep fingers crossed until August but Celia found herself doing so whenever she had a moment to quietly hope. Mathew was back from Dublin with no suggestion of him having to go again, that alone had breathed new life into her, the atmosphere at home seemed less strained and even William's sessions with the gramophone she'd endured without resentment for the 'Cigareets an' Whisky'.

"I saw Connor earlier," said Mathew, "I told him to call in, I knew you were intending to go with Hilda and grandma to Chapel tomorrow, to hear Rosemary sing so I suggested Monday, the bank holiday, that's alright isn't it? I think he was hoping for an invite, he remarked on it being Easter weekend last year that he first met us all."

"Of course it's alright, I wonder if he'll bring Beth?" In truth Celia was pleased, despite all his mystery she had a soft spot for Connor, he was apart from his own family and the fact that he chose to visit her's she found satisfying.

Emily stirred herself. "I'm surprised they're still seeing each other, Beth is so innocent, gullible even, and he's the opposite, the way he goes on about

Irish charm and little leprechauns, it's all nonsense, he might sweet talk Beth but I don't think anyone sees the real Connor, he most likely had a mighty falling out with his dad, being cocky like he is, and his mam persuaded him to find his fortune over here, just to keep the peace." Emily shoved her feet back into her shoes. "I ought to take him to London with me and set him loose, he'd be eaten alive within a week, they'd devour him simply to quieten his silly tongue."

"That's not very nice Emily," said Mathew, having completed his task with the bon bon dish he now stood in the doorway of the living room. "He's done nothing to upset you, and dad seems to like him, he can't be that bad if dad actually likes him."

Celia recognised Mathew's subtle reference to William's opinionated view of most folk, Mathew was right, if William approved of Connor O'Shea then he really must be a remarkable young man, most failed at William's first withering assessment.

"Well I can't see it working, not him and Beth, he needs a stern woman to keep him in check." Emily squeezed past her brother to gather up her abandoned shopping bags and take them to her bedroom. "My head dress has pink and mauve silk flowers all over it, I shall look like a fuchsia bush."

Mathew sighed as he listened to her tread on the stairs, crossing the room to Celia he whispered. "A prickly fuchsia bush at that!"

Annie felt proud of Rosemary, sitting in the choir, waiting to sing her solo, the child showed little sign of nervousness but Annie could only imagine how she must feel as the pews gradually became occupied and more expectant faces looked to the choir stalls, bedecked in their Sunday best, hats and gloves for the ladies, suits for the gents, making them appear less familiar, work clothes ever softened a character, no finery behind which to hide, but commonplace, equal.

This morning Hilda, Celia and Emily had joined Annie for the service, while seated at Annie's other side was Lizzie Sealey. Being Easter Sunday the congregation was bigger than usual and a visiting preacher was to take the service, a guest of the Reverend and Mrs.Goodwill, a most appropriate name for a man of the cloth. Annie had one day remarked on this to the Minister, his reply had shocked her but on thinking more about it she admired his honesty. 'My father was imprisoned for fraud, the Goodwill title passed to me not without a degree of shame and I received it not without a measure of resentment, perhaps I am best placed to redeem it, I can but try'.

The steward checked his watch, satisfied all 'faithful' were inside he closed the chapel door, the preacher mounted the steps to the pulpit and looking about the gathering smiled broadly. A particularly healthy example of man, ruddy cheeks, a full head of dark hair and a voice, strong and clear with conviction as he said. "Let us rejoice and be glad, our Redeemer is risen from the dead, praise The Lord. We shall begin by singing hymn number 215, *'The strife is o'er the battle won, now is the victor's triumph won'*."

The organist sent the first few introductory notes over the head and shoulders of the preacher, as demanding of response as would be a baton waving conductor, all stood and clutching their hymnals gave voice. Rosemary looked across to her mam who at that moment left the rousing 'Alleluia' to everyone else and blew a kiss. Now they settled in their pews anticipating the first prayer.

"We shall bow our heads and let the words speak to us." He commenced, 'Christ our Passover', his prayer of the resurrection and ascension and in the stillness that sense of thankfulness slipped silently along the rows of men, women and children, hushed was all distracting noise. Until just a few minutes into their prayers, someone outside began to shout, to call out alarmingly.

Annie's heart sank, she recognised the voice at once and poor Lizzie was shaking like a leaf.

"Come out 'ere woman an' bring that bag an'all or so 'elp me I'll come in there an' fetch it, 'e'll not mind me, Sealey, Private 476358."

"You stay here Lizzie, Fred knows me well enough, he'll likely go quiet when he sees me but he'd shout all the more at you." Needing to squeeze past Hilda, Celia and Emily, Annie whispered. "It's alright, stay with Lizzie." Hurriedly making her way down the aisle she nodded to the preacher and cast a quick glance at Reverend Goodwill, seated at the front with his wife, surely Fred Sealey would test the Minister's namesake like no other, and those not knowing Annie would be wondering why she didn't carry the bag, which hopefully might restore their peace, 'goodwill', it felt like a misplaced optimism as Annie clutched the heavy door latch to find escape. Relieved to be outside she willed the preacher to carry on.

Fred stood by the gate of the chapel yard, he was about to call out again but Annie put her fingers to her lips and shook her head. As if a divine hand had come down on his shoulder, Fred was mute. Annie stood before him, breathless from haste and anxiety.

"Sent you has she," he muttered under his breath.

"Sit a minute Fred," said Annie, "it's as well neither of us is broad about the beam or we wouldn't manage to perch here." Annie sat on the wall, her back against the railings and with a token sniff of intolerance, Fred sat alongside her.

"She's taken every last penny from the house, got it all locked away in that damn handbag, rather give it to 'im up there than let me 'ave a shillin'." He raised his face to the sky and spoke to the heavens. "It's nowt to do wi' you, 'ear me can yer, nay, I'm wrong side again, wrong side o' the bloody door this time."

Annie felt inside her pocket for the half crown she'd wrapped up in her hanky.

"He's happy to share Fred, if you need money then take this, I don't mind whether I put it in the collection plate or you have it instead." Annie held out the coin.

"I don't want your money, I want what's mine, inside Lizzie's bag." He fell silent for several seconds and appeared to calm. "Chaplain 'ould gather us round, I reckon 'e needed to see hope in our faces as much as we were desperate to find it in 'is. 'E'd lead us in prayer, and how we all begged to be 'delivered from evil', yet we could tell, chaplain's voice grew weaker each time, we knew 'e wer' strugglin'. I wanted to shout at the sky, it didn't feel like there was anywhere else, anyone else I could shout at, 'elp 'im can't yer, do summat'. Well I come to think that God 'ad a deaf ear an' we must 'ave been on that side 'cause 'e never answered, last time I saw chaplain 'e wer' arf' dead."

"I lost a son, John, he was RAF, you would have liked him, everyone did, he was all that a son should be, loving, kind, bright, I talk to him because he must be somewhere, with someone, something," said Annie. "What is it that you really want Fred, if it's not this half crown?"

"If I knew that I wouldn't keep lookin' in the bottom of a pint pot, I do....."

"Hush," Annie held up her hand, "listen Fred, that's my granddaughter singing, it's Rosemary."

Annie looked into Fred's eyes and smiled. The sound of a young girl's voice, made faint by the chapel walls, nevertheless fell upon their ears with a wonderful purity. When her singing ceased Fred stared at Annie in genuine bewilderment.

"Why did yer come out 'ere wi' me, yer should 'ave been inside listenin' to your granddaughter?"

"I won't answer you with anything but the truth Fred, I was afraid for Lizzie, I knew you wouldn't hurt me."

He shuffled his feet. "I'm sorry about your son, I didn't know that. I see your other son sometimes, though not so much lately, William isn't it? I go to me aunty Florrie's in an' out, to tidy up 'er bit o' front garden, clean the path, the odd job or two, she wer' good to me mam an' dad, they're both gone now, Purbeck Road, that's where she lives."

"Yes, that would be William," said Annie, "he lets a house on Purbeck Road, he'd be collecting the rent."

"Aye, that'd be it, collectin' 'is rent. 'E's not much like you is 'e?"

"William's my stepson, his mother died when he was an infant."

"Well there you go then, that explains that." He stood up, brushing the seat of his trousers with both hands. "Tell Lizzie I'll be at 'ome."

Annie gave him a look that sought assurance.

"I've never struck 'er wi' me fist, but I've lashed 'er wi' me tongue, yer can tell 'er it'll be alright, she needn't fret an' tell your young lass that Fred Sealey says she sings like a thrush."

He walked quietly away, as if whatever had driven his rancour was in retreat. A thrush and a blackbird, a girl and a troubled man, creatures great and small.

He must hear, somewhere John would be listening and would know how much his mother missed him.

A ring came at the front door. "I'll go, you finish your crossword."

Emily and Mathew had begged the puzzle page of the newspaper from William, who pored over the rest of the paper as though hidden somewhere between the lines of print was the infallible recipe for lifelong success.

"Hello Connor," said Celia, "I thought Beth might be with you, never mind you shall take her chocolate egg when you go, don't let me forget to give it to you."

Connor laughed. "I've not forgotten the way you put an Easter egg on my breakfast plate last year, I reckon that was the one thing above all else that made me decide on this city bein' Connor's 'place', an' now I'm returnin' the gesture." He carried a large box. "I know you'll share it with them all but the flowers are meant especially for you."

Connor beamed his pleasure as he turned the box around and held it out, through the cellophane panel Celia could see a big chocolate egg, decorated down the front with pink and purple sugar violets, 'Happy Easter' piped in white icing at either side.

"Oh my goodness Connor, a beautiful Thornton's egg, but you shouldn't have, it must have cost a fortune."

Celia felt concerned, while she was genuinely delighted and quite touched by his kindness, it should have been his own mother receiving such a gift, she couldn't help but voice her thoughts.

"Don't you worry about that Mrs.Eddowes, I'll likely be seein' mam next month, I'm due a bit o' time off so a trip on the ferry to see the family isn't far away, I'll think o' summat nice to take for mam, trouble is, knowing what, she don't crave much, except peace. I got a letter last week, all's well, though havin' said mam wouldn't tell me if it wasn't, shows a happy face to the world does mam, regardless of problems, like you do." Connor gave Celia a knowing look.

"Come through," she said hastily, a tremble of emotion threatening to support his intuitive remark, "they're in the living room, William too and any minute now Annie should arrive, William's mother, I don't imagine you've met her Connor."

He followed Celia through to where the others sat, Mathew was on his feet in an instant and greeted Connor warmly. Emily looked up from the crossword and cast a brief "Hello" accompanied by a somewhat grudging smile, while William put down his newspaper, saw the splendid Thornton's egg in Celia's hands and said.

"Whittle must be paying you too much if you can afford to be so generous."

Celia was about to say 'don't be so rude William', when the sound of the back door opening and Annie's voice calling out, "only me", moved the moment along.

Emily was at once animated, crossing the room to greet her grandma with a hug, then, in a sudden rush of politeness said.

"This is Connor O'Shea Grandma, you remember he stayed a while last year, Mathew worked in Dublin with Connor's dad."

"I've heard a lot about this young man," said Annie, she now stood before him, smiling, "you made a great impression on my dear friend Florence but sadly you've not yet called on her again, she keeps hoping that you will."

William's paper now fell from his lap, he reached to retrieve it, feeling a rush of blood to his head, more from what he'd just heard Annie say than from his sudden stoop. Florence Stanford, whatever was Connor doing at Mrs.Stanford's, his curiosity grew evermore pressing but Connor shook Annie's hand and said.

"Then I shall rectify the situation Mrs.Eddowes and it will be nothing but a pleasure."

William could contain himself no longer. "How do you know Florence Stanford?" Annie dare not let it show but she felt amused at William's obvious disbelief.

“It was a while ago now,” said Connor, “I was asked to deliver a message to the good lady and she was kind enough to insist I take tea with her, and her daughter as it turned out, Patricia.”

“Mrs.Bradshaw to you surely lad.” William’s tone was reproving.

“That’s what you’d expect I’m sure but in fact we are on Christian name terms, at their insistence, Florence and Patricia, now it’s not courteous to argue with a lady, let alone two.”

Annie glanced at Celia, who was quite clearly enjoying this moment as much as Annie herself.

“Look what Connor has brought for us all.” Celia held up her prized egg as if she held aloft the World Cup, indeed it did feel as if in some strange way she’d triumphed. William’s expression revealed his intense frustration at Connor’s revelation.

Celia placed the box on the table and looking directly at William declared it far too beautiful to eat just yet, for a few days they must relish the sight of it!

“Thank you so much Connor,” she planted a kiss on his cheek, “Beth is a lucky young woman.”

No one but Annie seemed to notice the way Emily’s face fell, perhaps Connor’s charm, of which Florence had spoken with such delight had found Emily also, a good thing then, that in just a few days her granddaughter would be back in London. It was a shame that heartache so often afflicted the young as they negotiated their way through those early years of love and attraction. At least Samuel had found happiness with Margaret, Annie so looked forward to the wedding, especially as Freddy and the family were coming for the day, except Faith’s husband Richard, although invited of course, someone needed to remain at the farm to tend the livestock. Annie had yet to persuade Charles, always he created problems and right up to the last minute she was never sure if he would actually go to the family’s special occasions.

"Grandma will know the answer," said Mathew, "there's only one we couldn't do, fourteen down, a six letter word and the clue is 'witness', it's A blank, blank E, blank T."

"Attest," said Annie, "as in to witness, to bear proof of." Mathew filled in the letters.

"Your talents are wasted Grandma, you could have run a big business, put Eddowes on the map." His words were spoken in jest but they held sufficient irony to send William behind his newspaper, where he could brood unseen.

CHAPTER FOURTEEN

July

"He's a good lad, one tellin's enough, picks it up quick, whether it's down to the army or natural ability I couldn't tell yer but he'll make a good mechanic, less inclined to swear than some, one young fella I took on made more sparks fly wi' his tongue than he did wi' the arc welder, I had every woman within arf mile radius on me case, had to send him up the road, works for Woolascroft now. It's been rumoured that the Queen might visit Mitchell Street, to see the new council housing when she comes to open the Royal Show at Wollaton, they best give Jake the day off or her majesty'll be blue blooded sure enough, blue bloody everythin' if he starts up."

Nat rubbed his hands with a piece of rag, more gesture than intent, as it appeared to have little effect, possibly due to the rag being saturated in oil and general filth.

"The car's all fixed up, carburettor wer' the problem, yer can tell just by listenin' sometimes, but at others you'll go mad tryin' to fathom it. Over the years I've come to realise that cars are like women, we see one we like the look of so we make that first fatal mistake an' get in the damn thing, enough leg room, fires up first time, nice tight clutch, good suspension, an' does a fair few miles to the gallon. Then we take another look at the outside, sturdy bonnet, nice roomy boot, suits our purpose, so we seal the deal, licensed, taxed an' ready for the road. It's runnin' sweet for a bit, yer look forward to a spin, then it gets sluggish uphill an' starts to splutter, so yer dig deep an' pay for best fuel, but then it develops a whinin' noise, fan belt slippin', get that sorted out an' radiator springs a leak, repair that an' battery loses a cell, plugs won't spark. For years yer coax it along because by then you've spent hours on your back underneath it, not to mention a fortune in money, 'til one day yer take a hard look at the bloody thing an' feel overcome wi' nostalgia for the first bike yer ever got yer legs astride of," Nat sniffed and let out a hefty sigh, "in my case it wer' an Ada, happy carefree mode o' transport wer' Ada," he laughed wickedly. "Spent a lot o' time free wheelin', when I think o' the fun we had back then!" He slapped George on the back. "Tell your sister Hilda she reared a good 'en, got more than a bit of his dad in him an'all, decent bloke is Jack Haynes."

George followed Nat to the area of the garage that passed for an office, walking by a very smart Daimler.

"Nice one that, bit o' class," said Nat, "she wanted it serviced, the Bradshaw woman." He flicked through a number of invoices. "Here yer go, that's the damage, I've knocked off the odd 3/6d, yer can thank young David over there for that, he's supposed to finish arf five but he wer' still at it gone six yesterday, determined to get an engine put back together."

George took the sheet of paper from Nat's fingers, down one side a row of oily thumb prints, looking like some kind of official stamp. A popular mechanic, many folk used 'Broadbent's Servicing and Repairs', he was reliable and reasonable, it wasn't unusual therefore to see a somewhat battered works vehicle parked alongside an elegant motor car, the latter belonging to someone in the professions, a surgeon, solicitor or accountant. Patricia Bradshaw didn't fit any such category, which was unfortunate and in the eyes of most folk the Daimler's number plate read STANFORD. Yet George suspected that when Nat rendered her account it would bear that same oily thumb print with which he stamped all the rest.

David pulled himself out from underneath a Wolseley, got to his feet and called across.

"Alright Uncle George?"

"Fine thanks David, come to see us soon, Liza would like that."

David gave a big grin and a thumbs up.

"Had your cousin in here the other day," said Nat, "Jack Wainwright. He's thinkin' o' buyin' a small, second hand car to take the family out of a weekend. He'll have to take a test first. 'I've not been behind the wheel since this', he said an scuffed the ground wi' his dummy leg. He'd moved vehicles durin' the war like a lot did. He asked if I'd let him have a go in summat we had in garage, just to see if he could manage the pedals, I keep an old runabout for when we go to a breakdown, get in there Jack lad, I said, drive it like you're chasin' Rommel. He took it across the yard an' reversed back as well as the next man, got out, looked at me an' said, 'there wer' no point in tryin' 'til I could afford a cheap set o' wheels'. That Daimler wer' here then, shinin' like fresh hewn coal, there's no bloody justice is there?" Nat shook his head in frustration. "Makes yer want to spit."

"My goodness, so many people." Celia looked up and down Western Boulevard and as far as she could see folk stood, waiting for a glimpse of the Queen.

"Let's cross over to the central reservation," said Rosie, "there's more grass an' Beryl can look for a four leafed clover while we wait, she's been tryin' to find one ever since your Emily picked one from the Boulevard, it could be another ten minutes before the royal car comes along. Keep hold of my arm Mam, I've got your bag it's alright."

Poor Audrey, her confusion became pitiful, Celia remembered so clearly the plight of her own mother when age and weariness gradually wore away the sharpness of her mind, until eventually reality was ever entwined with imagination and untangling the two, beyond anyone's hope. Rosie was tender hearted and Tommy a most placid man, it couldn't be too long away that

Audrey must live with family or be placed in care, either way it would hurt, Celia could vouch for that.

The sun shone warm from a cloudless sky, adding to everyone's sense of wellbeing and excitement. Nottingham hadn't been visited upon by royalty for many a year. The civic gatherings at which the Mayor paraded his authority fell far short of this day's anticipated events, a chance to see the young Queen Elizabeth in the flesh and furthermore, at the Royal Show, which was being viewed by some as a vast shop window where business both big and small might promote itself. Wollaton Park being chosen as the venue proved popular with everybody, it was an amenity of the city so favoured, with a lake, great expanses of mown grass, shrubs and flowers. The imposing main gates led visitors into the Park by way of 'lime tree avenue', a vision akin to the aisle of a magnificent cathedral, the trees rising on either side, not carved or chiselled by man's hand into worshipful designs but proclaiming God's glory through dappled sunlight of summer days, the all sheltering branches, like everlasting arms through threatening winds of winter. Commanding the view over all was Wollaton Hall with its elaborate façade and incredible interior, home to Nottingham's natural history collection. As Rosie once put it, 'what Noah had on the ark got stuffed in Wollaton Hall', not so much crammed in but preserved by the taxidermist, with exception of the honey bees, which were viewed behind glass but granted free exit and entry via a hole in the exterior wall of the building. Young Beryl, at her first experience of the wonders within could not understand why the animals didn't move. Rosie had explained as carefully as she could that they had all died and a kind man had been very clever and done something, which meant they looked like they were still alive. It did little to stem the child's tears and an early exit, with the promise of letting her hold Tilly's lead when they took aunty Celia's dog for a walk, proved the only acceptable comforter. Even Celia, while acknowledging the tremendous skill applied to the preservation of these deceased creatures, felt sad to see them in glass fronted cabinets, obliged to endure mankind's relentless curiosity. It had led her to believe that if the situation were to be reversed and all varieties of humankind, stuffed, and displayed in their natural habitat were put before the animals, few would be remotely interested.

"Are you too hot in that cardigan Mam?" Audrey did appear flushed in face. Let's try an' get close to a tree," said Rosie.

Beneath the leafy branches the sun's heat lost its intensity, it was pleasant and only young Beryl persisted in rooting about among the grass for that elusive four leafed clover.

"William's gone to Mitchell Street," said Celia, "the royal party is scheduled to stop there for only twenty minutes, just long enough to look at progress I suppose. Apparently the accommodation, when completed, will be quite different, modern, easier for the housewife. I think Dick Woolascroft has been asked to show Her Majesty the architect's plans and to explain the past problems of subsidence and how they've been addressed."

"I bet 'e's feelin' nervous, practisin' 'is bow an' makin; 'isself remember to sound 'is aitches, does William 'ave to speak an'all? It wouldn't be so bad for 'im, Annie taught 'em all to talk nicely, I can still remember the look on teacher's face when it wer' the turn of William or Freddy to read aloud a poem in school, she'd smile an' raise 'er eyes, like she'd just glimpsed Eden."

Celia sighed. "No, but knowing him I dare say he'll find a way, I'm sure he won't allow Dick all the limelight. Annie will be on Alfreton Road with Hilda and Rosemary, they were going to watch her go by from there."

Suddenly a ripple of animated voices travelled along the rows of people.

"It's them, it's the royal car." A man called out for all to hear and make ready their flags. The schoolchildren had been issued with hand held Union Jacks and given the day off lessons, while patriotic mams and grandmas had purchased flags from enterprising newsagents so's they too could wave their loyalty.

“Here you are Mam, she’s comin’.” Rosie put a flag in Audrey’s hand.

“Who is, who’s comin’?”

Rosie gave a troubled sigh. “The Queen Mam, it’s our Queen Elizabeth, look.”

At that moment a gleaming, open topped motor car drove serenely before their eyes, a pretty young woman waving her hand in carefully measured amounts to both left and right of the vehicle, the pale peach coloured feathers of her hat doing likewise. The jubilant throng responding with cheers and applause. Babies cried, dogs barked and a host of Union flags on extended arms demonstrated everyone’s delight through a display of unrestrained enthusiasm. Still leaning into the road, all eyes followed the two shining motor cars until they could be seen no more.

“Isn’t she tiny,” observed Beryl, “she looked a lot bigger on your television set Aunty Celia, I liked the colour of her outfit, when Beth marries Connor, if I’m a bridesmaid that’s the colour of dress I shall choose.”

Celia and Rosie exchanged amused looks but it was Audrey who innocently and touchingly created the abiding memory of this day. She began to sing, quite clearly, the national anthem. Folk stared bemused at the sight of an elderly woman standing in the shade of a tree, cardigan askew, slowly waving a Union flag and belatedly rendering the anthem to a queen now out of sight.

“Come on Mam.” Rosie took her mother gently by the arm and sniffled up the tears.

Celia swallowed a lump in her throat and clutched Beryl’s hand. “We’ll find a four leafed clover one day, you’ll see and we’ll press it between the pages of a book until it’s dried, like we did with the one Emily found. They’re very lucky, I shall make a point of looking every day, promise.”

Celia felt Beryl’s fingers tighten about her own but the girl said nothing. Despite all the jubilation, the excitement of seeing the Queen in the flesh, Celia suspected it would be the image of her grandma that remained with Beryl the longest.

"You must feel proud of Hilda, she's established a really good business, Patricia is always delighted with the results of her styling. My hair is naturally wavy and now it's become thin a simple shampoo over the kitchen sink is all that's required. When it needs a trim Caroline does the necessary so I declare myself to be of no use to Hilda."

Annie chuckled. "I think some days Florence, Hilda is thankful mother nature awarded that special flourish to the crowning glory of some, though she wouldn't want it to be common knowledge Hilda doesn't enjoy the perming process at all, if she had her way the twenties 'Bob' would be compulsory."

"Patricia has her eyebrows plucked," said Florence, "she thinks I don't notice but it gives her a curious startled expression. One of the students, Debora, is very much the modern Miss, I can't imagine where she buys her brassieres. I've heard the expression 'a nicely rounded bosom', but Debora's appears to be taking aim, honed at the nipples, cocked and ready to fire. It was amusing to see Connor's reaction the first time he met her, the poor lad physically flinched."

Annie had long ago stopped feeling shocked at Florence's unlikely observations, like Catherine Appleyard who often came out with remarks entirely unpredictable, both ladies were of some standing in the community but nothing more and nothing less than a natural character did either ever display. Annie chuckled.

"Women's undergarments have always been questionable, I remember aunt Bella's corsets. But the first one I saw was Mrs.Bacon's, hanging on the clothes line, I would have been about ten years old, it looked so formidable, I dared not ask but presumed it served some purpose for Mr.Bacon, I had no idea what mysteries lay underneath a man's clothing. How naive I was, not until I married Harold did I discover male anatomy, aunt Bella taught me my lessons but such a delicate subject she chose to leave to experience. Looking back I think it was Edna who enabled me some worldliness," Annie chuckled, "but I could never be sure how much was reality and how much was her wonderful imagination."

"How is Mr.Dodds?" Asked Florence.

A smile spread automatically across Annie's face. "Billy is, as ever, a loyal friend and today he is being taken to the show by Andrew Smithfield. It was so kind of Andrew, he called to ask Charles if he too would like to go," Annie paused and let out a long sigh, "anyway, Billy will thoroughly enjoy not just the show but Andrew's company, he seldom goes out and I know Susie feels concerned at her dad's reluctance to venture far beyond the house and garden."

"Loyal friends both, Annie dear, beyond price. Oh look, over there, it's Olive surely." Florence raised her arm to wave, it caught Olive Woolascroft's attention and she waved back, apparently now intending to cross the road and join them. "Are you well my dear, I've not seen you for some time," said Florence, "I imagine you came out to see the Queen, as we did and what a lovely spectacle it was."

"I did manage a glimpse, Dick was surprisingly nervous this morning, even his gut couldn't still the butterflies. I'm sure he'd made every preparation for Her Majesty's visit to the site at Mitchell Street but after he left the house I felt compelled to follow on alone. His father never permitted Cynthia to accompany him to any work site and Dick has kept up the tradition I'm afraid. I watched discreetly from a distance, the usual council officials were present, William was there Mrs.Eddowes and I could see Gordon Cheetham, it did feel strange, my husband in the company of our Queen. It can be difficult at times to feel proud of Dick, that must sound dreadful I'm sure, but if he could just let Fred's memory fade a little and be himself. Anyway I must hurry along, he'd likely be annoyed if he discovered I was watching him so I need to reach home before he does. I understand Patricia is one of the show committee, it will be a busy day for her, give her my best."

Olive was about to dash off but Florence caught hold of her arm.

"Yes indeed, and I do believe that like Dick she was suffering from nervousness. She wanted me to go to the show but while the spirit might be willing the flesh, especially of the legs and feet is sadly too weak. We are to hear all about it tomorrow, in every detail, Annie is coming to have lunch with us, why don't you come too Olive, it will be but a simple affair, sandwiches, some cake, but a firsthand account of events at the Park is sure to be fascinating, come around noon. I shall call you on the telephone this evening then Dick won't suspect you were anywhere near Mitchell Street, you must pretend I rang especially to invite you."

Annie felt obliged to hide her surprise, lunch at Castle Road had not been mentioned until this moment.

"Very well Florence, thank you, I would like to come." With a gracious smile Olive hurried away.

"I begin to realise Annie, that through the awkwardness over Anthony's unfortunate liaison we have been less than kind to poor Olive, how often the innocent must suffer simply by association. You will be there won't you, tell Charles I shall make it right but I do need to borrow you for just a little while tomorrow, Olive will feel more comfortable with you there as a ally so to speak, William being in business with Dick. It's time Patricia remedied the situation, I won't be here forever, she'll need family, I'm quite convinced that is why she encourages Connor, he has ambition and in her way she's being some kind of surrogate aunt, on hand to offer advice."

Inwardly, Annie questioned how much of an ally to Olive past events would allow her to be, and yet it was true, the woman had done no wrong, why should she suffer through association. It was that name Woolascroft, Florence must surely have been likening Olive's experiences to those of her own, Stanford, not merely a name but a charge of wrong doing, sufficient in itself to bring judgement, when in reality there was no case to answer.

"I shall do my best to be there Florence, but it must be for only an hour, Charles is on his own today whilst I'm in town."

Florence patted Annie's arm. "I understand dear, no more than an hour. Oh, in all the excitement I almost forgot to tell you, the solicitor telephoned yesterday, apparently the buyer is ready to exchange contracts, soon the house on Denman Street will be the responsibility of another, mother would be in full accord and Caroline's finances need no longer occupy my mind, I feel very relieved. Of course she would refuse to accept a large amount so I shall dispense it in modest measures, Caroline is always busy, she won't notice so much if I employ a little craft. No use growing old Annie if we don't grow artful too. Patricia has appeared entirely impartial on the subject, engaging as she does with the students and their youthful conversations I don't think my bit of simple business entered her mind much at all. I can understand why she enjoys these young people, they're bright, full of life. She did ask Connor you know if he would like to leave his rented accommodation on Denman Street to live at Castle Road. I confess to feeling admiration for him when he politely declined with a worthy explanation.

'I go to work of a mornin' with me dinner bag over me shoulder, a song in me head an' boots full o' determination. College folk set off with a pen in their pocket, books under their arm an' a head filled with dreams'.

For someone so young he does have a remarkable grasp of business, of course he spent time in the company of William when he first arrived, perhaps his knowledge and maturity is due to William's influence."

"I think Ireland could be a challenging place for a young man," said Annie, "still malleable, possible to be worked by older men into a design of their choosing and not yet confident of what they themselves really want to be.

In that situation a youth would grow up fast. Emily is expected home in just over a week from now, does Connor speak of Beth when he visits you and Patricia, I wonder how serious his intention?"

Florence detected a note of concern in Annie's voice. "Oh dear, do you sense Emily has a fondness for Connor? I can't recall him saying very much about Beth, but then he does seem more drawn to heavy industrial machines than to young women!"

"There's every probability Emily will teach at Harrow Road School so perhaps for the time at least she will feel more drawn to a classroom of lively children than to the complexities of courtship. Beth is a very homely young woman, like her mam, I think less needful of challenge than Emily. Aren't you glad we're the age that we are Florence, spared the desire for plucked eyebrows and gravity defying brassieres, too old to be lovelorn, wise enough to be resigned?"

Florence sighed. "Patricia will be introduced to the Queen of England today, it's almost impossible for me to believe that once she travelled to hospital in the cab of a corporation dustcart. Oh yes Annie, I am indeed glad to have got this far."

Dick sat in his car letting a moment of quietness drift over him. Whatever would his father have said, a Woolascroft in the company of royalty, the Queen no less, showing her the build, explaining the process. He would likely have scoffed at Dick's nerves, his chest tight, his face muscles taut from maintaining a suitably gracious smile and observed continually by council officials who were there to promote themselves and to rate his performance, oh yes, his father would have scoffed alright, Dick could hear him saying it, 'never be afraid o' top brass lad, they wouldn't get there without our shoulders to climb on an' the buggers know it'.

Mitchell Street had become a template for other authorities to copy, the mayor's chest expanded accordingly, the chief planning officer nodded his head in agreement each time Dick described a new approach, a deviation from the standard terraced street, an up to date type of dwelling for a post war population looking to the future, seeking more comfort, a not unrealistic expectation in return for hard work.

With every statement Dick made he'd swallowed hard on the figures, the decorators were already in some of the houses, it was fair to estimate the build complete on both sides of the street by Christmas, in fact he'd be surprised if most weren't occupied before then.

The contract to develop the other side of the street had gone some way to setting off the phenomenal cost of underpinning, if he was lucky he'd just about break even but that wouldn't satisfy Eddowes and Cheetham. They'd followed him today, breathing down his neck, protecting their interests and making sure they didn't miss a chance to stand under the spotlight, take a bow and be recognised.

With a hefty sigh Dick turned the key in the ignition, suddenly he felt hungry, breakfast had been no more than tea and a cigarette, not his usual start to the day but his stomach had baulked at the thought of porridge. Olive would doubtless want to know what the Queen was wearing, it was the way of women, naturally interested in what amounted to no more than trivia. As he'd been explaining to Her Majesty the principle of a back boiler hot water system he'd found it hard to believe that being first and foremost a young, married woman, she could hold any real curiosity for something so colourless and dull. Surely the Royal Show, with its many exhibits, would engage her imagination far more than modern plumbing and the benefits of piped gas. But for the council it was a coup, a royal stamp of approval for their enterprise and placed them ahead of their rivals in the local authority stakes. Dick began to understand all the more why his dad had sometimes employed questionable methods. Colver, thankfully yielded well, Mitchell Street was another matter. He'd heard that folk were cynically describing the groundworks as preparation for his mausoleum, it was ironic then that from the day the first earth mover went onto the site, in his mind Dick buried Charlie Holbrook beneath that build, every ton of aggregate and cement, every length of steel, each brick, tile and chimney pot made sure not a trace of Holbrook would ever leach out.

Dick drove home recounting as he went, pale peach coloured two piece with matching feathered hat, cream gloves, cream handbag and shoes, diamante brooch in the design of.....? For the life of him he couldn't remember, a flower, he couldn't go wrong with a flower surely. It wasn't much to ask after all, Olive's requests had ever been modest, fortunate given what would be his financial situation very soon.

A sudden pang of hunger from a belly that could be full of nothing but wind caused his foot to put more pressure on the accelerator, sod it, sod the bloody lot, what was done was done.

"Do come in Olive dear, what a lovely day again, sunshine entices everything, there's a peony flowering in the garden, I can't remember it ever looking so splendid, and a thrush is rearing young amongst the ivy on the back wall. Basil insisted the ivy be cut back, he believed it eventually weakened brickwork if left, Patricia and I agree that it looks so much more attractive than a bare wall and the birds must have somewhere suitable for their purposes. If one day the wall collapses at our feet we shall attribute the event more to Basil's intervention than to an ingress of ivy. In the meantime we enjoy the delightful song of the thrush and advance in hope."

Florence led Olive through to the sitting room where Patricia and Annie were perusing various leaflets and sheets of advertising material, which Patricia had gathered at the show, among them a particularly colourful catalogue of

'Wheatcrofts' Roses', the nursery specialising in that most English of blooms, the front cover displaying the Princess Elizabeth rose, one of their most popular varieties, a delicate shade of pink and abundant of petals.

"Hello Patricia, Mrs.Eddowes, the show was a great success I understand, it was all Mrs.Plowman could talk about this morning. She attended with her sister, although I do believe their attention was centred on the royal party more than on the trade stands." Realising they had no idea who Mrs.Plowman was, Olive quickly added, "Dorothy helps me in the house, only a couple of mornings each week, I've been better lately, I suppose I ought to manage without her, I know I could, but she's such a kindly woman with a growing family it doesn't seem right to dispense with her simply because my health isn't too bad at present, it's but a small amount of money though I imagine it's welcome in the Plowman household."

If such a revelation didn't incite Basil to send the back wall crumbling to dust then nothing would, an act of pure generosity and kindness, he'd be retching into a bucket wherever in the ether his day of reckoning had sent him! Florence's expression gave no hint as to her thoughts, she smiled warmly at her company, yet to Florence they were more than fanciful imagination. Patricia's need of pills, Caroline's need of funds, Julia's need of fulfilment, behind every dark cloud that appeared overhead, Florence pictured Basil, shrewdly manipulating its passage.

Over egg and cress sandwiches and locally grown strawberries the women chatted easily and any awkwardness at the beginning was very quickly gone. Patricia's account of events at Wollaton the previous day was both informative and entertaining.

Feeling relaxed, Olive related much of what Dick had told her about the Queen's time spent at Mitchell Street, she omitted his less than complimentary remarks about William and Gordon Cheetham, he'd obviously found them an irritation, 'if it hadn't been for the lass I'd have scratched the buggers off but a man can hardly relieve his torment by scratchin' when her majesty is at his elbow', had been the actual words used, redeeming himself by adding, 'she's a strikingly intelligent young lady, knew the significance of lime mortar'.

Annie put down the catalogue. "Harold's family lived on Mitchell Street," she said with a smile that indicated happy memories. "My first husband, Harold Boucher, his mam and dad, Samuel and Sarah, their other son Frank and five daughters, Nora the eldest of all, and Gertie, Jean, Mavis and Maggie. Number 69 Mitchell Street, it was such a happy house, how they all fitted into it was a mystery but they did. Nora when she retired from her work, went back there to look after her mam, until Sarah died, like most of the residents Nora's now living at Bilborough in a prefab. I have only good memories of number 69 apart from two exceptions, Harold was killed in an accident at the slaughter yard where he worked, seeing Sarah and Samuel's despair was more painful than words could ever rightly describe, then again when I had to tell them that Frank had been killed in France, the telegram had been sent to his wife, Ivy, she couldn't face the ordeal of telling them herself, both sons gone. But the world moves on and the new accommodation your husband has built there will provide happy homes for many folk I'm sure Mrs.Woolascroft."

"Please call me Olive, we do meet odd times, mostly at the post office, I've never considered us strangers, and not just because of Dick's association with William, you always smile and say 'Hello', not everyone does," she hesitated, "might I call you Annie? I feel even less of a stranger now, knowing your connection to No.69 Mitchell Street, Dick was determined to buy Mr.Holbrook's side, the odd numbers, I suppose he could have just as easily set his sights on the other side of the street, but I'm glad he didn't."

Ally, friend, acquaintance, Annie didn't feel the need to categorise Olive, in a strange way the name Woolascroft had lost some of its bite, perhaps it was remembering No.69 that enabled the softening, from now on it would be impossible not to connect Dick with Harold's childhood home, so in this instance only good had come of association. From someplace Harold's wisdom prevailed still, 'go on, have a mint, it'll do yer good', and it always did.

Annie's thoughts were pleasant as she sat watching Olive and Patricia deciding which rose to order for the garden. At the back of her mind something began to niggle, then she recalled the evening William had arrived unexpectedly at Winchester Street, asking about a man called Holbrook, so that was why the name had seemed familiar to her, she must have heard it when Nora spoke about her landlord. William's curiosity she'd sensed was far from idle, in the case of William it never was.

"Annie dear, we are all agreed, those strawberries were delicious, I know you have to return to Charles before too long but do tell him I shall call in a day or two with a treat, by way of thanks for sparing you today."

Florence's words brought Annie back to the present, and a glance at the clock, to her need of hurrying home.

Dick sank into the armchair, he'd been on his feet all day, up ladders, clambering over roof joists, checking with the masons that all was on time, their progress being vital to the decorators following on, but Mitchell Street was taking on a new look and despite his underlying anxiety over figures he considered the transformation an achievement of which to be proud. Each and every door would open to a living space that granted convenience, a practical kitchen, a small but adequate bathroom where a family might keep themselves healthily clean, bedrooms sufficiently clad to prevent winters of miserable shivering and a living room with a hearth freed of gloomy black lead, instead casting a cheerful smile in bright, shining tiles over the occupants gathered around it.

"I'm making a drink, which would you like, tea or coffee?"

Olive called out from the kitchen. His wife had not yet seen the new housing, yesterday her interest had extended beyond simply her majesty's mode of dress, Olive had stopped short of actually asking but he'd sensed her desire to be shown progress. His dad would never let his mother onto a building site, but life for women was changing, why shouldn't Olive see if she expressed interest?

"I'll have a glass of cold water, it's still so warm." He unfastened another button on his shirt and blew into the air.

Today the decorators had declared the paint to be drying almost as fast as they applied it and men working in the loft spaces had been running in sweat.

One of the carpenters brought his dog into work with him every day, a sort of grubby-white coloured mongrel the men nicknamed 'Scrubber', a good natured creature, plied with morsels from the numerous dinner bags, happy to wander the site like an affable foreman offering encouragement. But this afternoon it had been necessary to hose down poor Scrubber and making no attempt to shake itself, as would be a dog's normal practice following a good soaking, it flopped onto a mound of damp sand and steamed, looking like a piece of salt cod just lifted from boiling water.

"Here you are, would you like a piece of fruit as we didn't have pudding?" Olive placed the glass of water on the table beside him.

"No ta, it's too hot to be bothered with food. I suppose you had something suitably light and appropriately fancy at dear aunt Patricia's," he said, somewhat sarcastically.

"In fact we had egg sandwiches and some strawberries that Annie brought with her and very nice they were too." Dick looked at Olive enquiringly.

"Mrs.Eddowes was there, William's mother, you've heard me say before that Annie and Florence are good friends."

“Annie now is it?” Dick was still tetchy over the way William had pushed himself forward yesterday. “So what did you learn of Eddowes, anything that might help me fathom his mind? Some days I look at him and wonder what scheme he’s hatchin’, yer never see his true face, Cheetham I can read but that William, he’s deep.”

Although Olive didn’t say it, she nevertheless thought many folk would consider Dick to be ‘deep’.

“She’s a nice woman, we didn’t discuss William, or you for that matter. I did relate to them your description of the Queen, not so much her attire, they’d watched the royal car go by on Alfreton Road, but her informed conversation as you were showing her the council housing. Apparently Annie’s first husband and the family lived at Mitchell Street, Harold Boucher, he was killed tragically in an accident at the slaughter yard where he worked, very many years ago. It was so sad, they lost their other son in the Great War. Two boys and five girls lived with their mam and dad in one of those little houses. Annie described it as a happy home but for those two dreadful events.”

“Eddowes has never said, he actually made the first approach of Holbrook yet he never mentioned it.” Dick was bewildered.

“Well Annie is William’s stepmother, Mitchell Street was where her first husband lived.” Olive nibbled on a rich tea biscuit, content and pleased at being able to impart some knowledge of the place that so occupied her husband’s time.

“I wonder which side of the street they lived,” said Dick idly curious as to whether they’d dwelt on the odd side, significant to him, or the other, less relevant.

“Number 69, Annie remembers it so vividly, she was obviously very close to the family, 69 Mitchell Street was Harold Boucher’s happy childhood home.”

Dick stared at Olive in disbelief, as though in some, incomprehensible way his wife had this instant introduced him to the dreamer at No.69, to the smiley, optimistic face before which he'd promised great things. In his mind Dick grasped the outstretched hand and shook it warmly, relieving those persistent anxieties. Regardless of all else, a promise was a promise.

CHAPTER FIFTEEN

October

Emily rubbed the blackboard clean of chalk and looked around the classroom, the bell had sounded ten minutes ago, with the usual hurried routine her pupils had put away their books and placed their chairs upside down on their desks, a practice adopted in order to make life a little easier for the cleaner. Though the room was now empty of all life but herself, as Emily's gaze travelled the rows of desks in her mind she could see the faces, some less inclined to merge, holding her thoughts.

Alan Cook, a rogue if ever there was one yet frustratingly lovable. Peter Hughes, so studious, his spectacles of government issue, turning that young face to old, as though contained in his head might be years of accrued knowledge and wisdom. Little Daisy Underwood, similarly afflicted with those unkind glasses but applied for the purpose of correcting the vision in just one eye, sticking plaster obliterating any chance to even peep through the right hand lens, it changed altogether her natural prettiness. Serving as a comforter when a lesson presented challenge she would pick at the plaster causing the edges to fray and grow grubby, sadly her mother seemed not to notice and Emily looked forward to the day when Daisy would shed her ragged plumage and emerge a beautiful swan.

But it was Timmy Hitchins who caused Emily the most concern, so quiet, unusually so for a child of nine years, especially a boy. She'd observed him at playtime standing apart from the rest, reluctant to participate in their games. It was as if he tried to make himself invisible, his grey pullover and trousers, his long grey socks providing a measure of camouflage at the spot he positioned himself, by the pebble dashed wall of the lavatory block. Perhaps if his face could break to a smile that glimpse of brightness might attract a would be playmate.

His arithmetic was average, his writing neat but at reading he lagged behind. Emily had sat with him, quietly encouraging progress, yet still he struggled. The one thing she was desperate not to do was embarrass him in front of the others by asking him to read aloud, children could be cruel and while he could scarcely be described as a happy well integrated member of the class Emily had seen nothing to suggest Timmy was being teased or bullied, if anything she'd detected bewilderment amongst the others, not able to understand his detachment.

It had been just six weeks ago that Emily had walked through the school gates as Miss Eddowes, teacher of class four, Harrow Road School. She could sympathise with nervousness, College had instructed her well and the results of her finals had been excellent, yet despite arriving for her first day bearing these endorsements, when she'd been introduced by the Headmaster, Mr.Bishop to those expectant little faces in her class, Emily's stomach had turned somersaults and every squeak of the chalk when her unsteady hand jarred its passage across the blackboard had sent a rush of bile to her throat.

Such timidness very quickly eased in the company of twenty eight children who made no judgement of her, apart from Alan Cook, he'd raised his arm and ventured to observe, 'the seam up the back of your stocking's crooked Miss'.

She walked to the classroom door and was about to open it when she noticed something on the floor, beneath one of the desks. A pencil sharpener but not the regular type, this one was made to look like a football. She picked it up and slipped it into her pocket, it had been close to David Tucker's desk but could have easily rolled away from where it fell, she would hold it up in front of class tomorrow, the rightful owner could then make claim.

Mr.Bishop and Miss Cooper were in the staff room, everyone else had left.

"If you hang on just a minute Emily I'll walk with you, I've only to put these books into my bag and grab my coat."

Doreen Cooper was a friendly woman, indeed all the staff were pleasant, but it had been Doreen whom especially dispelled Emily's initial nervousness. They caught the same bus, though Doreen got off three stops before Emily, her chatter was always easy and most days they shared a chuckle. A woman in her late thirties and now happily engaged to one of the foremen at Bonham's, she'd felt able to speak to Emily of her first fiancé, he'd been killed in Normandy so close to the end of hostilities that it had inflicted on his family and Doreen heartache too great to bear. 'We fell to pieces, nothing functioned, I tried to teach but the poor children witnessed me in tears, I was granted a fortnight off. So little changes in just two weeks but what could I do but carry on, never were lessons so automated, Miss Cooper, the robot'. Doreen had related the tragedy to Emily with tears so close by one more word would have opened the floodgates.

"Come on, if we run we should just catch the No.13." Doreen was of slight build but tall and her long legs propelled her at quite a pace, Emily had sped along the pavement with her before, marvelling at her agility, shoulder bag heavy with books Doreen could nevertheless cover the ground like an athlete, so familiar with the surroundings she knew every raised paving and all the potholes, successfully avoiding them without lessening her stride.

Sometimes the bus would be about to pull away but presumably the regular conductor had got to know Doreen and would lean out from the platform, one hand poised over the bell, while pretending to wave a touchline flag with the other. Today they were out of luck as the rear of the No.13 could be seen in the distance.

"Sorry Emily, you'd have caught it if you'd not waited for me."

"It doesn't matter," said Emily, "we'll walk on towards the next stop, a 56 will likely be along soon." She hesitated, briefly undecided over her next remark. "What are your thoughts on dyslexia? I know some teachers are sceptical and view it as modern day nonsense, but we can no longer stand a child in the corner with a dunce's cap on their head. At St.Mary's the subject was debated and given credence, the notion being that for whatever reason, some don't recognise order in a word, they are blind to sequences that others register without difficulty."

"Why do you ask, is it just a general question or do you relate the condition to one of your pupils? I have an open mind, it strikes me entirely plausible but Mr.Bishop," Doreen sighed, "he'd pooh-pooh it as laziness and lack of ambition, I've not yet seen a dunce's cap come out from his desk drawer but more than a few moths fly out with his teaching methods. I remember at around the same time I started here Laura Innes applied for a post, she got it. Her young man was lost too, she tried to continue but after a little while she returned to Birmingham where her folks lived. Laura would get frustrated at the intransigence, she placed great emphasis on the importance of reading, be it the wording on a cigarette packet or a volume of the classics. She believed that the ability to read opened the way not just to simple pleasure, but to unlimited achievement. Unlocked the mind and liberated curiosity, allowing it to explore the vast expanse of wonders, there to be discovered. Bishop is due to retire next year so who knows, perhaps a new, enlightened broom will sweep the dust from the methods drawer."

Emily's pace had slowed as she listened. "It was my uncle John, I know they would have married if he'd not been killed." She took a deep breath and explained. "Laura stayed at grandma's while she worked at Harrow Road, everyone liked her, she was lovely, but the telegram came, of course I was very young then so didn't fully understand all that was happening, grownups decide what young ears should or shouldn't hear don't they? Laura tried hard but I think we all reminded her so much of John that she couldn't bear it. She writes still, not frequently but every few months grandma receives a letter. Laura's teaching but she doesn't mention a young man, I'm sure grandma hopes one day a letter will arrive, which tells her that Laura has found happiness. Isn't it strange how life weaves us into its pattern? The reason I asked you what you thought about dyslexia was because of Timmy Hitchins, I feel convinced he suffers from at least a degree of it. I want to help him, if he could read more confidently then I believe his shyness, his remoteness from other children would become less. At nine years of age his days need to be happy and well used, isn't it my job to make them so?"

"Try to give him more of your time, the most able will progress naturally. We could really do with some new books, that would help, we've been using the same ones for years, children are drawn to something different, especially when it's bright and fresh. When I go to the public library if there's a book with a colourful sleeve and crisp, unthumbed pages I always take that one out, I can't resist. Please ask your grandma if she will remember me to Laura when next she writes back to her. I wonder why the pattern has to be so dark in places. I liked Laura too, admired her in fact. I've been at Harrow Road all these years since and made little difference, if Laura had stayed she'd have made Bishop stand in the corner." Doreen laughed. "I shall mark my effort accordingly, 'not good enough'."

At that moment the sound of a car horn from behind caused both women to turn around, a vehicle was slowing down, the driver indicating his intention to pull up at the curb. For a few seconds the women were puzzled, it was Doreen who first realised who it was. She waved and called out.

"Hello Jack, I didn't know you had a car, you're a dark horse."

Only then did Emily recognise the man inside the vehicle, it was cousin Jack Wainwright, she'd not seen him since before starting at college.

“Do you need a lift ladies?” Said Jack, a wide grin on his face, “Chauffeur Jack at your service.” He leaned across to open the passenger door. “Maiden outin’, just collected it from the garage, Nat Broadbent found me a good ‘en, not too pricey. I’m afraid one will have to sit in the back. Hello young Emily, I confess it was Doreen I recognised, Ted an’ me work together at Bonham’s yer see.”

Emily at once made the connection, Ted was obviously Doreen’s fiancé, clambering into the back seat she laughed.

“All I can say Cousin Jack is that you are a far more attractive catch than the No.56 bus, is Myra alright?”

“Everyone’s fine Emily, I believe Myra bumped into your mam a few days ago in town, they ‘ad a good chin-wag. Of course we’ve both been kept abreast of events through your grandma Annie, proud as punch she is, of both you and Mathew.”

Doreen was confused, it showed in her expression, so Emily embarked upon an explanation.

“Jack’s mam, aunty Gertie had a brother Harold who was grandma’s first husband, my uncle George’s dad. But he was killed in a dreadful accident when uncle George was just a baby and eventually grandma remarried grandad, who’d been left with my dad and his younger brother uncle Freddy, when his wife died. Myra has always been like family because of aunty Edna and uncle Billy although they were no actual relation. Edna sadly died several years ago, she was grandma’s very best friend and Myra’s mum. Uncle Billy is a sweetheart, everyone loves him to bits, he used to be Harold’s best friend, I know it all sounds very complicated but it isn’t really , is it Jack?”

Jack smoothed his hands over the steering wheel and a look of deep satisfaction spread across his face.

“Next Saturday I’m takin’ Billy for a ride, I told Myra that before I take anybody else I’m goin’ to drive Billy up Strelley an’ out to Papplewick, show ‘im summat different. ‘E never asks for owt. Since me own dad died Billy’s been there for me, a rock. We went through some rough times Myra an’ me, Billy would quietly steer us through, never make a song an’ dance about it, I love that man an’ I don’t mind sayin’ it however soft it sounds.”

By now Doreen had abandoned all attempts at establishing who was related to whom but felt compelled to ask if he really did want to give Emily and herself a lift, shouldn’t they catch the bus and save the honour for Billy?

“You two damsels in distress can serve as my practice run,” said Jack, with a roguish twinkle in his eye. “Hats on backwards here we go.”

Jack stretched his arm out through the car window to indicate and put his dummy foot over the pedal, with a quick look in the rear mirror he gave a wink to Emily and off they went.

Doreen began to chat to Jack about Bonham’s and her fiancé Ted, while Emily sat behind them quietly pondering all the memories the last fifteen minutes or so had stirred. She reached for her hanky to blow a sniffle from her nose and her fingers found the pencil sharpener, which she’d completely forgotten about. How easy it was to forget, not until this afternoon had she in a long time thought about uncle John. Laura wouldn’t have allowed Timmy Hitchins to fall behind in his reading and neither would she, Mr.Bishop or no Mr.Bishop.

“I’m popping round to see Doris and Arthur for a little while,” said Celia, “while it’s quiet, your dad’s gone to Arnold and Mathew’s........”

“Out with Wendy Eathorne,” said Emily before Celia could complete the sentence. “He goes off so casually as if he was only nipping to the shop for a stick of liquorice, but we know different don’t we Mam.”

“Don’t tease him Emily, she’s the first young lady he’s been really smitten with, Mathew’s old enough to do what he likes in his spare time, leave him be. You'll be off with a chap one day and the last thing you'll want is your brother making fun."

The back door closed with a thud, though the kitchen window was open but a crack the draught was enough to send the door hard into its frame before Celia could grab the latch. Emily returned her attention to the exercise books on the living room table where she sat, smiling over her mam's words of caution. Mathew was in love surely that entitled her to a little sisterly mischief.

Meanwhile outside Celia wrapped her cardigan tightly about herself and hurried. It had got progressively windier throughout the morning until now, at mid-afternoon the trees were virtually bare of leaves from the relentless blow. Accumulations of withered foliage banked up against those walls offering sanctuary.

"Yes, got one!" Celia called out loud in her delight at having caught a leaf before it touched the ground. Another silly superstition but it pleased her, despite her promise to Beryl she'd not yet found a four leafed clover. Celia slipped the leaf into her pocket, no one had ever said what to do with a leaf once caught but good luck must surely be kept secure. In her mind the lucky horseshoe from her wedding cake, the good fortune bead given her by the Indian selling tea towels, the little brass Jack o' lantern talisman that came from her mother's house and now a lucky leaf, all would hold blessings in store, to be granted Celia's children at a time when they most needed them.

She reached the Bateman's back door, knocked once and went in, Doris kept it on the latch until dark but insisted Celia have a key, 'just in case dear'.

Emily licked the tiny gold star and stuck it to the page of Peter Hughes' exercise book, she'd set a spelling test, he'd answered all correctly. She left Timmy Hitchins' work until last, she sighed from frustration, out of twenty words only four easier ones were spelled correctly.

A knock came at the back door, purposeful, then twice more, whoever it was banged on the door loudly, so's to be heard above the noise of the wind.

“Botheration, persistent so and so.” Emily was tempted to ignore it and muttered tetchily as she went to the kitchen to answer. “Oh it’s you.” Standing at the threshold his hair blowing wildly across his forehead, trying to protect a bunch of chrysanthemums with one side of his jacket was Connor.

“Yer know Emily, you’ve all the charm of a gumboil, overwhelmin’ so it is.”

“Is that all you Irish ever talk about, charm?” Emily felt far from gracious, why wasn’t he with his sweet Miss Pearl.

“To be sure, we’re charmin’ folk yer see, over there ‘tis in the air, we breath it in from birth to death, invisible to the eye but a thing of beauty to the heart.”

Less than impressed Emily said. “There’s no one here, they’ve all gone out, must have known you were coming.”

Connor’s roar of laughter irked Emily all the more but if her mam discovered she had been rude it would upset her and Emily didn’t want that. While things between her mam and dad seemed better, still she sensed a tension, dormant for now, underlying but never far below the surface.

“You better come in before you're blown inside out.” Emily held the door tightly, defying its determination to slam, once closed she crossed to the window and shut it. “Mam cooked chips at dinnertime, she likes to let out the lingering smell of the fryer but in this gale enough’s enough.”

“When I wer’ walkin’ along, just before I reached the house, a branch came down off a tree on that central bit where all the grass is. It’s enough to make a nice bit o’ firewood so I nipped across the road to nab it before someone else does. I had to tuck me flowers inside your front gate while I did it, I’ve put the branch in your front garden on the bit o’ lawn, if yer tell me where your dad keeps his saw I’ll see to it, won’t take me more than ten minutes, just long enough for you to put the flowers in water an’ get the kettle on, the chrysanthemums are for your mother.”

The way he'd presumed she'd not been doing anything important annoyed her, Beth was likely shampooing her hair, she certainly wouldn't be puzzling her head over Tommy Hitchins. Emily's thoughts were unworthy as she held the kettle under the tap.

"Dad keeps tools in the shed, you'll have to look for a saw, I dare say there's one somewhere. Don't let the door slam, it shook the house when mam went out to the Batemans."

She took the flowers from the table and reached a vase down from the shelf, wondering how she could return to her marking in the living room without inviting Connor's nosiness.

Unable to resist she went to the window of the front room, there he was, in the teeth of the wind, jacket off, shirt sleeves rolled up, sawing up a sizeable branch of birch tree. Strong arms, broad back, unpolished, as God made him. The kettle began to whistle on the gas stove, Emily clenched her fingers in frustration.

"All done, I've stacked it in a corner of the coal shed, the twiggy bits'll do for kindlin', needs to dry out a bit but the branch wer' dyin' back, that's why it came down." Connor came in through the back door, his cheeks flushed from the weather. "Where is everybody then? Why aren't you out enjoyin' yourself on a Saturday afternoon? He pulled out a chair from the kitchen table and sat down.

Emily poured the steaming tea into cups. "Mam is only next door you must have heard her speak of the Batemans, Mathew is with his young lady and dad has gone to Arnold, why or what for I've not the slightest idea. I'm marking a spelling test, or trying to, some of us still have work to do at the weekend you know. That's the difference between a job and a profession."

"Well thanks for enlightenin' me, I've often puzzled over it but now it all makes sense. Them 'ladies of the night' pursue the oldest profession there is, so they say, an' I've heard that a Saturday can be their busiest day, I bet they give marks out o' ten an'all, I can just imagine it, 'you can do better' or 'try harder next time'. Emily's face turned bright red. "You asked for that Emily Eddowes, I've not been to college, nobody's ever given me a diploma but I've a brain an' I use it, I can even spell snob, e.m.i.l.y."

"Drink your tea Connor O'Shea, leave me alone." Emily hurried away to the living room.

Connor sighed, picked up his cup and went after her. She didn't speak as he crossed the room to stand behind her chair. He looked over her shoulder at the open exercise book on the table in front of her.

"What age are they?" He asked.

"Nine years mostly," she replied somewhat grudgingly but if conversation had moved on to the children then she would tolerate it.

"That poor little sod's strugglin', only got four right," said Connor, genuinely concerned. "Our Seamus wer' awful slow with his readin', mam had the patience of a Saint, she'd spend hours tryin' to help him. I reckon some young 'ens are frightened by school, they miss home an' their mams, teacher's the big bad wolf out to get them, poor little buggers, their brains shut up like a clam. I can picture mam now sittin' with Seamus, his readin' book open on the table, paper an' pencil ready. He could read the small words no bother but any with more than four or five letters an' he'd be stumped. Mam'd write down the longer words, one at a time, but spacin' the letters out, so they looked no more than part o' the alphabet, then she'd get Seamus to write down the word properly underneath where she'd written it. Gradually he began to understand, to recognise sequences. Yer see, he wer' at home, with the person he trusted most in the world, his brain stayed open an' he took it all in. Perhaps this kid's mam ought to sit him or her down an' try the same thing, who knows, it might help." He swallowed the last drop of his tea and was about to walk away.

“Show me exactly what you mean,” said Emily, “use this piece of paper, any word will do.”

He put down his cup and took the pencil, writing clearly, spacing the letters evenly he wrote,

t r u c e

truce.

Taking the pencil from his fingers Emily put a tick alongside the word. Though she didn’t say it, if Mrs.O’Shea’s approach worked for Timmy she would give Connor a pass, with merit.

One week later.

Annie had read the letter twice already, Francis wrote in such a way it was as if she sat with her, actually there chatting. Charles had declared himself to be aching all over and inclined to stay in bed so Annie had carried up breakfast, fetched his newspaper from the shop, taken him soup at midday, just minutes ago taken him a cup of tea and biscuits, and now sure in her mind that he wouldn’t be leaving his bed until the morning she dared to put several pieces of coal on the fire, picking them up with her fingers, if he heard the sound of a shovelful falling on to the grate he’d likely cast aside his aches and descend the stairs semi clad to retrieve all but two nubs, his prescribed amount. Last night by 8o’clock the room had become quite chill, it was apparent he intended no further nourishment of the sinking embers so Annie had filled a hot water bottle and found relief beneath the bed covers. She dare not ask why they must sit by such a feeble hearth, she spent no more than was necessary each week, neither of them had a large appetite, she cooked every day but in modest amounts. Their clothes endured, her skill with a needle and thread enabled that, yet Charles seemed intent on limiting comfort, as if denial in old age edged body and soul closer to demise in a state of readiness.

So to sit with her letter from Bonthorpe, the flames now growing higher in the grate, the house granting simple peace, allowed Annie hope of good things still to come. Faith and Richard were expecting a baby, she took the folds of notepaper from the envelope and again cherished the words written upon them. It was dated October 25th.

Dear Mam and Dad,

In our great joy and excitement we have merely shrugged our shoulders at the drop in milk price, gazed up stoically at the barn roof, damaged in last week's gales and waded undaunted through the deluge of rain water still occupying every gateway, all these events now insignificant alongside Faith's wonderful news, our first grandchild, due in April. The cows must wonder why they are serenaded with such gusto at each milking, I hear Freddy in song from indoors, a window open at the first catch provides more than enough chance for his cheerful melodies to fill my work space.

Grace is delighted of course but it was the reaction of Ivy and Reggie that touched my heart. They both look very old these days but when I gave them the news both tired faces were transformed. Molly is already knitting, isn't it wonderful how something so natural and familiar to all families can vitalise in an instant. Faith is remarkably laid back and relaxed, Richard's brother is as droll as ever, referring to it as 'the first lactation', he's brought a brand new galvanised bucket, onto which he's painted in bright yellow letters, 'Faith' and hung it up in the dairy.

I shall leave you to pass on the news to all the family, I know you will enjoy telling them.

The activities at Huttoft seem to increase almost at a monthly rate, they've recently secured an order for their barley from the brewery at Lincoln. Last year they bought in more acreage. It seems demand for the grain has almost exceeded supply, as Freddy says, be it a white pint or a brown one the farmer is key. Harold works all hours and Elizabeth sees little of him, so she has joined her local Women's Institute, 'a strong band of women sweeping the nation', is how someone described it, you can imagine the sort of comments that provoked among the menfolk! Elizabeth is undaunted and good for her.

I have begun to redecorate the living room, while most folk set about the task of 'spring cleaning' at that most appropriate time of year, on a farm the outdoor work is great and must take priority. Having put it off for so long it's now a source of shame, and anticipating visitors next April (big hint) I am putting able to it, only very straightforward, cream emulsion paint but it will be a good job done. Freddy says if I behave myself he might consider some nice new carpet, Grace and I have already been into Spalding to choose it. In the words of the song, 'Love is the sweetest thing'.

Must close now and get the meal on, take care and much love to everyone there.

Francis.

Annie smiled down at the letter, so many miles separated her from Bonthorpe yet never had she felt apart from Freddy and his family. Like George he included her, his plans, his ambitions, always he was open as he'd been when a boy. Hilda tended to 'do' first and tell of it after but never did Annie have to wait long to hear all about whatever happened to be her latest exploit. William seemed to confide in no one, she'd sensed for some time that Celia found far more pleasure in her friend of old, Rosie Spooner than she did William. Mathew and Emily had their own lives to lead, both loved their mam dearly but they couldn't fill the gaps that William's behaviour created.

Annie sat alone, her husband only a short staircase away, yet the house could have been empty but for herself, so distant was he. Not until the next tray was due would she hear a word to break the silence. The thought of Celia growing old in similar fashion brought actual pain to Annie. Rousing herself she quietly put two more nubs of coal on the fire and opened the damper, the flames responded, feeling like friends, cheerful company making the room less bare of life.

A sound caused her to look towards the scullery, the back door latch fell softly into place.

"George." Surprised to see him, her smile proclaimed her happiness. "Come and sit by the fire," she said in lowered tones, how pathetic it was that a fire needed to be so covert.

"Hello Mam." He crossed to the hearth and quietly asked, "Has dad gone out or is he.....?" He looked up at the ceiling.

"He said he felt aches all over, he's stayed in bed today, I don't think it's anything to worry about."

George wouldn't say it to upset her but he nevertheless thought she was right, a doctor wouldn't deem it cause for concern but it worried George, what sort of life did his mam have, certainly not a normal one. He unfastened his jacket and sat opposite her. "I suppose there are mixed blessings Mam." He smiled and held his hand out to the fire. At times George too had sat wondering why Charles would seemingly prefer to die of pneumonia rather than allow the grate a shovelful of coal. More than once last winter he'd called to find his mam working in the scullery with her coat on while Charles sat in the corner of the living room, staring at a fire that wouldn't warm a passing spider.

"We've had a letter from Francis, Faith is expecting a baby, they're all thrilled. You must read it and tell Liza, then by the time I've been to Celia's to give them the news and called at the salon to tell Hilda, all of Edna's family will know too." Annie handed him the envelope with such delight. George took it from her fingers and placed it on the arm of the chair, then he reached for her hands, holding them tightly between his own.

"There's something I have to tell you Mam, I've been at Susie's, Liza's there now, they all are, Annie and Alec, Myra and Jack. It was just after dinner, they'd eaten and Susie was clearing away. Billy had gone from the table to sit in his chair. Gillian was helping her mam and went from the scullery to pick up the tablecloth. She says Billy tried to stand, she supposed he needed the lavatory, but he fell forward, slumped to the floor. He's gone Mam, doctor came within ten minutes but there was no pulse. It was so quick Billy couldn't have known anything."

Annie's eyes filled with tears, she swayed back and forth in silent despair. George could no longer contain his own grief, he'd stayed strong for Liza, but this, he couldn't bear this. He took deep breaths and managed to speak.

"It's hard for Joe but Tommy is there now, I have to go back to Liza Mam, she needs me."

Annie nodded her head. "I should go to them."

"Leave it until the morning Mam, let Tommy do what he must, I'll tell them that you wanted to come but I persuaded you to wait 'til then, you can imagine what it's like there, they'll need you all the more tomorrow. I feel so sorry for Jack, he was that proud last Saturday to take Billy for a ride in the car, and Billy was made up, Susie said he was like a kiddie just back from their first trip to the seaside. That was only one week ago but we all know that Billy has barely lived since losing Edna, they're together again now Mam, picture them, I can and it's a happy picture, keep that vision safe, don't let anyone harm it." Again George looked up at the ceiling, "You hold on to it Mam." He handed her the letter. "Next time, I'll read it next time." He kissed her forehead and squeezed her hand. "Freddy will come, he loved Billy too, don't cry Mam, Edna would tell us all off if she saw us in tears. They're together again, Mr.and Mrs.Dodds, a first class union if ever there was one and we've had the privilege of knowing them all these years."

Annie watched him walk away through watery eyes, heard the back door latch as it closed quietly behind him, she felt unable to move herself but then came the sound of movement above, Charles called out from the top of the stairs.

"I heard a voice, was it George?"

He'd probably been listening though he'd pretend not to have heard. The fire had no place to hide. Annie wiped the tears from her cheeks with her hand, Charles was descending the stairs, Annie's chest near' crushed her lungs from the weight of pain yet she couldn't truly wish Billy to be anywhere else but with his beloved wife Edna.

"It's not even November yet." Charles kicked in the damper with his slippered foot before lowering himself to his chair. "Who's the letter from?" His eyes settled on the envelope in Annie's lap, she passed it to him, the writing on it almost illegible where falling tears had reached the ink.

"It's from Francis, a lovely letter as she ever writes." Annie hesitated, swallowing hard. "George came to tell me that Billy has passed away, just after dinner, he needed to hurry back to Liza, they are all at Susie's."

Charles made no reply, he took the letter from the envelope and began to read, what was going through his mind Annie couldn't know.

The flames had hastily retreated ahead of the threat, as if aware Charles would not abide their company. The fire and Annie both knew their lot.

"Is everything alright, yer seem very quiet?" Rosie reached for her coat, "I won't be long, I've a magazine for 'er, if she don't read it she'll look at the pictures."

"Your mam needs to be here, you can't keep dashin' over there every few hours. I'll go to see her landlord and 'ave a word with 'im, 'e won't care whose name's on the rent book so long as 'e gets his money. Thomas an' Samuel can live there, they're more than capable o' lookin' after the'selves but if it'll give you peace o' mind they can come here for their tea every day.

I hadn't realised until this mornin' that Thomas wer' so serious about Janet Yeats, at the funeral he never left her side, put 'is arm about the lass like 'e were desperate to keep her from hurtin'. You'd think that by now I'd be used to it, most times I go through the motions wi' me heart intact, but this mornin' I shed tears an' hurt with 'em all. Seein' our Joe so distraught, tryin' his best to get Susie through it. Myra wer' barely able to stand, her body convulsed with grief, leanin' on Jack an' tears streamin' down 'is face. Annie an' Alec Yeats, both suddenly showin' age, as poor lass stood at graveside she looked so much like Edna, an' George didn't know which way to turn, holdin' on to Liza, an' her lookin' like a ghost but desperate to help 'is mam, I thought Mrs.Eddowes might collapse at one point, perhaps she would 'ave if Freddy an' Mr.Smithfield hadn't been there at either side of her.

The young 'ens, Billy's grandchildren tugged at me heartstrings, when I held out the dish of earth an' saw their faces I could hardly get me breath. All of Annie Eddowes' family attended, Freddy came all the way from Bonthorpe, but no sign o' Charles. I reckon 'e's one o' them folk as can't face funerals, while some I see at virtually every one we do, if they're not there I know they must be poorly. Old workmates o' Billy's from the telephone exchange, all o' Jack Haynes' family, Billy loved that lad Victor. So many standin' in the cold, not just payin' their respects but grievin', unable to contain the pain of it, an' I wept with 'em.

I couldn't help thinkin' back, almost a couple o' years I reckon, we were instructed by a solicitor for the family. I don't see how I could rightly refer to it as a funeral. There was to be no notice placed in any newspaper, no service, simply burial. The daughter was there but nobody else except Moira Lacey, Bob's wife, she was the neighbour who found the old chap an' called the ambulance. The daughter wer' pleasant enough but all out dealin's wer' done through that Russe fella, so I didn't 'ave much to do with her. How could it be possible for a man to live his three score year an' ten, an' at the end of it all be so disregarded?

That much love, an' grief from the loss of it surrounded Billy Dodds' grave today, even the cemetery seemed to hang its head, utterly bereft. At Edna's funeral it was their dad's need of support that stayed the family, they 'ad to physically hold him fast or 'e'd 'ave fell into the grave with her. It makes yer realise just how much we all need one another. Your mam shall come to live here Rosie, her grandsons'll understand."

Rosie stood with tears pouring down her cheeks, Tommy got up from his chair and took her in his arms, neither spoke. Throughout their married life they'd shared moments of silence, when simply the presence of the other satisfied every need without the adornment of words. In stillness Tommy could feel his wife's heart beating steadily, his constant, the rhythm, which strengthened his own.

Rosie rubbed the back of her hand across her face and sniffed away emotion. "I'll only be an hour, Beryl will be home from school soon, tell 'er she needs to clean out them rabbits or there'll be no more talk of gettin' a budgerigar."

Andrew looked about the room, he imagined Henry Wicks sitting opposite him, chatting easily as so often they would do, then in his mind the image changed and became Rex Madden. Both gone, and now Billy Dodds too, Andrew felt intense isolation.

The funeral this morning had added great weight to his loneliness, the sight of Annie's misery and being unable to soothe it had sent his spirit to a place very dark. Ironically it had been Freddy who had rescued him and the words Freddy had spoken kept flooding back in waves of emotion.

‘Come stay with us for a few days Mr.Smithfield, a city man should see the ways of a farmer. I grew up in the city but the countryside beckoned to me like those looms and sewing machines must have called out to you. Humour me, allow me to be proud, to show you all that I’ve done. I’m not William, I don’t have his motivation, my pace is slower, my achievements won’t stand for generations like housing, crops come and go, animals live and die, but a man can put a certain stamp on his land, a stamp that identifies him and it’s that one thing that as a farmer makes me proud. Come to Bonthorpe, look at the farm, walk the fields with me and say, Freddy you’ve done well. Dad has never once told me that’.

The upset of Bobbers Mill felt to be so far back in time, yet over the years it had regularly tormented Andrew, and now Freddy’s invitation, genuinely extended, challenged his confidence. Had he any right, was he really entitled to speak those words Freddy needed to hear when they should come from his dad. What Andrew would give to have a son such as Freddy, what pride he would feel.

Charles had ever been a mystery to Andrew, his obvious contrariness, which Annie so loyally tried to hide. His apathy in business that led him to sell up. His blinkered view, from choice, even a horse given a chance would cast off its confines. But above all that, how could Charles bear to squander the privilege of telling a son like Freddy, ‘you’ve done well’.

When Andrew and Billy had sat watching the heavy horses at the Royal Show from out of the blue Billy had said, ‘Harold Boucher wer’ a smashin’ bloke’.

It had been the sight of the heavy horses pounding the ground of the show ring, muscles flexed in their effort to assist their handlers by pulling whatever the day’s labour required, that spectacle from Billy’s past stirred his memories. He’d told Andrew of Josiah Toft’s wagon that took the hides from the slaughter yard to the tannery, the way Harold would reach into his pocket for a mint and hold it out on the palm of his hand for the horse to take. Billy's reminiscences of the times he and Edna had shared with Harold and Annie had been an account of deepest friendship, then he'd added almost as a postscript, 'I don't believe Charles can help himself, Enid took his sense with her'.

Andrew was so grateful for that day at the show, those few hours he and Billy had spent together, talking, laughing, and lamenting the loss of a delicious Mazarelli ice cream. Following their return at the end of the war the family had found it too difficult to pick up the pieces, with the result that they'd never gone back to producing those wonderful ices. Now folk unwrapped what could only be described as an ice cream bar, which was then pushed into an oblong shaped, wafer receptacle, lacking all that tempting randomness every cone of Mazarelli's so lusciously displayed. Little children accepted it without question, having never known any other but for folk the age of Billy and Andrew, the modern ice cream experience represented an entire world of change.

Exhibits at the show had so thoroughly demonstrated the pace at which man's enterprise now began to leave far behind Billy and himself, Andrew had taken his friends hand and shaking it firmly said, 'Ours are now the simple years, the challenges all belong to the young'.

Andrew found himself drifting in the stillness of the room to a place of dreams. He closed his eyes, letting imagination transport him to Bonthorpe, to the farm, he was walking the fields with Freddy, seeing his pride, grasping his hand, and with such privilege saying, 'You've done well son'.

CHAPTER SIXTEEN

Late December.

"How about just there, that branch needs a bauble?" Annie encouraged Louise, her little fingers hesitating at the prickly needles of the Christmas tree. "Soon we shall be ready to put the fairy on the top, a few more baubles and tinsel then you can stand on a chair and fix her in place, where the wall lights will shine through her wings and make her especially pretty, like you."

Annie smiled down at the confused child, not old enough to understand grief, Louise knew only that her mam was different, she didn't laugh as she used to, the bedtime story no longer delivered those animated descriptions that engaged Louise's lively mind ahead of contented sleep and perhaps most troubling of all her mam displayed no excitement at the approach of Santa's visit. More puzzling to the child's innocence were her dad's well meant attempts to compensate, forcing his own cheerfulness until even one so young began to suspect pretence. For her brother Michael the situation took his nine year old mind to a place well beyond its natural dwelling, grandad had grown old and died, a fact the boy could accept, along with the tears and sadness but the misery of his mam and the plight of his dad he couldn't reconcile. Billy's death had devastated the entire family but Myra seemed unable to find a way past it, she functioned to the extent of putting a meal on the table and pursuing the housework as though programmed each morning by the turn of a switch. Trying to free his wife's heart from its weight of despair whilst hiding from their children his own mounting anxiety tested Jack's strength day on day with little relief but for young Michael's intuitive support. It would move Annie to tears that could find no release until she was out of sight, her walk from the bungalow to the bus stop being ever accompanied by a plea to The Almighty that no one would stop her and ask why she cried.

Christmas was only four days away, the city centre proclaimed the Season with colourful shop window displays and a tall, beautifully decorated tree adorned one end of slab square, lit at dusk by multi-coloured lights. This year feeling all the more festive having finally shed the limitations of rationing, folk made merry with abandon, which they considered 'well deserved'.

The previous evening George and Liza had gone to Thorpe Road, taking with them a Christmas tree, a box of the shiniest baubles Woolworths could offer, and several packs of gummed paper strips ideally suited to eager young fingers intent on making paper chains. Jack had gone up to the loft to bring down the box of decorations carefully packed away on the twelfth night of last Christmas and Annie had produced the fairy for the top of the tree, made from items found in her sewing box. This afternoon they'd set about the decorations as a surprise for Jack when he got home from work. Louise thread tinsel through the boughs while Michael wrapped the bucket in which the tree stood amid stones gathered from the garden with bright red crepe paper, transforming the dull grey galvanised pail, 'a sight for sore eyes' his happy description yet still his mam appeared numb. Annie had despatched her to the kitchen with the request for milk and biscuits for the children and some tea with a piece of Liza's sultana cake for themselves, Michael ever watchful had gone with her to help. Something had to be done, for everyone's sake and Annie racked her brain for a solution. Glancing at the clock confirmed half an hour was all the time she had before leaving to get her bus home, any later and Charles would create a scene, the play on the wireless occupied him until four, after that his concentration turned inward, his mood centred on the area about his chair, little existed or mattered outside the reach of his arm or the length of his gaze and compassion found entry to neither.

"Anybody home?"The back door opened and Charlie Jones, face beaming, stepped inside. "It's your friendly neighbourhood artist bearin' gifts."

Louise abandoned the tinsel and ran to the kitchen while Michael's face shed its look of anxiety and both besieged Charlie in their delight at seeing him.

Charlie Jones had that rare ability to raise the spirits of another without actual effort on his part, his personality gave off warmth, surely he must have his serious moments like everyone else but they were never apparent. He claimed the title of artist tongue in cheek, 'I may not paint people's faces but I do paint their lives' is how he put it. Inside folk's houses, the rooms in which they ate, washed and slept, outside, the walls, doors and windows that kept them from the elements. The day he and Bob Budgeon completed their painting of the bungalow's exterior on Thorpe Road Charlie had stood back to look at his work and said. 'it's smilin' sweet as the Mona Lisa'.

"I've had this in the van all day, Maureen asked me to drop it in on the way home." At the end of the table he put a parcel wrapped in colourful paper, along with an envelope. Charlie's hand rubbed Michael's hair. "Have yer been out carol singin' yet? Your dad an' me used to make ourselves a nice bit o' pocket money at this time o' year. We had an old malt tin on a bit o' string for folk to drop their pennies in. It got so we could tell by the way it clattered how much they'd giv' us. A sixpence made hardly any sound, we wer' pleased wi' a sixpence, a threepenny bit made more rattle 'cause it wer' heavier, that pleased us an'all. Pennies an' halfpennies made most noise, we'd be disappointed when it wer' only copper but every once in a while, somebody who was feelin' really happy 'ould drop in the old tin a florin or arf a crown, when one o' them big shiny silver coins went in they'd chime like the bells of All Saints an' me an' Jack'd sing another verse wi' a few nobs an' tiddly poms thrown in. It's a fact, folk allus give more when they're happy. This Christmas Maureen an' me couldn't be any happier, Shirley's goin' to 'ave a little brother or sister, next May, so if yer come round to our house Michael wi' a tin on a string we'll make it chime like the bells o' Notre Dame." Charlie burst into song. *'Christmas is comin' the goose is gettin' fat, please put a penny in the old man's hat. If yer haven't got a penny a ha'penny will do, if yer haven't got a ha'penny then God bless you'.*

"I'm so pleased for you Charlie, for you all." Annie was genuinely delighted. Charlie was well deserving of happiness and devoted to his family.

Myra's face broke to a smile, she actually smiled, pleasure showed in her eyes. "I am happy for you both Charlie," she said, "thank Maureen for thinking about us."

"Come here Mrs.Wainwright, give me a hug, I need a hug."

Myra chuckled and although she couldn't see them standing behind her, that sound, their mam laughing, brought joy to the faces of Michael and Louise in measure unseen for many weeks.

"Happy Christmas Myra," said Charlie, "wi' these two about it couldn't be any other." Looking down at Michael and Louise he gave a roguish wink. "Now best be on me way, can I give you a lift Mrs.Eddowes?"

Annie nodded. "Thank you Charlie, I'll get my coat." This day she was thankful to be leaving Myra with a trace of healing, it was a start and one they could build on.

Myra closed the door having waved them off. Jack would be home soon, she tried to picture him as a boy, singing carols with his best pal Charlie, counting up their takings in the old malt tin. If she made egg and chips for tea they could eat early and then Jack could drive them into town to see the big tree in front of the council house.

Louise stood holding the envelope that Charlie had brought. "Can I open the card Mam?"

"Yes, you can open it while I peel potatoes."

Within seconds Louise was calling out. "There's something inside the card."

Michael took from her fingers three tickets and read aloud. "Mother Goose, it's tickets for the pantomime, and there's a letter."

Myra left her task at the sink and sat down with the sheet of notepaper.

Dear Myra,

Shirley wants to go to the panto' and I think she's old enough this year to enjoy it, but if she had the company of Louise and Michael I know they would make it 'special' for her, I'm sure Charlie will have told you about the baby and future pantos' will hopefully include a brother or sister for Shirley but until then, please may we borrow the Wainwright family, Charlie says he's at a pantomime every day with Bob Budgeon and that Jack wouldn't be able to sit still long enough, men!

Love Maureen.

The tickets were for a matinee on January 14th.

Annie sat in the passenger seat of Charlie's van amid the various smells associated with his trade, linseed oil, turpentine, gloss paint and undercoat. Scraps of paper bearing hurried notes and reminders lay about her feet, while the pigeon hole beneath the dashboard overflowed with spent dinner wrappers and a couple of woollen hats. Adhering to the inside of the windscreen was a squashed beetle of some sort, Annie was trying to decide its identity when Charlie spoke.

"Sorry about the clutter Mrs.Eddowes, I shall 'ave a good clean up before we start again, Bob an' me are done now until after Christmas, folk don't want tradesmen in when it gets close, I don't blame 'em, it's family time."

"I'm grateful to you Charlie," said Annie, "to you and Maureen, I know Jack will have confided in you. Myra's been through a lot over the years, her nerves have been tested more than most but it will ease, she has tremendous strength really. This afternoon you made her smile, and learning that Maureen is expecting will set her to knitting, every little distraction helps."

“When I think back it’s hard to believe all that’s happened,” said Charlie, “Jack’s one o’ the best, ‘e never weakens, a bloke’s lucky if ‘e ‘as a mate like Jack.”

Annie retrieved a piece of paper that fell from the pigeon hole when they stopped at traffic lights.

“Don’t worry about that Mrs.Eddowes, this van is a sort of office an’ that pigeon hole is me desk drawer, perhaps one day I’ll have a proper one. Sometimes I wonder how a man manages to gather so much, not merely a desk, but offices, yards, workforce an’ a bit o’ swagger to get him noticed, hard work I suppose, an’ luck, surely some of it must be down to luck.

How’s your William gettin’ on these days, I heard he’d gone in with Dick Woolascroft? We did a bit o’ work for him at Mitchell Street, I suppose council were keen to move more tenants in, folk need to be housed and the council’s allus chasin’ revenue. To get the work completed Bob an me were offered hours, useful job, kept us busy for six weeks. I’m not one to pay much heed to gossip an’ rumour but one or two mouthy types are sayin’ Woolascroft took a loss on Mitchell Street. I aven’t sent in me bill yet, thought I’d wait until New Year but the decorators who began work on the site months back still ‘aven’t been paid. It’ll be alright I’m sure, the bigger the concern the less they like partin’ wi’ money, that applies to the council yer may depend, Woolascroft’s waitin’ on them for his final dues I shouldn’t wonder.”

“William’s not mentioned anything,” said Annie, “but seldom does he. I find it difficult to ask him about his business activities, he’s never been able to distinguish between genuine concern and nosiness.”

“You forget I said owt Mrs.Eddowes, Charlie Jones travels in hope, it’ll all come out in the wash.” He began to sing cheerfully as they drew closer to Winchester Street. Annie warmed to Charlie’s optimism, that wonderful personality of his, yet she feared trouble, William seemed to attract it and she too had heard people speculating over Dick Woolascroft's fortunes at Mitchell Street. All she could do was trust her niggling doubts to 'the wash'.

Emily knocked at the front door, this would be her fourth visit to the house and she dared to hope that a happier Timmy Hitchins would be at the threshold of Christmas, excitedly looking forward with his family to better times.

When Dora Hitchins had revealed to Emily the tragedy that had devastated them all, it had enabled her much clearer understanding of Timmy's quietness, his withdrawn behaviour when at school.

Timmy's elder sister Irene had died from meningitis at the age of ten, that had been a little over two years ago. At the time he and his infant sister had been taken to their grandma's, to be kept away from infection. When finally returning home to his mam and dad the trauma of being told that Irene had 'gone to Heaven' sent the boy into a remote world of his own, all efforts of family and friends failed to coax him out and it was their doctor who suggested a complete change of environment might help, new scenes, different faces may just ease away those bad memories. The family had moved from Burton upon Trent to Nottingham where Les Hitchins had secured a place at Briggs. They'd found a suitable house to rent through enquiring of James Cochran, the property agent and auctioneer, a man they'd discovered to be as quiet and contained as their own son. Timmy had been enrolled at Harrow Road School, where in the New Year little Susie would start attending. New scenes, different faces yet Timmy had continued to struggle until a few weeks ago.

Emily had taken courage and one Saturday afternoon called at the family's address where she'd carefully and sensitively explained her thoughts on Dyslexia. Dora Hitchins had in turn confided the recent history and their subsequent attempts at restoring Timmy's spirit. The anxious woman had been more than willing to be guided by Emily's conviction, which in truth had been strengthened by Connor O'Shea's description of his brother's experiences. Patiently and pleasantly mother and son had sat with pencil and paper, writing out the words over and over, reading sentences, enjoying the stories until now, almost at the end of a fraught year, young Timmy seemed to be grasping those all important sequences in writing, finding more confidence and his long absent smile.

A blurred image now appeared behind the mottled glass of the front door, it opened.

"Hello Miss Eddowes, come in, Dora's cuttin' Timmy's hair, she's nearly done."

Emily stepped inside. "Thank you Mrs.Lacey, is all well with you?"

"We're fine dear, lookin' forward to spendin' time with the family, it's what Christmas is all about isn't it, gettin' together?"

Emily liked Moira Lacey, the Hitchin's next door neighbour, she'd met her only a couple of times but the woman had a natural friendliness, not pushy or intrusive but comfortable, a genuine face among those prescribed by the doctor.

Timmy was just about on a chair, trying to wriggle his way free as his mam cleared his neck of hairs with a clothes brush. Susan sat at the table intent on some activity involving glue and glitter, the telltale clues being one sparkly cheek where her hand had rubbed at an irritation and a small piece of red crepe paper apparently stuck to her cardigan sleeve, waving with each movement of her arm, like a poppy head in the breeze.

"Hello Miss Eddowes," said Dora, "we were hopin' you'd call, they've been busy makin' cards, Les reckons homemade ones are the best, we've even made envelopes from scrap book paper, it's easy to fold you see. That's the second pot of Gloy an' I don't think the oil cloth will ever be the same again but most mantelpieces on the street will bear a special Christmas card, an' yours will too."

Susan required no further prompting, she hopped off the chair sending paper trimmings and glitter to the carpet and skipped across the room to the sideboard. She identified Miss Eddowes card by the pretty stick on label of a robin at the corner of the envelope, one of several that came in the post from the Spastic Society, a bright child, at only five years Susan couldn't yet read the names on the envelopes but she remembered what she'd been told, grandma's had a sticker with a candle pictured on it and aunty Maud's was the envelope with holly berries.

Eagerly she pressed it into Emily's hand. "For you, this one's for you."

"It's lovely havin' a family livin' next door," said Moira, "old Mr.Holbrook was a nice enough man an' we allus got on but to hear children playin' an' bein' able to chat with Dora makes the place come alive. Bob an' Les hit it off right away, they've a shared interest, bowls, they go regular' for a game o' bowls." Moira lowered her voice to a whisper so's Dora wouldn't hear in the kitchen where she'd gone to shake the towel and hair trimmings outside the back door, and put on the kettle. "I can't begin to imagine what it must be like to lose a child, Bob sees it workin' as he does at Handley's but I'm not sure I'd cope."

Dora came back into the living room. "You can open your card while you are here Miss Eddowes," she said giving Emily a look that implied the children would be disappointed if she didn't.

Sliding the card carefully from the handcrafted envelope Emily's eyes fell upon a joyful medley of colours, red, holly green, gold and silver, 'Happy Christmas' spelled out in glitter across the top. Inside written in Timmy's hand, To Miss Eddowes with love from the Hitchins family, only one word displayed evidence of correction, a second 'd' had been squeezed in before the 'o' in her name.

"I did that bit." Susan's finger pointed to the glitter while Timmy simply smiled, but it was a ready smile, not forced or faked.

"Thank you, it's the very best Christmas card I've ever received, it shall take pride of place on the mantelpiece."

Emily's thoughts at that moment turned to Connor. When he'd last called at Wollaton she'd sensed he was preoccupied with something. Whittle's men didn't finish until Friday, Saturday was Christmas Eve and Tuesday they were due into work again so it gave him no chance to travel home to Dublin. She imagined Connor would spend most of the weekend with Beth and the Searles. Emily had wanted to blurt out, 'come here for Christmas dinner', but how could she, her mam wouldn't have minded and though her dad would have uttered a token grunt of intolerance, come the day he'd have been civil, provided a tot of whisky was to hand, but Beth had doubtless claimed the day so Emily must 'deck the hall' with expected goodwill and welcome Wendy Eathorne to the table when she came for tea, at least Mathew was happy.

School was a daily distraction, it occupied fully Emily's waking hours but for two weeks the time was her own and irritatingly and illogically she wished for some of that time to be Connor's, she felt annoyed with herself, it was pathetic, yet on each occasion she'd called at the home of Timmy Hitchins the memory of Connor writing that word 'truce' drove her frustration further.

Mathew and his young lady seemed well suited, she did secretarial work, often covering for sickness or maternity leave, rather like a relief teacher but mainly for the legal profession. She modestly described her function as tying the ribbon bows around Wills and Deeds but Emily recognised Wendy's ability as being far beyond that, no doubt the first requirement of the legal secretary was complete discretion and the real nature of her work was securely bound between the folds of those ribboned documents.

Aunty Caroline had been especially interested on hearing of Wendy's work, presumably because of uncle Edmond's position with Chaucer, Caffin and Holt. It was perhaps unfortunate that neither of the boys had chosen to follow their dad into the legal profession, Nottingham maintained a goodly number of solicitors, all seemingly in demand, alive or dead mankind created a need of their services. Jonathon chose to study medicine and Gregory the Army, both admirable pursuits but requiring them to be miles away, this year they would be home for Christmas and Caroline had searched Burton's food hall for as many good things as she could afford, her student lodgers likewise homeward bound until the New Year.

"Try a slice of Tunis cake," said Dora, "I won it in the raffle at the Co-op it did have several little marzipan fruits on the top but Les can't resist marzipan so I'm afraid there's only one banana and a pear left."

The table still strewn with creativity they sat about the room with a plate on their lap and cup and saucer wherever a suitable spot presented itself. Emily sat alongside Timmy, so far this afternoon he'd been quiet, now gazing down at the piece of Tunis cake his mam had put on his plate he appeared pensive, then with no hint of uncertainty he declared.

"I want to join the Cubs, Alan Cook goes to Cubs and he told me they do all sorts o' stuff an' they go to places. Last summer they went campin' in a field. Alan knows how to thread a fishin' rod an' the best sort o' bait to use, he can recognise all the different birds' eggs an' knows where to find slow worms. I could start after Christmas, they have to sing sometimes but Alan says if you open your mouth wide an' look as if you know the words that'll do."

Emily looked across the room at his mam, for a minute or two the woman seemed unable to speak. Moira, their kindly neighbour granted Dora time to recover.

"We'll have to get you the uniform then, cap, shirt an' tie an' you best eat up that cake Timmy, a Cub needs his strength. Our Jimmy was in the Scouts, he thought about Boys Brigade first, but when he was a youth he had a mop of thick curls an' we didn't think that little pill box hat the Brigade wears would stay on his head, so he joined the Scouts instead. He loved it, reckoned he learned more useful lessons at Scouts than he did at school." Suddenly realising what she'd said in the company of a teacher Moira quickly added. "Intending no offence Miss Eddowes."

Emily was amused and not without a measure of accord, the three 'Rs' weren't sufficient knowledge by any means, practicalities held everything together, no one could exist on text book learning alone, be it Scouts or Boys Brigade, a youth would become a better man for owning common sense.

Timmy Hitchins was no longer remote from his classmates, his reading improved week on week, both Alan Cook and Connor O'Shea were deserving of Emily's gratitude. She took a hefty bite from her slice of cake, surely she was obliged to say thank you, it was only good manners, it was no skin off Beth's nose if she went to Denman Street, next Friday after Connor's work ended for Christmas break. The sweet, thick layer of chocolate on the cake melted in her mouth, coating her tongue with satisfaction, a truce, Miss Eddowes would so welcome a truce and Connor O'Shea had earned his pass, with merit.

Celia looked on the cake with some satisfaction, the first Christmas for many years that a woman might produce a Christmas cake, which could claim to have all the traditional elements, not least, the icing. She put the frill around it and smiled to herself, that more or less summed it up, rationing, life totally devoid of frills.

Mathew had gone to the Eathornes to see Wendy and Emily had declared her need to thank Connor for his help over a child's dyslexia. Celia had ventured to ask the nature of the condition, feeling bewildered at the notion that Connor was involved. Emily's explanation however had left her even more confused and so she'd set about creating the snow scene on top of the cake, a task within her own realm.

William sat in the living room watching his television, lately a number of things had become 'his', not exclusively, the family could use the gramophone, the wireless, the telephone, and the television but in the knowledge that such privilege was by his grace, not surprisingly it resulted in William often sitting alone. He'd been very quiet since his last Lodge meeting, Celia wondered if that too was subject to his grace and favour, the intrigues of the Free Masons she left to those with a wider understanding, such activities seemed far removed from the realities familiar to Celia.

Audrey Potts' dementia was now so advanced that even her living with Rosie and Tommy failed to lessen the anxiety dominating their days. The doors had to be kept locked or she would wander off and her actions could be unpredictable and distressing. The other day poor Rosie had found her mam with a tin of black boot polish, which Tommy had left on the stool in the scullery, Audrey had covered the entire front of the oak sideboard, in her way being helpful, and was proceeding to buffer it to a shine with one of Beryl's vests. They had to be constantly mindful of potential perils and the worry of not recognising any such reduced Rosie to a state of overwrought tearfulness by the end of each day.

Christopher and Beryl were cautioned to 'think for your grandma', but at nearly twenty one it was difficult to be ever reminding a young man when all the normal distractions of that age already occupied much of his mind and Beryl tried her best but when it all got too much she sought comfort in the company of her rabbits, and her budgerigar, which for its own good now lodged at aunty Kathleen's. One day Audrey had unfastened the door of the cage allowing it freedom, fortunately liberation went by way of the stairs and Rosie had managed to catch it in a bedroom with the help of a food umbrella. Celia's sympathies were genuine indeed and she called on her dear friend frequently, sitting with Audrey whilst Rosie went to the shops. It was a world apart from William's activities, he wouldn't understand frailty of the mind and the tragic consequences. When Celia had remarked one evening over their meal that he and Tommy had known one another since boyhood and that to ask Tommy if he'd like to go for a drink, just a casual hour at The Standard, would be a considerate thing to do, William's response had been beyond pathetic.

'Perhaps you'd like me to reserve our plot in the cemetery while I'm about it, a lot of business gets conducted over a pint you know, Handley's will attend to every detail and Tommy is Handley's after all'.

Celia had refused to bite her tongue telling him firmly that along with his television and his gramophone he could enjoy 'his' own society. Within minutes the black bedevilled disc filled the living room with *'Cigareets an' whisky'*, his adopted anthem and Celia had run next door to the Batemans before her ears ached as much as her heart.

Now she lowered the Christmas cake into the tin, it looked good, Mathew and Emily were no longer children, past all that excitement of being so close to Santa's visit, yet as a mother Celia still determined herself to make the time special.

The telephone began to ring, apparently William was not expecting a call as it continued to ring. Rubbing her fingers over her apron Celia hurried to the table in the hallway and picked up the receiver. "291233". She heard a series of pips and a click before someone on the other end of the line spoke, a man's voice, with a strong Irish accent.

"Is that Mrs.Eddowes, Mathew's mother?"

"Yes, it is."

"I'm sorry to trouble you but I need to get a message to my son, Connor O'Shea."

Celia was surprised but pleased to actually speak with someone from Connor's family at last, she responded happily.

"Of course, and it's no trouble Mr.O'Shea, no trouble at all, in fact our daughter Emily has gone to see him this evening, he helped her with a pupil whom she teaches you see and she needed to thank him."

Callum was finding words difficult, the last thing he wanted to do was alarm Connor but the lad should be aware, given the problems of the past Callum was anxious not to let Connor think he was the last to be told of any family matter.

"It's his mother Mrs.Eddowes she's been taken poorly, God love 'er she should have said before, pain, she's been in such pain but not until yesterday did she tell me, tryin' to hide it from the young 'ens she was. She's in the hospital and they're doin' tests but they suspect gallstones. Could yer explain to Connor, tell him no need to rush back home, this close to Christmas he couldn't get a ferry anyway, I'll............" The pips began again and then another click. "Sorry I've just put in more money. His sister Kathleen is a good girl she knows how to keep house while Maggie's in hospital, I'll ring again if that's alright with you, as soon as I know more. Regards to all of yers' for the season, especially that son o' yours Mrs.Eddowes, he's a grand young man so he is, a credit to yer, the fellas at factory all miss him." Again the sound of the pips. "Thanks a lot for everythin'."

The line cleared and with a heavy sigh Celia lowered the receiver. The poor man was quite clearly worried, gallstones, William would surely sympathise, he knew all about the pain of gallstones.

"Who was it?" He called out from the living room, despite his almost certain intent on listening Celia's few words must have failed to reach his ears, she explained and at once noticed a look of irritation come to William's face. He spoke tetchily." "I'd rather go now than tomorrow, Christmas Eve, what Connor's supposed to do I can't imagine but if they want him to know then I'll take the message and drive Emily back, save her bus fare. I'm surprised she's gone there, I thought she had little time for him, never appeared overjoyed to see him when he called here. Women, easier to plumb the ocean depths than to fathom the female mind. If he wants to ring Ireland then he can use the phone but he'll have to reverse the charge, long distance won't be cheap."

Celia rued her misplaced faith, William's sympathies were woefully limited and plainly did not extend to Connor's mother in Dublin.

William had driven but a few yards down the road when in the light of a street lamp he could see Emily walking along the pavement towards home, he pulled over and stopped, winding down the window on the passenger side he called out.

"You're back quick, was it worth bothering?"

She walked across and leant into the open window looking thoroughly fed up if not a little vague.

"He wasn't there, Barry Pointer opened the door and asked me in, so close to Christmas it seemed a little mean not to spend a few minutes with him. He insisted on pouring me a 'festive drink', as he called it, a cherry brandy, I had to beg a dry biscuit or it would have gone straight to my head, even then I negotiated every curb on the way to the bus stop like a toddler, whatever do they add to the cherries for goodness sake?"

William couldn't help but smile to himself, for all Emily's worldliness, gathered in London, she was innocently simple when it came to 'drink'. In his own experience alcohol at its introduction didn't merely shake the hand but the entire body and given chance would seize any opportunity to establish a long term relationship, he kept it at arm's length most of the time, only indulging its advances when his mood was so inclined.

"Well I'll have to drive to the Searles then, Connor's dad phoned with a message, Mrs.O'Shea is in hospital with suspected gallstones, not a thing the lad can do but they want him to be aware so muggins here must be the messenger boy."

Emily huffed sarcastically. "Oh you won't find him there, he's hob nobbing with his rich lady friend, Mrs.Bradshaw, Barry says Connor was invited to dine at Castle Road this evening, on Burton's finest no doubt."

Barry's words had actually been, 'He's gone for a tipple an' a mince pie with Mrs.Stanford, he won't be late back, the old lady's in bed by nine', but Emily was peeved and feeling less than gracious, if it wasn't Beth then it was Connor's ridiculous association with folk way out of his league.

"Bugger," said William, "I'll have to go there to tell him." Then a thought appeared to amuse him, he chuckled. "Connor can use her telephone to ring Ireland, you know how soft your mam is, she's likely to let him use mine when I'm not there without reversing the charge, better done on Patricia Bradshaw's phone, she can afford to please herself whether or not he puts his hand in his pocket. Do you want to come, extend your gratitude or whatever it is you feel so duty bound to offer Connor?"

"No, my thanks can wait, it doesn't matter. You had gallstones, they're painful aren't they, I hope Mrs.O'Shea will be alright?"

Emily's pique had begun to subside and now a measure of concern entered her mind.

William slowly wound up the window as he spoke. "Anything that afflicts the gut is painful, sticks an' stones break bones don't they? Let's hope the woman has bodily strength, at least a war didn't cast the stones, nothing hurls the sticks an' stones like a war does."

He lowered his foot on the pedal and as the engine revved Emily stepped back watching the car grow smaller in the distance. Connor was sure to be upset but Beth would be on hand to offer comfort, Emily sighed, if only she had a bottle of cherry brandy she could go to her bedroom, lay on her bed and spend Christmas under the spell of alcohol, ho, ho, bloody ho!

William pulled up outside the house that in the past had so impressed him, it sat square on its foundations, boldly looking out, even under night sky showing no sign of weakening, no trace of fatigue the less resilient abodes displayed when illuminated by the street lamp's glare. All those years ago he'd bowed to Stanford's authority misguidedly believing it would lead him to success, now young Connor stepped across its threshold with his head full of misplaced notions and only experience could teach him the true nature of things. Patricia Bradshaw would no more grant Connor entry to that exclusive, inner sanctum of wealth and influence than she would lead him to the sacred source of the Nile.

He'd be quick, deliver the message and take his leave, glancing in the mirror he straightened his tie, his chin looked shadowy, he'd not bothered to shave this morning, so be it, he owed them nothing, he was entitled to ring their doorbell clean shaven or otherwise, yet as William's steps took him ever closer to the front door an irrational nervousness crept over him, it tightened his breath, stifling an urge to curse out loud.

"Why it's William," said a surprised Florence, she opened the door wider, a genuine smile on her face, then an unsettling thought made her say. "Oh dear, please don't tell me that your mother is ill, I've not seen Annie for several days and she did look quite pale and tired."

"No, mother is well Mrs.Stanford, I need to speak briefly with Connor and I understand he's here, with you and Mrs.Bradshaw."

"Yes, do come in, Connor is chatting to Patricia, they have these discussions regularly, he's such a bright young man and Patricia does believe in encouraging the young folk but I'd swear she has a soft spot for Connor, I can understand why. He straddles both worlds, working hard as he does, driving heavy machinery yet constantly looking across the desk at those who daily drive him. Patricia now takes a much broader view of industry William, but enough of that, it's good to see you and this close to Christmas I am able to wish you and your family the very best of the Season, it is my sincere pleasure to do so."

"Thank you Mrs.Stanford, I shall pass on your good wishes to Celia, Mathew and Emily."

William's response was gracious enough but given with vague intent. She led him through to the drawing room where a lively fire crackled in the hearth, below a holly bough tastefully decorated, Connor's face on seeing William showed surprise and equally so Patricia's. Florence announced it was Connor with whom William wished to speak, Connor's immediate thought was of how William could know he was at Castle Road.

"Your father telephoned," said William, "your mother's been taken to hospital with suspected gallstones, he doesn't want you to rush back home, as he rightly points out there's little you could do but understandably he wanted you to know of the situation."

Patricia got to her feet at once. "You must return his call Connor, speak to your father, if only to ease his mind, the telephone is in the hall, please do feel free to use it."

Inwardly William felt smug, just as he'd predicted, it was worth the errand, calls to Ireland could go down on Patricia's bill.

"That's very kind of you Patricia but they don't have a telephone at home, dad would have been ringing from a public phone box." He glanced across at William as though seeking confirmation.

"It was Celia who answered lad so I can't tell you anymore than I have, your dad'll likely call again when there's more news, being Christmas I don't suppose many operations are performed unless considered emergencies. My gallstones got sorted out in the Yankee hospital at Leghorn, over there pretty much everything was an emergency."

“So you had gallstones Mr.Eddowes?” Said Connor. “Didn’t know that, anyway you’re livin’ proof they can be removed an’ the patient cured, poor mam she don’t deserve it, she’s had her share o’ pain one way or another.” He fell silent for a moment, pensive. Then he asked. “How did you know I was here?”

William appeared amused over something. “Emily went to Denman Street, according to Celia she needed to thank you for helping her with a boy from her class at the school. Your mate asked her in and gave her a cherry brandy, our Emily’s probably getting over it still, not used to alcohol you see, like her mother, too correct for indulgences. Now I’ve passed on the message I’ll be off, we’ll get word to you Connor when your dad calls again either at Denman Street or at the Searles’, I expect you’ll be spending most of Christmas with Beth won’t you?”

Connor nodded, while Patricia crossed to the side table.

“At least have a drink before you leave William, I rather think that whisky is your preference.”

He was about to decline but a niggling curiosity overruled his impatience to leave, Connor had been in animated discussion with Patricia, as Florence had led him to where they sat together William couldn’t help but overhear a snippet of their conversation.

‘It makes good sense, I’ll have a word with Dick.’ What was it that Patricia intended speaking about to Dick?

She put a glass of best malt in his hand. “Is all well with you William, we see and hear little of you these days?”

He could hardly respond truthfully by saying. ‘I’d feel a lot better if your nephew weren’t being so cagey’. Dick had avoided answering William’s concerns over Mitchell Street, rumours were circulating at The Lodge, both Cheetham and William had been quizzed at the last meeting, trying to sound confidently dismissive of their speculation proved difficult when in fact neither of them felt assured. If there really was no fire then the smoke was a mystery Dick needed to explain away. But so far he'd ducked the issue, his last excuse being Christmas.

'Not the time to be dwelling on business Eddowes, we shall go over everything in the New Year'.

Now William cast a lure, hoping to catch something if only a minnow.

"I'm surprised you're not a significant voice at Woolascroft's Mrs.Bradshaw, you are a relative of Dick's after all and having someone such as yourself on side could do him nothing but good."

Connor and Florence sat mute, both seemed to be engaged with their own thoughts. Patricia smiled, took a sip from her glass of sherry and quietly replied to William's remark.

"Dick has both you and Gordon Cheetham, I dare say there are times when he feels three is a crowd but with neither of his brothers sharing his aptitude for the trade Dick could do no other than accept a situation, which his father I am totally convinced, would have found intolerable. Fred allowed only the one son, Dick, to share the reins, immediate family and never to be a crowd. Dick is not his father however and even if he wore the same shoes and walked across the same thresholds, I am not immediate family but related only through my marriage to Anthony.

All that aside it is long past time you stopped addressing me as Mrs.Bradshaw, Patricia, please William. Our mothers are the best of friends, so should we be."

William forced a smile and swallowed the last of his whisky, whatever it was she and Connor had been discussing evidently would not be revealed to him tonight. Young people often chatted openly, Emily seemed to be softening in her opinion of Connor O'Shea, she had yet to deliver her thanks, if he casually mentioned the conversation between Patricia and Connor and the curious nature of it, then Emily might be more successful in discovering what lay behind their exchange. He got to his feet.

"I really must get back to Celia, try not to worry Connor, I'm sure your mother will receive the necessary treatment and make a full recovery. Thank you for the drink, Patricia, and a happy Christmas."

Florence went with him to the door. "I am fortunate William to have Annie as my friend and you are even more so to have such a fine mother, who regardless of events will always be 'on side' as you put it, she will do you nothing but good."

Florence had listened to the previous conversation recognising William's intention, the way he fished for answers to his own concerns, one face for show, another hidden. William could think of no words to make appropriate reply, nodding from politeness he bid Florence, "Goodnight" and walked away down the path, the beam from a street lamp allowing him to see two boys about to open the gate. Startled, they looked at one another and began to sing a carol, *'O come all ye faithful'*. William pushed past them and into his car without utterance, their singing ceased.

"Miserable bugger," said the one, while the other sniffed resignedly.

"Ignore him Phil', there's allus one stingy sod that can't be happy whether it's Christmas or Easter, we'll go next door an' see if we can prise a shillin' out o' them. Not all posh folk who live in nice houses are tight fisted, we got 'arf a crown from Mrs.Woolascroft last week remember, and a bar o' chocolate, she told us she enjoyed our singin' an' all, nice lady.

Since we moved into one o' them new places on Mitchell Street our mam's had nothin' but good to say about Dick Woolascroft. Reckon if she had one she'd hang a picture of him on the lavatory wall. No more shiverin' in a perishin' cold outside privy, not a word of a lie, sometimes in winter my hand'd be shakin' that much piddle'd go everywhere. Now we've even got a fancy mat to stand on, if mam'd put one down in the old place it'd have floated out under the door. Mod cons' Phil', that's what they call 'em, soon everybody'll 'ave mod cons'."

Alan whistled the tune of 'God rest ye merry gentlemen' and rattled their money tin, it sounded good, life felt good, despite the stingy old bloke who'd never be a merry gentleman while he had a hole in his backside!

CHAPTER SEVENTEEN

January 1956

"Daft bugger could have killed himself, what possessed the man, Whittle's pressin' charges, no bloody wonder. Drink, 'e must have downed a skinful, when coppers got there he wer' shoutin' like a madman. No man could knock to the ground a bloke the size o' Bill Whittle wi' out a might o' booze behind the punch. Stood in line o' the bulldozer cursin' Jerry to hell, picked up a piece o' rock an' hurled it like a grenade one o' the workmen told me. The drink addled his brain, they reckon 'e must have pictured a tank, a bloody tank an' when Whittle stopped the thing an' got down to confront the bloke his arm went out afore Whittle had a chance to open his mouth, bash, down 'e went an' the madman still rantin' over him, all the names under the sun.

Apparently they've told all the pubs not to serve him, off licences an'all. Some are sayin' it's a quack 'e needs, one o' them shrinks as feels your bumps. The war ended years ago, you moved on didn't yer?"

Nat Broadbent shook his head despairingly before sticking it back under the bonnet of Jack Wainwright's car where he tightened a jubilee clip, retrieved a couple of spanners from their temporary resting place on top of the engine before bringing the bonnet down with a satisfied 'clunk'.

"There you go Jack, just a bit o' perished rubber, all it needed wer' a length o' new hose, call it ten bob."

"I heard that Whittle wer' drivin' because the Irish lad's away, if O'Shea had been on the receivin' end o' that fist he'd likely be in a worse state," said Jack, "not a mark on Whittle's face, didn't break the skin but when he fell backwards he struck a piece of old angle iron, bruised his kidneys they reckon. O'Shea's gone home to see his mam, the woman's had some kind of operation, I only know through Annie Eddowes tellin' Myra. I've never been one for the drink, I can enjoy a pint in and out but thank God it don't tempt me like it does some."

Jack reached into his pocket, took out his wallet and handed Nat the money. "It can take a long time to forget hellfire Nat, sounds like the poor bloke's broke down, if only his problem could be cured with a bit o' new hose an' a jubilee clip. Thanks again Nat, I'll be on me way, 'tis past you're closin' up time but I knew somethin' weren't right so stoppin' on me way home from work seemed sensible. I said I'd drop Myra, Maureen Jones an' the kids at The Theatre Royal on Saturday afternoon, the panto, it's easier for Myra than the buses, they get busy especially when pantomime's on, I don't like her standin' on her bad leg."

Jack got into the driver's seat, turned the key in the ignition and waved back to Nat as he drove slowly across the yard to the road. He'd heard that the madman, as they described him, was Fred Sealey. Jack didn't know him as such but he'd heard of him. The fact that Nat mentioned no name suggested he was unaware and Jack's sympathy caused him not to speak it. A tank, may God help Fred Sealey, for it was likely no other could.

Connor sat on a capstan by the edge of the quay watching folk move about the place, only few in number, for today's chill did little to encourage a walk by the water unless of necessity. 'Dress warm Connor, the cold will find your marrow'. He smiled to himself, dear mother still nurturing, still minding him like a child. Perhaps a mother never sees the grown man, in her mind she pictures her child always. Connor had once heard someone say that a man lives his life in the mind, meaning mankind, womankind, all mere mortals.

All that he'd planned to ask, that he'd hoped to learn must wait, but for how long must it wait? His natural father had been killed in the war, that much he'd been told. If he'd not been wanted then to hell with them, that had been

Connors damnation of this man and the heartless grandad who'd sought not once to see his grandson.

Callum had met him at the dock, hugged him with those strong arms. ''Tis grand to see yer lad', his words ever genuine. But then he'd sighed, put a serious tone to his voice, a pleading look in his eyes and delivered a hard reality. 'The doctors were concerned at your mother's weariness, the gallstones they've removed and the operation went okay but they did some other tests, her heart's not good, there's a weakness, a murmur they called it, a heart murmur, given her age she needs to be careful, rest a bit each day and the biggest threat is stress, she mustn't get stressed'. His dad had looked hard into Connor's eyes, it was the unspoken words which carried the deepest meaning. He knew what Callum meant, don't go near the old haunts, stay away from trouble. In fact Connor had no intention of sitting down with the hot blooded types his past pursuits had led him into the company of. They were all talk anyway, tongues swilled in liquor 'til they worked loose, gabbled nonsense.

'What was grandad called and did he live in Nottingham'? That had been his intended question. It made sense, surely there was more to it than the fact Mathew Eddowes came from that place, that Callum worked for Raleigh and they based in Nottingham. Connor had not once heard his mother's maiden name spoken of and how could he ask her now when such a question was bound to upset her, he had a family, his family, why did he need to know about those who'd not cared, such a question she'd recognise as being laced with a dark curiosity. He now had money, a chance in life, affairs of the past were not his to claim, neither did they come with his inheritance, he was Connor O'Shea, the all English Irishman, a rare breed, yet he felt special for all the wrong reasons. Only one person might enable him to feel good in himself, Emily Eddowes, she tormented his thoughts, interrupted his sleep while sweet Beth, Miss Pearl administered regular doses of comfort, a pleasant medicine that slipped down easily but more and more left a nasty taste. He should tell her, somehow find the words and the courage to own up to the fact that it all started with a bet, then it simply drifted along, enjoyable, a relief from the workaday routine. Emily was out of reach, why couldn't he accept the truth of it.

The evening she'd come to Denman Street to tell him about the boy at school, for a moment he'd thought there was a spark, a reason for her visit beyond the spoken 'thank you' for what she deemed to be his part in enabling one of her pupils, Timmy Hitchins. He'd felt almost envious of the lad when she'd described her efforts, even spending time with him at his home, sitting by him, going over those troublesome words. But she couldn't resist, Emily just couldn't help herself, always some sarcasm, not merely a friendly prod in jest that meant nothing, but a belittling as Connor perceived it to be.

'Patricia Bradshaw will savour you for as long as the notion agrees with her, then she'll eat you alive, don't flatter yourself Connor O'Shea'.

When he'd responded by saying 'your grandma considers Florence and Patricia to be her friends, Emily for a second had hesitated before remarking, 'grandma sees everyone as a friend'.

Out of respect for Annie Eddowes he'd let the subject drop, on the few occasions he'd been in her company at Castle Road with Florence she'd given him a genuine smile and treated him as though they'd known one another for years, a nice lady whose virtues seemed not to have travelled down the line to Emily. Anyway, Barry's return from the off licence with one or two samples of Wrenshaw's ale proved a timely intervention and Emily's conversation had become immediately benign.

'Did you have a good Christmas Barry? My brother's sock drawer was somewhat overwhelmed, perhaps you enjoyed a little more variety, men are difficult to shop for. At least his young lady has imagination, Wendy gave him a season ticket for Trent Bridge so's he can watch the cricket, or bat n' ball as Rosie Spooner refers to it'.

Connors first thought had been lucky Mathew, not so much for receiving the season ticket but for having a girlfriend who understood the male mind. Beth had carefully wrapped in festive paper a leather bound diary, which on several evenings since he'd sat poised over, pen in hand. As yet only one entry, dated January 7th recorded Connor O'Shea's activity, it read. Packed a bag, leave early tomorrow, will ask the question this time.

"How's it goin' Connor, heard you'd emigrated, kicked you out already have they?"

The figure of Pat O'Driscoll pausing briefly to cast his cigarette end into the water caused Connor to step down from his perch on the capstan and call back.

"Too good for 'em Pat, they only want the tame variety, the likes o' you an' me put the fear o' God in 'em."

O'Driscoll now lowered his backside to the capstan. "Heard your mother wer' bad, in the hospital, she'll be right pleased to see you, your Seamus is a good lad but yer know what they're like, first born holds the soft spot."

"Gallstones," said Connor, "they got rid of 'em but her heart's not strong, must have peace an' quiet, no stress. I have to go back tomorrow, work, they let me take the week off, good hearted, compassionate buggers." Connor laughed.

His gaze now intent on the water he stretched out his arm to point. "What's that over there floatin'?" He moved closer to the wharf's edge. "Find a stick Pat, one long enough to pull it in."

A bottle bobbing on the surface, out of reach by about four feet had caught Connor's eye. Leaning against the wall of the building several yards to the rear of where they stood Pat spotted some lengths of timber, hurrying off to gather one suitable for the purpose he shouted over his shoulder.

"Keep it there."

Just how Connor was supposed to achieve that he couldn't imagine but Pat had never been the brightest of fools.

Carefully Connor eased the bottle towards them. "Slowly, slowly, catchee monkey," he whispered under his breath lest the wilful bottle hear. "Gotcha." Flinging the length of wood down and reaching with his other hand Connor managed to clutch his prize.

"I've always wanted to find a message in a bottle," he said, "America, it might have travelled across the vast Atlantic Ocean Pat, from the U.S. of A."

"Bet you'll 'ave to break the fickin' thing to get the message out, the cap'll be seized, rusted on, sure to be."

On closer inspection Connor couldn't help thinking that it appeared too clean to have been at sea for long, even the remains of a label with two letters still evident an M and an I.

"It's a bloody Miwadi bottle Pat, probably got chucked in yesterday." The cap succumbed to Connor's grip, the small roll of paper fell easily into his hand, he read the words written upon it. "Whoever finds this message, please write to me, I am Molly Hanrahan and I live at Garretstown, County Cork, Ireland."

"Jeysus, what a waste o' time that wer', stick it in a rubbish bin afore some other poor sod gets excited for nothin'."

Pat lit another cigarette to soothe his vexation, while Connor rubbed his hands together, the water was bitterly cold, he cupped them over his mouth and breathed into them until his fingers found feeling enough to put the roll of paper back into the Miwadi bottle and to screw on the cap as tightly as he could.

"No Pat, who are we to crush a dream." He pushed the bottle into his pocket. "I'll do what I can for Molly, tomorrow it shall go with me on the ferry an' when we're out in deep water I'll through it over the side, help it on its way, it'll be somethin' significant to write in me diary, 'today I sent Molly

Hanrahan's dream on its way'. Likely it'll be the only thing worth enterin'." Connor sighed, "I'm off to spend what time I've left with me mother. I'm not sure you're right about first borns Pat, reckon I've giv' her more sleepless nights than any o' the others." He slapped O'Driscoll on the shoulder. "Live a good 'en Pat," and with his hand over the bottle to prevent it from slipping from his pocket he walked away.

Pat retrieved the length of wood from the ground, took the half smoked cigarette briefly from his lips and spoke into the air.

"A diary, Connor O'Shea writes in a dairy, would yer believe such a thing, bugger me!"

Connor lay wakeful, his brothers slept soundly, their easy breathing confirmed it. They'd sat that afternoon, just the two of them, he and his mother, knowing that tomorrow would bring the goodbyes, Connor worried for her health, his mother worried for his happiness.

'I'm glad you have your young lady, perhaps you'll bring Beth to meet me one day', she'd said with a warm smile, in that instant lifting the tired lines of her face. Then a more searching question. 'Are you settled working for this Whittle's firm'?

He'd replied, 'Yes', his mother needed to believe he was content, he could hardly say, 'if I brought a young lady to meet you mother I'd hope that it would be Emily, and that he wouldn't rest until he was setting his own wage'. General chat was the least likely to put any little seeds of doubt inside his mother's head so he'd simply described the Christmas decorations in Nottingham's city centre, the new look coming to parts of the suburbs, fresh development, the modern local authority housing that folk admired but which some said had made a loss for the developer, a man named Dick Woolascroft. At that point his mother had asked, 'is he a family man'? Connor couldn't see any relevance in the question but women forever interested themselves in things for which men held not the slightest curiosity. Only a few days ago Beth had lowered her voice and spoken softly in his ear. 'Valerie Perry is expecting they say'. Well congratulations but why that intrigue, why the whispering as though it were some kind of revelation, no, when it came to interests men and women were very different, men practical, women whimsical.

Tomorrow when he hurled the Miwadi bottle into the deep water his own dream would be cast with it, what an entry in the diary that would be if one day he could write, 'today Emily Eddowes washed up on my doorstep'. But young women like Emily never became 'washed up', she would travel far beyond Connor's threshold and be found by someone special, for all the right reasons.

The door catch rattled and Barry felt grateful for the sound, it seemed pathetic, he wasn't a child, yet alone in the house waiting for Connor's return made events all the more alarming.

Connor lowered his rucksack to the floor and stretched himself to ease a stiffness in his back from sitting on the train. While he'd ventured to stretch his own legs along the corridor once or twice, the need of saying 'excuse me' each time to a particularly tall man who straddled the compartment with the longest legs Connor had ever seen made the disruption awkward, besides which the train had been besieged by supporters leaving a football match, and being full to capacity and beyond, a seat was ever up for grabs, it could be taken with all the competition of musical chairs.

"What's up with you?" Said Connor, "You look like death."

"Summat bad's 'appened, real bad Connor. It wer' last Wednesday afternoon, some bloke pissed out of his skull went mad, come onto the works site, stood right in the path o' the bulldozer, shoutin' an' swearin'. It wer' Whittle 'isself drivin'. 'E turned off, stopped but then the bloke started hurlin' rocks. Bill got down, yer know what 'e's like, did the bloke back off, no, 'e let go a punch that took Whittle off his feet, went backwards to the ground, landed on a piece of old angle iron. Coppers come, carted the bloke off an' 'e wer' still shoutin', summat German Unwin said, the mad bugger wer' rantin' like 'e wer' in the war. We worked on 'til knockin' off time, Unwin drove Whittle home an' his missus sent for the doctor. Not so much as a scratch on his face but pain in his lower back, the fall bruised his kidneys the doctor reckoned, told Whittle to rest up. Well last night 'e got so bad missus called the ambulance, it don't seem possible, dead Connor, Bill Whittle's agonna."

"What's supposed to happen on Monday, do we go in as usual?" Said Connor, his mind now racing way ahead of Barry's.

"I s'pose, what else can we do, Unwin'll know. They've arrested the bloke, 'e wer' in a cell all Wednesday night, 'e's in there again now can't see him comin' out any time soon. Winchester Street, they're sayin' the police took him away from Winchester Street."

Connor lowered himself to a chair and was silent. His thoughts went back to a conversation he'd had with Patricia Bradshaw. What a chance now for Woolascroft and for Connor himself if Patricia could manage to persuade her nephew. Even operating in competition with Whittle would have been a risk worth taking in Connor's view, the heavy plant, sourced sensibly, would pay for itself in but a few years. Woolascroft would shed that heaviest of costs and be independent of Whittle's services, especially if he was to take on the foundation work for some of the smaller builders, for a rate that kept them keen. For all folk said of Dick Woolascroft the man had vision. There was every likelihood that Mrs.Whittle would sell up, there were no offspring so no son to take on the business and she more interested in matters of the church, though theirs not a match made in Heaven by all accounts.

Connor hadn't touched a penny of his so called legacy, his grandad's money, it sat in the bank gathering a bit of fat. O'Shea might be small fry but he'd take his chances swimming in deeper water with the likes of Woolascroft and the wealthy Patricia, on his way, like Molly Hanrahan's message.

"You're very quiet Connor," said Barry. "Is it your mam, is she still poorly, I'm sorry here's me goin' on about Whittle and I haven't asked?"

"Mother's worn out I reckon Barry, she's worked hard, struggled through the years, now it's the family's turn to take care of her. The two young 'ens are good kids an' Kathleen's watchin' over her like a clucky hen but I wer' first born, so I'm the one who should make things easier for her, a bit o' comfort as she grows older. Get your jacket Barry, I'll treat yer to a plate o' pie an' mash at The Nelson, I've an appetite to satisfy, a big appetite."

Lizzie Sealey's fingers trembled in her lap, she sat in the gloom, the curtains allowing a sliver of light from the street lamp through a small gap at the top where they failed to meet entirely. Annie had found her with no fire in the grate, just ash and cooling embers as the neglected fire wasted away, the old blanket that covered Fred's weary armchair lay in a crumpled heap, only one corner of it stubbornly clinging to the grubby, worn upholstery of better days, evidence of Fred's resistance to the bustling activities of the police.

The street had been disturbed by their arrival at around three in the afternoon, Annie had been at George and Liza's so not until she got home did she learn of the trouble. Charles seemed remarkably well informed given that he'd been in bed showing no sign of stirring when she'd left and was well ensconced in his chair when she returned, a view of any type of event on the street would necessitate leaving the living room and going through the cold front room, a distance and inconvenience Charles never negotiated. This proved a blessing on the odd occasion that Myra called with the children. On their leaving Annie would lead them through to the front door, to save Myra walking on her bad leg across the yard and along the entry, even Charles accepted the sense of that, but it enabled Annie to pass unseen a sixpence to Michael and

Louise, their young fingers clutching the small silver coins and their kiss in exchange making her return to the living room much less lonely.

'I suppose you'll want to rush off to sit with the wretched woman', had been his first words as she'd stepped inside the living room. George had driven her home and so she had no clue to what he spoke of. 'They came for him in the black maria, you know it's serious when you see that. She screamed and wailed like a banshee. Whittle's dead, died in the early hours of this morning, Sealey'll be up for manslaughter now'.

Charles had delivered the news with sickening relish that sent actual pain to Annie's stomach. His knowledge had come through Sidney Regis, from next door. Much to Sid's wife's dismay he'd come home the previous week with a puppy, which had piddled and worse in copious amounts, but not yet of an age to be inoculated and therefore confined, a regular and earnest request for newspaper came to the back door of No.1 most days and Annie did her best to oblige. On learning of Charles' less than hospitable reception when in her absence Sid came with his request, she wouldn't anticipate seeing either Sid or his wife until the memory of Charles' cantankerous response faded somewhat.

'I told Regis I don't pay a paper bill each week so's he can clean up dogs mess he should buy his own newspapers and shut the damn dog in their coal shed 'til it knows how to cock it's leg and squat in what passes for their garden, the dog couldn't make it more of an eyesore than it is already'.

However Charles had lapped up Sid's description of events along the street before delivering his typical withering words of encouragement.

Poor Lizzie, she'd pulled the curtains across the window, withdrawing to the shadows as though taking on Fred's guilt, shielding herself from the fingers folk would point, the judgment they would pronounce over her, Lizzie Sealey, wife of a killer.

Through the course of the war so many men had killed and been killed, the peace had eventually been won yet Annie sensed Fred battled still. Lizzie sniffled up her misery and at last spoke to Annie.

"I only went to the Co-op for a few bits, they close for half day on a Wednesday so I went afore dinner. 'E wer' quiet, I told him I wouldn't be long, I made stew enough for twice the day before, I only had to warm it up. 'E wer' gone when I got home, went wi' nothin' in his belly but porridge from breakfast. I thought 'e might 'ave gone to Purbeck Road to do a job for his aunty Florrie, 'e does sometimes but when 'e still weren't back at tea time I didn't know what to think. They sent a young constable to tell me 'e'd be kept in a cell overnight to sober him up. That wer' when I looked to see if the money wer' still there. I've allus put a bit away, hid it, I'd never feed us or pay bills if I didn't. In the bottom o' me sewing basket, underneath all the buttons I keep in an old baccy tin. E'd found it, never left as much as sixpence in there, gone, drinkin' on an empty belly wi' all I had."

Annie wrapped her own hands around Lizzie's chilled fingers.

"We don't know what overcame Bill Whittle, something drastic, if Fred struck him on Wednesday and he lived until the early hours of this morning then only a post mortem will reveal the actual cause of death, you must be strong Lizzie. I shall relight your fire and make you a hot drink, you should rest then."

Annie busied herself, it was difficult to believe such a dreadful thing, Whittle, considered to be a man of solid stature must surely have suffered a heart attack or stroke. Either way it did seem serious for Fred. The police had told Lizzie that Bill Whittle had passed away in City Hospital at around 2-30am they'd said nothing more, removing Fred forcibly from his chair, from the house and into the waiting van in a matter of minutes.

The room now lit by the standard lamp, Annie put a cup of hot, sweet tea into Lizzie's hand, the fire crackled in the grate, relieving the sinister stillness.

“Eat the bread and butter, I shall come again early tomorrow morning but I need to go home now to make Charles’ tea.”

“Fred told me ‘e remembered seein’ Whittle walk away with one of his men, but most o’ what ‘e said when ‘e come home Thursday mornin’ I couldn’t make head nor tail of. It wer’ about Jerry, ‘how could I of thought Whittle wer’ a Kraut’ Fred said, ‘they were lean, hollow eyed, copper told me I called Whittle a Jerry bastard’. Them were ‘is words Annie, I can’t make sense of it.”

She took a piece of bread and butter and put it in her mouth while Annie swallowed hard on the irony. All the times she’d smiled when Lizzie pardoned her husband’s outbursts, ‘tis his war wound, give him ten minutes and he’ll be whistlin’ like a Billy blackbird. There was no mention, no pardon today, no anticipation of the cheerful blackbird, just despair.

Annie lay wide awake, she peered at the clock, nearly half past eleven. It was impossible to imagine Myra, Maureen and the children enjoyin Mother Goose at the theatre, they’d been in such a state of excitement for days, how could joy be so great in one part of the city while at another there was nothing but anguish. Rosemary was to sing a solo in Chapel tomorrow, Annie recalled sitting with Fred on the wall of the chapel yard last Easter Sunday. Suddenly there was a noise outside in the back yards, the yap of a puppy and the frustrated voice of Sid Regis. Thankfully Charles didn’t stir. She would smuggle round some newspapers when she had the chance. It had occurred to her many times when laying in the fire how often the image of someone famous or celebrated got screwed into an untidy ball around a knob of rancid dripping to be used as a firelighter. Even Sir Winston on his retirement last year had suffered the indignity, at least he’d not been obliged to soak up a puppy’s piddle, or worse. Annie’s feet couldn’t find warmth, the morning felt to be a long way off.

CHAPTER EIGHTEEN

Late February.

As she walked from the dull light of the concourse and onto the street the reality of her situation hit home. Until this moment her journey had felt positive, even chugging along on the train, tired from so much travelling, still she'd felt sure within herself that it was good, the future to be of her own making and no longer in the manipulative hands of any other. Now the hissing sound from a double decker bus as it braked at a zebra crossing felt to be directed at her, an unwelcoming gesture designed to undermine her confidence, a condemnation of past iniquities.

She had tried, it could not be said that Diane Roper had made no effort. New Zealand was a foreign place when she arrived there and was a foreign place still when she left. Perhaps Boots in their wisdom should have given her a post too, Steve thrived through the challenge, wearing his new found responsibility like a badge of honour while she grew more and more disillusioned, out of place and wearied from the effort of falsifying smiles, the pretence at being 'the good sort'.

For hours on end she'd been alone while he channelled his energies into proving himself the right man for the job. Well she just wasn't the right woman and suspected Steve had come to realise that too. The upset she'd anticipated, not without a degree of dread, in the event proved slight, while he'd stopped short of shrugging his shoulders and saying 'ah well', when she'd declared her misery and told him she wanted to leave, go back home, his reaction couldn't be described as dismayed, more acquiescent.

Finances were now Diane's big worry, her flight had cost Steve a lot of money and he'd given her funds to manage for a little while saying he'd make some arrangement, but they were both in no doubt, the separation would bring about an end to their marriage. With real intent she must find work and somewhere reasonable to live. In the immediate a cheap room at a boarding house for a couple of nights would give her chance to search the places to rent and situations vacant columns in The Evening Post. With so many shops surely one or two might be looking for a sales assistant, she appeared respectable and in the right situation Diane Roper could smile quite genuinely. Besides on leaving school she'd worked briefly at the hardware shop on Nuthall Road, until the proprietor fell foul of the law and was invited to be a guest of His Majesty. He'd exposed himself once too often and unwittingly before the wife of the J.P. as she'd been walking home from her voluntary work at a women's refuge. The shop premises were closed for the duration of his sentence, six months. Diane heard one customer remark, 'I never liked that brown overall 'e allus wore, made him look shifty at best o' times'. Thankfully during Diane's time at the shop the brown overall had remained buttoned and she'd applied for a position at Drews unscathed. Her work there had continued right up to her marrying Steve but he'd deemed wifely duties to be her role henceforth and so she'd become a lady of leisure, a kept woman. Well it was a role that bored her to death. Always the man 'deemed', William Eddowes had deemed himself God's gift to women, as though they should be eternally grateful for his attentions. She, Diane Roper was supposed to be in complete accord with their exchange of favours, as he referred to their times together, he'd made it sound no more than a casual swap, his want for her need. Had he never been taught the difference between the two? When a child, she'd often been told, 'I want doesn't get' while a need was never overlooked.

"Are you in need of a cab Missus?"

Lost in thought Diane had stood with her suitcase ignoring passing traffic, more intent on convincing herself that everything now would be better.

"I can't stop 'ere, follow me, I'll pull in at the taxi rank."

The nod of her head in response to his question was enough, he parked up and hurried back to relieve her of the suitcase.

"Why didn't yer stay on the concourse, taxis pull in an' out all day long there, new to the city are yer? You'll soon find your way about."

The man was only trying to be friendly and helpful but his chatter irritated her and yet of all people he'd be most likely to know where she might find a room for a sensible rate, taxi drivers made it their business to know such things.

Having installed both the case and his fare he looked up at his mirror, shuffled in his seat and grunted as he appeared to make some adjustment to his nether regions. Turning to look towards her he said.

"Where to then."

"I must find a room, for a couple of nights but not expensive, clean though." She added the last two words with emphasis and he chuckled.

"Well that rules out all the posh places on the first count an' one or two others I could mention on the second." He fell silent obviously thinking. "I reckon your best bet's The Crown, landlord there lets out a couple o' rooms above the bar, mostly to men on business, reps an' the like who just want a bed, a basin to have a shave an' a bite o' breakfast wi'out all the trimmin's. I've been told that at the Cedars yer get arf a grapefruit wi' a glace cherry stuck in it an' they cut the rind off the bacon. Your workin' man don't want a cherry to start 'is day an' the rind's best bit. The wife's cousin is landlord's missus at The Crown, she's alright is Mavis, keeps the place in good order, chances are you'll be the only one stoppin', some weeks she don't get anybody, depends who's on the roads. The bar can get a bit noisy for some folk I dare say."

"The Crown sounds like a good place to start," said Diane, "I can't imagine the noise will bother me, I'm too tired."

She felt relieved and amused at the irony, she might well find herself sleeping in a bed more used to accommodating a sales rep than the disenchanted wife of one.

"Where have yer travelled from missus?" He sensed this fare was not his usual pickup.

"New Zealand, the other side of the world," replied Diane, she wasn't about to satisfy his likely curiosity so diverted the conversation by saying. "I've been away almost two years, what's happened in my absence or is Nottingham unchanged?"

"Missus I could drive yer round the ring road 'til yer were dizzy an' still wouldn't 'ave time to tell yer what's 'appened in the past two years. Me an' pretty much every taxi driver gets to hear more than them at Evenin' Post, but we keep our mouths shut, wise old owls, that's us, we know enough to start a rebellion an' we've seen enough to rewrite that bloke Darwin's theory on species. You'll see the changes for yourself, they've tarted up the city centre, built new housin', an' there's a fancy new C&A where Drews used to be, you women like your fashion don't yer. Our Edie come home wi' a new frock from there, stripey affair wi' a belt fit to strangle an 'ernia, her mam daren't say owt, yer know what lasses are like, the more tellin' they get the more cussed they get, besides Edie's earnin' now, works at council offices."

His ramblings were harmless and Diane let the sound drift over her, responding with the odd, oh, well, my goodness, as she hoped it appropriate.

" 'Ere we are, The Crown, the bar'll be shut this time o' the afternoon so I'll park up the side an' wait, just in case the rooms are taken. Go to the back door, tell 'em it's me as brought yer."

"I don't know your name," said Diane.

He laughed. "Silly beggar, it's Eric, if she knows I've brought yer Mavis'll do her best to fix yer up."

Diane hurried, beginning to grow concerned over how much might be the cost of the cab, she'd needed to hail one when in London and physically shook when the driver asked for 17/6d. Perhaps surprisingly she'd never really needed to use the taxis in Nottingham, always the buses ran to wherever she needed to go.

The rear of the pub was far less inviting than the cream painted façade with its bright gold crown positioned regally above the front entrance. It was for a couple of nights, that's all, she determined herself and knocked loudly, trying to avoid as much delay as possible. Within seconds the back door opened and a man, presumably the landlord looked her up and down as though making mental measurement of her height.

"Yes," he said, the inflection in his voice confirming it a question. Diane explained. "Mavis, you're wanted." He called out so loudly she presumed the woman must be some distance off.

"If you do have a room I can tell Eric to go once I've retrieved my case from his taxi." Diane tried to impart her concern at what must be an ever increasing fare.

"You'll 'ave to wait for Mavis, she's comin', Eric won't sting yer." Within no more than a few seconds his wife appeared panting from the exertion of rushing downstairs. "Needs a room," he said and with no further ado, walked away.

"Eric is waiting to know if a room is available, he brought me here from the station." Diane's tone of anxiety was not lost on the sympathetic Mavis.

"Come on, I suppose you have a case, we'll fetch it and send Eric on his way, there's no one else staying tonight as far as I know but they can turn up late sometimes wantin' a room, while ever the bar's open they'll ask."

She came across as a friendly woman yet made no troublesome questions, Diane was relieved the journey had been long and tiring. She'd left from Wellington airport five days ago, travelling alone she'd felt nervous, afraid of missing a connection and finding herself marooned but spurred on by the conviction, she was now in charge of her own life.

"Hello Mavis, I told her she'd be alright wi' you, come all the way from New Zealand she has, been gone two years, puts us to shame, we've been no further than Skeggy, none of us. I only got as far as Loughborough in the war an' your Arthur did no better, two mile down at Birchdale wer' as far as 'e got." Eric handed the suitcase to Diane. "You'll manage won't yer, that'll be......" He paused before finally declaring. "Five shillin' Missus, if yer need drivin' to anywhere else just ring me number, I'd give yer one o' me cards but printin's not cheap an' Mavis'll give it to yer anyroad."

Diane put the case down, took the purse from her handbag and pressed two half crowns into his hand, along with an extra shilling by way of gratitude, he'd led her to Mavis after all and rightly or wrongly she felt entirely safe, if she was honest for the first time since leaving Wellington.

The room was clean, pleasant enough but bare of any ornamentation, those little curios, which made a space feel homely. Diane supposed it met the requirements of sales reps and businessmen merely occupying the room for no other purpose than sleep. Right now that was her intent too. She drew the curtains across the window shutting out the late afternoon light, a faint sound from below, Mavis and Arthur Monkton talking, a fuzzy reassurance that she was not alone soothed and allowed a calm to take hold her mind. She sat at the end of the bed, looking at her case momentarily debating whether to take out some fresh clothes and wash her face in the hand basin or surrender to sleep. She lay back and stared at the ceiling, at the lampshade that hung above her head, inanimate yet staring back at her, expressing its opinion through silent observation of her behaviour.

She kicked off her shoes, "There," she spoke in low tones to her shadowy observer, "I've cast off much more than a pair of old, laced up bootees, tomorrow morning I shall make a start, somewhere to live, a job, tomorrow is mine 'to deem'."

Even Annie felt the gaze of everyone on the bus scrutinizing Lizzie Sealey and herself, some observed in silence, others whispered their commentary for the benefit of those less vocal. She couldn't decide which was worse, the folk who presumed themselves sufficiently well informed to offer enlightenment, or those too weak to decline their tittle tattle. Poor Lizzie couldn't stop trembling, her face was ashen, the dark bags below her eyes held the weight of sleepless nights, her cheeks puffy and swollen from the constant wash of tears.

Fred was being held on remand in the prison awaiting trial. A post mortem revealed that Whittle had died from undetected internal bleeding, almost certainly caused by his falling back onto the piece of old angle iron when the punch sent him to the ground. Fred faced a charge of manslaughter. The police had advised Lizzie to apply for a visiting order, Fred was considered no further threat to anyone whilst in custody under enforced sobriety, he would be granted visiting rights.

Frightened of the unknown, Lizzie had asked Annie to go with her to Nottingham's prison, to wait for her, and despite Charles' harsh assault on Annie's frayed nerves she'd sat with Lizzie making sure the woman ate enough porridge to sustain her through the ordeal, put on her warm coat and hat, dressing her as Annie used to dress Hilda for school on cold mornings, and steered her towards the bus stop, passed folk who muttered mindless judgements at one already serving a most cruel sentence.

Now inside the bus, the familiar surroundings, which on any other day were no more than backdrop to routine had turned into a courtroom, like a change of scenery at a theatrical drama, and Lizzie Sealey sat in the dock.

"It's good to see the young people back," said Annie in an attempt at lightening the situation. "Caroline's students make such a difference to her days and my friend Florence says the big house on Castle Road is at last lived in, 'there is a great difference in living as opposed to merely dwelling you know Annie dear', was how she put it. Hilda hopes that Rosemary might choose to study at the university, if she were to pass all the entrance exams of course. David was always going to pursue work with his hands, he has a good head on him, like his dad, but needs to channel his ability into more physical activity, office work, 'the desk job' as they refer to that sort of thing wouldn't suit David. Rosemary enjoys her lessons, more so as she grows up, her music teacher encourages her singing. Emily says London is the place for anyone seeking a musical career. In London there are people whose job it is to discover what we call talent but what they call the arts. 'We have pictures hanging on the walls grandma', said Emily, 'in London they have works of art, we have books on the bookshelf, in London they have literary masterpieces in elegant glass fronted cabinets, we sing songs and whistle tunes, there they perform arias and cantatas'. Rosemary is to sing a solo in chapel on Sunday, we'll go together." Annie squeezed Lizzie's hand, the troubled woman looked into Annie's eyes with a vague emptiness that set her expression. Annie simply smiled, realising Lizzie hadn't heard a single word.

It was with relief that at last they stepped down onto the pavement, with but a few yards to walk to the prison entrance emotions became intensely mixed, the need of leaving the street and finding refuge would have them quicken their steps, yet that took them closer to a fearful place filled with offenders and somewhere among them, Fred.

Following the signs they reached a side door and were met at once by an official who asked their names, accepting that Annie had accompanied her friend and would wait in the appointed area. He looked over Lizzie's permit and checked both women for any items considered to be unsuitable and therefore not allowed. Annie wanted to tell him that Lizzie Sealey had already searched the depths of her soul, turned herself inside out looking for any way she might have prevented events of that day. His fumblings about Lizzie's person seemed feeble, little more than the stroke of a clothes brush by comparison.

Annie sat in the area designated neutral as she perceived it to be, for those not on official business but there as support for unfortunate folk who were. One other sat opposite her, a young woman, scanning the pages of a magazine and sucking a sweet of some sort, her legs crossed, the one on top moving gently up and down, reading something that amused her, she actually chuckled. Annie's thoughts in that instant being, just as herself the young woman was not immediate family of anyone incarcerated within but moral support for a neighbour or friend.

After half an hour or so had passed the sound of heavy doors along the corridor and footsteps drawing closer was welcomed by both Annie and the young woman who folded her magazine and put it in her shopping bag with a heavy sigh of relief. This was like no other waiting room, be it doctor or dentist.

Lizzie stood just outside the doorway as if her feet were unwilling to progress in any direction other than away from the place. Annie hurried across the waiting area, casting a brief goodbye to the young woman, took Lizzie's arm and joined her in thought, escape, they must escape this torment as quickly as they could.

Never had the streets felt so vital to life, to actually taking breath, air that moved freely on the wind, city noise today not an assault to the ears but rhythmic, a beat that confirmed life, a view open to the eyes whether they turned to left or right, up or down. Oh yes, if this was freedom then Annie could understand in a way never possible before why men fought to defend it.

"He looks different," said Lizzie.

Annie presumed it was the prison uniform that changed Fred's appearance, it would, but no, that wasn't it.

Lizzie continued. "His skin, there's a pinkness in his cheeks like a boy's an' they've cut his hair, 'e looks younger. When I come again 'e wants me to bring the tatty old cartoon book 'e found in France, the words are all in foreign, but I suppose a drawin's a drawin' wherever it comes from. I remember him showin' it to me soon after he got back, it's such a scruffy lookin' thing I couldn't understand why 'e'd kept it, it'd made 'im laugh, 'priceless this is Lizzie'. 'E held it to his lips an' kissed it. We don't know the 'arf of it really do we, two minutes later 'e 'ad tears in his eyes. Fred nearly died, army doctor saved him. We've both lived wi' his war wound an' these years on it still hurts. Do yer think they'll let him 'ave that old book?"

It was a question for which Annie had no answer other than to say. "We can but ask." Inwardly wondering if there might be too much of France in Fred's head already, which none of the prison's searching would ever uncover.

As they walked across the street to the bus stop Annie felt she must say it, not wanting to pry but worried for Lizzie there appeared no other way than to be direct.

"How are you managing Lizzie, do you have enough money?"

"They've giv' me some forms to apply for Social', I've to fill 'em in and take 'em to that place on Parliament Street, I've not done it yet, I'm hopeless when it comes to official stuff, I'll only get it all wrong."

Annie was about to respond when a voice called out.

"Good afternoon Annie." Andrew Smithfield now stood alongside them, he'd hurried to catch up, a little breathless he nevertheless said. "And it's Mrs.Sealey surely, you might remember me though it was a while ago."

How could she possibly forget that dreadful time when this gentleman had wiped up Fred's vomit now here he was again, meeting her on her way from the prison, what must he be thinking. Poor Lizzie wished for the ground to open up and swallow her.

"Where are you heading, I've the car parked around the corner, I could give you a lift? The opticians," he held up a small paper bag, "new spectacles, I've just come from there. A couple of weeks ago I told myself it was past time I had my eyes tested again. I found myself squinting at the crossword clues until I could scarcely tell an a from an e. We pretend not to notice old age as it stalks us, creeping up from behind. Like that game I've observed the children playing in the garden next door. 'What time is it Mr.Wolf?'

Annie chuckled. "Yes, Hilda and John when they were little would plead with William or Freddy to play that game, though William used to be truly frightening when he finally declared, 'time to eat you all up'. Freddy has always been far too gentle to ever seem scary."

On this occasion Annie was only too pleased to accept Andrew's offer of a lift and thereby avoid the uncomfortable atmosphere promised by the bus.

"We are on our way home now Andrew so a lift would be greatly appreciated wouldn't it Lizzie?"

Not a word found its way through Lizzie's trembling lips, kindness released so much emotion all she could do was weep.

"Come along my dear, it's quite chill out here, the car will offer shelter from that biting wind."

He gently led Lizzie along the pavement, glancing briefly at Annie. Safely ensconced in the back seat of Andrew's car, alongside Annie, Lizzie stared down into her lap where surely she must believe every misfortune had landed, Annie squeezed her arm and spoke softly.

"I'm sure Andrew would be happy to help you with the forms, I can think of no one better."

Lizzie looked up and Annie made her own search of those watery eyes for just a glimmer of hope, but they lowered again too quickly, the rest of the way they travelled in silence, Andrew glancing every few seconds in his mirror.

Still a few red embers were evident in the grate when they stepped inside Lizzie's living room, Annie made haste if she was quick then a couple of kindlers and a few nubs of coal might oblige to give warmth. Lizzie took of her coat and hat, went to the sideboard and picked a brown envelope from the drawer handing it to Andrew she said.

"They told me to fill these in."

For a few moments he looked puzzled but took the envelope and smiled his reassurance.

"Lizzie will need some help with rent and so on, she's not sure what to do, until now she's always managed you see, I told her you wouldn't mind going over the forms with her." Annie's words provided all the explanation Andrew needed.

"Indeed, I have new spectacles for that very purpose."

Sitting Lizzie down beside him at the table, with his never failing patience and care he took her through officialdom's questions and entered the appropriate responses, his expression showed sympathy and dismay, for Lizzie Sealey had no reserves of either money or hope.

Staying so long with Lizzie Annie knew that already Charles would have prepared his speech, to be orated on her return and designed to be unforgettable, she got to her feet.

"I must go now Lizzie, promise me you will eat something, you have bread and eggs, I'll call for you in the morning and we shall go to the Co-op."

Lizzie nodded and answered with a faint, "Thank you for goin' with me Annie an' thank you Mr.Smithfield for all your kindness." She assumed that her company would leave together as Annie had enabled him a timely departure also.

Andrew expected Annie to immediately hurry home so was bewildered when she stood alongside the car as though waiting to get in.

"Please let me." He opened the passenger side door and to his surprise Annie did indeed get in and sat down purposefully.

Now behind the wheel he hesitated before turning the key in the ignition, there must be a reason, at any other time Annie would have insisted on walking the short distance along the street to No.1, in fact she would have laughed at the suggestion of a lift for no more than a couple of hundred yards.

She sighed. "Is it true, did Dick Woolascroft make losses on the build at Mitchell Street?"

Now Andrew understood, she was worried about William's involvement but before he could reply she spoke again.

"I've heard rumours when in town but like you I pay little heed, often their limited knowledge is greatly exaggerated and best ignored, folk ever speculate. But when I called on Florence a few days ago Patricia was at home and Olive, Dick's wife was with them. She confided her anxiety, it seems Dick has been unusually quiet of late, apparently he's never enlightened her very much, keeps affairs of the firm close to his chest allowing her only what he considers incidental. His ponderous mood has convinced her that all is far from well. I thought you might be more reliably informed. We see William seldom these days."

Andrew opened the window a crack, already the warmth from their breath had begun to steam up the windscreen.

"I've heard such things too Annie, Mitchell Street posed a big challenge for whoever undertook the build there. The all vital foundation work must have cost Woolascroft dear but he would have known that at the outsct. I've heard it said that Woolascroft was determined to get his hands on Mitchell Street, no matter what, I find that hard to believe, it wouldn't make sense and yet knowing the problems subsidence had created he pursued it, went after a council contract and any work done for a local authority is bound to be less lucrative than for the private sector. In business there are times when, for whatever reason, it goes wrong. Bad judgment, market forces, labour problems all bring influence to bear. I would doubt Dick is in trouble to the degree of threat, that the firm is in danger of collapse, they must have made well at Colver and several individual builds that I've seen shout money to the onlooker, Dick would have swelled the coffers through those I'm convinced.

William must take the rough with the smooth I'm afraid Annie, there is never a guarantee. From what I've come to know of him William Eddowes seems never to draw the short straw, I wouldn't worry too much."

"It's not so much that I worry for William," said Annie, "it's Celia I feel concern for, he can be very difficult to live with if things are not going his way." She paused. "What do you think will happen to Fred Sealey?"

"A jail sentence of some length almost certainly, lawyers can be very persuasive but that is true on both counts, prosecution and defence. You and I may believe the presence of mitigating circumstances, drunkenness cannot be deemed one of them however. Disturbance of the mind through other factors possibly, but the law is short on sentiment, it works with hard facts only and the fact is, Bill Whittle died. I don't see how they can bring a case of murder, he won't hang Annie, but perhaps Lizzie will be as much a widow as Mrs.Whittle, both alone whatever the outcome."

"Thank you for helping her, I don't suppose they mean it but folk can be cruel when they don't stop to think. If you drop me off just short of the corner that would be kind."

Andrew started the car. Only as far as the corner but today Annie had sat by him and for a minute or two felt close, two elderly people travelling a couple of hundred yards together, yet for Andrew it was a passage worthy of committing to memory, along with the few others he used as comfort on the lonely evenings at Brassington.

This was the third entry in yesterday's Evening Post that she'd circled in pencil as being a possibility, a room with shared facilities at No.15 Mansfield Road. Of the previous two, one had been taken and the other could only have been claimed by an individual in desperate straits, she'd left the premises feeling itchy and still had the residue of a most unpleasant smell up her nose.

Diane rang the doorbell and waited, anticipating another waste of time. Very quickly it was answered by a man, not young, nor elderly, but old fashioned in his dress which made his appearance unusual, eccentric might be an apt word to apply she thought.

"I've come about the room." Diane glanced down at the newspaper she clutched in her left hand, along with her handbag.

"You best come in and have a look then, it won't stay empty for long, was a time when it took days, even weeks to get somebody but since the university started up them young folk from other places have grabbed at anywhere vacant and half decent. You'll not find a room like this for any less rent, the bed came from Burton's, me mother only bought the best, proud o' that bed she wer', right proud. Follow me."

Diane's thought in that instant was did his mother die in her Burton's bed, the way he looked and spoke suggested she was no longer with him.

The small hallway actually had a smell of polish about it, Diane could at least tick one box, on the wall a picture, the like of which she'd never seen before. A print of some kind she imagined, in muted brown shades, the subject, two monks sharing a bowl of spaghetti, they appeared to be relishing every strand as they sucked them up through pursed lips. It brought a smile to Diane's face, he noticed.

"You like it do yer. Father was a bookkeeper, did work for a client who couldn't pay his bill so father accepted that picture by way of settlement. He was told it originated in Italy, there is a faint signature but I can't make it out, don't suppose it's worth much, it's a lithograph, not original." They climbed the stairs to the landing where he opened the second door along. "I only let this room, I'm in another one and the third I use for storage. It's clean, I'm a great one for cleanliness, next to Godliness they say."

The room was of decent size, floor carpeted, worn a little at the doorway but otherwise in fair condition. The curtains were lined and fell from the pelmet to the skirting board. A chest of drawers, wardrobe and bedside table all matching and a pretty little chair with flower patterned upholstery. The bed was indeed impressive, a dark oak headboard with a fancy carved top, the foot of the bed also of oak but plain. A couple of simple prints adorned the walls along with a mirror.

"Well is it what you're looking for, if it is then I'll show you the bathroom and scullery, you'll have the use of them of course and I don't mind a lodger joining me in the living room at Christmas, I always put up the decorations, mother loved all that sort o' thing. I eat my main meal at midday so's I'm out o' the way in the evenings, I expect you work, most of them do."

"The room will do me very well I'm sure, I would like to see the other facilities though, if they appear suitable then I'd hope to move in today."

"Fair enough," he turned to the door behind them, opened it and stood to one side, a bath like any other and a wash basin more or less filled the space, only the biting cold that struck her face when she stepped inside for a moment caused her to hesitate, he'd noticed her shiver. "Faces north, you'll not linger in the bath this time o' year but you'll be glad o' the cool in summer."

On first sight the scullery appeared to be unchanged since Mrs.Micawber occupied it. An old black leaded range, shelving on heavy wall brackets, flagstone floor and deep sink with huge brass taps but just as the rest of the house, it shone with cleanliness. It may not be what she'd envisaged when starting her search for somewhere to dwell but the rent was reasonable and the longer she dithered the less time she had to pursue that other urgent matter, employment. He opened a door at the side.

"Fine pantry this is, mother used to fill this with preserves, you'll have the bottom shelf and I'll use the top one, we'd have to share the slab and the meat safe. Dustbin's out the back so's the clothes line. I like the bed to be changed once a week and I boil the whites meself, you'll do your own washing in the sink, there's a wringer out the back. The electric fire in the bedroom works off the meter and so long as yer don't sit in there all day long with it turned on it's included in the rent but I don't make any adjustment in the summer, flat rate all year round, take it or leave it and money up front every month. I don't allow any hanky panky, mother'd turn in her grave."

He looked hard at Diane as though instantly quashing any notion she might have of entertaining, he need not have bothered, the room would be entirely for her own use, no one else's. Her only niggling concern was his dear, departed mother who almost certainly breathed her last in that bed. It would have to do regardless, no ghost would dare to roam the household for fear of being scrubbed of its soul, with flesh and bone gone that's all that remained and Ajax would show little mercy she felt sure.

"I'll take it thank you. I'm Diane Roper and your name is Mr. ......?"

"Robotham, Claude Robotham, embalmer retired."

He extended his hand. Dear God, it grew more daunting by the minute yet Diane shook his hand and said.

"I shall fetch my things, you'll want me to pay you now then?"

He didn't need to affirm it, at once producing from his pocket a rent book and pen. "Is it Miss Roper?" He'd looked to see if she wore a ring when she first arrived. She'd removed it once aboard the aeroplane from Wellington, she was travelling light. In truth she'd debated whether to keep it on and declare herself a widow if anyone asked, or take it off and avoid searching questions, while the latter had felt favourable it was because she couldn't bring herself to speak of Steve as dead. Their marriage was over but they were both alive, despite everything she couldn't even think of him in that way, he would find somebody else, be happy and successful, so she'd slipped the ring from her finger and become the single woman. The few people she'd known who might remember her, to them she would simply say the marriage had failed, they would accept that, besides it was true and folk were sympathetic of failure while they could be envious of success. William Eddowes was successful, damn the man. No hanky panky, Diane Roper would readily sign to that agreement, she sought no favours, no favours at all.

"Yes, Miss Roper, you'll find me no bother Mr.Robotham, you'll hardly know I'm here."

When his aunt Patricia entered the office, closing the door firmly behind her and sat down at the other side of his desk Dick couldn't have felt more surprised. Since the death of his father, not once had she come to the yard, in fact he couldn't remember the last time, so why now? Perhaps she'd come to pick some flesh from what remained on the bones, like everyone else she would have heard that Mitchell Street had been a disaster for the firm.

"How are you Dick?"

What you really mean is am I broke, that was his thinking but he managed a smile and said.

"Well my dear Aunt, sound of wind an' limb and not yet succumbed to madness despite the general opinion. How can I help you, I don't imagine you've come here without a purpose in mind?"

"We can surely dispense with the aunt bit, I'm too young to be anything of an aunt to you Dick and you've never really thought of me as one anyway.

Patricia seems altogether more sensible, even Olive finds no difficulty in addressing me less formally, she calls on mother and me from time to time as I'm sure you're aware and we enjoy her company. While there is another purpose to my visit, first and foremost I do genuinely enquire after your health and well being, though you possibly doubt that.

Neither of us grows any younger Dick, we've both struggled one way or another, trying to live up to our fathers, but it's time we agreed a more cooperative approach. In both cases they dominated what we did and how we did it, now we are our own agents, free to make our own decisions."

Dick listened patiently, anticipating some kind of gracious offer, a subtle salvage operation to redeem Olive's sinking husband. He might have guessed she'd fall for Patricia's carefully calculated questioning, veiled as it would doubtless have been in more innocent, casual conversation. When he'd asked Patricia three years ago to invest her response had been immediately negative, he'd surmised she would only be interested in a controlling share, unwilling to trust him at the helm whilst she slept. Now she saw the time as ideal to secure just that. Well he was still solvent, Cheetham and Eddowes were far from happy, the latter was relentless in his bitterness but Woolascroft's had won a contract to build an estate of modern housing at Bulwell and this site presented none of the challenges they'd had to overcome at Mitchell Street, mainly being the connection to Dick's nemesis Charlie Holbrook. Dick was rid of that thorn in his side, he'd dealt with it, he was the biggest loser, it had been Dick's own money that had paid for the deed to Mitchell Street, 'the odd side', Holbrook's miserable houses but he felt no regret. Whatever Patricia had come to offer he would not be patronised.

"I think you should consider expansion," said Patricia, "when folk suppose you to be ailing, that's when they take weakness for granted and how they do prey on any perceived weakness." She got to her feet suddenly, picked up the chair and carried it to Dick's side of the desk placing it down beside where he sat. "We have been separated by unnecessary obstacles that stubbornly persisted in standing in our way," she sat down, "it's a nonsense that we should tolerate no longer.

So much of the initial outlay you would save if all foundation work was done by Woolascroft's and not contracted out to Whittles. Connor has told me that Whittles profits are to be envied, he believes that you would recoup your money in no more than a year or two if you acquired some heavy plant."

Dick at this point raised his hand. "Now just hold on there, you wait a minute Patricia. I'm not about to go under as some folk seem to think but neither am I in any position to put money into costly machinery. I don't know what kind of fairy tale you and Olive have come up with between you, and why you would give even a modicum of consideration to the half baked schemes that young Irish navvy spouts God knows. He's most likely a devious mouthpiece of William Eddowes, that's who you refer to isn't it, the Irish lad who lodged at the Eddowes' place a couple of years back. You're being used Patricia." Dick laughed sarcastically.

"You're wrong Dick, Connor is bright, his mind works well beyond his years, so bright he'd be more than capable of running that side of the business if you'd agree to let him in. He inherited some money from his grandfather, unlike many young men who would have squandered it on, 'a good time', he's waited an opportunity to better himself, and what's wrong with that. I've had long conversations with him, he calls often to see mother and me, we've grown very fond of him. I recognise potential when I see it and I can discern reliability too, far better now than at any time in my life before. He deserves a chance, we both had a head start, Fred made you his replacement and father did likewise with me."

"For Heaven's sake woman, can you hear yourself? It's pathetic, do you actually believe you can turn him into the son you never had, comes the day that we must face the fact, it's too late, too bloody late, for you an' me both.

He's got family back in Ireland, Eddowes told me, the father worked at the Raleigh factory in Dublin with Eddowes' lad. The economy of Ireland's in the doldrums, his folk see more opportunity for their son in England but they don't expect him to take over the place, nor for some desperate, middle aged woman to covet him. You're foolin' yourself Patricia. Your mother's likely too afraid to say it for fear of sending you into some God awful depression. This firm'll survive, more than that, it'll grow, but now's hardly the right time to be tellin' me I should expand an' certainly not to further the ambition of some fantasy Irish prodigy."

Patricia got up from the chair, crossed to the window and looked out over the yard. She spoke without turning to face him.

"It was the message, if he'd knocked at the door to tell us we had a loose slate on the roof or that crows were nesting in the chimney pot I'd have dismissed all memory of Connor O'Shea. You see Dick, he'd come to deliver to us, to mother and me a message from Rex Madden, the very last words Rex uttered. It just happened to be Connor to whom Rex entrusted the message that night of the gas leak in Denman Street. 'Tell Mrs.Stanford I never blamed her, I never blamed her nor Patricia'." Now she turned to face Dick. "I can't forget that message." She had tears in her eyes. "I can't forget the message or the messenger, don't you ever feel the need to give something back Dick?"

He let out a long troubled breath. "Sit down Patricia. Just how the lad could have any such knowledge of Whittle's profits begs a question, but I dare say he's right. I don't understand quite what it is you propose, you must have assumed before coming here that I'd be in no position to put up money for any new venture, so how do you plan to operate this scheme of yours?"

His words had been harsh, he shouldn't have spoken to Patricia so heartlessly and he shouldn't blame Olive for voicing her worries, apart from Dorothy Plowman, God forbid, who else did she have to confide in.

Patricia sank onto the chair beside him as if all strength had drained from her. She took a hanky from her pocket and wiped her face before speaking.

"I would put money into the firm but not claim any return on it for five years, and then only if my convictions had proved correct, I'd make sure it didn't result in any cost to you Dick."

She'd been right in what she'd said at the beginning, he'd not really thought of Patricia as aunt, yet here she was, sitting by him, defences down and he felt a curious connection, they shared past events, events that had shaped their lives.

"I expect O'Shea has heard the same whispers I have, Whittle's widow is inclined to sell up," said Dick. "If the business is as lucrative as we believe then they'll be lining up, she won't be selling off machines, she'll be putting the whole bloody lot up for sale."

Patricia was quiet for a moment, thinking. "The topic of discussion at The Lodge no doubt, father's favourite place, there he pursued his own kind of faith, worshiped with the chosen ones."

Dick scoffed. "I've not attended in months, Eddowes can recite their conversations and exchanges word by word including the odd punctuation when someone coughs up an intrigue, so it renders my presence unnecessary. I shall be excommunicated in due course I shouldn't wonder, defrocked, dismissed as an embarrassment." He sighed. "There's only room for so many Indians to dance around the totem pole after all."

Patricia sensed his weariness, not a physical tiredness but that exhaustion of spirit, of eagerness so present in younger days but now diminished through years of trying to live up to expectation.

"Perhaps I should meet with Mrs.Whittle," she said, "the poor woman might prefer to be approached by another woman in the first instance."

"You may not be the first instance," observed Dick, "anyway, could you find the money for a business like that?"

“Probably, but I’d need your support, furthermore I’d need you to front it. Whatever I do folk will deem it to be ‘Stanford’. While they speculate over your losses at Mitchell Street they nevertheless give you all the credit for creating the kind of homes that until now the less fortunate saw slight hope of ever knowing, even less of dwelling in. Goodwill doesn’t follow me readily Dick, but attitudes mellow in time and folk begin to see you in a kinder light.”

“Tell O’Shea to come and see me, but not here, I don’t want Eddowes or Cheetham to get a whiff of this. At home, ask him to come to the house, tomorrow evening, if he really has knowledge of Whittle’s affairs I’d like to know how he came by it. Then I’ll judge for myself just how bright he is.”

It was entirely spontaneous, she couldn’t have stopped herself if she’d wanted to. Patricia kissed his cheek. “It’s not too late to be agreeable at least, we’ve been distant as family for long enough Dick.”

He laughed a little scornfully. “You women are all the same, that’s Olive’s eternal cry, ‘it’s never too late’. Remember me to your mother.”

Dick walked Patricia to the door and watched as she crossed the yard to the open gates. Men were realistic, they recognised the truth, the hard facts and for Dick Woolascroft it was too late, far too bloody late.

CHAPTER NINETEEN

Late April.

"You need only to attend the service William," said Celia, "Mathew will go back to the house with me afterwards but Rosie and Tommy are Mathew's Godparents and you've known them virtually all your life, don't be so selfish. How they must have struggled, poor Audrey couldn't help it but her dementia made everyday difficult, you don't realise how lucky you are. I know what it's like, I'd sit with mother trying not to cry in front of her because by then she didn't even recognise me and seeing someone crying upset her terribly, but when I walked away from the place, feeling wretched, I couldn't suppress the tears regardless of who else might see me. You've been spared so far William and I hope with all my heart that Annie never loses her mind in the way mother and Audrey did, it hurts, it pains like a bereavement. Rosie lost her mother months and months ago, today is that unavoidable ordeal, to be endured of necessity, we must support them through it, and show respect."

Mathew stood in the scullery, looking out of the window, dismayed at the atmosphere, his mam and dad's raised voices reaching him from the living room where they argued yet again. Why did his dad determine himself to be so confrontational? Emily was fortunate to be missing today's row, they'd both, he and Emily, retreated to their bedrooms or taken themselves out somewhere several times over the past few weeks and always the troubles began through their dad's unreasonable attitude. Outside the sun shone, Mathew wasn't looking forward to the funeral if indeed anyone ever did embrace such occasions with thoughts of pleasure. Billy Dodds had been the last one he'd attended, he and Samuel Boucher had stood together, the heartbreak they'd witnessed rendered emotions raw and the pain took days to fade. Sunlight seemed to comfort somehow, the absence of clouds allowed a belief in Heaven while dull grey sky challenged, allowing only harrowed hope, there'd been no sun when they laid Billy to rest.

At last his mother called out. "We're ready now Mathew, did you put that clean handkerchief in your pocket?"

He sighed, crossed to the doorway of the living room and smiling at his mam said. "Yes, and I've bolted the back door, Emily has her front door key but dad will be back anyway." He cast a despairing glance at William who occupied the black suit kept for sombre occasions with equally dark demeanour.

Once inside the car Celia fell silent, the awkwardness of having to explain to Tommy, with some fabricated excuse, the reason why William hadn't come thankfully she hadn't now to face, it was relief enough to enable the calm and Mathew sitting in the front with his dad drew a deep breath, as if testing the air and subconsciously he was, 'you could have cut the air with a knife', an expression he'd heard at some point during his growing up, now he knew exactly what it meant.

Audrey Potts had found peace ten days ago. While Rosie had wept all over Celia she could not have wished her mother's situation to continue. It had reached a pitiful depth of torment until that morning when Rosie had literally caught her mam as she collapsed, exhausted, spent, emptied of the madness that had contorted her every thought. It had been merciful. Tommy's brother Joe and Bob Lacey would see to everything, the family must get through today, pick up the pieces and begin again.

After the service at St.Andrew's Rosie would be inviting all those attending back to the house, for refreshment, tea, sandwiches and some cakes. Celia had helped with the baking, taking Beryl under her wing, coaxing her to mix the sponges and ice the sweet buns. The boys being older were better able to cope with the upset but young Beryl struggled. William was adamant, he would not go to the wake, as he called it, Celia could only hope that Tommy might understand, Rosie was aware of just how contrary William could be and she'd probably confided to Tommy those times when Celia had let down her guard and cried in the company of her friend.

As he drove William's mind was distracted, the meeting he'd had with Dick Woolascroft the previous afternoon still echoed in his head, galled his stomach and filled him with angry resentment, he was in no mood for today's demands.

"I'll park as close to the church as I can, I don't suppose there'll be many beyond the family, unless someone offers you two a lift then I'll drive you to Tommy's but I shan't come in, you can catch the bus home, it's good weather."

Neither Celia nor Mathew made comment, William's attitude was too pathetic to warrant one.

Annie had said she would wait for them, so they could walk into church together. As they drove by Celia could see her standing to one side of the lichgates. In fact several cars were parked along the street, the space immediately outside the church was left clear for the cortège.

William pulled up the handbrake as if it were the trigger of some remarkable piece of weaponry, designed to fire all tribulations into oblivion.

Mathew stepped onto the pavement and opened the door for his mother while his dad stood for a few seconds, his hand still on the open driver's door, as if undecided.

"What's the matter?" Asked Celia.

"Nothing's the matter, I just don't happen to be one of those folk who rush to a funeral as if afraid of missing the last ticket, that's all."

Celia was too dignified to voice it at such a time but her thought had been of William's eagerness to attend Fred Woolascroft's funeral when he barely knew the man. She couldn't have known that William's own thought's had travelled back to the days of youth, of times spent on these very streets kicking a ball about with Tommy Spooner, of sharing a first cigarette, a Player's Weight, the ordinary kind. People were making their way.

"Come along we should hurry," said Celia, "the hearse will be here soon and Annie is waiting for us."

William slammed the car door shut, closing it on the past and followed them.

Mathew kissed his grandma's cheek and she squeezed his hand. Over the course of a lifetime the need to be present, to attend out of respect, could become almost familiar, but to witness through love was never so, no matter what age, and for the young the ordered sequence of a funeral service could make chill the warmest day and weak the strongest stomach.

"Let's go in now," said Annie, "I think most are here." She smiled encouragement at Mathew, he took her arm.

"Are you alright Grandma?" He asked. Despite feeling old and noticing William's quietness she answered positively, but confidence waned with the years and even the church path seemed steeper as they made their way to the open door.

Hilda had noticed Janet's almost withdrawn mood, never one to chatter mindlessly like her workmate Sheila but today especially so. She was sure to be with Thomas Spooner in thought. Although Janet had said she would go with him to his grandma's funeral he'd gently said 'no'. He and Samuel were two of the bearers, 'I wouldn't be able to hold your hand'. Knowing the loss of Billy was still raw in Janet thoughtful Thomas had persuaded her to stay at work and allow her mind to be occupied by less distressing events.

Hilda was styling Patricia Bradshaw's hair, gossip regularly came into the salon, mostly nonsense. Often Hilda 'turned off', it could become tedious after a while. In the past she had gathered more edifying knowledge from reading the children's comic strips than from those salon rumours, which grew out of boredom. However, the revelation Jack had brought home the previous evening was definitely not one to be aired over a wash basin of shampoo and its fall out to be swept up with the clippings, it was more suited to the front page of The Evening Post. Dick Woolascroft had bought out Whittle's, lock, stock and barrel, in association with his aunt, Patricia Bradshaw. Now here she was, sitting in front of a mirror while Hilda did her hair, showing not the slightest hint of its truth, and not even the incessantly vocal Mrs.Whale, presently being permed by Janet would dare to utter one single sound on the subject, if indeed any whiff of it had come her way.

Jack was inclined to accept the news as true, it had originated from Jed Unwin, one of the foremen at Whittle's. Shockwaves would spread across the city on a tide of intrigue, only a month or two ago folk had been declaring Dick Woolascroft to be on the verge of bankruptcy, even allowing for the inevitable exaggeration it was a turnaround of epic dimension. Woolascroft and Patricia, Bradshaw everyone knew were far from close, this would be a twist in the plot no one could have predicted and in the likely opinion of most, leave the ending wide open. Yet Whittle's employees would be relieved, their jobs had felt less secure, a new boss might put an altogether different stamp on things but taken over by Woolascroft's, a local firm that had traditionally used Whittle's for all their foundation work, that sort of new boss could feel nothing less than reassuring.

Hilda held up the hand mirror for Mrs.Bradshaw to view the back of her hair.

"Thank you my dear, that feels much better. I've been busy of late, it had grown too long and mother is convinced that collar length hair results in more visits to the drycleaners, that's why I bought a coat with a fur collar. 'When you think it's become dirty mother we'll simply take the scissors to it and give it a trim', I can't resist teasing her."

It seemed to be a generational thing, the one before ever displaying a need of economy as though it was able to see the future through naturally wiser eyes. It was hard to believe the cost of dry cleaning could possibly make any significant impact on Patricia Bradshaw's finances. On the other hand, investing in Whittle's with Dick Woolascroft, if in fact she had, might make a huge difference, Florence with her accrued wisdom may well be concerned.

Hilda took the smart fur collared coat from the stand, only then discovering that Mrs.Whale had acquired a new coat too, her usual tired looking dog tooth check had been replaced by a much more attractive fashion, dark red with a grey fleck. Hilda sneaked a peek at the label, C&A, the new shop, which claimed to be both fashionable and affordable. Now Hilda held Mrs.Bradshaw's coat for her to slip her arms into the sleeves and though not really her intention, human nature being what it is Hilda cast her eyes over that label also, C&A, well who'd have thought it!

The salon closed an hour earlier on a Wednesday, at 4o'clock, Janet would be anxious to get away, to see Thomas. It was half past three, now Patricia Bradshaw had gone Hilda's time could be spent on finishing Mrs.Whale's hair and she could let Janet go. Rosemary was old enough to walk home on her own from school and let herself in while David was never back from work before half five. The early days at the salon had been difficult, needing to be in two places at the same time, it would have been impossible without Annie, now the situation was much eased. It had been worth the challenge, as a family they were happy and able to feel secure, far from wealthy but comfortably off.

"She's a rum 'en, to look at her these days yer wouldn't think she'd been in the madhouse would yer, there's no accountin' for folk?" Mrs.Whale now sat in the chair while Hilda did the necessary, her tongue had found release, with Janet being so quiet and given the fact that Patricia Bradshaw occupied a seat only a stride away from her, not until this moment had she ventured to air her opinions, which came straight from Mrs.Whale's assumed authority on most subjects. "She's never married again, I suppose if you've got her sort o' money you'd not be able to tell if a fella wer' chasin' yer for that or for the other. An' they never 'ad a kid, it might have been him as couldn't make one but she's allus had a barren look about 'er."

Hilda sighed and drew the brush through Mrs.Whale's' hair, the waves and curls transforming her appearance, making her look almost genteel.

"There you are, your crowning glory." Holding up the mirror for her to approve the end result Hilda hoped for a speedy departure without further tiresome observations, but apparently she must endure one more as Mrs.Whale sniffed up breath to enable her next delivery.

"Bert says that Sealey fella's case comes up next week, at the Assizes, Crown Court, too serious for Magistrates'. Last murder must 'ave been all o' five years ago, an' over some woman it wer'. It don't take much to get a man's dander up, they'll fight for a pastime. It's that ego business, the dominant male they call it don't they? Well my Bert's the dormant male, I swear if Elijah were to blow 'is horn outside our back door it wouldn't wake Bert's ego. Yer know it's bad when they get tried at Crown Court, that Sealey fella could swing. Ah well, at least my Bert'll never be in the dock." She looked into the mirror, turning her head slightly from side to side. "Our mam allus said that a woman's hair wer' her crowning glory, very nice Hilda love, very nice."

Wishing she'd never uttered the word 'crowning' Hilda took the red coat with the grey flecks from the stand and fed Mrs.Whale's arms into it with great haste, escorting her to the door and turning the sign to closed. Little wonder that at the end of her working day Hilda looked forward to the comparative ignorance of Bliss Street.

Rosie's small front room had never before received so much company, Tommy was well respected and popular with folk, which must account for the number now sipping tea and eating the results of both Rosie and Celia's efforts yesterday. Encouraged by Annie Beryl helped serve, taking some solace from overhearing several people remark on how light the sponge cakes.

The women tended to contain themselves indoors, while many of the men had wandered outside to the yard forming small groups, some feeling the need of a smoke, others desperate to loosen their ties without attracting stern looks from their wives. All ignoring young Beryl's rabbits that pressed their noses to the wire of the hutch as if taking advantage of the chance to sniffle up tobacco fumes!

"Thanks for comin' Will," said Tommy, "to be honest, I didn't think you would." Folk imagine that I'm so used to these occasions I don't feel tested, that I simply do the necessary without thinking about it, truth is every single one gets to me, even complete strangers. It's not the dead, they're no challenge, it's the responsibility of bein' what the livin' want me to be. Joe relieved me today, so I could stand with Rosie and the young 'ens. Audrey hadn't been livin' in this world for a long time an' where she'd gone Rosie couldn't reach her. I felt as helpless as I did all them years ago when Rosie miscarried. One day Will, before it's too late, you an' me should stand on Bobbers Mill Bridge as the train goes underneath, for old times' sake, while we both still live in this world."

For a few seconds William made no reply, it had struck him that no one other than Tommy addressed him as Will' apart from Freddy, whom he saw seldom. While children, and then youths, finally becoming men Tommy had ever addressed him in that old familiar way as though nothing between them changed. Yet the uncomplicated friendship of those earlier years was in every way different to the shallow, devious company William found himself rubbing shoulders with these days. Tommy was a constant, straightforward, honest,

William realised just how far he'd strayed. He felt in his pocket for his silver cigarette case and actually had his fingers upon it, but something changed his mind.

"Can you remember that night at the Institute Tommy, when they had a send off for Alf before he left Player's to go farming at Huttoft? We went outside to the street an' lit a fag, nattered for a bit. Then after you'd walked away I spotted a sixpence shining in the lamplight, felt like a fortune back then, there it was, just waiting for me to pick it up and you'd walked straight past it, that made it all the more of a fortune, mine were the spoils.

You'll hear soon enough anyway, now the deal's done. Woolascroft the man has taken over Whittle's, nothing to do with Woolascroft's the firm, entirely separate business apparently. This time I walked straight past the shining fortune and Dick picked it up, though I suspect it was Patricia Bradshaw who dropped it.

Mitchell Street made the firm a lot leaner and there's no way Dick could have found the money, why he bought those houses off Charlie Holbrook God knows, used his own money and lost the lot. Perhaps aunt Patricia's taken pity on him." William hesitated. "I wasn't going to come in for tea, it was your Joe persuaded me. He shook my hand, firm, genuine, 'Tommy would appreciate it William', he said 'for old times' sake'."

Tommy hardly knew what to say but in the event Rosie came to his rescue.

"You need to come Tommy," she said, "Joyce and Kathleen are leaving now." She smiled nervously at William. "I wouldn't have managed without Celia."

William was far too insensitive to realize that she referred to past traumas and not just to her mother's wake.

"Tell her I need to be going if you will Rosie, and Mathew, unless he's going to make his own way home."

"Yes, of course, thank you for comin'."

William Eddowes always made her feel somehow inadequate and anxious, like the feeling she got before an arithmetic test at school. Tommy was the opposite, she always felt safe from all threat with Tommy, he made every test go away.

Annie was busy in the scullery, gathering the cups and saucers for washing up, the room that granted sanctuary. She began to recognise that trait of aunt Bella's becoming present in herself, the need of finding a quiet corner, a shell in which to withdraw. Celia and Mathew appeared, William lingered in the doorway.

"We're off now Mam, Beryl's picking up the plates, she'll help you I know it's where she'd rather be." Celia kissed Annie's cheek, both women understood perfectly.

"Goodbye Grandma, I'll pop in at the weekend, bring Wendy."

Annie detected Mathew's apprehension, Charles was never a convivial host, thankfully the weather had warmed and so any unaccustomed visitor might be spared onset hypothermia, though his manner could inflict a chill depending on his mood of the day. William merely nodded his head, rather like a covert bid at an auction sale.

"Goodbye William, there's a letter at home, from Bonthorpe, still no news of Faith's baby but a heart warming account of events about the farm and as always, Francis and Freddy send you their best. Why don't you call in and read it, see your dad, if only for a few minutes?"

Annie tried her best, today had stirred many memories, the Spooners, especially Tommy had travelled the years with her family and walked with them still, as loyal as ever. William had chosen less reliable travelling companions. She wondered if today might cause him to feel regret. It was impossible to read a mere nod of the head but that was all he'd offered, it would be easier to read the tea leaves in the bottom of the cups, though Annie preferred to tip everyone's destiny into the old pail, believing it best not to know.

It was done, Patricia was happy, Conner O'Shea was strutting about like a dog with two dicks and as for himself, well Dick was strangely indifferent. This was not his risk but neither was it a risk for Patricia. Whittle's business was rock solid, only that driven faith she had in the young Irishman could threaten her, in business any judgement made by the heart and not the head left the door open to the unwanted. Yet when O'Shea had come to the house that evening and answered Dick's questions, each time with informed, confident answers, like Patricia Dick had glimpsed a spark, and often that was all it took to ignite fire, one spark could turn lifeless black into brilliance.

When he'd probed the circumstance that enabled O'Shea positive knowledge of Whittle's success and discovered it was through a friend, Beth, who worked in the office, at first Dick had felt critical of the somewhat devious means, even more so when O'Shea was at pains to explain that the said young lady was not an intended. That old fashioned term, 'one's intended'. Dick couldn't help wondering if Beth was aware of how Connor chose to describe her, if he'd been a man in the dock his manner would have given away his guilt. In that instant Dick had passed judgement, then frowned on his own hypocrisy, it was just the kind of thing he would have done years ago, he'd used people to advance himself. In fact he could see a lot of the young Dick Woolascroft in Patricia's Irish prodigy, that same determination, regardless.

It was age and experience now made them different characters, Dick found himself looking forward to home at the end of a day, to being in the innocent company of his wife, that constant, which Olive had become. It had taken him all these years to appreciate her loyalty, the dignity she refused to adulterate with snide remarks, those petty insults many folk traded in their attempt to win an argument. These days Olive would confront him over his decisions but only ever with carefully chosen words, which served their purpose, he'd turn them over in his mind, apply their caution or encouragement, whichever might be the case. His father must be turning in his grave, perhaps Connor O'Shea might quell Fred's unrest, a determined young man with a devious streak, not afraid to bulldoze his way to success, just the type of fodder on which Fred Woolascroft had grown fat, ideal putty for his hands to mould.

Six thousand pounds was a princely sum for any young man to have at his disposal. O'Shea had skilfully talked his way in, but more than that, he'd bought his way in. When Dick had probed the ability of one so young to make an investment, albeit modest overall, and learned firsthand from Connor of his inheritance, that too had proved persuasive, his grandfather must have thought a great deal of the lad, and when Connor declared, 'I've sat with it, let it grow, waiting for the right opportunity', such mature thinking seemed to endorse the grandfather's belief. Only time would tell.

In theory the two companies should make profits for each other and in practice Dick couldn't see why that couldn't be so. But Patricia must depend more on her head, he could understand why she'd torn up Basil's cloak and sent it to the bottom of the rag pile, but sentiment could cost dear in business, he could vouch for that, Mitchell Street, the odd side, he'd allowed his heart to rule.

Foundation work had begun already on the site at Bulwell, every trench dug, each ton shifted, ultimately became an entry on the accounts of both Whittle's and Woolascroft's, incomings or outgoings. Dick's name used for Patricia's purpose had guaranteed a favourable rate for his own firm and while legally the two were entirely separate entities, in principle it was a sort of marriage, but of convenience, for appearances' sake Patricia would have it to be, Dick had simply been unopposing. Eddowes wouldn't see it that way, not until the benefits became clear, there was truth in the notion that two people could abide together more economically than one on their own.

Dick looked at the clock, everyone else had gone, the yard was deserted. No doubt by this time tomorrow all manner of speculation would be passed about and the name Woolascroft kicked like a ball from one side of opinion to the other. It made him remember that afternoon, following his mother's funeral of earlier in the day, when he'd walked along Mitchell Street and joined in the kick about with two boys, when he'd met the dreamer at No.69.

'Dick's goin' to shake things up around here'. Folk could say and think whatever they liked, he'd kept his promise. Whenever he had a moment of doubting himself, knowing he'd been as good as his word restored his spirit.

He took his jacket from the hook, his keys from the drawer, and laughed, a full, out loud laugh, despite everything he felt entitled.

Mathew had gone next door to see the Batemans, too late now to go back into work it seemed a good opportunity, he was fond of the elderly couple. Emily had arrived home with some class work to mark, the pupils had advanced under her more up to date approach, she had achieved to secure a number of new books and the standard of reading had definitely improved, even Timmy Hitchins was sufficiently confident to take a turn at reading to the class. So these days it was a reasonably cheerful Emily who left the house each weekday morning and returned late afternoon feeling her job well done. Her bus ride today however had not been uneventful, she'd found herself sitting alongside Ernie Searle, he'd an appointment at the dentist. 'Kathleen's gone to the funeral, hard day for Rosie', he'd said with genuine sympathy. But it was his other remark that puzzled her. 'Summat's up with our Beth, her mam could tell she'd been cryin' but when she asked what was the matter all Beth said wer' nothing mam, nothing's the matter. Things must have been difficult at Whittle's since Bill died but Beth's gone in every day, doin' her best, if somebody's spoken out o' turn an' upset her it's a bad job, she's a good lass is our Beth. If Peter's heard somethin' then he's not said owt but he's about as sensitive as a firebrick, goes in to work of a mornin', does his job 'til knockin' off time then leaves it all behind, his sister takes everythin' to heart, soft like her mam is Beth'.

That was as far as the conversation went before Ernie got off at his stop. Emily had thought to ask her dad if he'd heard anything untoward regarding Whittle's but when she'd mentioned it to her mam Celia had cautioned her to leave it for now. Since getting back from Tommy's William had been subdued and she was loth for anything to disturb the peace. Whittle's might prove an agitation, Celia suspected that not all was well with William's affairs and few subjects felt to be safe, even a comment on the weather might invite some caustic remark in response.

The phone began to ring in the hallway, William made no move so Celia answered.

"291233."

William's ears pricked up, Celia was animated, excited, to the other extreme of earlier. The funeral service had caused many tears, Gwendolyn he imagined was operating the floodgates, poor Audrey Potts had been up against a champion in the madness stakes, Audrey could do no better than 'also ran'.

After several minutes Celia put down the receiver and hurried into the living room where he sat, calling out to Emily at the same time.

"That was Francis, Faith's had her baby, a week overdue but all's well. A boy, 8lbs14 ½ ozs. John Henry."

William had ever puzzled over the way women announced the precise weight of a baby, like a butcher at every transaction over his counter. If the infant was safely born what possible difference could half an ounce make? Celia chattered on.

"I told mam to give Francis our telephone number, a letter would take too long and it would be silly for them to pay for a telegram. John, I'm so pleased that they've named the baby John. Of course they want us to take the news to Annie as soon as we can, if you don't want to go William I'll take the bus. After all the sadness of this afternoon Annie needs cheering, besides I know she's been anxious hoping every day to hear."

Emily now joined them. "Uncle Freddy will be so happy, we must visit them in a week or two, take grandma, but you could go to Winchester Street now at least Dad, even grandad will be pleased I'm sure, you're not going anywhere this evening are you, it wouldn't take you long anyway?"

Celia's excitement suddenly dimmed at the prospect of William's awkwardness, his face showed no joy at the news. She had no way of knowing how much Emily's innocent words had tormented him, he felt it, the irony, going nowhere summed up his current circumstances.

William got up from his chair. "Alright, if that's what you want I shall take the news to Winchester Street, every last half ounce of it."

News could be a weighty business, a burden to carry. He looked over at the small side table, his whisky was low in the bottle, on the way home from delivering the 8lbs 14½ ozs he'd call at the off licence, wet the infants head as it were, raise a glass. To that at least he was entitled.

CHAPTER TWENTY

Late June.

Edgar brought the hatchet down on the piece of wood and felt his nerves shudder as another kindler flew across the yard. At early summer his activities would seem premature but he could not be still. He'd taken Elizabeth to Joyce where she'd be happily occupied with some kind of pastime most likely planned well ahead of this day.

Valerie had gone into labour five hours ago, Peggy and the midwife were with her and as each minute passed Edgar willed his son or daughter, whichever it might be, to enter the world safely and to cry out to him through the open bedroom window above.

Suddenly a head popped over the garden wall.

"Anythin' yet? I've been listenin', I told Harry to turn the wireless off so's I could hear. 'Educatin' Archie', 'e tunes into that every week, I've sent him down the pub, not much educatin' goes on there but at least I'll hear the baby when it stretches its lungs, no sound quite like it, allus made me milk flow."

Edgar put down the hatchet. "No, not yet Mrs.Tilsley, but Joyce says it'll wait 'til dark, most babies do." He'd checked the living room clock not long ago, almost half past eight. Not since listening in faint hope as a child for the sound of Santa's reindeers had he so longed for darkness to fall.

"Yer can't hurry it," said Mrs.Tilsley, "an' if it's a boy, well, I reckon they go back to sleep for a bit halfway through. Our Alf took two days. Me mam, bless her, come wi' her bag o' wool an' needles thinkin' she'd start a sock while she waited but by the time the lazy little beggar finely popped out she'd knitted two pairs o' knee length an' a balaclava."

With that note of encouragement duly delivered, thankfully she disappeared. Two days! Edgar's stomach knotted at the thought. He looked skyward, at last night clouds were gathering, he picked up the hatchet, breathed deep and returned to his wood chopping.

"Just another ten minutes Elizabeth then you must get ready for bed, it's school tomorrow."

Joyce had made up the bed in readiness, it had been arranged weeks ago, when Valerie started Elizabeth would stay with her grandma Joyce until the baby was born. Joyce had explored the toy shops for likely distractions, a jigsaw of cats and a sewing set had lain in the sideboard drawer awaiting their usefulness. Elizabeth, while excited at the prospect of a baby brother or sister was now at an age to be anxious for her mam.

William had come home from work and on finding Joyce and Elizabeth busily engaged with needle and thread at once guessed the situation, his reaction had been to declare to the child. 'After tea we'll walk to the corner an' you can choose some sweets at the shop before they shut. We'll buy a bit o' chocolate for your grandma an' somethin' for your mam as well'.

Joyce regularly counted her blessings. William had struggled with his emotions all those years ago when baby Elizabeth had suddenly come to dwell under his roof. It had been a tense time for them all yet as the months went by William had grown fond of the bundle of innocence. How his own mother would have loved her, a little girl, all those sons but no daughter. Florrie Haynes would have cherished the infant, any unfortunate circumstances surrounding Elizabeth's entry to the world would have failed to plant a single shred of doubt in Florrie's mind. William would do this for his mam.

Now William sat in the corner, contentedly observing the scene, his Joyce, a grandma, a role she filled with ease. Tonight they would both play their part, he'd piggy back Elizabeth up the stairs, tuck her up in bed and call for Joyce to come and kiss her goodnight, just as Edgar had always done until he and Valerie married and set up their own home. Despite the mixed feelings it had proved good, as a family should be, and soon there would be another member. Edgar would bring word, all they could do was wait.

Joyce encouraged Elizabeth's efforts, guiding the little fingers until they grasped the sequence, pushing the needle through the back of the cloth, then up again. For Joyce it required little concentration and her mind was elsewhere, with her niece Beth.

Connor had seemed relaxed and comfortable in Beth's company on the occasions they'd called in. Both William and herself had imagined them to be a settled couple. Connor was like most men folk, never too attentive whilst being observed, but that was their way, a young woman might persuade a boyfriend to hold hands but kissing and cuddling was reserved for the back row of the cinema or other suitably dark places. The arch of the viaduct probably freed the ardour of most young men when wanting to canoodle, Joyce had heard it referred to as 'the rutting ground'.

Connor had told Beth that though he cared for her as a close friend he was afraid her feelings ran deeper than his own and so to save even greater hurt he felt they should spend less time together, especially as he must now concentrate more on his responsibilities at Whittle's. That had been two months ago and though Beth had tried to cope with the awkwardness of working herself in the office at Whittle's it had proved too much and she'd handed in her notice three weeks ago. In fairness to Connor he'd tried to dissuade her from leaving but to no avail. Beth had hidden herself away, withdrawn and miserable, her mam's sympathy had further cocooned her. It had been Tommy who'd rescued the situation, at least for the time being. The young woman who'd been doing the paperwork at Handley's for the past six years had left to have her second child, Beth was capable of taking on the work and uncles Tommy and Joe would make sure that their niece found her smile again. Beth's brother Peter had vent' his feelings one evening after work, seeking out Connor at Whittle's yard and confronting him. For several days Connor had sported a black eye, though Peter could not really claim bravado as Connor had offered no resistance and no retaliation.

'I reckon O'Shea knew 'e had it comin' an' thought it wer' nothin' more than 'e deserved', had been Peter's frustrated view of the incident.

"Come on now Elizabeth," said Joyce, "bed, tuck your needle in the cloth and put it in the box, you can do some more tomorrow."

William got to his feet. "Here we go Princess, up the timbered hill." He lowered himself so's she could climb onto his back, Joyce looked on and as they disappeared up the stairs she made another count of her blessings.

It was almost six o'clock when the back door latch lifted quietly and Edgar came in. Joyce had been up since five, unable to sleep she'd been glad to tiptoe to the scullery to make some tea, William had followed just a few minutes after. He left the house each workday morning at a little after six, still at the pit but now a foreman and popular with the men, he saw no reason to change what had become familiar. Some of the miners looked on him as an extension of his brother Jack, that same solid character, firm but fair. Jack would often pull his leg. 'You're a Godsend to the Union Will, they know any gripe or grouse will be 'arf chewed by you afore I have to bite on it'.

Under Jack's management the pit operated with little disturbance, the work was still filthy black, and dangerous, but the men were heard to sing and whistle these days far more than they cursed and swore.

William was putting his flask and sandwiches into his dinner bag, while Joyce was running water on the dishes in the sink, Edgar looked from one to the other with a beam on his face that could have outshone a full moon.

"It's a boy, I couldn't come 'til now, he finally arrived a quarter to one this mornin'. Peggy wer' asleep on her feet so when the midwife left I sent her to bed for a bit."

"Is everything alright?" Joyce couldn't rest until she knew both baby and Valerie were well.

Edgar grinned and hugging Joyce kissed her. "They're both lovely, Valerie's tired o' course but Master Perry's doin' everythin' he's supposed to, he soon found out where food comes from an' he's got all the right engineerin'."

William laughed, "Congratulations lad, you're not goin' in to the factory today surely." Edgar had left the pit and secured a place at Briggs a few years back.

"No, I've already squared it with the boss, I'll make up the hours in overtime, it's Friday tomorrow anyway so I shan't go in 'til Monday. Come round when you can, he's a fine chap."

"What weight is he," asked Joyce, "an' have you named him yet?"

"You women want to know the weight, breadth an' length, midwife even measured the circumference of his head," said Edgar with a chuckle. "He wer' 8lbs somethin', I can't remember how many ounces, I wer' shakin' like a leaf, a proper bundle o' nerves by then. But I can tell you his name. Luke, William, Peggy wanted him to have a biblical name, Valerie an' me both like Luke an' William is for his grandad."

William threw his strong arms about Edgar. "God bless yer Son," when he released his hold Edgar glimpsed tears in William's eyes, but within seconds, dinner bag over his shoulder, he was through the door and gone.

"By break time everybody at pit will know," said Joyce. "Shall I take Elizabeth to school?"

She hoped Edgar would let the child miss lessons today.

"Bring her home Joyce, she'll be aching to see Luke an' Valerie'll want to see her."

It was the answer Joyce hoped for. "Tell Peggy I'll make a pot of stew, enough for all of us an' when William's got in from his shift an' had a bath we'll come round, I won't be able to contain him 'til he's seen his grandson. Best you tell Peggy now, it'll save her havin' to think about cookin' today. Elizabeth's fast asleep still, I won't hurry her. Be sure to tell Peggy that we won't stay long this evenin', Valerie needs her peace."

Joyce sat alone in the quietness. So many memories joined her at the scullery table, some brushed her fingers with kindness, others stung her knuckles in rebuke, they visited her still from time to time, when she was by herself, when she let them in. Luke William Perry. Joyce was happier than words could adequately express, yet she wept, not a distressed sobbing but a silent flow of tears. Only the memories were present to witness and they wouldn't tell, they never did, in all the many times they'd sat with her, despite everything, in that respect they were compassionate.

Celia had tried hard to persuade William to drive the family to Bonthorpe but in vain, so he could like it or lump it, George would take them, in fact George had suggested it before she had time to ask. The disappointing though predictable element was Charles, he'd declared himself too ill and too old to go gadding about the countryside, it should be the young ones bringing the child to see its great grandparents. Annie knew that if she went, leaving him on his own for all the hours they would be away, then for days after his temper would flare at the least little thing, she was too old to bear the strain, he'd achieved his aim, making it impossible for her to ride with George and the others. Freddy would understand, while William was always ready to judge he held little perception of the reality, whereas Freddy was aware. Perhaps Richard and Faith might come after harvest, when the farm work eased a little, bring the baby. All the family could gather at Winchester Street to meet John then Charles need only stake claim to the chair in the corner and pretend to be pleased.

And so on Sunday, George, Liza, Celia and Emily would go to Bonthorpe, taking with them Annie's love along with some skilfully knitted and crocheted outfits for her great grandson.

Celia had arranged to meet Rosie in town today, at ten o'clock. Friday could often prove to be the best day to buy fruit and veg from the barrow boys, Saturday's clamour gave the shrewd traders an opportunity to off load one or two less fresh items if the individuals buying didn't watch their sleight of hand.

Emily had seemed a bit out of sorts lately, in the spring she'd been fine, delighted with her pupils' progress but of late her cheerful chatter had been replaced with periods of silence, as though miles away in thought, she would go into the front room and play quietly on the piano, something she'd rarely done since starting at Harrow Road. A mother's intuition allowed Celia to suspect Connor as the cause of her daughter's remoteness, though it was unlikely he held any awareness of Emily's feelings.

News had slowly seeped, Beth had been put aside by the ambitious O'Shea who now embraced only his new found position of importance as a foreman at Whittle's, ranking alongside the seasoned Jed Unwin.

Celia had sensed some time ago that Emily was jealous of Beth's friendship with Connor, her less than complimentary remarks directed at the young Irishman were designed to cover up her true feelings, a mother recognised these things. The situation must now torment Emily all the more, Connor no longer with Beth meant she could befriend him without feeling guilty, it was easy to think and say, but hard to do. Beth was hurting and if what folk were saying were true then Connor O'Shea was best left to his ambitions, any self respecting young woman would avoid him. He'd inveigled his way into Patricia Bradshaw's affairs with an eye to advancement and poor Beth had been cast off like a worn shirt.

Yet Celia couldn't subscribe to this move against Connor, it wasn't in his nature to be heartless. Rosie had learned from her niece his actual words, his truthful concern at Beth's depth of feeling being greater than his own and his wish for her to meet the right man, which he was not.

Heartache was the most painful condition at any age but for the young, with as yet little experience of life's knocks it could be even more crushing. Celia would look for something nice in the shops, a pretty blouse for summer might cheer up Emily. The main purpose of the shopping trip was to find a gift for baby John, fruit and veg were necessities and sought with care but never enthusiasm, searching the baby wear department at Burton's however would give Rosie and herself great pleasure. Celia looked forward to again having a genuine reason to handle those delicate items, the pretty ribbons, cute rattles and teething rings, skin soft cot sheets and tiny bootees. She sighed at the thought of how much easier it was to relieve the discomfort of a baby's wind than to take away the pain of a grown daughter's heartache.

The foundation work at Bulwell was almost finished, Dick had gone there to see for himself the progress. Working two offices until Patricia was confident in her knowledge of the business, Dick had endured long days in recent weeks. A replacement had been found for Beth Searle, a week's trial had proved Sonia Holloway to be suitable. As Dick had pointed out, in due course Patricia might decide it sensible to hire a manager, while at this early stage she was enjoying the challenge herself, albeit with Dick's help, in time the responsibility may become too much.

Connor was foreman on the Bulwell site today while Jed Unwin was overseeing a difficult job at Clifton, where the digger work was close to a water main, the last thing anyone wanted was for the pipe to be ruptured. Any resentment at working with one as young as Connor and on the same level as himself Unwin had soon abandoned, O'Shea was capable. Connor was also intelligent enough to realise that in his situation a degree of tact would serve him well, sufficiently wise to recognise that to keep his own counsel over his investment in the firm would allow him a better relationship with the men.

Unwin had accepted management's decision whether it be attributed to Patricia Bradshaw or Dick Woolascroft, he'd kept his job and knew how to do it, beyond that he was disinclined to concern himself.

"When do you expect the plant to drive off site?" Asked Dick. "Later today would suit me O'Shea, the sooner bricks go up the better, at this stage every site looks a bloody mess but once the masons get goin' a man can see some order."

Connor laughed. "Can't wait to be rid of us Mr.Woolascroft, me mother is more philosophical, when it's time to spring clean an' all the furniture gets pulled out, pictures took off the wall an' curtains put to wash she'll say, 'you have to be a mess before you can be tidy'. Five of us kids in the house, her an' me father, I reckon a bit o' mess is healthy, stops a man from gettin' above himself.

I went to a place with Mr.Eddowes once, he'd been rentin' it out, the tenants had moved on. Most folk leave somethin' o' themselves behind, but that house hadn't got as much as a scuff mark to record their existence. We'll be gone tonight Mr.Woolascroft if I have to work the men into overtime but I shall leave a bit o' meself here somewhere, to record the mess as bein' Connor O'Shea's, own it for what it is."

Dick smiled, he began to understand Patricia's liking for this young Irishman, some folk challenged, made life harder than it need be, O'Shea had an easy manner about him, the very opposite of William Eddowes, chafing, forever chafing. It was to be expected, Cheetham wasn't happy either, but this build at Bulwell would better their fortunes and back at Dick's office another costing was underway, this time for an extension to the University Building. Patricia's connections were proving useful, Dick could do no other than admit that to himself so he could hardly judge O'Shea for having recognised the opportunity she presented. He slapped Connor on the back.

"See you at the next mess then O'Shea." As he walked away to his vehicle Dick felt strangely at ease.

"How is Beth now?" Asked Celia. "Working at Handley's with Tommy and Joe in a different environment must help. I haven't seen Connor for some time, I know his mother isn't very well. I suppose I should feel cross with him but he's easy to like and young after all. I dare say that when he first started at Whittle's he felt a bit lost, Beth would have been a friendly face, a pretty one too. A first love. We've both known the bewilderment of that haven't we? I remember you and William were soft on one another at school and I thought I was in love with Norris Singleton, I made him a Christmas card and bought a man's cotton handkerchief with my own money to put inside it. Then William smiled at me, who would believe that a simple smile could perform such magic, even without the dimming of lights or a drum roll it can turn the heart from a steadily beating pump to an out of control spinning top and you've no idea how. You probably didn't like me much at that time."

Rosie sniffed. "We were just kids, what did we know about love, our Beryl loves her rabbits more than I ever loved William an' he never really cared much for me. You were lucky, you didn't have a bosom the lads wanted to play with, that's all it was, I don't think they ever noticed the rest o' me, even Tommy enjoyed a fumble, but he did care, not like the others. You'll always have to compete with William's other love, himself, before anyone else, I'm convinced he loves himself."

“Celia thread her arm through Rosie’s. “Come on, let’s lose ourselves in the baby wear department and we’ll pop into ladies fashion to see Liza, she’s quite excited about going to Bonthorpe on Sunday, besides, I want to look for something to cheer up Emily, she’s been a bit down lately.”

The two women walked through Burton’s arcade looking at the attractive window displays. Annie would say ‘a cat can look at a king’, expensive furnishings and rich fabrics, fine bone china and sparkling cut glass, wonderful hats to complement elegant outfits, not items on the average shopping list but anyone might look and admire. Inside the infant department any woman with maternal feelings couldn't fail to be charmed, smocked bodices, lacy bonnets, embroidered pram covers, all in delicate pastel shades and purest white.

Surely it was Joyce Haynes looking at a pale blue romper suit, she’d not noticed them. “Cooee.” Rosie called across.

Joyce looked up and her face broke into a wide grin as she held up the romper. “Early hours of this mornin’, a boy.” Celia and Rosie hurried over to her. “I sent word to Kathleen an’ she was goin’ to let everybody know, Beth would have told Tommy when she got to work. Luke William, 8lbs 5ozs, he’s beautiful. I didn’t dare to buy blue or pink until we knew, this is for Elizabeth to give to her little brother.”

“Congratulations Joyce, give our love to them all. That’s three new babies in a row. Faith last April, Maureen Jones last month and now Valerie.” With a rush of emotion Celia hugged Joyce tightly.

“Look at me soft ‘apeth, new borns allus make me cry.” Rosie dabbed her eyes with a hanky, laughing at the same time. For the next half hour or so they shopped together, parting company only when their purchases in that department were done.

“I’ll just have a quick look in fashions Rosie,” said Celia, “Liza will know of any really good buys and if I can’t find anything we’ll try C&A, I haven’t been in there yet.”

"I have," said Rosie, "they've some nice stuff, I don't suppose it's the same quality as Burton's but Beryl's growin' so fast it wouldn't be sensible to pay too much for her clothes until she's older. I got her a pretty frock an' bolero for the summer an' they weren't all that dear. I used to give Joyce bits an' pieces when Beryl grew out of them, for Elizabeth. I didn't know what to do when Edgar married Valerie, it's difficult isn't it?"

"I'm sure Valerie would appreciate help as much as Joyce did," said Celia. "I don't really know her but I can't imagine she's proud, I don't mean that in any way nastily, it all worked out well in the end didn't it?"

Rosie nodded agreement and they stepped inside ladies fashion. An impressive array of the most stylish clothing met them, along with a scented air from the many sample bottles, dabbed frequently onto wrists, which were than waved about to set the perfume. It was far from Rosie's usual shopping ground and if she could have seen just one mannequin with an ample bosom she might have felt less out of place but all were like beanpoles.

"There's Liza," said Celia, "she's serving a customer, let's look at this rail of blouses while we wait until she's free." The choice was considerable but the prices at the upper range of what Celia felt she could afford.

"Can I help you Madam?" A rather grand voice halted Celia and Rosie in their search of the rail. A tall, smartly dressed woman now stood by them, Rosie wondered if she should stick out her tongue and show both sides of her hands, like she was required to do when the school nurse paid a visit, surely any moment now she would feel this figure of authority intent on exploring her scalp for head lice. "Are you both seeking to purchase, we do have a selection for the fuller figure." The woman's gaze fell upon Rosie who in that instant was compelled to scratch her head and sense again the shame of being sent home with a note.

"We're just looking thank you," said Celia, "for a gift for my daughter."

"I see, well if you require any assistance our fully trained ladies are on hand to help." She smiled but with one of those synthetic expressions that looked the part but held no real substance.

"A sales assistant like her could close the Co-op," observed Rosie. "I bet she's never set foot in Moffat's an' she's sure to have one o' them double barrelled names, Lady Flat Chested of La de dah."

"Shush she might hear you," said Celia with a chuckle, "Liza's free now, even if I don't buy anything I must say hello to her."

Whispering the nature of their encounter Liza listened with amusement.

"Take no notice, that's Mrs.Warneck, head of department, she's alright really been here for donkeys' years, one of a dying breed in this day an' age, she epitomises the stiff upper lip."

"Uhm, I bet she does," said Rosie with feeling.

Celia explained their purpose and Liza led them to a stand of reduced items.

"End of lines but there's one or two you might like, I know there's a nice skirt, it would suit Emily."

Liza had come up trumps, indeed it was in every way suitable, the right size and colour, and reasonably priced.

"I shall put it in one of the store's special bags, for the more select customer which of course you are." Liza winked roguishly.

Her purchases now completed Celia confirmed the time she and Emily were to be ready for George to collect them on Sunday morning and they left.

"We've to walk past C&A, you ought to take a quick peek in there, compare the prices then you'll know for another time." It was almost midday and Celia wanted to catch the half past twelve bus but Rosie had been patient while she shopped for Emily's present in Burton's so a brief scan of C&A was only fair.

The store was busy, being brightly lit and colourful made it seem more so. Celia took a quick look at several price tags, they would certainly tempt folk and the various racks and counters displayed all manner of attire. In their need to hurry neither Celia nor Rosie noticed a sales assistant a few yards away, staring at them intently. Yes, it was her, Diane Roper observed the two women, one she'd not seen before but the other she recognised, William Eddowes' wife. It had been just a brief encounter when handing over the keys to Moreleigh but it was definitely the same woman, and she carried a fancy bag emblazoned with 'Burton's', in gold lettering. To date Diane had received but a pittance from Steve, all he could afford to send his note said, he'd cast her a crumb. She'd heard folk talking about Woolascroft's, how they'd taken over Whittle's. William had interest in Woolascroft's, that she knew. Men like him never failed to make money, he led a charmed life, how he must be raking it in and his lady wife enjoying the spending of it. The Burton's bag stung her like a slap in the face, she watched the two women hurry out through the door and bit hard on her own meagre finances. If soon she didn't gather sufficient money to feel in control of her life she'd go mad, while the thought of sitting in the living room at Christmas with the weird embalmer and his deceased mother, abiding still at that house, which week on week grew creepier, drove her mind to depths of despair.

Annie had called on Lizzie Sealey to make sure she was coping. Found guilty of manslaughter the powers that be had ordered Fred to be detained for the duration of his sentence, not at Nottingham prison where he'd been held on remand, but at Leeds, locally referred to as Armley Goal, an execution site though Fred would not hang. It seemed particularly harsh on Lizzie, as if a contrary malice determined her hardship. How was the unfortunate woman supposed to visit her husband, it required a lengthy train journey and with

Lizzie's limited means it was prohibitively costly. Annie couldn't accompany her to Leeds, the situation seemed hopeless.

Then yet again, Andrew Smithfield came to Lizzie's aid, he'd read the report in the newspaper of Fred's trial and sentence, concerning himself right away over the difficulty Leeds presented. Last week he'd driven Lizzie all the way to Armley Goal, waited while she was with Fred, then taken her to a tearoom for some hot, sweet tea before bringing her back to her front door. Annie had been with Lizzie when he called for her and when she'd stood on the pavement waving as the car pulled away her gratitude had been immense, to have such a friend was surely to have riches beyond price.

Lizzie's spirits had been bolstered as a result, Andrew's kindness enabled her to better cope with the now odd thoughtless remark. As with all such dramatic events folk seized upon at the time, talking of little else, gradually their obsession had faded and they'd moved on until the next upheaval took over their tongues and minds.

Andrew would be happy to take Lizzie again in a week or two.

When Annie had enquired after Fred, Lizzie's reply had hardly filled her with confidence.

'A man sat opposite me, it looked like Fred so I suppose it must have been him. They let him have his old cartoon book in Nottingham, perhaps they have different rules at Leeds'.

That dreadful tragedy of last January seemed to feed on misery, ever growing, spreading its reach and whether intentionally or not, catching the innocent and unrelated in its grip. Lizzie's predicament was bad enough but Bill Whittle's widow, being obliged to sell the business as she must have viewed her position, enabled yet another serving of misery. William festered within from Dick's apparent gain over his own and Celia bore the brunt. Poor Beth too had become a casualty of the situation, Connor now intent on proving Patricia's faith in him to be merited had left no space in his days for the homely

Beth. All these thoughts went through Annie's mind as she walked back home. If only Charles had clutched at the chance of going to the farm, instead he would sit in the corner, speaking hardly at all, glancing at the clock as though willing his time away.

As she approached the back door of No.1 she could hear a woman's voice escaping from the opening at the top of the window, it was familiar. She hurried inside to find Gertie and Jean sitting on the old sofa below the window, looking fraught. Charles glowered at Annie as though she might have returned from some devious assignation. He spoke.

"They've been here half an hour already."

"Oh, I'm sorry Gertie, Jean, I shall put the kettle on right away."

"We've been at City Hospital Annie, Nora's had a fall, broken her hip the doctor said, she's in a poorly way. Her neighbour came to tell us, Nora gave her Maggie's telephone number but no one answered. It happened in the early hours an' by the time Mrs.Wilson found her Nora was cold even though the temperature in the house was mild. The ambulance man said it was shock, regardless of the time of year a fall and injury like that always causes the casualty to feel cold. Once they got Nora safely into the ambulance Mrs.Wilson hurried back to the phone box and tried Maggie again but still no reply so she caught the bus and came to us. We've managed to get hold of Maggie since and she'll let Mavis know."

Annie sank onto a chair, she'd visited Nora just twice since her move to Bilborough. Mitchell Street had been so much closer and No.69 had always been special, sitting there in that simple house with Nora Annie had relived memories, felt a closeness to Harold, now she regretted not spending more time with her.

"I shall go to see Nora this evening, I believe visiting is seven to eight."

“They have to do an operation,” said Jean, “they said not to visit until tomorrow but to ring the hospital late afternoon, not before five, they should be able to tell us more then.

Mrs.Wilson found her on the lavatory floor, at least that’s inside the house, imagine how much worse it would have been if it had happened on the cobbles at No.69.”

Charles stared at the hearth making no attempt at conversation, he embarrassed Annie, what must Gertie and Jean think of him and how much of his sullen indifference had they endured through the course of that half an hour while waiting for her to come back from Lizzie’s. Anyone else would have tried to comfort, to encourage hope. Perhaps Charles, like Armley Gaol, imposed different rules.

CHAPTER TWENTY ONE

Late August.

'You can't draw blood from a stone'. Diane was resigned to accepting the truth of the old adage. She folded the sheet of paper and slid it back inside the envelope, ten pounds, Steve had thrown her but another crumb. He had no assets and the balance of his account at the bank in Wellington had been reduced to virtually nothing as a result of paying her fare back to England, along with money to see her through until securing a job. It was the best he could do, take it or leave it, hardly a love letter but it was she, after all who'd 'left it'.

Just then a knock came at her bedroom door, it opened and Claude Robotham appeared she'd completely forgotten it was this evening he collected her bed linen for laundering and handed her clean sheets and pillowslips. Normally she would have the neatly folded linen ready for the weekly ritual, it was the same every time, as though they must not introduce any change to the sequence for fear of upsetting the ether, disturbing the gods.

"I'm going away on Friday," he said. Diane's expression couldn't fail to reveal her surprise, would they now be turned to pillars of salt! "I go to the coast every year in August, when mother was alive we would spend a week at Chapel St. Leonards, now I go for a couple of days, she expects me to paddle my feet. Mother was a great believer in the benefits to the feet of salt water. I shall catch a train on Friday morning and return Sunday evening. You have your keys so be sure to lock up when you go out. I trust our initial agreement will be adhered to?" He gave Diane a vaguely critical look.

Why doesn't he just come out with it, she thought, did he suppose that the minute his back was turned she would become a harlot, prostitute his mother's bloody bed. "I shall be diligent in securing all doors and windows when leaving the house and remain as celibate as a vestal virgin." She took the clean linen from him, put it down on the chair while she quickly stripped the bed, rolling the sheets and pillowslips into a neat bundle and handing it to him with a most ambiguous smile. "You can rely on me Mr.Robotham and enjoy your paddle in the full knowledge that No.15 Mansfield Road will continue to be a house of utter respectability."

"Yes, well, that's alright then." He nodded his head, turned and hurried away down the stairs.

Did he even know what hanky panky meant? Dipping his toes in the sea at Chapel St. Leonards was likely to be the extent of his abandon. She sighed, took the clean linen from the chair and made up the bed, tucking the sheets under the edge of the mattress with such force that she caught her hand on the bed frame splitting a finger nail. "Hell an' damnation." Frustration drove her curses, and her mind to finding a way out of her predicament. She was entitled to a life, even the weird embalmer was escaping his confines for the weekend. She would cast those tormenting names to fate, Steve Roper, Claude Robotham and William Eddowes, she would turn them over and over in her mind like a tombola and allow fate to decide which name came out first, then claim her prize.

Beth had settled in well at Handley's with her uncles and the kindly Bob Lacey. The nature of her work, typing, keeping ledgers, filing and answering the telephone was not so very different to her role at Whittle's, the nature of the business itself however was a world away from Bill Whittle's type of operation. The days at Handley's were always busy but gentleness prevailed, a respectful awareness at all times of life's slender thread. While the men could swap yarns over their dinner break, sitting as they did on the bench in the yard, only quiet concentration was ever given to the mortal remains in their care. On starting

Beth had imagined a creepy, fearful place and so had felt surprised at her own sense of calm when seated in the office as her first day progressed. Responding to an individual on the telephone whose desperate call was for Tommy or Joe to come had taught Beth to look forward, not back. Those who grieved the death of a loved one, until a passage of time enabled them to do otherwise, could only look back and seek comfort from memories. Beth missed Connor, but he'd not died, she had no call to grieve.

Payment had arrived in this morning's first post of the bill for Mrs. Oates' funeral. It had been viewed by everyone as particularly sad, so soon after the birth of Valerie's baby. When Peggy had not called as promised and still not come to see them the following day Edgar had gone to her home, after work that evening, to see if she was unwell. The back door was on the latch, he'd gone inside, called her name but the house was silent except for the ticking of the clock. Upstairs he'd found Peggy in bed, lifeless. For whatever reason, be it old age or a consuming weariness, her heart had ceased to beat. Edgar could do no other than fetch Valerie but how it pained him, Luke was barely a month old. Tommy had arrived there to find Valerie in a most anguished state of despair, she'd poured out her misery and Tommy had left there knowing that for Valerie, even looking back failed to offer solace. Peggy had lived for years with a man whose temper had ruled the household, sending her sons away from her, at the very first opportunity they'd left home to escape Tom Oates' belt and the dreaded riding crop he kept for special occasions!

The funeral had been just a week ago, Valerie had endured it only by clinging to Edgar throughout, looking on as Tommy must, he'd recognised devotion, whether or not Dick Woolascroft was Elizabeth's true father mattered not an iota, it was of no significance to either the husband and wife standing as one at Peggy's grave, or to anyone else, love made it so.

Typical of Edgar he'd settled the account without delay, the very next day he'd come to Handley's to ask for the bill. Valerie's brothers had attended the funeral and insisted on paying their share. Gradually Elizabeth and Luke would direct their mother's mind forward, to the future and memories would become less sharp.

Beth opened the filing cabinet and fingered through the dividers until she came to 'O' in the index. There appeared to be far fewer of those, not the most common initial. O'Shea, surely someone's account had been filed under the name O'Shea? Beth took the sheet of paper from the drawer, Handley's had carried out a funeral, the deceased being a Charles Holbrook, a solicitor, Julian Russe had instructed Handley's on behalf of Mr.Holbrook's daughter, Margaret O'Shea. It was dated February 1954. Beth placed the Oates' account, marked paid, in the drawer alphabetically, before an Ogden and the bewildering O'Shea. At that moment Tommy came into the office.

"Have you seen my glasses Beth, I've left them somewhere?"

"No, I've not noticed then Uncle Tommy." She hesitated for a moment, should she say something? Tommy wouldn't mind. "When I was putting the Oates' account into the filing cabinet I saw an entry in the name of O'Shea." The questioning look on Beth's face made Tommy sigh, in Beth's world only one O'Shea existed.

"Beth love, I can remember the funeral, it was a sad, bleak affair. Mr.Holbrook's daughter lives in Ireland, she came but apart from Bob's wife Moira, no one else attended, Moira found the poor old chap and called the ambulance, she and Bob live in the house next door. No family to mourn his passing but one daughter. Connor has brothers and sisters, his mam and dad, I bet there's a lot more in that family, Celia Eddowes has spoken of him to Rosie so I know it's true. You have to realise that in Ireland there must be hundreds of O'Shea's, and O'Donnells, O'Malleys, O'Connors, O'Haras, over there everybody's an O', somethin'." He chuckled. That Mrs.O'Shea might be a relative of Connors, I've even heard it said that we're all related to Adam an' Eve but me mam never got a Christmas card from em'. I best go search for me glasses, I've lost three pairs over the years, they've never come to light, Bob reckons they must have got shut in the coffins and departed with the corpses, if they did then I hope they gave the souls a better view of Heaven. I had to put his favourite pigeon in with one chap, I were only in me teens back then, perhaps he flew to them pearly gates faster than anybody else eh Beth." Tommy gave her a hug. "Move on love, give Valerie a bit of your time, there's always somebody with a bigger misery than your own an' Elizabeth could do with a distraction, take her out on her bike, bring her to our place to play with Beryl's rabbits." With that, he was away through the door.

Beth pushed in the drawer of the filing cabinet and returned to her work, only then spotting a pair of spectacles on the window ledge. Hurrying to the door she called out. "Uncle Tommy," but he'd already gone outside to the yard. She went to find him where he was searching the glove compartment of the hearse. She waved them in the air when he turned to look. "Under our noses all the time and still we didn't see."

A tap at the door caused Dick to look up, Sylvia, his wages clerk come secretary stepped inside pushing the door to behind her.

"There's a lady asking to speak with Mr.Eddowes, I explained that he's here at odd times only but she seems anxious, do you want me to send her away?"

Dick was working on figures for a maintenance job, some painting and general repair to the Alms Houses at Wollaton, not highly profitable but useful to the firm nonetheless. All such jobs kept Woolascroft's in the minds of folk while providing a learning situation for apprentices. He was thoughtful for a second or two.

"Now she's here you may as well send her through Sylvia."

Not since the day Patricia came to the yard had he received a lady caller and one asking for Eddowes made him curious.

"In here," said Sylvia, holding the door for the woman then closing it behind her with a quick glance at Dick.

He felt amused, wondering if Sylvia would resist the temptation to put her ear to the door panel. This woman Dick had never seen before, not unattractive but quite obviously agitated, her fingers loosening and tightening repeatedly at the sides of a clutch bag, as if trying to produce a tune. "Take a seat my dear." Dick offered a smile in an attempt to calm her nervousness.

"I've only a few minutes." Diane knew she would be late back from her dinner break at C&A but this was the only chance she had. "I need to speak to William Eddowes, I imagined I'd find him here, it's a matter of importance."

Dick's impression was of a woman in her forties, possibly younger but far from confident, ill at ease.

"I'm afraid Mr.Eddowes comes and goes at irregular intervals, depending on his various activities but as I've not seen him for a day or two I'd be very surprised if he didn't appear soon, certainly before the end of the week, I'm never permitted to avoid his scrutiny for long. I can of course give you his home address if that would help or his telephone number, his wife would be glad to take a message if he weren't there." Dick noticed the fingers again tighten around her bag.

"No, it's business you see, it would be much easier if I could speak to him directly. Would you be kind enough to give him my address? I'll write it down if I could beg a piece of paper and a pen. It's an urgent matter, if you would stress the importance of him meeting me there on Saturday afternoon or Sunday morning." Dick handed her a notepad and pen. She put her bag down on the desk and hastily wrote her name and address before passing both pen and pad back to him with a faint, "Thank you."

"Don't worry my dear, I shall see William receives it in time to set aside an hour at the weekend. Saturday afternoon or Sunday morning you said?"

"Yes, I'm at home then, remember to tell him that it's a business matter."

Dick glanced at the note pad. Diane Roper. 15, Mansfield Road. "You can rely on it being done Miss Roper, anything business related Mr.Eddowes pursues without delay, you may rest assured of that."

He watched her walk away, dash away in fact. Another pressing engagement perhaps, Diane Roper was clearly a busy lady.

Joyce gently put Luke down in his crib, the air was warm, a welcome breeze drifted in through the open window, along with the sound of Elizabeth's skipping rhyme. Joyce couldn't help thinking that thc start of autumn term would be a blessing for the child. Home had been a difficult place for Elizabeth these past few weeks. Joyce had spent almost all her time with Valerie and the children, Edgar had to work. William was understanding of the situation and provided Joyce was home each evening and overnight, made no demands on her time. With no lessons to occupy Elizabeth and Valerie so emotional and prone to tearful episodes it was for Joyce to be even more of a grandma. Rosie had been good as gold, calling as often as she could, sometimes with her dear friend Celia Eddowes. One day a knock had come to Edgar's back door and Joyce had been surprised, not so much at finding Annie Eddowes there but Mrs.Stanford as well. Never in a month of Sundays would Joyce have expected to put the kettle on to boil in order to make tea for Florence Stanford. Yet the hour or so had passed so easily. Children didn't notice differences, feel awkwardness at what the adult perceived as class divide and Elizabeth had responded to both Annie and Florence's encouragement, showing them her needlework and a poem that she'd written for her baby brother. Joyce's initial nervousness had very soon faded and just as she'd ever been in the company of Annie, so too she had become at ease chatting with Florence.

Luke's eyelids closed within seconds of Joyce laying him down, already his face was fuller, his limbs showing creases at the joints as week on week they grew fleshier. Valerie was blessed in having a baby so content as to sleep between feeds. Edgar was stoic, hurrying home from the factory and right away taking both Luke in his pram and Elizabeth on her bicycle round the block, often calling at the corner shop for a little something to take back to Valerie. It gave her the opportunity to prepare their meal and relax for ten minutes and relieved Joyce to go home to William.

The most distressing task had been to empty Peggy's things from the house she'd lived in for many years. One of Valerie's brothers had stayed on after the funeral to help. Edgar had paid her rent for the month of August, to grant them the necessary time. When he'd turned the key in the lock and walked away on that last evening a wave of sadness swept over him, shouldn't life offer more? Peggy Oates received a meagre share of happiness but one thought comforted him. She had seen and held her grandson amid great joy, entitlement denied her at Elizabeth's birth through Tom's harsh authority.

Valerie began to feel better, Joyce had managed to coax her outside of the house on most days the past week, reminding her that soon the mild weather would be gone and Luke should have the benefit of fresh air, autumn brought the shorter days and winter the most uninviting cold winds, it would be unfortunate not to seize what was left of summer.

It was while at the embankment the previous Sunday morning that they'd seen Connor, he was sitting alone on the steps, throwing bits of bread to the ducks and swans. Given all that they'd heard in recent weeks of his ambitious plans and selfishness it was an unlikely scene to behold. For a moment they'd been undecided, should they go over to him or quickly move on? Joyce knew only too well what it was like to be judged, so too did Valerie, they'd pushed the pram to the top of the steps and called his name. When he looked around it was genuine pleasure that came to his face, a broad smile. On his feet and standing beside them in seconds he'd given both a peck on the cheek and gazed down at the pram. 'What a fine chap you are Master Perry'. He'd put his hand out to touch Luke, who'd then wrapped his little fingers around Connor's forefinger. Without looking up he'd said, 'I'm sorry for the way things worked out, she's a good 'en Beth, the sort o' girl a man needs, trouble is us fellas' pay more dues to our wants than to our needs, don't have the good sense of you ladies, Beth deserves to be happy, I just wasn't the one'. With that he'd smiled vaguely and walked away. Although Joyce couldn't understand why, she'd fought back tears and sensed Connor was no more happy than was Beth.

"It's a good job you decided to look in today Eddowes," said Dick, "cuttin' it fine in fact."

William looked at him tetchily. "What the devil are you muttering about, if you needed me to sign something you only had to telephone, Celia would have answered if I wasn't home and passed on the message."

"That's exactly what I told Miss Roper but she insisted I give you this, she needs to speak to you personally and with urgency, either tomorrow afternoon or Sunday morning, she was most precise." Dick handed the sheet of notepaper to William who now had the look of a man caught cheating at cards. He read the words written upon it and mumbled something inaudible. "Business she said, must be crucial if so brief the opportunity to discuss it, best not spend too long hesitating Eddowes, he who does so is lost, as the saying goes." The sarcasm in Dick's voice irked William.

"And you should mind your own bloody business Woolascroft, while you're poking your nose into mine dear aunt Patricia could be mounting a takeover."

Dick laughed. "What do you take me for William, there's only one kind o' business that woman is about."

William was defensive. "I've not seen the woman in more than two years and bloody hell Woolascroft, you're in no position to judge me, not with your past, when it comes to being thick skinned you've the hide of a rhino. How can you be so two faced as to mock me when for all these years another man has reared your kid?"

"What do you mean?" Dick's tone had changed, no longer merely an idle taunting of William for the satisfaction of watching him squirm, it was now purposeful, intent on truthful answers. Did Eddowes really know what Dick, for so long had sought to find out?

It was William's turn to laugh. "Boot's on the other foot now isn't it Woolascroft? Talk about the fire calling the kettle, you take it to another level. Everybody knows it was you who put a kid in Valerie Oates' belly all those years ago then sat back to watch Edgar Perry, poor daft sod, raise it. You're a hypocrite Dick, you hide behind swank, decent house, big business, successful self made old man and an obedient wife, large aren't yer, well one day somebody'll cut you down to size an' I hope I'm there to witness."

Dick let William finish his tirade. "Sit down for God's sake man." Dick crossed the room to a cupboard, took from within, two tumblers and a bottle of whisky. Returning to his desk he poured a tot into each glass and placed one in front of William, then took a packet of cigarettes from his pocket, offering one across the desk.

No, I prefer my own brand, creature of habit, 'stick with what suits,' that's my motto."

Dick sat down, took a sip from his glass and lit a cigarette.

"Folk think they know, truth is they don't actually think at all an' sometimes it's easier to let it be. Valerie Oates came to this place, to this very room, all dolled up, asking me to give her a job. I sat in this same chair realising she'd put on her finery, powdered her nose an' painted her lips bright red believing she needed to present herself on a plate, then I'd not refuse, that was my reputation, Woolascroft the philanderer, I'd not bother my head one jot over the fact she'd had a baby out of wedlock. I'd find work for her, Dick Woolascroft wouldn't judge." He drew on his cigarette, mentally reliving that long gone moment. "I told her 'no', there was nothing here for her. I remember saying those words with the intent of inflicting hurt, I wasn't what she thought me to be. She had her hand on that door handle, about to leave." Dick pointed to the door. "Conscience made me change my mind, who was I to condemn, to even criticize I had no right, so I called her back and told her she could do up the men's wages, a week's trial. She was good, couldn't fault her work. By the end of the week I was in no doubt over her ability and certain in my mind that had I as much as laid my hand over one of hers she'd have slapped me in the face with the other. Valerie Oates' baby was nothing to do with me." Dick picked up his glass and emptied it with one swig. "Your turn Eddowes."

William now calmed by Dick's salutary account, sighed, looked down at the tumbler of whisky as if within its amber content lay pardon, and slowly spoke his own account. "Her husband works for Boot's, sales rep. But he must be good at his job as they offered him promotion if he went to New Zealand, to advance their set up over there. They emigrated, more than two years ago, I didn't know they were back, I didn't need to know, their absence was of no importance, her absence didn't occupy my mind."

"She isn't wearing a ring," said Dick. "I couldn't help but notice, her fingers clutched at her bag like a child clings to a comforter, she was nervous. Meet with her, find out what's wrong, but be careful William, you've a good family, we're too old you an' me to cope without them as understand us, remember your own motto, 'stick with what suits'."

William got to his feet before raising the glass of whisky to his lips and swallowing his measure. “Well who’d of thought it? Edgar Perry’s the father after all, bugger me.”

Dick wanted to respond by saying, ‘anyone with a half decent mind’, but why waste his breath, such an observation would be wasted on William Eddowes.

Emily walked along Sherwood Road feeling miserable. Today she just couldn't bear it, Mathew had made his escape, taking himself to the Eathornes, to see Wendy as he usually did on a Saturday. For her mam’s sake Emily had stayed, hoping it would stop but her dad’s mood persisted, whatever ailed him was the fault of everyone but himself. Last night he’d been quiet, sticking his head in the newspaper and barely uttering a word but this morning he was like a bear woken too early from winter sleep. When he’d resorted to putting that infernal record on the gramophone, playing it over and over, her mam had gone to the Batemans and Emily had fled his excess of Cigareets an’ Whisky, thinking of no place to go other than to grandma’s. She felt misery beyond description, if she didn’t confide in someone she’d despair. Grandma was different she’d understand, she wouldn’t be shocked. It wasn’t as if they’d just finished with one another, Beth must be getting over it by now and grandma wouldn’t judge Connor, she never judged anyone.

Emily turned the corner of Winchester Street and stood at the entry to the back yard of No.1. ‘Please let grandad be in bed’, she whispered the words in hope. A quick peep through the window confirmed his chair to be unoccupied and opening the back door as quietly as she could she felt such relief to see Annie at the sink peeling potatoes.

Emily was frustrated at her own weakness, when at the school she was confident, and forthright when discussing the needs of the children, she would express an opinion on many topics yet on the subject of Connor O’Shea she often spoke nonsense quite knowingly and couldn't help herself. She envied

Mathew, he had found happiness with Wendy Eathorne, it strengthened him. Emily needed someone too and though she'd always given the impression of being unimpressed by Connor, irritated by him even, the truth was the opposite. His boldness she secretly applauded, his untamed approach to life she admired and his Irish charm found her heartstrings and made music deep within her.

Annie dropped the potato back into the bowl and wiped her hands. She was surprised to see Emily at this time of day.

"Is everything alright? I'm glad you've come now, there's too much lamb for just your grandad and me and it's much nicer hot than eating it cold on the second day." She gave Emily a hug sensing not all was well.

"Is grandad in bed?"

Annie nodded. "I'll finish these potatoes and then put them on over a low light. I can turn off the oven, the meat can rest while we go for a walk if you'd like to."

Emily's smile answered for her. Glancing at the clock, twenty past twelve, Annie called up the stairs. "We won't be long, just popping out for ten minutes, Emily's here, she'll have dinner with us when we get back."

A muttered response managed to reach Annie's ears. "Get the paper while you're out and a packet of twenty."

Barely a week left of August, it had been a pleasant month and still the sun lit the streets, causing the cobbles worn smooth with age, to glint. It cheered any weary spirit, unlike the gloom of winter when the cobbles day on day displayed nothing to encourage mirth, only a sombre grey the length of the street, as if they vied with the river Trent to be the most depressed. That too would then wind its way through the city, lost of its summer sparkle once winter cloud and smoky fog stole its sunny disposition.

"What do you think of Connor Grandma? Is he so very bad, surely if he didn't hold deep feelings for Beth then he did the right thing?"

Annie wasn't surprised by her granddaughter's question, for some time she'd recognised Emily's fondness of him, the more she'd tried to disguise it the more apparent it had become.

"I like Connor, at first he seemed to puzzle us all, we couldn't quite fathom him could we? I dare say he found us far from straight forward, folk tend to hold back, be reserved until getting to better know one another. I'm sure Beth will soon hurt less and recognise his honesty. It couldn't have been easy for him and by all accounts he spoke only truth to Beth when he explained his feelings, even owning up to a wager he made with Barry Pointer, that he would achieve to persuade Beth to go to the pictures with him. I don't believe he deceived her, the friendship simply moved happily along with the months but Beth developed a much stronger attachment than did Connor, in the end he couldn't let that continue, a selfish, uncaring man, while it suited his purpose would have. Connor did the decent thing."

Emily kissed Annie's cheek. "I love you Grandma." She hesitated. "Sometimes mam and dad argue, I've given up trying to work out whose fault it is, dad can be moody and difficult, mam challenges him but that makes him worse so then she goes to the Batemans, Mathew goes to Wendy and I begin to think that I shall go mad. I like Connor, would it be too forward of me to call on him, ask how he is, as a friend?"

"I'm sure he would appreciate your calling on him, after all it was with your mam and dad that he stayed when he first came over from Ireland, and Mathew of course worked alongside Connor's dad at Raleigh in Dublin. We all need a good friend, be content with that for now and see what happens, allow time for Beth to move on. After dinner, we'll clear away and while grandad listens to the wireless I'll go home with you, spend an hour with your mam and dad. I've a letter from Bonthorpe, Celia enjoys reading news of the farm, she'll be pleased to learn that Grace now has a young man, don't laugh, he's an artificial inseminator."

“Isn’t that someone who puts a cow in the family way? Emily chuckled.

“That might not be the literal translation but near enough. Freddy used to refer to him as ‘the bull in the bowler hat’, most farmers do apparently but since he’s been dating Grace Freddy’s felt obliged to shed the word bull as his job description so now would you believe he’s become, ‘love in a rubber glove’. Grace made pretence of disapproval but knowing her dad will have his fun and wouldn’t bother if he didn’t like Solomon, she goes along with it. Solomon East, though he likes to be called Sol. I sense from reading Francis’s letter that he’s a very nice young man.” Annie squeezed Emily’s arm. “It’ll be alright, you’ll see, before too long you’ll have a very nice young man of your own.”

William stood on the pavement for a moment or two, looking up at the house, this was the one No.15. In all the many times he’d gone to Morleigh never had he felt anxious, he’d been master over the situation, sure of himself. Today he’d forced his feet to reach the step of this place and even now, standing outside the front door, his better sense made attempt at cautioning him, it could only lead to trouble, here was no rent to collect and his stomach would take no repast. He clenched his knuckles and knocked at the door. It was answered within seconds, there she was, Diane. He began to speak, to protest her note.

“For Heaven’s sake, just get inside before some busy body sees or they’ll tell the weird embalmer that while he was dipping his toes I turned his mausoleum into a house of ill repute.”

William’s bluster was ignored as she virtually pulled him over the threshold and closed the door as if denying him escape.

“What do you want Diane?”

“Oh William, such a gent, more than two years but not, how are you Diane, good to see you,” she scoffed, “I should know better than to expect pleasantry, or even courtesy, ‘what do you want Diane’ is far more your style, ever direct. I don’t want anything, would you believe I can resist your unmatched charms, I can live without them, suppress the female urge. Perhaps I’ve benefited from a change of water, developed immunity, this is business, as clean and clinical as was Morleigh the day we left.”

“Where is your husband Diane?”

She couldn't allow her resolve to weaken. “I need to go from this place and you are in a position to help me with that, I have ears, I know you are doing well for yourself.”

He ignored her, turning and walking along the hallway, William needed to know they were without company. She called him back.

“We can’t go into his living room, that would never do, so you have a choice, either my bedroom or the scullery?”

“For God’s sake Diane, what’s this all about, if you can’t say something sensible then I’m off.”

“Come in here, this is common ground, I dare say you’d consider that appropriate for Diane Roper, common, cheap, anybody’s.” She led the bewildered William to the scullery and pointed to a stool. “Do take a seat.”

William was losing patience but sat down and awaited an explanation.

Diane stood with her back to the sink, one had resting on the draining board, she pointed with her foot to a mark on the floor. “Oh dear, I shall have to get busy with a mop or he’ll throw a fit. Steve is in New Zealand expanding Boot’s empire, while I am here existing on a shrinking budget in the house of Claude Robotham, embalmer retired, along with the ever present spirit of his dear, departed mother who probably lies under the flagstones beneath our feet. I can’t stand it William, I need somewhere to live, the smallest, simplest abode will do, but where I can be on my own if I choose to be or with a friend when I so please."

"You mean you've left Steve?" William slowly began to realise the situation. Now subdued she nodded. "I don't have any rental properties other than Moreleigh and a family moved in there soon after you left. What do you expect me to do about your problems Diane, they're of your own making?"

Now she moved from the sink and stood in front of him. "I'm not asking for sympathy William, you're making money, don't try to tell me otherwise, I've seen your wife with a fancy Burton's bag, oh don't worry I didn't approach her, she was with a fat friend. I need a loan, I shall pay back every penny, it may be several months before Steve can send me more money, my flight cost him dear, he has a decent job but it doesn't pay that much. You can charge me interest if you want, it's not a lot anyway, fifty pounds, enough to rent a space of my own. My wages barely cover what I'm paying Robotham and a mite of food, I haven't had a stitch of new clothing since I came back last February, I could little afford the price of a card of knicker elastic last week."

William listened but was still puzzled. "What's wrong with this Robotham fella, and where is he? Has he been bothering you?"

Diane knew exactly what William was thinking. "If you mean has he offered me any favours then the answer's no, unless you count the offer of being allowed to sit with him and the ghost of Christmas past, sharing a candle and singing *'joy to the world'*, come December 25th. The man gives me the creeps, he comes back from Chapel St. Leonards tomorrow afternoon, that's why you had to come now or tomorrow morning. I'm not permitted to bring any company here, if he found out I'd let you in I'd be out on the street with my few belongings and the curse of doom around my neck for evermore."

"What if I say no, I'm sure a woman as resourceful as you will have a backup plan." William reached into his jacket pocket for his cigarette case.

"Heaven forbid you can't smoke in here, I shall need to robustly polish the stool when you're gone in case some trace of your occupation remains. Anyway, why would you say no if it's a business transaction? The bank wouldn't give me the time of day if I went to them, a shop girl whose husband is on the other side of the world. Steve is a decent man, he'll send me money as soon as he's able, not once was he late with your rent and you know it."

William sighed, "And just how am I supposed to get this money to you if I can't come here?"

"I work at C&A, every weekday and on Saturday mornings, you'll find me there. If you want me to sign an agreement then I will."

William wondered how she'd managed to survive from February until now and he not know she was back. It would suggest her intent to be genuine, she wasn't seeking to make trouble.

"I shan't wait forever you know, if I extend the loan it won't be for an indefinite period. You say it was early in the year that you left New Zealand so your husband has earned for several months since then, presumably over the course of the next six months he should recover sufficiently his finances and be in a position to discharge the debt, if he is indeed as decent and reliable as you claim him to be."

He gave Diane a stern look, she was equally determined, sensing she had it almost in the bag.

"Of course he will, he'll send me money and I'll repay the loan, our business completed William."

"If I agree to this you will give me your word that at no time will you go anywhere near my wife. The way you handed her the keys made her suspicious, she's no fool, I won't stand for that Diane."

She sniffled. "That was ages ago, I've moved on, when I leave this miserable house for my new place of abode I'll take a note with the new address to Woolascroft's, you can collect it from there, I imagine you'll want to know where I am so you can make sure I don't abscond."

"No, not there." William's response was immediate and firm. "You can post it to Wollaton, if it's addressed to me only then Celia won't open it, she's very correct in that way, her father's influence. It might be best to use block capitals nevertheless, I've heard it said that a woman's handwriting clearly identifies itself over a man's style, it's as much for your sake as for mine, Celia would never see it as business no matter how I explained."

"Very well, if you prefer, although Mr.Woolascroft seemed quite affable. It won't take too long I hope to set up our agreement."

William got down from the stool. "You'll be gone from here long before Christmas. I shall find you at C&A, make a purchase, no doubt you'll be eager to offer assistance," he couldn't resist voicing the aside.

As he walked away along Mansfield Road he felt relieved, an hour earlier his mind had been troubled, Diane had felt like a threat. Dick need not concern himself, everything was entirely respectable, Eddowes would bring no scandal to the gates of Woolascroft's yard, no slight to the company name, Eddowes was as reputable as Dick himself. William laughed out loud at the notion as he neared his car, what a bloody farce life was, a nonsense from start to finish.

Celia folded the letter and handed it back to Annie. "We so enjoyed our time with them all, it was brief but one of those rare days always to be remembered. It was especially rewarding to watch George and Freddy together, chatting, laughing constantly. William never allows himself to be at ease, not even with his own brother. Liza was in her element at the farm, I think all those years at Halam have put the countryside at her heart, George will take her there again before too long I'm sure."

Just then the sound of the back door opening brought a hush to the living room, it couldn't be Mathew, he always called out. Celia looked at Annie and smiled feebly, poor Emily stood and was about to go to her bedroom when William appeared in the doorway.

"Ah good, I suspected Mathew might not be home yet but four of us should manage to eat it all. I stopped at the shop on the boulevard to get a paper and I fancied some ice cream so I've a block of Neapolitan and a packet of wafers, they're on the scullery table, you're good at assembling them Emily, my hands are too big, they always crack the wafers. There's a bunch of carnations as well, they were selling them at the allotments."

He crossed the room and sat down in his chair, even in his absence neither of the women had ventured to occupy it. Annie knew him so well, he had a smugness about him, she felt anxious, almost anticipating an upset, which he planned to reveal when they'd relaxed under the comfort of his better demeanour, when they least expected it.

Emily returned carrying a tray. "Which flavour do you like best Grandma? There's chocolate, vanilla, raspberry, coffee and lime?"

"I really don't mind, I know your dad likes coffee flavour."

Emily cut the block into slices and sandwiched them between the wafers, putting the lime and coffee portions together.

"There you are Dad, in the absence of Mathew you have a double decker."

Quietness prevailed while they licked away at their treat, which Celia accepted as William's apology, he could never bring himself to utter the word sorry. After several minutes and with a satisfied smack of his lips, William wiped the stickiness from his fingers with his hanky and picked up his newspaper, spreading it in front of his face as was his practice, listening to every word spoken on the other side of the screen it created.

"How is Nora now Annie?" Asked Celia. "I know George has been to the hospital to visit his aunty but I've not had chance to speak with him for several days."

"The doctor is pleased with her progress and hopes to discharge her next week but she won't be able to go home to Bilborough. Nora is eighty next birthday and quite frail, Gertie and Jean have persuaded her to live with them, it's the only possibility really. I don't think she was at Bilborough long enough to develop an attachment to the place. Her rent is paid up to the end of this month but because it's stood empty for two months already she's given the landlord written notice and Mavis and Maggie have begun to pack her belongings. There's not that much to clear, dear Nora gave numerous items to her nephews and nieces when she left Mitchell Street, we'd all had bits and pieces of Sarah's over the years, there would be little point in giving us older ones anything more, the youngsters will value items that belonged to their grandma and grandad, Nora knows that."

William's ears pricked up, never was he more intent than when listening to conversation not directed at him, he considered everything 'his business' and thus had every right to 'mind it'.

Nora would have been living in a one bedroom prefab, such simple houses never stayed empty for very long, he must find Diane at C&A on Monday morning. A self satisfied smile came to his face, the time was now right for him to spread the news he'd overheard when buying the paper, in fact until then he'd not given a thought to ice cream but William liked to choose his moment. Laying the paper down onto his lap he looked from one to the other and said.

"Jed Unwin's wife was in the shop, of course you can never be sure how much is true, folk do like to exaggerate. She was saying that Connor O'Shea's mother passed away yesterday, we've had no telephone call from Ireland but I imagine Patricia Bradshaw would be the first contact these days."

He lifted the newspaper once more, from behind its pages listening for their reaction, awaiting the sound of their shock, while on the scullery table a bunch of forgotten carnations woefully awaited water.

CHAPTER TWENTY TWO

Early November.

Olive put her book down on the occasional table, removed her reading glasses to rub her eyes and glanced at the clock, ten minutes to eight. Dick she knew had intended driving to Long Eaton in the afternoon, to look over the planned site of new housing, destined to become social housing run by the council. He'd not actually said at what time he expected to be home but it did seem late, it had been dark for hours. She'd eaten earlier. Crohn's disease prevented her from taking more than a slice of bread and butter or one or two plain biscuits after 5o'clock. Dick's meal was plated up and just before seven she'd covered it and placed it over a saucepan of hot water where it gently simmered still on the stove, surely he'd be back at any moment. Unable to relax she abandoned her book and went to the kitchen, lifted the cover from the plate to check the food wasn't drying and was about to turn off the gas when the back door opened.

"Damn fireworks, if I could have caught the little sods they'd have still been rubbing their backsides come Christmas. It was lucky I got back to the yard when I did or the whole lot could have gone up in smoke, kids larkin' about. They chucked a firecracker over the wall, I was actually turning the key in the office door and saw sparks dartin' along the ground. There's that much combustible stuff, I've told the men time and again to lock it away. I put the damn thing out with a bucket o' water an' made safe the yard, in as much as a builder's yard can be made safe, then I thought if I sat quiet in the dark I might catch the little buggers, you know what young lads are like, once the devil's in 'em they don't know when to stop. I waited 'til I couldn't feel me feet from cold, the only unwanted company was a rat, it stopped in its tracks an' looked at me like I wer' the intruder, in me own yard. I'd had enough by then, done what I could so I locked the big gates an' got in the car to come home. I'd only been drivin' five minutes or so when I saw a young couple, hand in hand, walkin' along in their own little sphere, they didn't notice me, they wouldn't have noticed if the four horsemen of the apocalypse had rode by on white chargers. It was Connor O'Shea an' though I've seen her no more than once or twice I'd swear the lass wer' Eddowes daughter. Patricia told me he wer' gettin' over the death of his mother, that he'd calmed. When he first got home from Dublin, after the funeral, he worked like a man possessed. Eddowes hasn't said anythin', makes me wonder if he's aware, can't see it pleasin' him."

"Why do you say that?" Asked Olive. As she carried the hot plate to the table. "Eat your meal before it spoils."

Dick spread his jacket over the back of the chair and sat down with a weary sigh.

"Eddowes knows Patricia has an able mind and O'Shea has managed to find his way inside it, Eddowes hasn't, that simple, jealousy."

Dick set about eating and Olive sat by him thinking. When she'd called on Florence the previous week Annie had been there, through the course of conversation Olive had learned of Emily's fondness for Connor but Annie had made a remark, which might suggest Dick's observation to be correct. 'I think all dads are possessive of their daughters but Emily hopes Connor will grow on William'.

"It was very sad Connor's mother dying at what must have been a comparatively young age, I believe she had a weakness of the heart. If you think William isn't likely to be very welcoming of the young man then perhaps we should invite him and Emily here, for a simple tea one Sunday evening. It must be awkward for Emily's mother, how could she encourage Connor to spend time with them at Wollaton if things are as you describe."

Dick swallowed a mouthful of potato and took a sip of water. "I wouldn't concern yourself, invite them by all means if you want but I reckon Eddowes spends enough time away from the house to enable his missus to smuggle in O'Shea for an hour or so. William has his own distractions!" His tone implied intrigue and Olive gave Dick a quizzical look but at that moment their thoughts were interrupted by the sound of fire bells.

"Guy Fawkes has a lot to answer for," said Dick, "the Brigade are on their way to somethin'."

"Will the yard be alright?" Olive was anxious given earlier events.

"If it was the yard I daresay the phone would have rung by now or somebody'd be bangin' on the door, could be anywhere."

Having finished his meal Dick got to his feet and made for the living room, as he crossed the hallway the telephone began to ring. Olive tensed, when a child she'd witnessed fire consume a house and even though no one perished or suffered injury it remained vivid in her memory. She heard Dick say "no bother" and he replaced the handset after just a second or so. He turned to her, laughing. "Wrong number. I don't know about you but I could do with a proper drink."

Olive gathered up his plate and laid it in the sink, she would likely suffer as a consequence but tonight she'd risk a tot of brandy, live a little. Her mind lingered still with Connor's mother, Olive did hope that the unfortunate woman had somehow managed to 'live a little'. Life was a jackpot, often without rhyme or reason and death was unpredictable, making no allowance for loose ends, for the unprepared. She would invite Annie's granddaughter Emily and her young Irishman for tea, she would do that for Celia and for Mrs.O'Shea, a measure of women's fellowship in what felt to be a man's world still.

The next morning brought news of the fire, not the fault of a stray firework, in fact nothing whatsoever to do with Guy Fawkes but the devastating result of an overheated fryer at the chip shop. Annie waited her turn at the Post

Office, listening to folk as they related their individual versions of last night's mayhem. They ranged in magnitude from the burning of Atlanta to Dante's Inferno, Cicely Rule's description Annie thought to be within the bounds of reality.

"Went up like one o' Jerry's incendiary bombs, heat from the flames cracked the tiles, by the time Brigade put it out the whole place wer' as sticky as a fly paper, all that grease. Yer can still smell it from a mile away, I don't envy them as live down wind of it. I once forgot, went to bed an' left some belly fat in the oven o' the range all night. Cheetham give it me, he wer' in a good mood 'cause he'd had a winnin' line on the pools. 'Here you are Mrs.Rule', he said, 'it'll render down nicely'. When I come down over stairs next mornin' the scullery smelled like the banks o' the Ganges, burned to a cinder. I heard after that it wer' one o' them weeks when the payout wer' nothin' to get excited about, well Cheetham couldn't have it back even if he'd asked. It took me three days o' soakin' an' scrubbin' to redeem me pan. They'll be insured, very particular is Albert Hickling, I've never had chips from him wrapped in News o' the World, always the Telegraph or Times."

At last it was Mrs.Rule's turn to be served, Annie had come simply for stamps, now she considered herself oversupplied.

Walking away from the Post Office Annie's thoughts were of Emily. Connor's return from Ireland, travelling as he'd been with the grief of losing his mother, had compelled Emily to find him at Denman Street. Whether it was raw emotion or Emily's long held want of him no one would ever really know. 'He needed someone to love him Grandma', the words Emily had spoken to Annie when confiding her relief. Since then, when work permitted, they'd spend time together, often walking through the arboretum or Wollaton Park. Sitting in the camellia house on a Sunday afternoon, watching small children running up and down the paths between the rich green shrubs, calling to each other, creating an echo, a pastime enjoyed by Emily herself with Mathew, before the war and the subsequent military camps, which seemed to appear overnight with the arrival of the Americans. When William had come to hear of it his temper flared beyond all reason, while he'd never really shown Connor much hospitality this seemed extreme and completely uncalled for. Annie could only put it down to William's resentment of Connor's association with Patricia Bradshaw, pathetic though that was, it nevertheless troubled her deeply. In so many ways William was like his dad, all those years ago when Charles had driven Hilda from home simply because of her love for Jack Haynes, whom he resented for some warped reason, Annie had wept from the pain of it and witnessed Hilda's regard for her dad shrink through the intensity of his selfish assault of her feelings. Annie would not let William do to Emily what Charles had so cruelly done to Hilda, if his manner persisted then she could do no other than intervene. The fact that in law he had no sanction over the young couple was some comfort, Emily was twenty one. But if his attitude sent their daughter away from home amid bitterness, then Celia would suffer.

If only William could find an interest away from his business dealings, something to engage his mind without making demands upon it. Other men enjoyed sport, got together if not to actively take part then to be a spectator at least. It built friendships, created pleasure and relaxation. Like Charles, William seemed ever to distance himself, abiding in self imposed isolation, as if afraid the hand of friendship might somehow scratch his veneer.

Liza was taking this week off from her work at Burton's and George too had arranged a week of leave from Raleigh to coincide. Tomorrow the two of them were to go to Bonthorpe, Francis had insisted they stay, if only for a short while so the plan was they'd return on Friday, bringing Faith, Richard and baby John with them. Annie so looked forward to seeing them, especially the baby. George had thoughtfully suggested they stay with Liza and himself for the two nights, visiting the various family and friends by day. On Sunday he would drive them to Midland Station where they would catch the train back to

Steeping, Freddy of course would pick them up at that end. Charles should cope with the arrangements as it would cause little disturbance of his routine, apart from the fact that on this occasion he must accept the necessity of a decent fire in the grate, the weather was chill and an infant must be kept warm.

So deep in thought was Annie that she failed to notice a vehicle slowing down until it stopped at the curb and a voice called out.

"Can I give you a lift Annie?" It was Tommy Spooner, he wound down the window to enable his broad smile to reach her unimpeded. "I'm only going back to Handley's, had to collect the hearse from Nat Broadbent's, needed a few bits done to it so if yer don't mind ridin' with the undertaker?"

Annie chucked. "Whilst I'm not feeling ready for it just yet Tommy, nevertheless when the time comes I can think of no one Annie Eddowes would care to be conveyed by other than you."

She walked around to the passenger side and sat down beside him, nodding her head solemnly, as she had observed Bob Lacey do when discreetly instructing the bearers. Tommy responded by driving slowly forward and touching his forehead lightly.

"Dignified, that's what you an' me are Mrs.E, dignified. Saw your David at the garage, had his head under the bonnet of Gordon Cheetham's delivery van. Nat says the lad'll make a top notch mechanic."

Annie smiled. "David will always do his best, he's loyal, he'd not want any vehicle he'd repaired to cause the slightest dent to Mr.Broadbent's reputation. How is dear Rosie? It's almost impossible to speak of loyalty and not at once think of your Rosie."

"Better than nothin'," said Tommy roguishly. "Nearly everybody I meet asks me that, she don't realise how much regard folk have for her, can't recognise her own qualities, just because she struggled a bit at school she doubts herself. She knows how I answer if it's somebody like you who we've known for years, it's a bit o' fun, I tell her 'can't have you gettin' too full of yourself', then she'll wallop me backside an' pull a face." Tommy sighed. "I'd be lost without her Annie, I thank the Lord everyday for my Rosie."

"I don't suppose you've seen William since Audrey's funeral," said Annie.

"No, but it's as much my fault as his, I should call on him, drag him out of himself. When we were lads we made one another's fun, even back then he were full o' big ideas. I used to pull his leg, then he'd chase me round the block 'til neither of us had breath left. We'd share a bit o' chocolate when one or the other had some, in fact we shared all sorts, secrets, daft jokes, discoveries, I reckon early teens is full o' discoveries," Tommy chuckled, "some things a lad can't learn at school. Then war come, I don't think any of us wer' same after that. When we got back from the funeral an' we stood talkin', out in the yard, while the women wer' servin' the tea, I thought for a few minutes Will' let his guard down, as if he wer' tryin' to find that old simplicity him an' me shared. Somewhere beneath all that grand exterior is the William who cut his teeth on the tough back streets o' this city, who rubbed the seat out of his pants slidin' down railway embankment an' learned' to whistle on a blade o' grass from the old meadows, like all of us lads did. I'll knock on his door Annie an' ask him if he's comin' out, like I used to."

Annie smiled she was entirely at ease in Tommy's company, safe from harm. She found herself confiding in him, telling of William's resentment of Connor, her fears for Emily and Celia.

"I hope Beth will understand, if she and Connor had not split up Emily would never have sought his company but losing his mother was so sad and Emily felt compelled to call on him."

"Don't fret over it Annie, Beth told me that she sensed quite early on that Connor was attracted to Emily, deep down she knows it wasn't to be, but the lass took it bad all the same. She's a lot better now, she went to the pictures last Saturday with a young chap who works at Players with Ernie. Beth'll be alright, she's movin' on. Soon after she started at Handley's she come across an account in the filing cabinet, O'Shea, it was in the name of O'Shea. Bless her she clutched at that connection like a drowning man grabs at a leaf floatin' by. I told her there must be hundreds of O'Shea's in Ireland, nearly everybody over there is an 'O' somethin' or other. We did Charlie Holbrook's funeral." Tommy hesitated. "It's the first requirement of the job, to keep everythin' to meself, but I know you won't say anythin' Annie. It wer' a bleak affair, the daughter lives in Ireland, she come over briefly, for his burial an' to empty the house of his personal stuff. That's how Moira met her, Bob an' Moira Lacey live in the house next door, it wer' Moira who found the poor old fella an' called the ambulance. She said Margaret O'Shea was a nice woman, shy an' work worn, not what Moira expected. Apart from seein' her at the cemetery I had no other dealings with her, a solicitor instructed Handley's on her behalf an' he settled the account. They're all different, some folk want a big send off while others can only cope with a modest affair an' it's my privilege to see to it, whatever the 'it' might be.

Beth can pull out the drawer of the filing cabinet these days and not even notice the O'Shea, yet at the time, in her mind, there was only one in all Ireland, in all the world even." Tommy laughed. "Love is a powerful thing Annie, a mighty powerful thing."

Tommy had dropped her off at Sherwood road. 'Best not drive the hearse into Winchester Street, folk'll wonder who's died an' if they saw you get out you'd have half the neighbourhood at your door afore you'd had chance to take off your coat'. Dear Tommy, he was not unlike Billy, a strong arm yet a gentle nature. His conversation however had troubled her, it had brought back to mind the evening when William had called, his purpose apparently being to gather some knowledge of Charlie Holbrook from his dad whom he presumed would be able to enlighten him. Was there yet another revelation awaiting William's chosen moment to be shed over the unsuspecting? Had he achieved one evening in The Standard to enable the recall of some suitably drink primed individual who like Charles, years ago had joined in the speculation over a young woman's disappearance, in the absence of proof devising their own theory, nominating Dick Woolascroft as the cause of Margaret Holbrook's banishment to relatives in Ireland?

Annie's tread was weary as she turned into Winchester Street, her eyes following that river of cold, grey cobbles, making its way not to a great expanse of sparkling blue ocean, but to more of the same. All she could was trust Tommy's wisdom and believe Ireland to be populated by hundreds of O'Shea's of which Connor was one, but unrelated to Charlie Holbrook's daughter.

William left the house under the pretext of attending his Lodge, since extending the loan to Diane he'd determined himself to stay away from her. Although he'd told her of the prefab in Bilborough she'd chosen to go her own way and rented a one bedroom, terraced house on Monsall Street. As they'd agreed, she'd written the address on a piece of notepaper and mailed it to Wollaton. Celia paid no attention to his correspondence, her correctness at times tormented him, why did she never give in to temptation, why must she be always so dependable? George was due back from Bonthorpe tomorrow with Faith, Richard and the baby, hence Celia's feverish activity. Baking, cleaning, still she was icing cakes. William's nose had taken all it could of spiced fruit cake and lavender polish, he had no tolerance of it, no reserve of good humour, which he'd be expected to shower on the visiting relatives. Now he sat inside the car debating with his conscience, it put up a sound argument but the need to reassure himself of Diane's intention to clear the debt entitled him to call on her, to see for himself evidence of her thriftiness, he'd not provided her with money to spend idly. William's powers of persuasion were triumphant over his less forthright conscience, he turned the key in the ignition and drove to Monsall Street.

William stepped out from his car and gazed up and down the row of houses, then likewise across the street to the opposite side. Not unlike Mitchell Street before Woolascroft granted it a change of identity, a passport to the new, modern world. Here the stamp of time remained, indelibly set into the red faced brickwork, which showed its embarrassment by shrinking away from his scrutiny, thoughtlessly enabled by the beam from the smug streetlamp, that having been granted the up to date brilliance of electricity.

William knocked on the door, she must be in, a light was showing through the curtains. He heard the sound of heavy bolts, top and bottom of the door being pulled back. The look of surprise on Diane's face in that instant amused him.

"Too late for 'penny for the Guy' and too early to be carol singers, so a convenient time for me to pay a visit Diane."

She spoke in lowered tones. "Well as you can see I've not done a moonlight flit owing you a fortune so you can go home a happy man."

"I won't keep you," said William, "but surely I might come in for a few minutes now that I'm here, good manners will cost neither of us."

Suddenly someone coughed, so Diane was not alone, William put one foot on the threshold. In a much louder voice she said.

"It's not really convenient Mr.Eddowes, I have a friend with me but if it will take but a few minutes then I suppose you best come in." She stood aside, thinking that it could serve a purpose for him to see that she posed no threat to his domestic harmony. "Come through." She led him into a small living room where sat a man of similar age to Diane, at once he got to his feet, crossed the room and offered his hand to William.

"Clive Adler, pleased to meet you Mr......?"

"William Eddowes." The two shook hands, both looking to Diane for some kind of introduction.

"This is Mr.Eddowes Clive, he's kindly advised me on some financial matters in recent weeks, he happened to be in the neighbourhood so decided to call, to check his suggestions had proved helpful."

"Well that sounds to be outside my realm of expertise, now if you asked me where the rump ends an' sirloin starts I could tell you exactly Mr.Eddowes. I work at Cheetham's, deliverin' sometimes but mainly in cuttin' room, jointin' an' makin' sausages. That's where I'll be spendin' all me time in a few weeks. The build up to Christmas keeps a butcher on his feet for hours on end, don't do his till any harm though. Where I worked before, if I played me cards right I got a bonus, I've only been at Cheetham's a couple o' months so unless he's a big hearted sort I don't reckon I can count on one this Christmas. We had to move house, me an' the old man. Uncle Bill had a stroke, that's dad's brother, there wer' nobody as could look after him so needs must as they say. As it turned out uncle Bill had another stroke an' died but landlord wer' happy for us to take over tenancy an I'd got work at Cheetham's so we stayed put. Nice to meet you Mr.Eddowes but I'll be off, leave you to talk to Diane in private, money matters are best discussed without distraction." He leaned forward and kissed Diane on the cheek. "I can let myself out, goodnight to you both."

Diane followed him as far as the door of the living room, he turned before opening the front door and glanced back at her, with a smile he briefly raised his hand to wave and was gone.

"It doesn't take you long does it Diane?" William lowered himself into the armchair by the fire and lifting the poker from its resting place prodded at the coals. "So you've swapped your weird embalmer for a butchers assistant, you really know how to live." He laughed mockingly.

"He's a friend, I like him, met him a couple of weeks ago, on the bus, people do have friends you know William."

“Do you always bolt the door top and bottom when entertaining friends?” His manner annoyed her, she prickled.

“Mind your own bloody business, you judge everybody by your standards. Clive wasn’t in my bed was he? He was fully clad, not as much as his tie undone. What have you come here for anyway?”

William searched the room for any evidence to suggest his money was being spent on female whims, ornamentation was sparse and old fashioned, not an obvious choice for a woman like Diane. Let furnished it was clean but a little shabby, the armchair in which he sat had seen better days. The carpet was worn at his feet and in one corner the wallpaper was peeling off where dampness mottled the plaster beneath.

“Why would you prefer this dump to a recently erected prefab?” He was genuinely puzzled.

“Because William, Bilborough is two bus rides away from the city centre where I work, that would mean six days a week I’d have to pay the fare to go back and forth out of a wage that wouldn’t provide a blue tit with peanuts, Monsall Street, on a fine day, is close enough for me to walk to C&A thereby saving vital pennies, a policy I’m sure you’d applaud.”

“You shouldn’t make mention of my name again to this Clive Adler, he’ll likely forget it then. The last thing I want is for Cheetham to know my business.”

Diane laughed. “You’re so transparent William Eddowes, but you needn’t worry, when next I see Clive I doubt if either of us will give you the slightest thought. How is your wife, I’ve not seen her in the store since that day, I imagine she prefers Burton’s, from what I was able to observe she and her friend made only a swift perusal of C&A’s offerings?”

William sniffed but ignored her question, instead responding with. "I don't suppose you've any whisky?" the way Diane raised her eyebrows was answer in itself. "Put the damn kettle on then," he said tetchily, "your financial adviser needs a beverage of some sort."

Diane went to the scullery smiling to herself. For all his largesse, his self importance William Eddowes was so naive, fifty pounds was no more than she deemed herself owed. The law imposed no obligation on Steve to send her money, it had been she who had deserted the marriage. Eventually after a given period divorce would become automatic. She called back to William.

"Do you want a biscuit with your tea, they're Thin Arrowroot, good for the digestion?"

CHAPTER TWENTY THREE

Mid December

"Are you sure you really don't mind, it sounds very lively in there?"

Emily and Connor stood on the pavement outside the door of the dance hall, the full bodied notes of big band music even though the door was closed, appeared to inspire lavish garlands of tinsel, hanging on either side, to sway with the beat. The coloured lamps above the entrance enticing festive spirit to shimmy inside on each eager gust of wind that seized its opportunity to share in the merriment when the door opened, revealing the scene within.

"I'm sure Em', mam would want us to be happy. Me dad'll be decoratin' a tree for the young ens, tryin' to make it as normal as he can, don't mean we're not thinkin' about her, it's the opposite. Christmas back in Ireland is the one time o' year when ordinary, humble homes dare to glitter. Some of the Catholic Churches have that much gildin' a workin man with one or two sins to his name can be blinded by it, rendered sightless before the image of his redeemer, an' that makes redemption hard to find. Me dad's Catholic though he seldom attends Mass, but at Christmas when mam put up the decorations, the holly bough above the mantelpiece with red ribbon bows an' gold stars, he'd break off just a small sprig o' greenery with a couple of berries on it an' perch it on top the frame that held the Holy Picture. He didn't do that because it was the image of the Virgin Mary, but because Mary was a mother. When we go there next week I bet you that sprig of holly will be above the picture, only this year it'll have a red ribbon an' a gold star as well, for mam. We'll go inside Em' an' we'll dance for her, every bit o' gilt an' glitter'll sparkle to the memory of Maggie O'Shea." Connor took Emily's hand and led her inside where two women dressed as elves were taking entry money. Now the sound level rose to match the excitement as folk filled the floor, couples whirling their way from one end to the other, a kaleidoscope of continually changing sequences in vibrant colour.

Emily nervously wondered if Beth would be present, she'd heard that for a few weeks now Beth had been dating a young man who worked at Player's. Already she'd spotted some familiar faces. Samuel and Margaret had said they were coming and Mathew hoped he and Wendy would make it. Some hours of overtime had been on offer at Raleigh for the last few weeks and with an eye to the future Mathew had been working late every Tuesday and Friday since the start of last month. Emily suspected an engagement ring might appear at Christmas, she'd seen her brother's love for Wendy Eathorne grow deeper and deeper and could understand why he might dream of marriage, a place to live with his wife, a peaceful place where lurked no discord, where no unpredictable menace had made its abode.

They could put it off no longer, a week today they were to catch the train to Liverpool and then the ferry to Dublin. Connor had asked her to go with him, to meet his family, to support Callum as he tried to hold everything together without his beloved Maggie. Emily knew her mam would understand and would busy herself buying some small treats for Connor's brothers and sisters, which she'd send with her love. Mathew would be delighted that at last Emily was to see Ireland. Still he spoke of Dublin, of his workmates at the factory, especially Connor's dad, with fondness in his voice. But Emily felt dread of her dad's reaction when they stood before him and declared their intent, despite the fact they were to return by New Year's Eve.

Emily herself couldn't but feel guilt at knowing that Christmas for her mam would be unbearable as a result. Where in his ill temper could her dad go when everywhere was closed, no business meetings to attend, no building works to observe? Could her mam really spend every moment of Christmas with the Batemans, would that wretched record achieve to drown out every note of, 'O come all ye faithful'?

"Hello you two". An urgent voice interrupted Emily's fears, hurrying towards them before the band struck up again were Samuel and Margaret. "We've been keeping an eye out for you, Mathew and Wendy should be here at any minute, he won't let Raleigh stand in the way of a bit o' fun."

As if awaiting their cue, the sudden draught as the door opened swept Mathew and Wendy inside amid cheers and laughter. Mathew sported in his buttonhole a flower made from gold foil and a sprig of mistletoe.

"Well fellas," said Connor, "if we haven't got the three prettiest girls in the entire place. Time we were sweepin' them off their feet, come on Em', before your brother an' cousin beg a dance, I'll be charmed to put an arm about Margaret an' Wendy in a while but you're the first name on me little card Emily Eddowes." He patted his breast pocket with the palm of his hand, Emily knew that Connor's little card was really his heart.

The band played on and the atmosphere grew more carefree with every minute. Emily had spotted Beth in the arms of a young man, she looked happy, it was reassuring. Emily wondered if Connor too had seen the couple, his remark in Emily's ear confirmed that he had.

"God bless Beth an' the man who's restored her smile."

It was just before the end of the interval as the band began to pick up their instruments that a loud voice called out. "Give us a song Charlie Jones."

Charlie had persuaded Maureen to leave the children with their grandma and go dancing. Since the baby was born she'd taken no time out for herself, he'd declared this to Bob Budgeon as they'd painted the newly refurbished chip shop, a job that had come their way through Bob's girlfriend Glynis Hopwood. 'I told Mr.Hickling that Jones an' Budgeon wer' the best decorators this side o' Macclesfield' had been her proud announcement.

Bob couldn't let the chance pass, the lively sound created by the band was exciting but the melody that as if by magic, floated from within his mate Charlie when he opened his mouth to sing left anyone listening spellbound. Cheers now erupted from the crowd, cries of 'come on Charlie', filled the air with eager anticipation.

Maureen laughed. "It's no use love, they won't stop until you sing to them."

He sighed, gave her a kiss and made his way to the bandstand. Folk watched as Charlie whispered in the bandleader's ear. A hush descended, all eyes now set upon the familiar figure, seen regularly about the city in paint spattered overalls, an unlikely performer yet to those who knew him, a star. Charlie took the podium.

"I'll sing but only if every one of yer gets to the floor to dance life into this place where we all live, love and lay our heads, this is for Nottingham and all her children."

Hands were instantly put together to produce joyful clapping. Charlie nodded to the bandleader, who raised his baton and the magic commenced.

"Love is the sweetest thing,

there's nothing else on earth could bring

such happiness to everything,

that's love's old story."

Emily felt Connor's cheek against her own, nothing else at that moment held any importance. She couldn't be aware of Wendy Eathorne's curiosity as Mathew whirled her round the dance floor, passing close by Connor and Emily. A curiosity driven deeper through the knowledge that she must not mention it to anyone, not even Mathew. Complete discretion was the first requirement of the job, any failing on Wendy's part to observe the code of ethics would deny her all opportunity of work in the future, the legal profession was unforgiving of misconduct.

Julian Russe's secretary Ruth was on a fortnights holiday and Wendy had been instructed as temporary cover. This morning Mr.Russe had dictated a letter addressed to a Callum O'Shea of Dublin. It confirmed the title deed of a property, following the death of his wife Margaret O'Shea, there being no Will to specify otherwise and prior to in her sole ownership, in law now passed to him and thereby rendered him landlord of the said property and of the current tenant. This necessitated a new contract to be agreed and signed by both parties, of the one part Callum O'Shea and of the other, Leslie John Hitchins. Mr.O'Shea was to respond, stating his wishes on the matter. The existing tenancy agreement called for renewal every twelve month period and became due again on the first day of May 1957. Wendy had made a copy of the letter as was standard practice and filed it, with other documentation in the name of Margaret O'Shea, née Holbrook. It surely must be a file relating to the affairs of Connor's late mother. It would suggest a family connection to Nottingham, which existed long before he came over from Dublin to seek better prospects. Mathew, through casual conversation, had revealed to Wendy the poor economic conditions prevailing Ireland and spoken of his regard for Connor's father, Callum, who wanted his son to find opportunities in England where industry appeared to be thriving. Nottingham had been the obvious place for Connor to go in the first instance as Mathew had been able to describe the city's assets and suggest Connor stay with his mam and dad while he explored a little. Mathew hadn't mentioned an English side of Connor's family, it did seem odd?

Now Charlie's singing ended and the place was at once filled with rapturous applause. Bob Budgeon looked as proud as any man could look and kissed Glynis over and over in his glee.

Mathew chuckled. "You women have your friends and you natter together, share your pleasures, but I've never seen any woman display the unbridled jubilation a man can show when his best mate triumphs. Charlie

Jones is wasted painting folk's houses he should be making records or entertaining large audiences in the best music halls."

Wendy looked across to where Emily and Connor stood clapping enthusiastically.

"Has Connor made a good mate since settling here, it must be difficult, having an Irish background, we've all heard of the differences, which exist between the Irish and the English?"

"In my experience there's little difference, they sing and dance more than we do, they speak the same language but with a coating of melted butter over every word, so it slides from the tongue, effortless and unrehearsed. They love with a passion and live the same way, I reckon most English folk could slot into Irish ways and barely notice while Irish could equally well merge with ours. Differences? No, I saw no differences. As for Connor, I believe he's found a good mate alright." Mathew chuckled. "He and Emily were invited to tea at Dick Woolascroft's a couple of weeks back and according to Emily they got on like a house on fire. 'Tis the charm of the Irish don't yer know, 'tis the little people, skipping away with our heart strings." Mathew spoke the words with an Irish accent and laughed. "The invitation probably came about through grandma getting to know Mrs.Woolascroft. Some say Dick's mellowing with age, if Connor's happy then it's nothing to do with anyone else, except our Emily and she's as happy as a sandboy. Besides, they're related Mrs.Bradshaw and Dick, so I suppose it follows that Connor would get to know him, through her. Come on Miss Eathorne, this one's a boogie."

Mathew took her hand and pulled Wendy into the throng, she couldn't resist his high spirits, his infectious mischief. It would soon be Christmas and life was good. To the strains of 'Chatanooga choo choo', Nottingham's children boogied.

Emily busied herself marking the children's work, yesterday she'd set the class an arithmetic test. Normally she would have done the marking last night but the dance had claimed her time so now she calmed her nervousness with an application of nine year old calculation, it never failed to divert her mind away from other more regular matters. Connor would come at around half past seven to talk to her dad about their proposed trip to Dublin.

'You fret too much Em', he'd said, 'your father'll be alright with it, we're both responsible adults'. Indeed they were but right now Emily felt less assured than Peter Smith who'd managed to multiply 9 by 9 and reach an answer of 99. Connor's confident approach had done little to dispel her own trepidation, it was almost a quarter past. William sat by the fire with his Financial Times while Celia was in the kitchen, ironing. The ticking of the clock brought ever closer the moment when her dad's temper would surely ignite.

The doorbell rang, Emily felt a sickliness of stomach as she heard her mam's footsteps crossing the hallway and a tone of surprise in her voice when she spoke to the caller.

"Tommy, come in, is everything alright?"

"We're all fine Celia, it's William I've come to see, is he at home?"

Celia was so pleased to find Tommy at the door, if a little curious as to why he sought William but Tommy's expression would suggest nothing untoward and she led him to the living room without concern.

"It's Tommy, to see you William." Casting a smile Tommy's way Celia said. "I'll turn off the iron and make some tea."

"Don't bother with that Celia, I've come to drag him out for an hour, pour a pint of Wrenshaw's down him."

William looked up from his paper and Tommy recognised alarm in his eyes. Despite all of William's would be indifference his first thoughts on seeing Tommy were for his dad and Annie.

"Just a social call Will', long overdue an'all. Do you remember the conversation you an' me had the day of Audrey's funeral? I do, an' I'm not goin' to let another year end before we share an hour over a pint." He turned to Emily. "Hello Emily love, I expect you're lookin' forward to some time off from the three 'R's', I reckon whether you're teachin' 'em or learnin' 'em the three 'R's' can get tiresome. I can remember wishin' Mr.Dunn'd go up in a puff of smoke some days. Instantaneous combustion, with nothin' left but his watch an' chain an' the damn whistle he allus kept on a cord about his neck. Kickin' a ball around the streets seemed like a far better way of spendin' me time back then." Tommy crossed the room and sat down opposite William. "Perhaps if I'd paid more attention I'd be doin' something different but life evolved. If I'm honest then I'd have to admit to never really harbourin' fine ambitions, one thing simply led to another, like it wer' meant to be."

"Isn't that so for everybody?" Said William. "I can remember wanting to be all sorts of things, ideas used to come into my head every night when my eyes closed and they'd grow bigger when I woke up next morning, but fate has its own plans, fate writes the script, puts words in your mouth an' works you like a puppet."

Tommy could hear Celia in the kitchen ironing, a familiar sound. Sometimes when Rosie was about the same task that slight creaking of the ironing board and the way she'd hum to herself lulled him to a deep contentment.

"At Christmas our Thomas is goin' to propose to Janet Yeats, he whispered it to Rosie. I don't believe the lads have ever kept anything secret from their mam, they've avoided spillin' the beans to their old dad a few times I dare say but not their mam. I reckon we were the same, then war come an' dad wer' gone." Tommy sighed. "I hear your Mathew's serious about his young lady. We're the veterans now Will', been there, done that, got the scars." Tommy chuckled. "Get your coat Eddowes, we deserve that pint."

Emily was anxious, her dad needed to be there when Connor arrived but at that moment a knock came to the back door and Connor's voice called out.

"Only me from over the sea Mrs.Eddowes."

Emily tensed. It didn't escape Tommy's notice, William's shoulders too stiffened at that moment. Tommy recalled the conversation with Annie that day in the hearse, perhaps he should postpone their pint and leave, yet that would be to abandon Emily and Celia to William's ill humour, his stance surely confirmed intent of objection, a determination to be unpleasant.

"Go through Connor," said Celia, "Mr.Spooner's called to see William, have you met him before?"

"I've met both uncle Tommy and uncle Joe, when I was with Beth, good sorts, don't suppose they're too keen on me though."

Tommy stood up. "Good to see you again Connor, no need to feel awkward lad, Beth's moved on, no harm done." They shook hands.

Emily sat mute, afraid to as much as blink. William remained seated but Connor offered his hand firmly.

"How do Mr.Eddowes? Haven't seen you in a while, not to speak to anyway, all bein' well next year should find us diggin' out foundations at Long Eaton, things are on the up."

William took Connor's hand grudgingly and muttered a vague response.

"How's your dad Connor? We were all really sorry to hear about your mam, this'll be a tough Christmas for him and your brothers and sisters."

"Dad's bearin' up Mr.Spooner, it's kind of you to ask."

"It's Tommy lad, everybody calls me Tommy, I'm only ever mister when I'm wearin' that black hat, I reckon it must change the look of me, like that bowler hat you had Will'. Without it you looked like every other lad but when yer put that on, not 'til yer spoke did we know it wer' you. Only Father Ryan at St.Joseph's is the exception, they've a church cat there called Tommy so he always refers to me as Brother Thomas an' Joe as simply Joe. Makes me sound like an old Friar who should be spending time in a walled garden tendin' a hive o' bees."

Connor smiled. "Back home, when I wer' a kid, the priest wer' called Father Amos so we boys nicknamed the altar boy amen. Amos an' Amen, like Tweedle Dum an' Tweedle Dee in party frocks. I shall never get to Heaven but from what I've learned about Amen, neither will he! I'm goin' to Dublin at the end of next week, for Christmas, to help me dad get through it, an' to be there for the others, Maeve an' Eoin, the two youngest are strugglin', God love 'em." Connor hesitated for a second or two. "Mother had a house here in Nottingham, her father left it to her when he died, she'd been rentin' it out. Me dad knew he must sort things out, there's always legal stuff after a death isn't there? He's been in touch with a solicitor but documents an' official papers worry him. That sort o' thing don't come easy to dad. I think in time he'll sell the house, use the proceeds to enable him more time at home. Kathleen can't carry on doin' what mam did, it wouldn't be right, she's entitled to a life of her own. If me dad had a bit of money he could work less hours at Raleigh, be with the young ens more. I've asked Emily to come with me, to meet 'em all an' she's lookin' forward to it aren't you Em'?"

Emily hadn't dared to look at her dad, she merely nodded and uttered a faint, "Yes."

Celia stood in the doorway, willing Tommy's presence to limit William's harshness. He got to his feet and spoke.

"Emily's wanted to see Ireland ever since Mathew came back waxing lyrical. I don't imagine the middle of winter is the best time for crossing the water on the ferry but I dare say she'll find her sea legs. Tommy and I are going to The Standard, you're welcome to come but knowing you two lovebirds, you'll have other plans."

His gaze fell upon Emily who in turn looked at Connor.

"Jimmy Stewart film, 'It's a Wonderful Life', but thanks anyway Mr.Eddowes, another time an' you're on."

Emily finally allowed herself a deep breath while Celia clung to the door frame, her legs weak from relief. Only Tommy had recognised the light behind William's eyes change the instant Connor said his mother had a house in Nottingham, and how that light brightened even further when Connor said his father would likely sell the place. At least the women had been spared William's rancour, including Annie, at her age she shouldn't be so anxious. Now the prospect of sitting in the pub with William, his mind set on yet another 'ambition', gave Tommy little cheer and if he could have turned back the clock, then he'd have taunted William Eddowes with a gibe and raced him round the back streets 'til neither had breath left in them.

Armley Goal. Three days later.

Fred clasped his hands to his ears, the alarms piercing the air like the scream of mortars, they didn't stop, and shouting, men were yelling, loud bangs, metal against metal, men against tanks, fear against fire. Yet no smell, always there was stench. He stared, trembling at the bottom of his cell door, would blood seep under it, would it be blasted from its hinges, then would come the stench, like no other, burning entrails, seared flesh, the agonised cries sent into dense, swirling clouds of destruction that transported a man to no place recognised on God's earth. He grabbed the pillow from his bunk and thrust his face into it, that smelled of nothing but himself, of his own scalp. His leg shook, every sinew wrenched from its resting place, he couldn't stop it, he couldn't hold it still because then the pillow would fall from his face and there would be the stench, that smell of death, it penetrated skin 'til nowhere could a man be free of it. Awake or asleep, it clung to his nostrils and tainted every breath right up to his last, until it was all over.

The noise stopped, in the silence Fred awaited the aftermath, how many would be left, would Captain be alive still? Someone moved towards him, heavy steps, urgent. The cell door opened with one last sound of metal against metal. Fred hunched himself tighter, burying his head further into the pillow.

The warder crossed the narrow space to where Fred was and wrenched the pillow from him.

"For God's sake Sealey." The warder shook his head in disgust at the sight of Fred's urine soaked trousers.

"Is it over Sir?" Fred looked up like a puppy in fear of punishment. Captain was alive, he was still alive.

"It stinks in here." The warder leaned forward and spat into the bucket. "You stink Sealey."

Fred sniffed the air. "No Sir, there is no stench." His face, pale and lined by bewilderment Fred looked down at himself, piss, not blood, just piss!

The warder couldn't know that though the prison guards had quelled a riot, Fred Sealey had survived a war.

Celia sat on the bus into town, the blesséd relief of last Saturday allowed her to approach Christmas shopping with happiness the past few weeks had been denied. Today she was without her friend Rosie because she wanted to find in the shops a particularly nice present for both Tommy and Rosie, a surprise for her two most loyal friends, convinced in her mind it had been the calming presence of Tommy that had curbed William's resentment of Connor and granted Emily an untroubled passage to Dublin on Friday. Today was Tuesday so Celia needed to make her purchases then tomorrow she could wrap and label everything. She felt great sympathy for Connor's father, at least she could send one or two nice things for his family. The bank must be her first port of call. Not every week by any means but periodically Celia made a point of withdrawing a modest sum of money from their joint account. She never squandered it and William had made no remark. Since spending an hour in the pub with Tommy his manner had been quite pleasant. When in town the previous week she'd seen a set of cufflinks in the window of H.Samuel, they were a little more than she would normally spend on his present but it had been a difficult year for William, she'd heard folk talking about Mitchell Street, Woolascrofts' losses and then had come Patricia's takeover of Whittle's, that had stung him hard and he prickled still. While he believed his wife had no business acumen and Celia chose to distance herself from his dealings, she nevertheless did recognise the cause of his frustrations, her understanding was sufficient to enable her that.

"Hello Celia, I've not seen you in weeks, how is everyone?" Susie Spooner sat down beside her. "Joe said Tommy had been out for a drink with William, a bit of nostalgia I expect, Tommy and Will' spent a lot of time together when they were growing up."

"We're all well, I think Mathew and Wendy might get engaged either Christmas or New Year and Emily's going to Dublin with Connor, of course it will be a sad Christmas for the O'Sheas but I know Emily will help all she can. How about all yours?"

"If I don't tell someone I shall burst," said Susie. "We've lived on Monsall Street for donkey's years, I didn't dare to hope of one day moving. We've always had good neighbours but there's not a lot to raise the spirits there these days. William might already be aware but you know what businessmen are like, keep everything close to their chest." Susie giggled like a schoolgirl about to impart censored information. "Joe's put down a deposit on one of the new houses Woolascroft's are building at Bulwell. They're not finished yet but he's seen the plans, as the houses will be at completion and Dick Woolascroft expects them to be snapped up quick, we're not the only ones to have put money down against one. Your William seems always to have his eye on the ball doesn't he, folk are saying that the Bulwell development should restore Woolascrofts' fortunes. Of course William's rental properties must provide a useful, regular income. Joe saw him one evening coming out of a house just a few doors along from us, he didn't see Joe in the car. Joe remarked how much the landlord William does look." Susie laughed. "One day we shall see him, silk hanky peeping from his breast pocket, bowler hat, spats and carrying a silver topped Malacca walking cane. I'm getting off at the next stop, the girls have given me an early Christmas present, a real treat, I'm to have a perm and manicure at Hilda's salon." She got to her feet. "Love to everybody."

The bus pulled in at the next stop and Susie waved as she walked away. Through the window Celia waved back feeling pleased for Susie and Joe. Even if William was aware it would be unlikely he'd say anything, Celia knew so little of his business affairs. Landlord of a house on Monsall Street? She didn't even know that. But today her thoughts were on other more pleasing things, the shops were bright with seasonal decorations and attractive goods. She might treat herself to a bite of lunch at Griffins Café. Walking cane and spats indeed, although a bowler hat did in fact reside on the top shelf of the wardrobe. Celia smiled from amusement as she gathered up the handles of her bag in readiness.

"Next stop, city centre." The conductor called out over the heads of the passengers before returning to the stairwell of the bus whistling the tune of *'While shepherds watched'*. Bank first then H.Samuel. Celia hummed with him as she waited to alight, happy, today she might even be merry, as if reading her mind the conductor winked. It had been many a year since a man winked at her and she laughed.

"Mind as yer go Missus," he said, "there'll be pickpockets about, slick as monkeys they are."

Celia nodded and thanked him. As she stepped down from the platform to the pavement the Salvation Army Band began to play outside Jessops. She took a half crown from her purse and dropped it in the collection tin.

“God bless you,” said the young woman, her face framed by her bonnet, the big deep, red ribbon bow beneath her chin adding to her prettiness, “and a happy Christmas.”

CHAPTER TWENTY FOUR

"I wonder what happened to Molly Hanrahan's message?" Said Connor. He stared down at the water, from where they stood, hands clasped over the rail of the deck.

"Who's Molly Hanrahan?" Asked a curious Emily. The skin on her face tingling from the salty air, the smell of the sea, so different from any earthbound smell, hung about her nose just as it had done the day they came across from Liverpool. Now on the way back and the wind fresher, as though chasing them home, the ferry carved its way through the water like a plough crossing a field of deep loam. Seagulls screeched overhead, ever optimistic of another ailing passenger, casting the content of their stomach over the side. Emily had been relieved to find herself unaffected by seasickness, her stomach was truly stoic but her heart pitched and tossed on a swell of emotion when she thought of Connor's dad, Callum, crying and waving at the quayside.

"When I came over to see the family last January I fished a bottle out of the water by the quay at Dublin. It had a message inside, from Molly Hanrahan, but it'd only travelled from a bit further round the coast so I took it with me an' threw it in the water, on the way back, out deep where it had a chance of travellin' far away. If but half of what's happened to our family has befell that Miwadi bottle then it could be in the South China Seas by now wonderin' if it wer' ever really a Miwadi, with its label gone it could be anythin' from lemonade to vinegar. Sometimes a man can feel like he's lost his original label. Sniffin' the neck of a bottle can help if there's a trace left but by the time it's drifted in an' out with the current an' weathered a storm or two chances are its identity'll never be known." Emily gave Connor a puzzled look. He laughed. "I used to wonder how you could be so unlike your grandma, spiky an' self important when Mrs.Eddowes is gentle as a lamb. Then I realised you were no blood relation, Annie bein' your dad's stepmother."

"Goodness was I that bad? Said Emily, having to acknowledge to herself that his remark did hold some truth.

"Oh you were worse," said Connor, "I'm tryin' to be polite." Both laughed, but after a few seconds Connor spoke again with a more serious tone to his voice. "I never knew me grandad on me mam's side, he wer' a funny bugger, did nothin' for mam while he lived but left her his house when he pegged out, left me a bit o' money too. I've persuaded dad to wait 'til Spring to sell the place, with the economy in England strengthenin' and Nottingham's industries reflectin' that he stands a chance of good money for it if he waits a while. He's a soft hearted man is me dad, he wouldn't want to cause upset to the folks who rent the house. He says they're good tenants, no trouble. Of course me dad's never seen the place, nor have I. The solicitor mam met when she had to sort things out, followin' grandad's death seems to think the Hitchins are decent, reliable people. Leslie and Dora Hitchins, couple o' kids, rent always paid on time. Ideally dad wants to sell to an investor, somebody lookin' for a property to let, that way the family could stay put."

"I can scarce believe it," said Emily. "I've been in that house several times, Timmy Hitchins the boy who was struggling at school with reading and spelling. It must be them, his mother is Dora and his father is Les and he has a sister Susan, they're living where presumably your grandad used to live."

Connor was silent for a moment or two, his immediate reaction to sniff the neck of the bottle, find a trace. His mam had chosen to deny him sight of the label, she must have had her reasons and losing her pained still, it felt disloyal and drove the hurt even deeper.

"We could call on them if you like," said Emily, "Timmy's moved up a class so I don't see as much of him now but Dora wouldn't mind. I've met their neighbour Moira, she's lived there for many years, she knew your grandad, in fact it was Moira who found him unwell and called for an ambulance. What a coincidence!"

"One day perhaps," said Connor, "when dad's close to sellin', leave it be for now Em'. I promised to call on Patricia an' Florence New Years Day, just for an hour, you'll come won't you?"

Emily hesitated. "I've been absent all over Christmas, I do need to spend some time with mam and dad, school will start again soon."

"I don't suppose the neighbour mentioned a name?" Connor ventured a peek at the label, his mam would understand wouldn't she?

Emily tried to recall. "I think she did but it didn't mean anything to me at the time, it's no good I can't remember, but can't you ask your dad?"

"There are lots of things I'd like to ask my dad Em'." He put his arm about her waist, spray from the waves delivered more stinging saltiness. He turned his face to Emily, smiled wistfully, and kissed her.

Celia had resolved to keep the peace, to say nothing to William until after Christmas and New Year. Mathew had proposed to Wendy and now spent time with his 'fiancé. Emily had returned from Ireland recounting her stay with Connor's family, even William had listened with interest, much to Celia's surprise, but now she understood, oh how well she understood, his pleasantness, his contrived attempts at agreeable conversation, he'd actually complimented her on the moistness of the Christmas cake.

They were back, Celia had seen the Roper woman, working in C&A. It was her alright, never could she forget that face and William's subterfuge would not work this time. They had seen the New Year in together, Mathew, Wendy, Emily and Connor, all seated by the wireless awaiting the chimes of Big Ben. William had kissed her and even then she'd maintained the calm but later today, when they were alone, Celia would demand answers. Where was he when he claimed to be attending meetings at his Lodge, where had he been when coming home late for his tea? How long had he been renting out a house at Monsall Street and could he look her in the eye and deny the tenants being no other but Steve and Diane Roper? Steve Roper too was entitled to the truth as much as herself, he was a decent, hard working man.

Celia laid the breakfast table, movement above confirmed they were all stirring. She knew Emily had agreed to go with Connor to Castle Road later this morning, to wish Patricia and her mother the best of the Season. Mathew was to go to the Eathornes but before that, both intended calling to see their grandma and grandad at Winchester Street. It presented Celia with the overdue opportunity to challenge William before the New Year progressed, for her sanity's sake she must call him to account.

Stirring the smooth porridge Celia recognised the irony but it was necessary if she was to keep it from spoiling, after all, she had been making the porridge for nigh on thirty years, so stir she must.

Annie willed Charles to dress and come down, it was New Years Day. Mathew and Emily had come with a gift for him, it was surely cigarettes beneath the wrapping paper but what else could they present him with when he displayed no interest in events round about him. They had eagerly pressed into her hands a brightly wrapped parcel and urged her to open it. A lovely lambswool cardigan in a pretty shade of blue.

"For the best Grandma in all the world," said Emily, while Mathew squeezed her hand fondly.

"Happy New Year Grandma," he said with a waver to his voice. His own utter happiness with Wendy made all the more apparent his grandma's lack of it. If only he could change things. "I best be going, Wendy's mother is getting the meal ready for midday so's we can go to the park, to feed the deer afterwards and walk around the lake before it gets too cold. You're alright for a bit aren't you Emily?"

She nodded. "I told Connor I'd go straight to Castle Road from here, the bus isn't until twenty past."

The clock showed the time to be just before eleven. They waved through the window as Mathew crossed the yard, and saw him look up at the bedroom window, in case his grandad was watching but there was no sound above their heads. Emily chatted away, describing Connor's brothers and sisters, the house where they lived, his dad Callum, a strong man yet gentle and touchingly dignified.

"You would like him Grandma, he's so kind and devoted to his family. One night Connor went out for a drink with his brother Seamus and Kathleen took the opportunity to visit her friend Theresa while Callum and I were there to see the youngest to bed. The two of us sat quietly and Callum spoke to me of his wife, his dear Maggie. We both cried and I thought of you. A long time ago Maggie lost an infant, Callum said it was as if Rowan just wasn't meant to live. You lost little Danny didn't you? I told him you would understand more than anyone. One day you shall meet Callum O'Shea Grandma." Emily gazed up at the ceiling and whispered. "If only grandad understood." She kissed Annie's cheek. "Mam seems quiet yet dad is remarkably cheerful, I couldn't believe it the evening Connor told dad I'd agreed to go with him to Dublin, I'd been dreading his reaction but in the event he raised no objection. I've asked her if everything's alright, she didn't actually answer, 'We shall go to the Sales together before you start back to work, find one or two bottom drawer bargains', that was her reply, a little evasive I thought but perhaps it's just me being silly."

Annie patted Emily's hand. "I shall go there this afternoon, spend an hour with them both. You shouldn't worry, I expect your mam is simply tired.

Christmas brings a lot of extra work for a wife and mother, as one day Emily dear you will discover for yourself."

Charles had eaten and now sat in the corner, his demeanour unchanged, no sign of any New Year resolution to be less ungracious had Annie glimpsed as she cleared away the dinner dishes.

"I'm going to Wollaton, to see William and Celia for an hour, then I shall go on to George and Liza. The young ones are busy doing what young folk do, William and Celia will be on their own, I don't suppose you want to come with me?"

He shook his head and cleared his throat, sending spittle into the grate where despite the fire being in retreat of his imposed neglect, it sizzled a brave defiance.

"Do you really prefer to sit here alone, fully aware that many more New Years have passed than the few we might hope yet to see?"

"Tell them I've got a cold coming, they wouldn't thank me for bringing that to their door," his pathetic response.

Annie sighed, took her hat and coat from the hook and left him to his thoughts, whatever the nature of them might be.

The street was quiet, as if no one wanted to make a mark on the first clean page of the year, no blot or smudge to spoil its freshness. Edna used to feel anxious at this time, 'It's like goin' up a class at school, mam'd tell me how happy I wer' goin' to be yet I wanted everythin' to stay the same, I could cope with the same'. Annie smiled at the memory but she knew what Edna had meant. As she walked along Sherwood Road to the bus stop Annie thought of what Emily had said about Connor's mother. Maggie O'Shea had lost an infant, a long time ago. 'It was as though Rowan was not meant to live'. Annie dared to believe that Emily's young man was truly none other than Callum O'Shea's son, that if Dick Woolascroft had fathered a child with Margaret Holbrook then it was not Connor. Charles had never really accepted Danny as his own and when her spirits had been at there lowest ebb Annie too had felt that her infant son had not been meant to live.

Furthermore she had witnessed firsthand the misery of discovering a concealed birthright and no matter how good and kind the intent, the element of resentment and mistrust seemed never to diminish. Since that desperate evening when Anthony Hemsley, in his frustration of Charles' malice, had opened the long untouched history book, revealing the factual account, destroying forever the previously accepted gentler version, nothing had been as before.

Only one other stood at the bus stop, Mrs.Casley from No.7.

"Have you had a good Christmas Mrs.Eddowes? We got through that without any bother but would you believe, Bobby, our Betty's youngest wer' rushed to hospital last Saturday with appendicitis. I told him not to swallow the date stones but kids don't listen do they? Still, like Betty said, it's one less thing to worry about this year. The daft beggars sang to him last night, 'should old appendix be forgot'." She chuckled. "Happy New Year to you an' all yours Mrs.Eddowes, here it comes." She put out her arm for the bus, while Annie softly murmured the words to herself.

'For the sake of auld lang syne'.

Celia put the cup and saucer in William's hand. "That was the last of the brandy, if you want some in your coffee tomorrow you will have to go to the off licence."

"You must have put a lot in the cake, unless you've turned to the bottle." He looked at her, amused by the notion, as if his perpetually correct wife would ever as much as 'sneak a peek' at a vice as it ran past her on its way to easier prey.

She sat down opposite him, he took a sip from the coffee and placed it on the mantelpiece at his shoulder. "It's too hot yet," he said.

"How long have the Ropers been back? Celia's eyes were intent on his face."

"How should I know, who told you they were back?"

"I saw her, the Roper woman, she's working at C&A, and she saw me, that woman smiled at me, with a certain kind of smile. There are those that bring sweetness to a day, open, genuine smiles. Her's was the other sort, the kind that turns a day sour. You've been seeing her haven't you?"

"Christmas must have addled your brain woman, you're talking rubbish." William's voice rose up the scale in his annoyance. "Why would I know the Roper's movements across the globe, I don't go shopping at C&A so how could I have seen her?"

"Those special meetings at the Lodge, your so called business appointments, you must think I'm without one whit of intelligence, but I'm not. You look me in the eye and tell me that the Ropers are not renting a house of yours, on Monsall Street, go on, deny it if you dare."

"The Ropers are not renting any property of mine, and as for Monsall Street, I wouldn't choose to have a house there if the golden goose nested in the chimney and the doorbell played God Save the Queen."

"You were seen coming out of a house on Monsall Street, it was dark but the streetlamp illuminated your pathetic activities William. So, I shall ask again, are the Ropers living in a rental property of yours and does her husband know that you keep her company when he's away selling for Boot's?"

William took a deep breath. "It's not at all what you've convinced yourself of. She came back, he's in New Zealand still. I don't know what happened out there and neither do I care. She was renting a place on Mansfield Road but the landlord, for some obscure reason, made her uneasy. I didn't know she was back here, not until Dick Woolascroft handed me a note. She'd called at the yard, presuming I'd be there, she left her address, told Dick she needed to see me urgently, she stressed it was a business matter."

Celia raised her hands in disbelief and scoffed but he continued.

"She needed to borrow money, so she could rent somewhere else and buy clothing, she'd travelled with only the bare essentials. He'll send her money when he's earned enough, but paying her fare and putting funds in her purse when she left virtually cleaned him out. Diane will repay the loan as soon as he sends a cheque. I did suggest she try for Nora's prefab at Bilborough but it would have been too far out apparently, the bus fares to and fro would take from her wages more than she could afford. So there, now you know."

Celia stood, her chest tight, she wanted to slap his face, hit him hard, put a dent in his sickeningly smooth expression.

"You expect me to believe that hogwash, oh I can well believe you've given her money, you may not shop at C&A but you buy what you want from one of their assistants and you pay for it with our money, 'our' money William. You're so bloody foolish, is it really worth a few minutes of Eddowes' ego when you get bored, when Dick Woolascroft leaves you behind, when Patricia Bradshaw fails to notice your existence? Is Diane Roper so intoxicating that you in your stupor don't see what she's playing at?"

In sheer frustration William got to his feet, raising his arms to his head in despair of Celia's condemnation, her misguided belief in his failing. His elbow caught the cup and saucer, sending them both to the hearth where they shattered into fragments amid pools of coffee and that reaching the flames causing the fire to hiss its disgust at their wanting behaviour.

"Celia wept, tears streaming down her face. "Now see what you've done."

William's temper flared. "What I've done! There's no reasoning with you Celia Tozer, you're losing your mind, going mad like your mother."

Their voices rose to such a pitch that Annie, approaching the back door felt alarm, their arguing frighteningly intense. Catching her breath she opened the door just as a tremendous draught almost wrenched the latch from her fingers. William had grabbed his coat from the hallstand and stormed out the front door in the instant Annie had entered through the back.

"Celia," she called out, first looking in the living room where she at once saw the broken china, the spilled coffee. Then it began, in the front room the gramophone had started to play that silly song.

"In here, I'm in here." Celia stared down at the spinning disc, her face wet from crying.

"What is it, what's happened, where is William?" Annie crossed the room to where she stood.

"He'll be at an important meeting." Celia lifted the arm of the gramophone, sniffed, then dragged the needle across the record, gouging a deep scratch into its surface. It ground to a discordant halt, feebly she sang words of nonsense, *"they drive you crazy they drive you insane."*

"Come along, let's clean up the mess before Mathew or Emily comes home." Annie put her arm around Celia while more tears flowed, her gaze lighting on a card on the windowledge. Happy New Year, the words in gold printed upon it. Annie's stomach ached for the want of a small helping of peace.

Florence put a shovel of coal on the fire, the room was comfortably warm allowing a sense of wellbeing. Julia had come home for Christmas, looking well. Waving goodbye last Saturday had been hard but knowing she was returning to Exeter to see in the New Year with friends eased Florence's mind. It was comforting, she wouldn't be here forever, Julia needed friends perhaps more than she needed an ageing mother. Caroline had gone by train to

Birmingham where Jonathon now worked as a junior doctor. She was to stay at his flat and Gregory would join them, on the 25th and 26th, before returning to Sandhurst. Selected for officer training he was destined to be apart from his family for much of the time. Caroline, when she'd telephoned last night, described him as very sure of military life, now sporting a moustache and standing taller than at any time before.

Patricia had gone to the front door with Connor and Emily, to see them off. Florence recalled that first meeting, when Connor had come to the house with the message from Rex. How those few words uttered by Rex just before he died had influenced the household since. All the years he'd been at Basil's beck and call, without leave to influence even one hour, yet now his influence was felt far more than Basil's.

Olive came to the house quite frequently and chatted openly, even Dick had called on Christmas Eve and sat for an hour without any of the stiffness, which had bound his nature in the past. But it was Connor, young Connor O'Shea who more than anyone had brought about such change in Patricia, and though Florence couldn't rightly define how, it was surely the young Irishman who'd achieved to remove the obstacle, for so long standing in the way of relations between Patricia and Dick.

If Connor and Emily's romance continued then back into the mix would inevitably come William.

"You look deep in thought Mother," said Patricia, "I'll give you a penny for them."

Florence smiled. "My dear, a penny couldn't make purchase of even the least so perhaps it's as well that none is for sale. Open that box of chocolates young Connor and Emily brought for our indulgence Patricia, I feel the childlike want of a strawberry cream."

CHAPTER TWENTY FIVE

Early February.

Annie, though sympathetic of poor Lizzie Sealey's plight nevertheless struggled to find sufficient confidence for this day's trials. In the telephone box her legs had trembled, not from cold but from the prospect of today's challenges. Andrew had answered the call with a degree of surprise in his voice, as though aware of Charles' awkwardness when faced with a change to his routine. Annie tried to hide his contrariness from anyone outside the family but some were more perceptive than others and she suspected Edna, albeit out of love and concern, had confided one or two observations to Andrew over the years.

On her last visit, before Christmas, Lizzie had been distressed by Fred's health. Physically weakened and mentally confused she'd described him as 'crumpled up, like an empty discarded cigarette packet'. Today was his birthday and Lizzie was desperate for him not to be without a visitor but she was far too poorly, close to pneumonia, a chill had advanced to very much more over the last three weeks. Annie recognised the circumstances that had contributed to Lizzie's condition, a hand to mouth existence with little to encourage her spirit, Lizzie had neglected herself and as a result now lay in bed at the General Hospital where she would be nursed back to health and receive medication. Yet Lizzie's first and vital need she had begged Annie to meet. Between gasps of laboured breath Lizzie had managed to utter 'two pairs of socks, I knitted them myself, in the sideboard, take them to Fred, for his birthday, February the fifth, you an' Mr.Smithfield'. She'd pressed her house key into Annie's hand, then smiled, comforted.

Declaring this to Charles had been the greatest trial but now as she waited for Andrew to arrive, Annie's stomach churned. It was half past ten, she'd taken Charles his breakfast, prepared a pan of soup and a piece of boiled brisket, fetched his paper and cigarettes, stoked the fire, backed it up with some slack to burn slowly and put a bottle of beer by his place at the table. He lay in bed, his mood so harsh she'd felt the chill of it follow her down the stairs when she'd carried away his tray. Her return would no doubt be greeted by a full day's measure of bad temper, wreaked upon her in a first, bitter dose, then dispensed at regular intervals with nothing to take away the taste.

A knock came at the front door, she pulled on her coat, gathered her bag and called up the stairwell.

"Mr.Smithfield's here, I'll be back as soon as I can, don't let your fire go out."

The only sound in reply was an exaggerated clearing of the throat as he spat his noisy objection into the spittoon. At least Andrew was spared any discomfort, if Charles had been up then Andrew's good manners would have required him to first pass the time of day with Charles before leaving for Leeds, no such cordiality would have passed from Charles in return.

"Good morning Annie, the early frost has cleared, we are in good time and so the journey need not be too hurried." He held open the passenger door, his manner as ever, kindly and gentle. Taking her bag he placed it on the back seat. "Would you like a blanket for your knees Annie?"

"No thank you Andrew, really I'm quite alright. As a child, living with aunt Bella, I grew used to the nature of winter, so many lessons taught to me then have proved invaluable through the years since."

"You have with you the necessary order?" He looked at her and laughed, realising his nonsense. "As if you, of all people would forget, don't mind my foolishness Annie, it's just that more and more often these days I find myself having to write down anything important otherwise I wouldn't remember, there is a part of my brain that spends much time asleep."

"I have it in my pocket, a 'compassionate visiting order'. It's hard to recognise compassion in something so official, the wording regulated and impersonal. They will allow him the socks won't they? Surely they couldn't consider them inappropriate."

Andrew took a cloth from beneath the dashboard and wiped condensation from the windscreen.

"I'm sure they will pose no problem, of course they'll check them before giving them to Fred but not even the most devious of minds could knit into a sock any aid of escape and dear Mrs.Sealey hasn't the slightest capacity for deceit. All will be well Annie, never fear."

Having travelled safely and without hindrance it was a little after one when they reached the prison. Andrew parked the car a short distance along the road.

"I filled a thermos flask Annie, simply tea but I think you should have a warm drink before going inside." He reached over to the back seat and retrieved it. "I ventured to add a little sugar, a strengthener if you will." He poured the tea, still steaming into the flask cup and passed it to Annie. "You first my dear."

"You're very kind Andrew, indeed Lizzie has been overcome by the many kindnesses you have shown her. She is of course in the best place, her health is not good but her need to see Fred I'm sure will be a factor in her recovery." Annie drank the warming tea and felt grateful for it. Andrew noticed the slight tremor in her hands.

"I shall walk with you and wait in the small ante-room, as I do when with Mrs.Sealey. I sit trying to imagine the scene beyond public view and though my better sense tells me it is of this modern time I can't help picturing the dark interior of a workhouse. Who knows, perhaps one day I shall be so driven by curiosity as to commit a felonious act and thus discover the true nature of things."

Annie smiled, handing him the cup she said. "You do know that curiosity killed the cat?"

Their chatter was light and served to fill the twenty minutes or so until it was time to make their way.

It was a most intimidating place where even the innocent and blameless felt that firm hand of the law at their back as they entered and despite being entirely upright couldn't help wondering if they too might find themselves denied liberty, spirited away, disappearing without trace, transported to 'the new world', to new born colonies.

Annie took the visiting order from her pocket and gave it to the official, a woman, she looked at it intently then transferred her scrutiny to Annie, making a search of her person, urgent hands travelling about her clothing, it created the most alien experience. Then came the turn of the socks. The woman slowly coaxed her hand down the length of each, as though anticipating a bite from some kind of small animal therein concealed. All this she did without speaking, the uniform declaring her authority without need of stating it. Finally she allowed herself a feeble smile along with a disconcerting remark.

"Warm socks eh, lucky fella, I could do wi' some o' them meself."

Fred raised his face as Annie sat down in front of him. "Hello Fred, Lizzie couldn't come today because she's unwell, a chest infection, so I've come instead."

He stared at her with a vague look in his eyes. "Are you Red Cross?"

"It's Annie, Annie Eddowes, it's your birthday, Lizzie's knitted some nice warm socks for you." She laid them on the table, he fingered them carefully.

"Parcel from home, what did you say you're name was?"

"Annie, its Annie Eddowes, a neighbour from Winchester Street."

"Are you Red Cross? At night they take out the dead, them as don't make it, I hear 'em. Food comes, we get food." Fred was convulsed by a bout of coughing, it took his breath away for a moment. "They won't let me have a cigarette, they give one to Albert Champion, they took 'is leg off an' he could still feel 'is toes yer know. Are you Red Cross? Good nurses, the Red Cross."

Annie's fingers entwined with each other, this was unbearable.

"You remember Lizzie, your wife Lizzie." Annie spoke slowly, hoping Fred might connect with her name, find a way through his confusion to recognise his wife.

"I hear 'em at night, they move the dead by night, them as don't make it. You know, you nurses know what they do. You'll be alright Lizzie, we're a way from the front, Captain comes, 'ave yer seen 'im? They won't let me 'ave a cigarette, they give one to Albert, 'e could still feel 'is toes, they took 'is leg off."

Andrew got to his feet and hurried to where Annie stood at the doorway, tears falling, her lip trembling.

"Come along my dear." His thoughtfulness allowed him to make no question, leading her gently by the arm they stepped outside, into free air where Annie could contain her misery no longer. Her shoulders shook from sobbing while he held her in his arms. Her crying eased and she reached into her pocket for a hanky, taking deep breaths.

"We'll walk to the car Annie, find warmth and those things familiar."

She nodded, grateful for his understanding, he asked nothing, recognising her need of quietness, until she chose to be otherwise.

Andrew was able to imagine the cause of Annie's distress, on the last occasion he'd brought Lizzie to this place, she'd walked with him to the car after spending time with her husband and said nothing but, 'Billy blackbird doesn't whistle anymore'. Few words but they spoke volumes.

Now he and Annie travelled in silence too, not an awkward or uncomfortable silence, but an allowance of time spent processing thoughts, uninterrupted by conversation.

Eventually Annie began to relate the tragedy, Fred's mind lost in a maze, man-made, not of nature's design, round and round went his tormented mind, but found no way out. Andrew listened, his sadness sincere and his concern for Annie's deep distress causing him anxiety of his own.

"Won't you grant yourself just a few minutes to recover your strength Annie, to take a nip of brandy. A brief interlude at Brassington before moving on to Winchester Street. I know that you face every day with fortitude but this particular day has been especially taxing?"

"It's kind of you Andrew, but I really must get back, Charles is never alone for so many hours. His sympathies seldom extend very far and they certainly don't reach Fred Sealey in Leeds."

Andrew sighed. "I used to think William a little short on sympathy, various things would happen at the factory, events to sadden the less contained individual and yet William seemed always to be removed from them, intent on pursuing his aims and not to be diverted, perhaps he inherited the ways of his father, it is often the case. I have tried all my life not to allow my father's character to enter my own, he had little to recommend him as a man and nothing to entitle him, a gentleman."

Following the upset on New Year's Day Annie had sought to find William alone. She'd cautioned him to speak nothing less than the absolute truth. Through his initial bluster he'd explained, and while it was pitiful, he had confessed to being unfaithful before the Ropers emigrated, though insisting he had done nothing disloyal to Celia since. William could achieve to pardon himself and be persuasive when seeking to appease others, offering only as much regret as he deemed necessary. Yet Annie had found it difficult to disbelieve him, he'd shown what she felt was genuine desire for Celia and himself to be restored to a better situation. The household at Wollaton functioned on a knife's edge, Annie tried constantly to maintain the balance, while Charles appeared detached from it all.

"You were very close to your aunt Alicia weren't you Andrew? I never really had a mother or father, not in my life at any rate, aunt Bella was both. I believe I was fortunate in spite of losing my parents before reaching an age of recollection, I was given the very best of aunt Bella. Like her I have never sparkled as many women do, I've not become worldly through travel or attained any position of importance but I have found satisfaction in seeing the good in my children. William has tested me more than the others but I think even he can recognise a failing, and correct it."

"We are, who we are, when all's said and done." Andrew gave a hefty sigh.

Now drawing near to Winchester Street and the light fading, the day's end was close. He slowed the car to turn the corner, pulling up but a few yards from No.1.

"Thank you Andrew, I am so grateful, I shall tell Lizzie that the socks were delivered, and on Fred's birthday." Emotion thread a tremor through her voice and drove an ache to her stomach as she looked towards the front door of home.

Andrew hesitated for a second, but this would likely be the only opportunity. He'd been feeling very old of late.

"I've loved you for years Annie, you must know that, but you need be neither alarmed nor embarrassed for it's not a romantic notion, it has no impassioned urgency, rather it dwells quietly, deep within my very bones, it threads through the marrow that keeps me alive. I have long since accepted that in this life I shall have no easement but one day we shall both, in turn, depart this life and I dare to hope for some small concession in the next. Through the barred window of his cell Fred Sealey sees not enough light, I think we should keep that hope for him also."

Annie nodded, afraid to attempt a single sound, setting her eyes on the streetlamp. Andrew had stirred a memory, words from long ago, from a distant past and in them Annie could barely recognise any relevance to 'this life'.

May every window open to the sun
And life for you be full of pleasant ways
So that you may, as the Seasons run
Look out upon a world of happy days.